THE GOLDEN TOWER

Book Two of
The Warriors of Estavia

FIONA PATTON

DAW BOOKS, INC.

DONALD A. WOLLHEIM, FOUNDER
375 Hudson Street, New York, NY 10014
ELIZABETH R. WOLLHEIM
SHEILA E. GILBERT
PUBLISHERS
www.dawbooks.com

First Paperback Printing, November 2009
1 2 3 4 5 6 7 8 9

DAW TRADEMARK REGISTERED
U.S. PAT. AND TM. OFF. AND FOREIGN COUNTRIES
—MARCA REGISTRADA
HECHO EN U.S.A.

PRINTED IN THE U.S.A.

To Mama and Papa
For ohana
"Nobody gets left behind. Or forgotten."

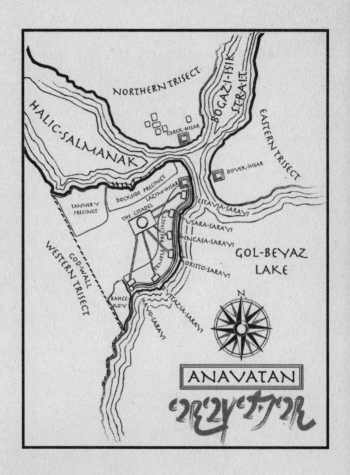

I

Spar

"Children encompass a lifetime's labor in their creation, housing within their unformed potential all the promises made by the Gods: the prosperity of the harvest, the comfort of the aged, the defense of the home, the richness of artistic endeavor, and the light shining in the depths of unknowable time.

"A child of the Gods is a flaming arrow shot into those depths to illuminate the future."

—The Chronicles of Anavatan: City of the Gods. Book twenty-eight: The Age of Creation and Destruction. By: Ihsan, First Scribe to Ystazia, God of the Arts

"Children are ungrateful little rodents who only remember your failures and inconsistencies.

"Gods are worse."

—Favorite saying of Niklon, owner of The Kedi-Meyhane Inn and Tavern, Western Dockside Precinct

THE CITY OF ANAVATAN was a sparkling jewel in Low Summer, moving from warm, sun-drenched days to cool, silken nights with the effortless grace of a dancer. As the late afternoon sun cast orange fingers of light across its delicate minarets and crenellated marble towers, the six great statues of the Gods built on the southern wall above Gol-Beyaz Lake, looked out across Their city, each one holding the symbols of Their patronage aloft: leaf-green and earth-brown Havo, bigender God of Seasonal Bounty, brandishing a scythe and flail; multihued Ystazia, God of the Arts, pressing Her reed pipe to Her lips; Oristo, bi-gender God of Hearth and Home, cradling the symbols of Anavatan, bread and fire, in ruddy-brown arms; icy-white and unknowable Incasa, God of Prophecy, holding His ever-present opalescent dice frozen in the final movement of casting them toward the future; Usara, God of Healing, with one pale blue hand gripping a fistful of medicinal herbs, the other held open to all those who sought His care or respite; and finally Estavia, midnight black and crimson-eyed God of Battles, Her silver swords pointing toward the city's traditional enemies: Volinsk and Rostov across the northern sea and the Yuruk nomads on the western wild lands.

Beneath Their marble feet, the life of Their city moved at a steady pace, secure in the love and protection of its Gods. Priests, farmers, tradespeople, thieves, and beggars alike took their ease in the many open-air cafes, drinking raki beneath sweeping cinar trees, while in the marketplaces, merchants lingered before their open doorways listening to the cries of the salap and sweetmeat sellers. On the docks the stiff breeze off silver Gol-Beyaz Lake—home of the Gods—snapped at the fishmongers' drying lines and perfumed the air with the aroma of fresh, clean water. Everywhere the sense of security and prosperity wrapped about the city like a balm.

Standing under the canvas awning of an urn-smith's shop, a blond-haired youth in the blue tunic of the Battle God's temple infantry took in the idyllic scene with a cynical frown. Before him, Ystazia-Caddesi, the largest of the many artisan streets in Anavatan's Temple

Precinct, stretched from the Arts God's temple on the southern shore, to the Derneke-Mahalle Citadel, seat of Anavatan's civil authority, in the center of the city. Along its cobblestoned length one could find examples of the finest metallurgy, jewelry, glassware, and pottery in the known world; the very best of those in the shops and stalls closest to the temple itself.

Glancing down the length of the bustling avenue, the youth gave a dismissive snort. Despite the garrison guards posted at each intersection, he'd never seen such lax security. Four years ago he'd have made off with half the trinkets strewn so carelessly on the tables and carts before the shop windows without a second thought.

But four years ago he'd been a street thief, a lifter, unfettered by duties or responsibilities. Not like today.

He scowled resentfully and, sensing his mood, the large red dog lying patiently at his feet, glanced up with a questioning whine.

The youth laid a hand on its head reassuringly. " 'S all right, Jaq," he murmured.

Mollified, the dog dropped its head back onto its paws again. They'd been standing there for over an hour, watching the slowly thinning crowds go by, but as long as they remained in the shade, the dog was patient.

Beside them, the man leaning against the shop's clay and timber wall was not. Like the youth, he was wearing the blue tunic of Estavia's infantry, but unlike him, he was also wearing the sword and embossed leather cuirass of a full ghazi-priest at Estavia-Sarayi, the Battle God's temple. Thick, dark hair falling just short of his equally dark eyes, he smiled absently in response to a young weaver's appreciative leer before casting the youth an impatient glance.

"Well?" he demanded, rubbing at a thin red scar that cut through the growth of beard on his left cheek. "Are we going in, or are you going to spend what's left of the day picking fleas out of your arse?"

A flash of annoyance came and went in the youth's blue eyes. "Twenty years old and you still act like an idiot, Brax," he snarled.

The other shrugged. "Fifteen years old and you still act like a cantankerous old man, Spar."

"Fourteen."

"Tanay says you were born on the fifty-ninth Day of Ystazia. That's tomorrow. Tonight, actually, at dusk."

Ignoring the distracting reference to Estavia's temple Chamberlain, Spar shook his head. "Then I'll be fifteen *at dusk*, not now," he insisted.

"Close enough."

"No, it's not."

Glancing up at the setting sun, Brax shook his head and then bent to dig a bit of grit from between his sandal and the sole of his foot. "You have an entire year before they try to stuff you into Sable Company black, you know," he said, deliberately bringing up the touchy subject of Spar's looming adult oaths. "Why worry about it now?"

"I'm not worrying about *anything* now."

Taking in the other's stiff stance, furrowed brow, and angry expression, Brax lifted one quizzical eyebrow. They'd spent most of their early lives together as kardon—brothers—facing off against the uncertain future of poverty and disease that life on the western docks afforded, trusting no one but each other. Those days might be long behind them, but Brax still knew Spar better than anyone alive.

As Spar ignored his expression, Brax continued to stare at him until finally the youth gave an explosive snort. "Sable Company black or Cyan Company blue, it's all the same," he snapped.

"No, it's not. In Sable Company you're a seer, in Cyan Company you're a ghazi-warrior."

"Ghazi-*priest*."

"Seer-*priest*."

"Like I said, it's all the same."

Brax tipped his head to one side. "Point," he acknowledged.

"Yeah, the one on top of your head that's turned you into a God-worshiping thug with half a brain and no sense of self-preservation."

"Maybe." Brax shrugged off both the heretical and the personal insults with practiced ease. "But you gotta do something to keep yourself fed and warm," he said, returning to the Dockside accent of their childhood. "An' if it's not gonna be as a Sable Company seer, what's it gonna be, then?"

His words reminded Spar of the desperation of their early days just as he'd meant them to, but the youth was in no mood to be distracted by the past or to be made grudgingly grateful for the present. Not today.

Today, Elif was dying.

Accepting the piece of dried apricot Brax held out as a peace offering, he chewed at it savagely as if he could put off the inevitable by force of will alone, but the thought would not be banished.

Elif, the most powerful seer-priest in the Battle God's Sable Company was dying. She'd sent Spar, the only official delinkos—apprentice—she'd taken on in over two decades, to choose her funerary urn; a singular honor.

A singular honor Spar didn't want.

Glaring at the row of brass, clay, and porcelain burial urns lined up neatly beneath the shop window, he narrowed his eyes. Desperate or not, life used to be a lot simpler, he thought as the shadow of the past rose up like a fog to obscure his thinking. He and Brax had relied on each other, not on Gods or priests or seers, or anyone else, not even on their abayos Cindar, the master thief who'd kept them fed and safe in exchange for their services as delinkon. But Cindar had attacked a troop of garrison guards in a drunken rage and been struck down in the streets when Spar had been only nine. Brax had tried to protect him from the sight, but Spar had already *seen* it.

His eyes darkened slightly. He knew things, *saw* things. He'd *seen* Cindar's death moments before it happened and had seen the hungry spirits of the wild lands that had taken advantage of that death to grow strong enough to break through the Gods' protection of Anavatan later that night. Stripped of their own protection with Cindar gone, he and Brax had been attacked by thousands of the vicious, wraithlike creatures until Brax had called out for help, the force of his need strong enough to summon a God: Estavia, God of those selfsame guards who'd killed Cindar.

"Save us, God of Battles, and I will pledge you my life, my worship, AND MY LAST DROP OF BLOOD, FOREVER!"

Brax's words—burned into his memory like a brand— had destroyed their old life completely because Estavia *had* saved him, had saved *them*, and catapulted them from a life of poverty on the Dockside streets to one of unimaginable opportunity in the glittering temple of Estavia-Sarayi among Her most elite fighting force; the ghazi-priests and battle-seers who protected Anavatan and the twelve lakeside villages around Gol-Beyaz. Brax had repaid Her gift by giving himself over to Her will with an absolute devotion that had both astonished and frightened Spar in its unwavering intensity. Long before the temple had accepted his adult oaths, he'd become one of the *sworn*, those who pledged their worship to the Gods.

Spar himself was still unsworn but protected by the vows of their new abayon—parents—Kemal and Yashar of Cyan Company, until he turned sixteen.

In one year and one day.

The shadows that fingered across the market street before him belied the thought. In one year and one hour, he amended darkly.

After that he would be expected to give his oaths, his mind, body, spirit, abilities, and future to Estavia, God of Battles, the deity who'd saved their lives, given them food, shelter, safety, security, and learning beyond anything they ever would have had under Cindar, just as Brax had done. On the surface it seemed like a simple choice, an unbalanced choice, but Spar was still unsure whether he owed the God, *any God*, that much power over him. Especially a God of War.

The words he'd seen years ago scrawled on a Dockside wharf came back to him.

Gods are big, and they'll do you if you let them.

Across the avenue, he saw a priest of Oristo turn her head toward them and stilled the ingrained urge to melt swiftly into the background. Old habits died hard, and the Hearth God's abayos-priests had spent most of his and Brax's childhood trying to pull them off the streets and into their own temple's protective custody. But the woman's gaze slid past him, focusing on the uniform that marked Brax as one of Estavia's temple elite rather than a mere garrison guard. She caught his eye, nodded to him as one might do to an equal, and Spar felt rather than saw Brax's shoulders stiffen.

He smiled faintly. Old habits did indeed die hard. Perhaps Brax wasn't so caught up in the temple life after all.

But then the moment passed and Brax returned her nod and, as the priest continued on her way, Spar stilled a new urge to scowl resentfully at his kardos.

"Gods'll turn you into a mark. So will Their priests."

Cindar's words. Four years ago Spar had accepted them without question, but four years of dining at the Battle God's overflowing table and that argument was beginning to wear thin. So why was he still holding back?

"Gods'll get you killed."

No one's words but his own, spoken in the privacy of his own thoughts, but no less true for all of that.

"If it's not gonna be as a Sable Company seer, what's it gonna be, then?"

Point, he acknowledged at Brax with a silent scowl.

If he walked away from all that security, what would he have in its place?

Nothing. Not even Brax.

He thrust aside the thought and the accompanying twist of fear it always provoked. There had to be a path, a "stream" as the Anavatanon seers called the many possible futures they envisioned, that offered both security and independence; a stream that kept Brax beside him just as he was now. He knew it was out there, hovering just beyond his grasp; if he wanted it, it could not elude him for long.

Eyes darkening to the black of a moonless night, he reached out, down into a place another abayos had shown him, a place where even the Gods were hesitant to travel, a place beyond death, as opaque as Gol-Beyaz was bright: the dark place.

It stretched out before him like a vast black ocean, every answer to every question lying just below the surface. He had only to cast his net out and draw them up like a silvery catch of tchiros fish to know them all.

He cast, and the key to his answer rose up at once as if it had been waiting for him: a creature made of power and formed by passion, no longer spirit and not yet a God, but hovering as close to Its own adulthood as Spar was to his. A creature, a Godling, given the domain of Creation and Destruction as a birthing gift by the God of Prophecy Himself and just as unwilling to accept it as Spar was to accept the mantle of a battle-seer of Estavia.

It stared back at him with all the self-aware ferocity of a half-tamed wild animal, but under the pressure of Spar's black gaze, It merged and shifted until a tall, ebony tower stood before him.

In the last four years the creature's ability to take on more complex forms had been growing with Its understanding of the world, and so now Spar fixed It with a steady glare as he spoke a single word.

"Hisar."

The name the God of Prophecy had laid upon It four years ago caused a ripple of disquiet to mar Its smooth facade. A dozen images passed across Its surface until, with a resentful flicker, It became a gray-eyed, brown-haired man of Brax's age, clad in meadow grasses and fire, a triumphant and sardonic smile, both cruel and promising, playing across Its lips. A man both familiar and unwelcome.

Graize.

Spar narrowed his eyes. At thirteen, Graize had been Brax's most dangerous enemy and Spar's only prophetic rival on the western docks of their childhood. He'd been snatched away by the spirits the night Estavia had answered Brax's call, only to reappear on the field of battle allied with Anavatan's enemies, the nomadic Yuruk of the Berbat-Dunya wild lands. Graize had fashioned Hisar from those selfsame spirits, bringing the Godling to a conscious and cohesive whole with the aid of Incasa that had nearly cost Brax his life four years ago. They hadn't seen him since, but from what the Godling had shown him, Graize was still in the game.

Taking note of Spar's warning expression, the Godling's Graize-seeming laughed at him as It held up three mottled turtle shells.

"Place your shine, place your shine," It jeered at him in Graize's singsong accent, spinning the shells in mid-air. *"Which shell has your future under it? Place your shine, place your shine."*

Spar reached out to snatch all three shells away at once, but as he touched them, they disappeared.

"Spar, the sun's going down."

Hisar and Its Graize-seeming vanished as well.

"Spar?"

Turning, he focused on Brax's face with some difficulty, his eyes returning to their natural blue.

"What?"

"The sun. Is going down. The priests of Havo are about to start the Evening Invocations."

"So?"

"So it's time. Close your eyes, make a wish or do whatever it is you do, pick an urn, and let's go.

"You know it has to be done," Brax added in a gentler tone. "Why not just face it and get it over with, yeah? Then you can stop fretting about it."

In a rush, all the resentment and denial Spar had built up that afternoon drained away to be replaced by a dull sense of loss. Elif was dying and there was nothing he could do to stop it. Another person he cared about, another person he'd allowed into his heart, was leaving him. Again.

As he turned toward the shop door, the dog made to follow, but Brax reached out and caught him by the collar.

"Stay, Jaq," he ordered softly. "He'll only be a moment."

✦

It was full dark by the time they returned to Estavia-Sarayi, the Invocations were over, and the people of the city had retired to their suppers, leaving the hushed and perfumed evening to the crickets and the nightingales. The huge, front portcullis gate was already closed, but after identifying themselves to the Sable Company battle-seers, the traditional sentinels, at the inner gate-house, they were allowed inside a small, side door.

Making their way down the temple's dark entrance tunnel, Spar clutched the cloth-wrapped urn against his chest, feeling his heart beating treasonously fast. Five years ago they'd made this very same walk for the first time, Brax holding onto the back of his jacket to keep him from bolting. Now he felt rather than saw Brax almost reach for him again, but realizing that his hesitation tonight was due to an entirely different reason, dropped his hands to his sides and, resisting the urge to take hold of Jaq's collar, Spar squared his shoulders, Brax's words from that first night echoing in his mind.

"Confident and like we're meant to be here."
Because whether he liked it or not, they were.
Elif was dying.
"Shut up."
Another person he ...
"Shut up!"
"Why not just face it and get it over with?"
"Because ... I don't want her to go, but I can't stop her."

Emerging onto the main parade square, he and Brax ducked under a carved marble archway festooned with morning glory vines, then followed an open cloister that flanked the kitchen wing until they came to a familiar wooden door, and slipped inside the temple proper.

The shadowy, lamplit hallway was empty of people. Bypassing the more public areas, they took a small set of stone steps two at a time, then followed a maze of silent passageways, the clicking of Jaq's toenails on the polished tiles the only sound to be heard. They met no one. It was as if the entire temple was deserted.

"Everyone's at supper," Brax supplied unnecessarily.

"Everyone's in hiding," Spar corrected. "Waiting."

They passed under a black-painted archway carved to represent a huge raven, blank white eyes of prophecy staring down at them, and he shivered. They were in the seers' wing now and the air of somber grieving hung in the air like a pall, masking a deeper, feral anticipation that made his head ache from the force of it.

Elif was dying, and everyone was waiting. Everyone, including the God of Battles.

At the end of a quiet passageway they came to a simple wooden door guarded by a sixteen-year-old armored seer-delinkos. Scowling, Spar squared his shoulders and strode purposely forward, the urn in his arms held out like a weapon. The delinkos, his eyes red-rimmed from the effort not to cry on duty, stared down at it as if it were a coiled snake, then pushed the door open a crack. He caught a glimpse of a dozen or so black-clad people hovering in the shadowy outer chamber, the oil lamps on the walls casting a funerary glow over their solemn features. The smell of ritual incense wafted out to them, and as Brax pressed his wrist against his nose to stifle a sneeze, Spar turned.

"This'll take all night," he said, his eyes already clouded over with the more traditional milky-white mist of a seer's gaze. "Don't wait up."

Brax frowned. "What about Jaq?" he asked, his tone betraying his hesitation to send Spar into the shrouded room alone. "She always did like to see him," he pressed. "It might give her some comfort, yeah?"

Spar chewed at his lip, his desire to keep the solid presence of the dog at his side warring with his need to stay focused on the task at hand. The battle-seers of Estavia were as sharp as silver needles, and they would be especially sensitive tonight. If he was going to remain independent in both thought and deed, he needed to keep his wits equally sharp. He couldn't afford to let any of his own grief show, and Jaq would make that too hard; he always knew when Spar was upset.

"No, she'll only take comfort in Estavia now," he answered, allowing a tiny amount of the bitterness Brax would detect anyway to color his voice. "You'd better take him back with you."

The familiar nod of understanding that Brax made before he turned to go brought the past sweeping through Spar's mind again. The black tower rose up suddenly like a warning beacon in the darkness, and he caught Brax's sleeve suddenly, his own expression uncharacteristically open. "Everything's going to change after tonight," he said urgently. "You know that, right? Everything's gonna speed up like a runaway cart from now on?"

Brax gave him a carefully neutral but reassuring

shrug in response. "That's only a problem if we let it run over us," he answered. "So we make sure we keep out of its way just like old times, yeah? You warn me when the cart's coming, and I'll shove us both into a doorway."

"And we stay there until *I* say the danger's past?"

"Don't we always?"

"No. *You* don't always."

"Sure I do."

"No, you don't . . ."

The delinkos at Elif's door gave a meaningful cough, and Spar turned the full force of a Dockside glare on him before returning his attention to Brax. "We keep out of its way until *I* say the danger's past," he repeated, "and everything stays like it was; you and me, safe and together, just like old times. You move before then, and the cart's gonna hit you like a typhoon."

"You're mixing your metaphors," Brax said mildly.

Spar gave an unimpressed snort. "Big words from someone who just learned how to read," he retorted. "You just remember what I said."

"Yeah, sure. Hey . . ." Catching the youth by the sleeve, Brax held out a small cloth-wrapped package of his own. "Fortune for fifteen, yeah?" he said casually.

"Yeah."

"It's just, you know . . . silver."

Spar nodded. "Right. Silver's good. Thanks."

Tucking the package into his shirt, Spar slipped through the door, casting Brax one last warning glance as he went.

Peering out from the dark place, the black tower pressed against Spar's eyes, as excited by Elif's approaching death as Spar was hesitant, and as careless of Brax's reaction to Its presence as Spar was cautious. As the door closed behind them, It, too, cast him a warning glance before turning Its feral attention to the room beyond. Elif was dying and everyone was waiting, including the God of Battles and the newly born Godling of Creation and Destruction. Fortune and fifteen would have to wait as well.

✦

She was dying.

Lying in the bedchamber beyond, the words and thoughts of her juniors fluttering about her like so many tiny moths, Elif, oldest and most exalted battle-seer of Estavia, rolled the words across her tongue.

She was dying. She'd known it since last night, and she wished they'd all just shut up about it already and let her concentrate on doing it. With an exasperated gesture, she smacked the tiny moths from her mind with a well-practiced slap.

She was dying. She could feel it through the whispering chill that had begun in her fingers and toes and slowly crept up until her hands and feet were numb; she could feel it in the soft faltering of her heartbeat and in the fading of her prophetic vision as the streams of possibility decreased, one by one; she could feel it in the growing awareness of the God of Battles made restless in Her sleep beneath the waves of Gol-Beyaz by the advent of the single stream that would soon carry Elif into Estavia's embrace.

The image of a small, light fishing boat, like the ones her kardon had used to catch tchiros in when she was young, bobbed against the shoreline of her mind, coming closer with each labored breath. Soon, it promised, soon, but not just yet, there was still one fish left swimming outside the shining net of her prophetic vision to be scooped up.

Her sudden, impatient desire to be finished with everything, both physical and symbolic, spoke the fish's name aloud.

"Spar."

Her ever-faithful attendant, Murad, bent over her in concern.

"He'll be here soon, Sayin. Will you take some broth while you wait?"

Elif bit back a waspish retort. She was past the need for eating now, all she wanted to do was climb into her little boat and be done with it, but saying so would hurt Murad's feelings, so she simply shook her head as patiently as she was able. But honestly, where, by Usara's blue-painted bollocks, was that child with her urn?

The boat retreated back to the dark waves beyond her sight as her annoyance brought on a weak fit of coughing. Murad lift her head, and she sipped at the cup of lemon-scented water pressed against her lips until the coughing eased. Beyond her bed, the sense of fearful anticipation eased as well as the many seers crammed into her quarters relaxed. It was not yet time. Soon, but not yet.

Around her, the room was warm and somberly dark as was proper at a deathbed vigil. The warmth she could sense through the many woolen blankets her seer-delon had piled on top of her as if they were preparing her body for the heaviness of death. She'd said as much that morning, but only the temple's Marshal, Brayazi-Delin, had thought it funny. Now, surrounded by her Sable Company Honor Guard, she didn't see the point in repeating it. Most battle-seers had no sense of humor. This hadn't changed in the sixty-five years she'd spent at Estavia-Sarayi trying to set them a good example.

Ungrateful, stuffy little buggers.

The darkness she could sense through the ever-shifting patterns of now-muted color that danced across her inward vision; her life's final yellows and pinks of daylight's communion with the past and present already retreating before the onslaught of dusk's deep blue and the future night's opaque and immutable indigo.

And because she'd heard the Evening Invocations beyond her window, she added with a sarcastic sneer. Sometimes the ordinary details were the most important.

Many of her juniors would have disagreed with her, she knew, but that was hardly surprising. After all, they were not the subtle and dissembling Oracles of Incasa, that most slippery God of Prophecy and Probability; they were the handpicked warriors of the very unsubtle God of Battles, made even more elite by their prophetic talents, but still predominantly warriors; only the biggest and most obvious visions offered up by Estavia Herself were even recognized.

And most of them were too young to appreciate the simple and prosaic details of everyday prophecy anyway, she added with a sniff. There'd been only one out of the hundreds of delon she'd taught over the years who'd ever appreciated them, and he'd turned out to be the most stubborn and annoying of them all.

And he was late, she added peevishly. What was he playing at? Did he think she had all the blistering night to wait for him?

She gave an irritated snort that Murad misread as another cough. The attendant gently wiped her cheeks with a warm cloth that smelled of lilacs and, despite her pique, Elif smiled as the scent took her back to her abia's gardens in Camus-Koy, so many decades ago.

She'd played in those gardens each and every spring of her childhood, building temples in their midst and breathing in the honey-sweet odor of their blossoms until she was quite intoxicated by it. The day she'd turned nine years old she'd stolen outside before the dawn to stand beneath their heavily laden purple-and-white branches and thought about her future.

Most of her older kardon had chosen to worship Havo, but it had become obvious even at this tender age that little "Elifin" had the power of prophecy. The Senior Oracle at Incasa-Cami had already come to interview her twice. He'd promised her a life of learning and influence beyond her wildest dreams, maybe even as far as the glittering temple of Incasa-Sarayi in the exotic city of Anavatan. She'd been tempted, very tempted, but in her dreams she saw a vast, snow-clad mountain covered in crimson mist and a small child with hair the color of ripening wheat and eyes as black as pitch standing beside a tall, shimmering tower that barred her way. The child was clad in armor, and that had led her instead to Estavia-Cami and then to Estavia-Sarayi and the rigorous life of one of Anavatan's premier battle-seers.

Once her decision had been made, the child of her vision had disappeared, and in truth she'd all but forgotten him until the day, some sixty-eight years later, when a pale-haired ten-year-old Spar had returned from the Yuruk attack at Serin-Koy, his bright blue eyes flickering with a darkness as black as pitch and his guarded destiny filled with the images of a tall, shimmering tower that stared back at her with a feral intensity that both worried and intrigued her.

They'd played an intricate game of cat-and-mouse ever since, she and her cynical, suspicious little vision-child. Spar had refused to commit himself to any one stream, but Elif had dreamed him armored, a dream that had determined the course of her own, long life, and he was going to make some small move in that direction before she died or she wasn't going to go at all, not by Havo's brawny butt, she wasn't.

The sudden agitation of the streams caused by his arrival interrupted her thoughts, and she raised her head, opening her eyes to stare into his. The tall tower behind his gaze stared back at her and bared Its teeth.

✦

Hisar had felt Spar's discomfort with the number of people in the room as soon as they'd entered it. No, not with the *number* of people, It amended after a moment's consideration, with the *kind* of people, with what they could do, with what they *were*.

"Seers."

The word undulated through Spar's mind with its own special resonance, a mixture of mistrust and dislike covering an older, more pervasive layer of fear, like a dirty bandage wrapped about an ancient wound long ago hardened into scar tissue.

Pleased with the image, Hisar dug deeper, down beneath the layers of bandaging and scars.

Spar didn't like seers. They *saw things*. Things that Spar didn't want them to see, things inside him that he liked to keep hidden: scared things, vulnerable things.

Hisar could see those things without even trying, but didn't usually understand them. Not yet anyway. Idly, It wondered if Spar would feel the same mistrust and dislike toward It one day. If he would feel the same fear. Right now he usually just felt annoyed. Hisar didn't mind annoyed; annoyed was fun to play with. It uncovered things.

Shifting back and forth through Its various human-seemings, Hisar finally settled on Its favorite: a youth named Caleb who'd been Graize's kardos while he'd lived among the Yuruk. Caleb with his lean, lithe body, almond-shaped dark eyes, and bright, inquisitive mind. Caleb had enjoyed uncovering things as much as Hisar did, and unlike Hisar, he'd usually understood them. Besides, Caleb was . . . physical, and Hisar liked physical. It was simple and easy to anticipate. Looking out through Caleb's and Spar's eyes, Hisar studied the room before them as they would have done: physically.

Four black-clad battle-seers—one of whom Hisar recognized as their kaptin—stood sentinel at each corner of a narrow pallet covered with blankets, standing as still and as silent as the great ravens of the Berbat-Dunya wild lands could stand as they waited for word of a newly killed feast on the wind. Except, Hisar amended, that these ravens wore the harsh expression of suppressed grief upon their faces whereas the ravens of the wild lands only wore expressions of greed and hunger. Crouched nearby, an attendant, lines of sorrow marring smooth, bi-gender features, also waited, guarding the pallet as if from the raven-clad seers themselves.

Hisar could feel Spar's growing unease as they approached, but it was the wasted figure swaddled in blankets on the pallet itself that was causing his reaction this time. When she opened her all-too-seeing blinded eyes to stare at them, Hisar couldn't help but bare Its teeth at her. Fighting down a sudden welling of fear, It forced Itself to stare back at her as Caleb might have done. As Spar was struggling to do. Seeing the physical body and not the metaphysical threat. Or at the very least, denying it.

By looking in this way, Hisar saw an old, old woman, her chestnut-colored skin so fine and thin that it looked as if it had been washed over with a paintbrush, stretched across the bones of her face so tightly that each one stood out in sharp relief. Her ward-painted cheeks were deeply sunken, and her lips drawn down over a toothless mouth. Her breathing had a frighteningly forced and ragged quality as if each breath was being made by concentrated will alone, but her eyes glowed with an otherworldly strength that made Hisar want to shudder. She was close to death, so very close, and she did not fear it.

Spar had been dreading this meeting. His outer thoughts said he was afraid that Elif would open her milky-white eyes and coerce him into some constrictive deathbed promise that would destroy his hold on his own fate. His inner thoughts betrayed his fear of losing another person that he loved to death. And far, far below that, youth's fear of age. Spar was not afraid of death, but that didn't mean that he wasn't afraid of a dying old woman. When she gestured at him with one wizened, clawlike hand, he moved forward as if fighting his way through waist-high water, and Hisar fought with him. Then, tucking the cloth-wrapped bundle into her arms, Spar knelt beside the pallet, just out of her reach.

Elif smiled faintly.

"Freyiz predicted it," she whispered harshly.

The mention of Incasa's most powerful oracle at such

a time caused the seers in the room to start in surprise, and she cast them an irritated glance.

"Her most important prophecy," she continued after a moment when Spar's expression remained deliberately impassive. "A child of great potential still unformed standing on the streets of Anavatan; the twin dogs of creation and destruction crouched at its feet. The child was ringed by silver swords and golden knives, and its eyes were filled with fire. It drew strength from Anavatan's unsworn and was to be born under the cover of Havo's Dance.

"A new God, born from the spirits of the wild lands."

Recognizing the story of Its own birth, Hisar bent forward eagerly but came up short as Spar threw up an impenetrable black net of power between them, his thoughts spitting forth like so many angry black snakes.

"Don't touch her!" he hissed.

Hisar reared back, an earlier memory of Spar's black net making It suddenly angry. *"I wasn't going to!"* It protested.

"Yes, you were, and don't. She's a seer and she's sworn to a God. She'll see you."

"So? She's knows about me already."

"Knowing and seeing *are two different things. Do you want the Gods to see you, too? Really* see *you? Do you want to be brought under Their domination like some half-grown, half-wild little dog in a wolf pack?"*

Stung, Hisar narrowed Caleb's eyes. *"I'm not afraid of Gods or seers,"* It snarled. *"Not like you."*

A dry cough brought their attention snapping back to Elif.

"We all thought her vision was fulfilled that terrible night on the streets of Anavatan, but it was only the beginning," she wheezed, struggling to force out each word, one by one. "The child, the God, was born but remained unformed. It lived and grew and drew strength for a year before It took shape on the battlements of

Estavia-Sarayi." She raised one wizened finger in warning. "But the twin dogs of creation and destruction were still crouched at Its feet and the weapons that surrounded It remained.

"And they still do."

Her mist-filled eyes widened painfully. "I predicted it so many years ago," she whispered almost to herself. "Although I didn't know it at the time, I thought the figures in my dream were only there to show me the course of my own life. Now I know differently."

She gave a rueful chuckle. "The young always think that everything's always about them, don't they, Spar-Delin? But now, with so many years of prophecy behind me, so many signs, so many meanings, and so much learning past, I've learned that nothing's certain. A prophecy can actually mean something quite different than what you thought it meant at first; what you were *sure* it meant at first." She clenched one bony fist, then relaxed it against the blankets. "And so my first vision becomes my final vision, and I see it for what it truly is."

The seers in the room leaned forward once more as she raised her head, speaking as much to them now as to Spar. "A child armed and armored and a shimmering tower, strong and defensible, standing before a snow-clad mountain covered in a crimson mist; a mist of danger and of death," she intoned, her voice suddenly strong and clear. "A child and a tower raised to defend the City of the Gods."

She gave a shallow sigh, falling back against her pillow with an exhausted air. "I don't know if they'll be strong enough for what's to come," she rasped weakly. "I've done all I can, and there's no time left to help them now."

Her blinded gaze turned inward. "You might have told me sooner," she added in an admonishing voice, her pique giving her a fresh burst of vigor. "I could have done so much more for them. But not now."

She coughed a fine spattering of blood across the white woolen blankets like a spray of crimson raindrops and stared down at them as if actually seeing them. Then, catching hold of Spar's arm, she drew him down with surprising strength. "I suppose that means you're off the hook, little tchiros," she whispered in his ear. "At least you're off of mine." Pressing a coin into his palm, she gave him a toothless smile, but her eyes were frighteningly bright. "One day soon you'll *have* to choose, Delin. Make a strong choice when you do. That's all I ask. And remember, obscurity's not found in prophecy, but in the prophets who seed their own desires into their reading of it. Make that your fortune for fifteen."

Her hand fell back, and in the midst of fighting the urge to jerk himself away from her, Spar froze as the scent of lilacs suddenly filled the room. The air around the pallet seemed to swell and darken and a great pressure welled up all around them, like the breath the world might take before a storm. Then, between one heartbeat and the next, the God of Battles exploded into the room, and Spar was flung away from the pallet like a rag doll by the force of Her coming, his bond with Hisar shredded instantly.

In the tiny confines of the room, Estavia seemed impossibly huge, taking up all the spaces that ever were. As one, Her seers fell to their knees before Her and even Murad stumbled back from the pallet. Fighting back a welling of angry tears, Spar struggled to his feet and, fists clenched, took one step forward, but the God had eyes only for Elif. Her spinning swords streaked downward, impaling the elderly seer in the chest and, gasping, Elif's eyes snapped open impossibly wide. The white mist of her visioning shot up the blades to reveal the rich brown color of her eyes' true nature for the first time in years, her arms reached out for Her God, and she was received. The sound of waves and wind swept the scent of flowers from the room and then her spirit and her Deity disappeared together.

Battle-Seer Elif of Estavia-Sarayi was dead.

Weeping openly, a junior seer stumbled to the window and gave a signal. As the great bell atop the armory tower began to toll, Spar wiped a smear of blood from his lip and fled the room.

✦

The Godling caught up with him before his running feet took him back beneath the raven archway, but it wasn't until he finally collapsed, exhausted, on the farthest battlements overlooking Gol-Beyaz, now dark and still, that It swooped down to hover before his eyes, half in and half out of the physical realm.

"What was that?" It demanded.

Fists pressed against his brow to ease a pounding headache that threatened to split his skull wide open, Spar glared at the half-translucent figure of Hisar's Caleb-seeming.

"You know what that was," he spat, not trusting his inner voice to speak the words as dispassionately as he needed to. "That was death. You've seen death before."

"Not like that. That was . . . frightening."

Pulling himself together, Spar gave an explosive snort. "Yeah, well, that was death with a God mixed in."

"I didn't like it."

"Neither did I."

Perching an inch above the battlements, Hisar drew Its knees up to Its chin. *"Are you all right?"* It asked suddenly.

Spar glared at it, the headache still thrumming across his eyes. "I'm fine, why?"

"You don't look fine."

"Looks aren't everything."

"You don't feel *fine either."*

"Whatever. Just leave it alone, will you?"

The Caleb-seeming wavered uncertainly, then solidified once more as Hisar cocked an ear toward the tolling bell. *"Did the seer go down into the dark place after she died?"* It asked, willing to change the subject.

"Her name was Elif, and no." Spar didn't bother to hide the note of bitterness that crept into his voice. "She went down into the *silver* place, into Gol-Beyaz to dwell with the Gods."

To become silver?"

"Yes."

"Because she wanted to? Because she was sworn to a God?"

"Yes."

"You're not sworn to a God. Don't you want to go down into Gol-Beyaz and become silver, too?"

Spar bit back an angry retort, then just shook his head. "No."

"Why not?"

"Because."

"Because why?"

"Just . . ." Spar took a deep breath to still the sudden overloud pounding of his heart. Sometimes he forgot that Hisar had only been four years in the world. "Because I like the dark place better," he explained slowly. "It's quiet."

After a long moment, Hisar shook Its head. *"No,"* It corrected in a small voice. *"It's not quiet, Spar; it's silent. It makes me feel . . ."* It paused.

"What?"

Hisar didn't answer for a long time, then finally the Caleb-seeming shrugged. *"Lonely."*

Spar frowned. "Do *you* want to go down into Gol-Beyaz?" he asked, trying the hide his reluctance to ask the question at all. "And become silver?" The naked fear in his voice made him scowl, but he held Hisar's gaze until It shrugged again.

"No," It answered slowly. *"Not if you don't want to. I'll . . . stay with you here. I don't* need *to be silver."*

Resisting the urge to make a careless or sarcastic reply, Spar merely nodded, doing his best to ignore the sudden gout of relief that made his legs feel traitorously weak.

They sat for a long time, saying nothing, and then Hisar glanced at him with a worried expression.

"Those things she ... I mean Elif, said about towers and mountains," It asked, changing the subject. *"Were they about me?"*

Rubbing his temples, Spar just shrugged. "Probably," he answered.

"What did they mean?"

Spar's brows drew down. *"A child and a tower raised to defend the City of the Gods."* He snorted. *"Try a more blatant ruse, why don't you?"*

Hisar blinked in confusion, unsure if the other's mental muttering was meant to be overheard or not. *"Spar?"*

"They meant I wasn't the only one Elif was trying to trap into a deathbed promise," Spar answered.

"Will I have to do what she said?"

Make a strong choice, that's all I ask.

"No." Spar shook his head emphatically. "You never have to do anything just because someone else says you do. But we will have to be on our guard. Both of us. Things are moving fast." The image of the runaway cart flashed between them. "And far too many seers are about to get far too interested in them."

"And far too many Gods," Hisar added, glancing back at Gol-Beyaz as if It feared that Its Elders were already approaching.

"Far too many," Spar agreed. His gaze drew inward. "And They probably won't even give you the warning of a fortune for fifteen present.

"But that's all right," he concluded firmly, "We've fought off Gods before, yeah?"

The memory of Its final push into the physical world, as much as Spar's words, caused Hisar's form to shimmer until It stood, looking out at him with Brax's dark brown eyes. "Yeah," It answered, pushing the words into the physical realm as It had been pushed and trying to sound as confident as Brax would have sounded.

Spar nodded his approval of the attempt and encouraged, Hisar turned to glance at him shyly.

"Spar?"

"What?"

"If we aren't gonna to be black and we aren't gonna be silver, what color are we gonna be?" It asked, still using Brax's voice.

Clutching the coin Elif had given him in his hand until the edge bit into his palm, Spar watched a shaft of early morning prophecy cast a golden glow across the waters of Gol-Beyaz.

"I have an idea," he said quietly. "But we're going to need help."

"Whose help?"

"I'm not sure yet." He turned to see Hisar's Brax-seeming waver in Its uncertainty. "Maybe Brax's," he answered suddenly.

Hisar gave Spar a disbelieving frown. Brax had fought It on the battlements of Estavia-Sarayi four years ago. Hisar had drunk from the burning power that was Brax's essence and the strength of it had been like nothing the Godling had ever experienced before. It still dreamed of it, still longed for it, but the memory of Brax's fear and revulsion and the pain of Estavia's violent response made It wince. "Brax doesn't like me," It replied in a terse voice. "He doesn't trust me."

"Because you tried to eat him," Spar snorted.

"Not exactly . . . eat."

"The difference doesn't exactly matter."

"So why would he help me?"

"Because I asked him to."

"Just because of that?"

"Yes."

Hisar was quiet for a long time. The rising sun glistened in Its eyes and with a renewed frown, It shifted back to Its more comfortable Caleb-seeming. *"Why is it always about Brax?"* It mused almost to Itself, Its voice echoing in his thoughts once again.

"What?"

"Brax, why does everyone always think about Brax?"

Spar glared at It in suspicion. "Everyone doesn't," he replied with a warning growl.

"You and Graize do."

"No, we ... no, I don't." Spar's eyes narrowed. "Graize does?" he asked.

Hisar tossed Its head carelessly. *"Only all the time."*

"Why?"

"I don't know."

"You haven't asked him?"

The Caleb-seeming dimmed. *"No."*

"Why not?"

"We don't ... talk."

Spar's expression softened to one of sympathetic concern. "Don't you link with him and speak in his thoughts like you do with me?" he asked more gently.

The Caleb-seeming dimmed still farther. *"No."*

"Why not?"

"We don't ... he doesn't think of me that way."

"What way?"

"Like a ..." The Godling struggled to put the difference into words, then shrugged. *"Just leave it, will you?"* It echoed in Spar's own voice, and when Spar nodded with a faintly sardonic smile, Its form solidified a little. *"So will you ask Brax to help?"* It asked in a small voice.

Spar nodded again.

"When?"

"The next time I see him."

"And ... he'll help us?"

"Yes."

"How?"

"Again, I'm not sure yet."

"Should I talk to him?"

Spar's opinion about the outcome of that idea was clear on his face. "I wouldn't," he cautioned. "Not just yet anyway. Let me talk to him first."

"But he will *help us if you ask him?"*

Spar gave a deep sigh. "Yes, Hisar," he repeated. "If I ask him, he'll help us."

"So what color will we be after he helps us?" It insisted.

Recognizing that the Godling was not going to leave the subject alone until It got some kind of an answer, Spar opened his hand to show It the coin nestled in his palm, the form of a watchtower etched into its surface. "Gold," he answered.

Hisar blinked. *"Gold? What's gold?"*

"Gold is new."

"Is new good?"

"Maybe. That's the thing about new, it could go either way: creation or destruction."

"Like Freyiz's prophecy?"

"Yes."

Hisar frowned. *"But I thought you said we didn't have to do what anyone else said. Isn't that doing what Freyiz said?"*

"No."

"But . . ."

Spar raised one hand. "It's too soon for answers. We've set our boat into the current; we've chosen a color. Now we have to wait and see how the streams are flowing and then choose a course that takes us to that color."

"And you'll tell me when it's time for that."

"I won't have to; you'll know it."

"But you'll tell me anyway? You'll talk to me?"

The point was obvious, and Spar nodded patiently. "Yes, Hisar. I'll talk to you."

"And I won't have to . . . die to be gold?" It asked, Its voice suddenly low and frightened.

"No."

"Because I don't want to die, Spar, not even to be gold."

"You won't have to."

"Promise?"

"Yes."

Finally satisfied, Hisar's Caleb-seeming solidified completely and, turning toward the armory tower, the seer and the Godling listened as the bell sounded over and over, the former frowning thoughtfully and the latter content to leave the details to the future now that It had Its answer.

With Brax's help, It would be gold. And, unlike Elif, It wouldn't die. Spar had promised.

2

Brax

BRAX STARED, UNSEEING, into the darkness. The tolling of the armory bell had awakened him long before dawn. Lying in bed, he'd listened as each somber note sounded, echoed across the silent temple grounds, faded, and then sounded again. Once, twice, too many times for anyone except the bell ringer to keep track of and maybe not even then. Elif had been eighty-one years old. The bell would probably toll all morning. Nobody would sleep deeply today.

Throwing back the sheet, he worked his way out from under the snoring dog sprawled across his legs and rose stiffly. Jaq usually bedded down with Spar, and Brax was not used to sleeping in one spot all night. It made his body ache. Rubbing at the twisting scar on his left elbow where a blow taken on the field at Serin-Koy had nearly shattered his arm four years ago, he used the pot and then crossed naked to the window. The early morning breeze whispered across his skin, following the buzz of Estavia's lien through his limbs. Her presence felt still and sleepy this morning, sated from Elif's joining.

The God would be that much more powerful now, a greater source of strength for Her warriors on the battlefield and for the God-Wall of power and protection that stretched all the way from Anavatan's Gerek-Hisar in the north to Anahtar-Hisar to the south. That was the way of it: Her people strengthened Her with their reverence, and She strengthened them with Her will.

"God-worshiping thug with half a brain and no sense of self-preservation."

Spar's voice echoed in his mind as loudly as if he were standing right beside him, and Brax silently acknowledged the ring of truth in the words, but he'd made his choice on the blood-slicked cobblestones of Liman-Caddesi and had never regretted it. She kept them safe, both of them, and he would defend Her wall as he'd promised, whatever it took.

Peering through the fine latticework which covered the window, he stared out at the paling darkness. It would be a bright, clear morning. On the shores of Gol-Beyaz the mist would burn off quickly, giving the village watchtowers a clear line of sight all the way to the western ridge of the Berbat-Dunya wild lands, and on the turrets and minarets of Anavatan, the priests of Havo would see the entire city spread out before them.

Spar would be up there somewhere now that Elif was dead, crouched on the battlements, staring out at the eastern sky, and making his first silent predictions for the morning.

Rubbing at the short growth of beard along his jaw, Brax frowned. He should have been up there with him. In the old days, he would have been; standing beside him, waiting patiently to learn if the day's trade would be prosperous or dangerous and even after they'd come to live at Estavia-Sarayi, exchanging the trade of theft for the trade of war, he'd gone more out of habit and for the company than for any need to know the future, but ever since he'd sworn his adult oaths, they'd had less and less time to stand together.

He'd had to rely on others to keep Spar safe: Kemal and Yashar. And Jaq.

Turning, he glared across at the sleeping animal.

"Hey, you great lump, get up and go find Spar."

The dog opened one reproachful eye to stare back

at him then, with a loud grunt, heaved himself off the pallet. Pushing the chamber door open with his nose, he slipped out into the corridor beyond, the hard clicking sound of his toenails against the marble floor marking his path. Brax heard the faint greeting of the night duty sentinel at the outer door and the sound of it being unbarred, and turned back to the window.

A faint feathering of wings against the latticework made him frown.

"Everything's going to change after tonight. You know that, right?"

Brax shook head with an exasperated sigh. Runaway carts and, whatever else Spar had said ... everything had already changed. The days of two young Dockside lifters united against a world of marks and garrison guards on the streets of Anavatan had vanished the night they'd stepped into the world of Gods and priests.

But even before that, Brax had known Spar wouldn't stay a ragged little pickpocket forever. He was better than that. He was a seer, not a thief.

"And not a foot soldier either," he told himself sternly. "Whatever the color of his tunic is right now, Spar'll never stand beside you in Cyan Company, so you'd better get used to it."

That had been why he'd honored Spar's unspoken request to face Elif's death without him last night because last night Sable Company had gathered to attend Elif's deathbed joining with Estavia. Sable Company and Spar.

The image of another presence, immature and feral, gazing out from deep within Spar's eyes, made him pause. Sable Company, Spar, and the spirit creature born on the walls of Anavatan four years ago, he amended darkly.

A chill passed through him as he remembered that night, crouched on the temple battlements, sleet and rain in equal measure pelting him in the face, and the rising storm called up by Havo's Dance threatening to hurl him down into the dark waters of Gol-Beyaz. A deafening crack of thunder had summoned the spirit Hisar into the physical world and, desperate for the power that fed Its kind, It had flung Itself on Brax like a huge, ethereal leech.

He remembered the shock of pain as It had driven Its half-formed claws and teeth into his chest, and the hazy dreamlike quality of Its feeding. He'd fought It with every ounce of strength he'd possessed, but it had taken both Spar and Estavia to drive It away. The memory of Its attack still tainted his dreams with an icy weakness, and although Spar now insisted that Hisar was no longer a threat, Brax had no intention of ever letting It get that close to him again. It was a spirit. Spirits were dangerous. Always. They'd nearly destroyed the city four years ago. He hadn't forgotten that even if Spar had.

A dawn bird trilling its greeting to the approaching sun brought him back to the present and, shaking off the lingering chill, he crossed to his chamber's tiny altar and lit a stick of sandalwood incense off the nearby oil lamp. Breathing in the heavy scent, he reached down into the place where Estavia's presence warmed his thoughts, waiting until the sense of peace and belonging steadied his hand, before picking up the goat's hair brush lying beside its marble inkpot.

When they'd first come to Estavia-Sarayi, Brax and Spar had been housed in the huge golden guest suite usually reserved for visiting dignitaries, then in the small delin-room off the bedchamber of their new abayon, Kemal and Yashar. When Brax had taken his adult vows, he'd moved to single quarters of his own—not that he was in them much, he admitted; he spent most of his nights with Brin and Bazmin, two of his fellow Cyan Company ghazi—but in each room, he'd painted the symbols of Estavia's protection on his body every morning as all of Her warriors did.

Now, dipping the tip of the brush in the inkpot, he felt Her hand wrap about his and together they drew the symbols of Her city, Her temple, and Her second infantry company on his shield arm, then himself, Spar, Jaq, Kemal, and Yashar on his chest. Finally, changing hands, they painted Her wall—the private symbol She'd gifted him with on the shores of Gol-Beyaz four years ago when he'd sworn to be Her Champion—on his sword arm. More than just pictures, the symbols were the written reminders of his oaths, the written reminders that he was Her Champion, Her favorite.

The brown bead he wore on a string about his neck knocked against his chest, and he smiled. He was Her Champion, but he was also Spar's kardos which was why, although he painted Estavia's wards on his body each morning, he also wore the bead that Spar had given him four years ago. Because that was the point: he'd given his word to keep Spar safe and he would do whatever he must to ensure he stayed that way.

Moments later, dressed in blue tunic and sandals, he joined the other early risers and those just coming off night duty on their way to breakfast. Few stopped to talk; the tolling bell discouraged thought of anything this morning but Battle-Seer Elif late of Sable Company.

As he crossed the silent central courtyard, Brax passed several Sable Company delinkon standing reverently beside the bench where she'd liked to hold court, and allowed himself a short bark of laughter. Whatever the strength of her prophetic sight, Brax would always remember Elif as a caustic old woman with a cackling laugh and a wicked sense of humor. She could even make Spar crack a smile from time to time; and that was no mean feat. He would miss that.

As a passing gardener-delinkos gave him a blatantly seductive leer, he smiled back at him and carried on toward the commissary wing, noting that it was already brightly lit despite the early hour. Obviously, he wasn't the only one driven out of bed by Elif's death bell this morning. She'd have appreciated that. She always had been a very early riser.

A flutter of wings passed his cheek, and he brushed them aside as he spotted two shadowy figures waiting in the commissary doorway. Brin and Bazmin pounced on him a moment later, falling into step on either side like overprotective bodyguards—or a pair of lifters about to pick his pocket—he added cynically. He ignored them, and the twins exchanged a meaningful glance over his head, their smooth features bearing the same predatory expression.

No more than a year older than him, the two bigender ghazi had taken it upon themselves to help Brax through the accelerated training that Estavia had demanded of Her newest favorite and, under their persistent tutelage, he'd even learned to read well enough to finally be named ghazi-priest last winter. They'd become his closest friends other than Spar, but he didn't trust them. Not as far as he could throw them. They were both notorious gossips, and if they'd been waiting for him outside in the dark instead of inside in the warm camaraderie of the Cyan Company dining hall, they obviously wanted to get an early start on their morning's information mongering. And there was only one topic of interest this morning: Elif's deathbed prophecy.

Now Bazmin threw a proprietary arm over his shoulder before cocking an ear toward the sound of the tolling bell. "That will be going on all day."

"Likely," Brax allowed cautiously, knowing this was just the opening volley.

"I imagine the priests of Usara are already preparing Elif's body since Spar fetched her urn in such a timely fashion," Brin added.

Brax gave a noncommittal grunt. Everyone had known that Elif's health had been failing for weeks. The priests of Usara'd probably had their unguents and herbs ready for just as long, so this was not what the twins were fishing for.

"So what sort of urn did he choose?" Bazmin asked casually.

"I've no idea."

"Weren't you there?"

"Not in the shop, no. Someone had to wait with Jaq. Why?"

"No reason. I ask only because you were gone for so long we began to wonder if you'd been waylaid by the sex trade bawds of Ystazia-Sarayi. With your looks, you could make a fortune for them."

"Very funny." Brax shot Bazmin an irritated glance which the other ghazi happily ignored. Thanks to Temple Chamberlain Tanay's vigilant ministrations, Brax had finally outgrown the pinched-underfed look that fourteen years on the streets had left on his body. He'd filled out and shot up by at least six inches, outgrowing tunics and sandals at an alarming pace. The sudden interest caused whenever he swam, bathed, or even trained was a constant source of distraction for him and amusement for the twins.

"So . . . how's Spar?" Brin now asked in a falsely casual voice as they passed through the commissary's mosaic antechamber.

Brax just shrugged. "He's fine," he answered in a neutral tone, making his way through the press of people heading for the main refectory hall. He and Spar did not discuss each other's business with anyone else, especially the twins. They were already the subject of far too much temple gossip as it was; and much of that was because of the twins themselves.

"It must be hard to lose your abayos," Brin continued.

Brax's chest tightened. He should have been up on the battlements with him, not down here fencing with the twins. "He's used to it," he snapped, the twinge of guilt making him short. "She's not the first."

"That's true."

The twins fell silent, obviously regrouping. The unspoken agreement at Estavia-Sarayi was that Brax and Spar's unlawful childhood was not discussed in public, and both Brax and Spar found that funnier than the rest of the temple did. You were what you were; being uncomfortable about the past wasn't going to change it.

"We'd hoped to see him this morning," Brin continued after a moment. "We have his fortune for fifteen gift."

"You'll see him at Invocation. And if not there, then at the noon meal."

"What did you get him?" Bazmin asked bluntly.

"Silver."

"Very original."

"Hm." Brax lengthened his stride, passing quickly into the main hall and, despite their added height, the twins had to hurry to catch up to him.

"So, were there a lot of seers huddled about Elif's rooms last night?" Bazmin asked in a hushed whisper as Brax made for the central table piled high with food and drink.

"Probably the lot," Brax answered, reaching for a plate.

"How many did you see?"

"One. On guard outside the door."

Bazmin shot him an exasperated expression before catching up a plate as well. "I heard that Kaptin Liel's stood death duty at her bedside for the last three days."

"Marshal Brayazi was there most of yesterday, too," Brin added. "And every one of the city's temple leaders have come to see her, including retired First Oracle Freyiz and the new First Oracle Bessic of Incasa-Sarayi himself. He came yesterday when the two of you were off fetching Elif's urn. I heard that he was very put out to find Spar missing. Funny, you'd think a First Oracle would *know* he wasn't here. Pass me a plate, will you?"

Brax obliged with a scowl. The Head of Incasa's temple had been after Spar ever since he'd foreseen the Yuruk attack on Serin-Koy five years ago—their priests hated sharing their God's gift with other seers even though they pretended not to. Up to this point, the combined defense of Elif, Kaptin Liel, and Marshal Brayazi had kept Bessic at bay, but now, with Elif gone and Spar so close to his adult oaths, his attempts were only going to increase.

Brax's sword hand itched to solve the problem himself, and he covered it up by catching up a huge piece of honey-covered flatbread, wondering now if the twins were actually giving out information this morning instead of seeking it and what it was going to cost him if they were.

"Bessic probably just came to horn in on Elif's deathbed prophecy," Bazmin said with a disdainful sniff. "They say that when a seer's close to death, their ability's particularly strong. There's all kinds of stories about Incasa's oracle-seers seeing directly into the heart of their God's own prophecy moments before their joining, and Estavia's been know to pass messages of danger to Her temple through Her own dying seers."

They both looked expectantly at Brax who accepted a small cup of black coffee from a hovering server of Oristo without comment.

"Sometimes, though, it's nothing too special," Brin allowed with a careless shrug. "It's more like a personal eulogy made to remember the seer by; that's all."

"Do you think Elif made a deathbed prophecy?" Bazmin asked, prodding Brax gently in the ribs when he once again refused to be drawn into their speculation.

"I don't know," Brax snapped as half his coffee splashed out onto the floor from the motion.

The server immediately refilled his cup, and Brax gave her a smile of thanks that nearly made her faint. "Thank you, Hanee."

She gave him a besotted smile in return. "My pleasure, Ghazi," she murmured.

"Didn't Spar tell you?" Bazmin insisted, maneuvering between them with practiced ease.

"No. Why don't you go ask him yourself?"

"Because he'll only say something rude."

"So will I in a moment."

"Do that, and Hanee will know you for the coarse, unlettered brute you really are and not the smooth doe-eyed lover of her dreams." Bazmin winked at the server, who blushed.

"Get stiffed, Baz," Brax growled.

"There isn't time, dear one," Bazmin replied with a chuckle, unfazed by the threat. As Brin reached past them both for the salap jug, filling two tall crystal glasses with the foaming liquid, Bazmin gave Brax an innocent look. "Do you think we'll be returning to Alev-Hisar after the funeral?"

"What?" Momentarily thrown off by the change of subject, Brax just blinked.

"Alev-Hisar," Brin repeated for the other twin with exaggerated patience. "You know, the southern watch-tower we've been assigned to this season."

"Of course we will, why wouldn't we be?" Brax added a slice of fresh melon to his plate before fixing the other two ghazi with a suspicious glare. "The Petchan raids have increased. Marshal Brayazi wanted a show of strength in the south all season. You know that."

Brin just shrugged. "Word is that Kaptin Julide has some important new strategy to discuss with the command council after Elif's funeral. Word is that strategy might involve a raid of our own."

In the act of reaching for another slice, Brax turned, finally interested despite himself. "What, up into the mountains?" he asked.

"Could be," Brin answered, deftly maneuvering under Brax's arm to snag the same piece. "To the grasslands, anyway. Apparently the Sable Company seers have discerned a shift in the Petchan power base that suggests they might have a new leader."

Brax frowned. The last time they'd heard of a new leader, it had been Graize at the head of an army of Yuruk five years ago. Spar had said their old enemy was still alive, so it might be him stirring up trouble once again.

"He has all the survival luck of a cockroach," Brax groused to himself as his injured elbow began to throb at the memory.

He had to remember to speak to Spar about the possibility, but even if this new leader wasn't Graize, maybe they'd get lucky and both of them would die of the pox.

Catching up a handful of dates, he threw them on his plate with enough force to send half of them tumbling onto the floor. As the twins bent to pick them up for him, he scowled at them both.

"And how do you know what the Sable Company seers have discerned, anyway," he demanded.

"Oh, we have our sources. Elif wasn't the only talented prophet at Estavia-Sarayi, you know."

Something in Bazmin's tone gave Brax pause. "Spar told you?"

"Spar wrote to us," Brin replied smugly.

"He wrote to *you*."

"Maybe he forgot you could read."

"Not funny."

"Yes, it is." Bazmin caught him by the arm, drawing him away from a crowd of Verdant Company archers who'd just arrived at the table. "He knows you don't discuss what he tells you. He knows we do. He wanted to give Cyan Company the heads up. Something's happening, something the infantry ghazi are going to need to know about."

"Everything's going to change after tonight. You know that, right?"

"We thought he might have gone into detail yesterday when you went into the city together," Brin added, passing Bazmin a handful of Brax's fallen dates.

"Everything's gonna speed up like a runaway cart."

"He didn't."

"He will." Piling the dates back onto Brax's plate, Bazmin gave him a meaningful look. "And when he does, you should tell us."

"Why?"

"For the same reason. To give Cyan Company the heads up. We're the ones who have to face the enemy, the more information we have the more effectively we can do it, yes?"

"Whatever."

"Brax."

"I'll think about it. Now, leave me alone, will you? I want to eat in peace."

Turning his back on them, Brax headed toward the Cyan Company dining hall. Sharing another glance, this one of speculation tinged with triumph, the twins finished filling their own plates, before following him.

✦

The blue-and-gold-tiled infantry hall was abuzz with quiet conversation this early in the morning. It slackened off for a moment when Brax entered, but on seeing that Spar was not with him, the gathered warriors returned to their breakfasts at once. As Brin and Bazmin veered off in the direction of Kaptin Julide's table, Brax spotted his abayon seated at their usual place by the west garden window. Yashar, the older and taller of the two men, motioned him over with a wave.

"When did you get in, Braxin-Delin?" he demanded as Brax took the seat offered beside him.

"Late yesterday afternoon, Aba."

"And you didn't think to come find us?"

"I imagine he had other things on his mind," Kemal supplied.

Yashar harrumphed into his teacup. "How long are you here for?"

"Just two days."

Kemal nodded thoughtfully. "Think you might have time to run through some sword training with this year's delinkon later this morning?"

Brax smiled faintly. "I might, why?"

"I have Assembly."

"And Yashar . . . ?"

The older man grunted. "Is having his spleen pulled out."

"They can't be that bad."

"They're not, really." Yashar allowed. "But I'm sure they'd much rather learn from Estavia's Champion. Besides, it's what delin do for their aged abayon. They help out, take some of the weight off their weakening shoulders, share the . . ."

"Fine, I'll do it." Brax threw his arms into the air in mock surrender, giving both men a fond look.

Five years ago when Estavia had led him and Spar to Her temple She'd all but given them to Kemal and Yashar. The twenty-four- and twenty-six-year-old ghazi-warriors had suddenly found themselves in the unenviable position of being abayon to the youngest delinkon in the temple's history. Little more than a decade older than Brax himself, they'd done their best to finish his raising and see him through the unique fighting apprenticeship served under the Battle God's watchful eye, while at the same time trying to give Spar the childhood he'd never really had, and wasn't sure he wanted.

When Brax was inducted into the ranks of Cyan Company as a full ghazi-priest last winter, he'd been posted to Alev-Hisar. Kemal and Yashar had remained at Estavia-Sarayi so that Spar might continue his prophetic studies under Elif and Kaptin Liel. Brax hadn't realized how much he'd missed them both until now.

As if sensing his thoughts, Kemal stroked two fingers through his beard as he studied Brax intently.

"You look well, all in one piece despite our absence," he noted. "When we learned of the Petchan attacks against Kinor-Koy this spring, we worried after you."

"It was a few cattle raids, nothing more," Brax replied, swallowing his coffee in one gulp. A passing delinkos refilled it almost at once, and he nodded his thanks as his abayon exchanged a private grin.

"You might have written to tell us that," Yashar pointed out once the delinkos was out of earshot again.

Brax shrugged. "You know I'm not that good with a pen. Besides, Spar would have told you if he'd sensed anything wrong."

"Yes, well, as you know, digging words out of Spar is much the same as digging pearls out of oysters. Sometimes you need a shucking knife," Kemal observed.

Brax just snorted.

"He did say that he thought the raids had increased in both number and ferocity," Yashar supplied.

"He thought—or the Sable Company seers thought?"

"Apparently, the Kinor-Koy farmers bringing a load of vinegar and honey to the temple kitchens thought."

Biting into his bread, Brax frowned. "For someone who doesn't talk much, he sure hears a lot," he groused.

Yashar nodded. "That's the way of it," he said sagely. "Those who keep their ears open and their mouths shut walk the secret paths of the world."

Both Brax and Kemal paused to stare at him and he snickered at their expressions. "Elif told me that the day I arrived," he explained. "It's always stuck in my head."

"Hm. She once told me that I held my sword like a swineherd," Kemal offered, taking a sip of his own coffee.

Brax's brows drew down into a vee. "Do swineherds carry swords?" he asked.

"No. I think she meant that I shouldn't poke at people as if they were pigs."

"I don't see why not," Yashar countered, "pigs are just as likely to poke back as people."

"Perhaps. Not everything she said made sense," the other man allowed. "Sometimes she just liked to take the piss on you, play the wise old woman card."

"More often than not she liked to play the cantankerous, bossy old woman card. With everyone," Yashar snorted.

Leaning back, Kemal lifted his cup toward the tolling bell in a silent salute. "She had the right to, I suppose," he mused. "She trained just about everyone at Estavia-Sarayi in one way or another from Marshal Brayazi on down. She'll be sorely missed."

Turning his own cup between his fingers, Brax frowned reflectively. "Then why did Sable Company bar her door last night?" he asked. "Wouldn't some of those people want to be with her at the end?"

Yashar shrugged. "That's also the way of it. A deathbed watch is attended to by family or those closest in lieu of family. Elif served as a Sable Company battleseer for over sixty years. It was their right to guard her journey to the God as jealously as they saw fit."

"So she had no actual family?"

"Her abayon died a long time ago, of course. And her kardon and their delon as well. Very few are so fortunate as to make eight full decades in this world. Few enough make six."

"Few enough make three," Kemal said quietly. "My abayon were no more than a few years past that when they both died. I was only four, but I remember that Bayard, Badahir, and Chian stood watch at their sickbed for over three days."

"But you didn't?" Brax asked.

Kemal shook his head. "No. They'd taken a contagious fever, and the priests of Usara feared the four youngest wouldn't be strong enough to fight it off. We stayed with Maydir." He smiled sadly. "I remember she brought us to play under their infirmary window at Usara-Cami. Radiard and Nathu kept trying to get us to sing some nonsense song they'd made up, but Zondi was crying too hard. Our abayon died that night, but Bayard always says it gave them comfort to hear us together. Even if we were squabbling."

Brax frowned thoughtfully. "Do you wish you'd been with them at the end?"

Kemal shook his head. "I was too young to understand what was going on. My memories of them are few, but they're memories of health and laughter—not of sickness and pain. Bayard and the others gave me that, and I honor them for it. That's what older kardon do. They shield you from sadness as long as they can. Then, later, you shield them."

Brax stirred the tip of his finger in his coffee for a moment.

"I never knew my first abayon," he said after a time. "Neither did Spar. We don't even know if we share one or both of them. But we probably don't," he allowed. "We don't look anything alike. Sometimes we wondered if Cindar might be our blood abayos, but he'd never talk about it." He paused. "I'm glad of that actually; it used to make Spar sad to think about them."

Yashar and Kemal exchanged a glance. "You could find out, you know," the younger man said gently. "They might still be alive. The priests of Oristo are very talented in that regard. You could go to Chamberlain Tanay. The Hearth God would tell her if she asked."

"It's not that important," Brax replied in a carefully neutral tone. All his life he'd been taught to mistrust the priests of Oristo and, even though he trusted Tanay more than almost anyone else, he still couldn't bring himself to ask for her help as one of them. As a kind of abayos, yes, always; as a priest of Oristo, no. Chewing at his bread with a little more force than necessary, he stared out the window at the shadowy gardens beyond. "So Elif had no delon of her own?" he asked, by way of changing the subject.

Kemal shook his head. "It's not all that uncommon," he explained. "Especially among battle-seers. The Gods demands a level of commitment to Their visions that precludes most other relationships, and by the time many seers are ready to settle down and start raising

delon, it's too late. Not everyone has a pair of half-
growns gifted to them by Estavia Herself."

Brax acknowledged the compliment with an absent
nod. "She must have been lonely, though," he noted.
"Didn't she ever have an arkados?"

Yashar laughed out loud. "If some of her more outrageous stories can be believed, she had a great many," he
replied. "But none who outlived her."

"She lived a rich and passionate life," Kemal added,
"And she died surrounded by people who loved and
respected her. A good death for a good life. Those of us
who are sworn to the Battle God don't always get that
luxury. We die on the battlefield or in the infirmary, unaware of our friends and family, even though they may
be standing right beside us. That's why it's comforting
to know that you're never really alone, that Estavia's
always with you even in the darkest and most pain-filled
moments; and at the very end, She'll come for you and
you'll never be alone again. Not ever."

He and Yashar pressed a hand against their chests
and Brax echoed the motion, feeling the God's lien
buzzing against his fingertips and knowing that his
abayon felt the same thing.

"And those who are left behind?" he asked quietly.

"Will join with you in the Gods' embrace when it's
finally their time."

"Even if they're sworn to different Gods," Yashar
added, anticipating Brax's next question.

Kemal nodded. "Gol-Beyaz is large. There's room for
everyone."

Brax fixed them both with an intense stare. "Even for
the *unsworn*, Aban?" he asked pointedly.

The two older men exchanged a glance. "Spar will
swear, Brax," Kemal said gently. "He just needs time to understand that nobody's going to try and force him to make
a decision that isn't right for him. It really is his choice."

"But what if he doesn't?"

Kemal sighed. "I don't know. You'll have to ask Estavia, but She probably won't have an answer for you; the God of Battle is more concerned with the present than with the future."

"You're saying I should ask Incasa, then?"

Yashar almost snorted coffee out his nose. "Only if you want a cryptic pile of rubbish that makes no sense. Better to ask Oristo."

"Oristo will probably just tell me to eat more vegetables and stop worrying about it."

"Likewise Havo."

"Likewise Usara," Kemal added.

"And Ystazia?"

The two older men paused. "Ystazia might have an answer for you," Yashar allowed. "Take Her something pretty made of colored glass and you might be able to get Her attention. They say She's mesmerized by prisms. They make rainbows."

"Better yet, why don't you just go and ask Ihsan," Kemal suggested. "He's been compiling Elif's life history in the temple library for the past six months. Just trade him a story or two about her; a private one he may not have heard. The priests of Ystazia are always greedy for knowledge."

"You'll probably find Spar there, too," Yashar added. "Tell him we have his fortune for fifteen present waiting for him."

"I will." As the first notes of Havo's Morning Invocation filtered in over the sound of the tolling bell, Brax scooped the last of his breakfast into his hand as he stood. "So what did you get him?" he asked.

"Silver."

"Very original."

"It's tradition. Fifteen needs to start saving for the future if it's going to have any fortune at all."

"Oh, you're supposed to save it?" Brax asked with exaggerated surprise.

Yashar's eyes narrowed. "You are. Why, what did you do with yours?"

Brax grinned. "I spent it. Life's too short to hoard your shine," he answered using the street term for money deliberately to tease the older man.

"Tell that to Elif."

"Point. I'll try to remember it next time I get a handful of silver. See you at Invocation." Popping a date into his mouth, Brax smiled at both men before heading for the door, feeling better than he had since he'd woken up.

3

The Funeral

ESTAVIA'S MORNING INVOCATION passed with a quiet solemnity. Elif's death had cast a pall over the temple that wouldn't be lifted until after her funeral. The companies mustered in the main courtyard, positioned as they would be on the battlefield with the infantry: Azure, Cyan, Sapphire, and Indigo Companies in the center; the mounted cavalry, Bronze Company, as the vanguard; the Sable Company battle-seers to the rear; and the Verdant and Turquoise Company archers on the flanks.

Standing beside Brin and Bazmin, Brax felt Estavia's presence stir within him, still sated and sleepy from Elif's joining as Marshal Brayazi sang the first note. When the Battle God finally made a hazy appearance, he felt Her great hand whisper through his hair and along his sword arm, lingering for a moment on the spot where She'd scored the symbol of Her wall five years ago, and then She was gone. He could almost see Elif's milky white eyes staring out at him in the crimson afterimage; then it, too, disappeared.

Marshal Brayazi dismissed the troops. As one, Sable Company made for the seer's shrine. While the rest broke into smaller groups to reminisce about the passing of their most venerable elder, he went looking for Spar.

He hadn't expected to see him at Invocation.

Noncombatants took up a position on a series of long, marble benches beneath a stand of cinar trees on the southern end of the courtyard. On the best of days the row of huge warhorse rear ends blocked Brax's view of just about everything, and even if he could have seen those seated, Spar liked to move about, one morning sitting in front, the next behind, one evening to the left, the following to the right; wherever the winds of his vision took him.

Or maybe just to make it appear that way, Brax allowed. Seers were supposed to be unpredictable and mysterious, and they were granted a lot of leeway because of it. A lifetime on the streets had taught them both that perception was far more important than reality, and Spar had always been a master at playing perception to his own, best advantage. He'd been that way from the very first day when Cindar'd returned to their dingy third-floor room with the wide-eyed four year old in tow and shoved him unceremoniously at nine-year-old Brax.

"This is Spar. He's gonna be working with us from now on, 'cause you've gotten too buggerin' big to fit through the upper-story windows. Learn him what he needs to know. Get him ready for tonight."

Spar had turned an innocently expectant smile on Brax, and the older boy had seen just the faintest hint of the cynical lifter he was destined to become sparkling in his big, blue eyes.

Spar had been a very fast learner and a natural actor, able to become either completely invisible or the center of attention from one moment to the next. Brax had seen him go from hard-eyed lifter sizing up a possible mark to terrified, underfed, and lost delos to disdainful and arrogant seer in the blink of an eye. He was not unpredictable. And he was not mysterious. Not if you paid attention.

Brax always paid attention, even when Spar believed he didn't.

Now, weaving through the clumps of warriors who still lingered in the courtyard, he ducked into the finely-wrought colonnade covered in morning glory vines that marched along the front facade of a small, northwest pavilion. Here, half a dozen scribes of Ystazia kept rooms, recording what events they deemed worthy of posterity and tutoring those few warriors who wanted a more advanced instruction in poetry, mathematics, or philosophy than the Battle God's temple usually offered. As a consequence, Brax only came here when he was looking for Spar and had exhausted all the high, lonely places he usually haunted. But today Yashar's suggestion was the most likely. Spar would be closeted with his old teacher, Ihsan, the serenely patient priest of Ystazia whose love of learning had earned him a trust very rarely given.

Taking the pavilion's winding, white marble stairs two at a time, Brax emerged into a small, hushed corridor, and then, resisting the urge to wipe his hands on his tunic like a nervous delinkos, he pushed open the small, wooden door that led to the temple library.

During their second year at Estavia-Sarayi, Ihsan had taken both Brax and Spar to visit The Bibliotheca, the largest collection of books, manuscripts, and scrolls in the known world. Housed in the very heart of the Arts God's temple, it stood three stories high, its intricate mosaic ceiling supported by a dozen multihued marble pillars drawn from the bottom of Gol-Beyaz itself. Brightly-patterned woven carpets covered its floors, and vast tapestries and gilt-framed paintings hung above the polished mahogany shelves that lined its walls. The silk cushions strategically scattered before the tall, stained-glass windows and the musicians playing quietly in the upper gallery had lent a hushed and studious air to a room that Brax had found both intimidating and overwhelming.

But Spar had been completely entranced.

Spar had always loved books. Even when he'd been

very young, he'd been happiest hovering about the book stalls, running his fingers along their leather-bound spines and dreaming of the stories they contained. Afraid that the bookmongers—ever sensitive to one of their own—might lure his most useful delinkos away from him, Cindar had forbidden them to go anywhere near the stalls. However, knowing only too well what kind of life the master lifter would eventually lead them to—prison—Brax had taken Spar there as often as possible.

When it became obvious that, even weeks after their visit to Ystazia's library, Spar could think of little else, Brax had finally taken him aside and asked in as sincere a tone as he could manage if he wanted to enter Ystazia-Sarayi as a librarian-delinkos. The half-starved expression of longing the other boy had done his best to conceal had almost confirmed his worst fears, but then he'd just shaken his head.

Brax had cocked his own to one side in skeptical disbelief.

"You sure? You've always loved books. Wouldn't you like to spend the rest of your life surrounded by them?"

Spar had regarded him seriously.

"No. Books can take you over as much as any God can."

"Would that be such a terrible thing? Really?"

"Yes."

He'd never mentioned the Bibliotheca again.

By contrast, the library at Estavia-Sarayi was ridiculously small. Made up of two small rooms, an upper entrance gallery which housed its twelve leather-bound volumes, and a lower reading and meditation room just large enough to contain a mangel to warm the space in bad weather, a low table for lessons, and half a dozen cushions. Crossing to the slim railing that separated the two, Brax peered over the edge. As he'd suspected, with Ystazia's Invocation just ended, Spar and Ihsan were already seated at the table together, youth and elder bent over several neatly stacked piles of parchment paper, scribbling diligently.

The fine golden whiskers that had just begun to scatter across Spar's cheeks in the last year glinted in the sunlight, and Brax paused a moment to take notice of the extra thickness in his shoulder-length blond hair and the new breadth of muscle across his back, which suggested Brax wasn't the only one to have benefited from life under Chamberlain Tanay's tender care in the last five years. And if the set of his shoulders was still tight, and his expression still guarded, they were less so than they'd been. Spar had blossomed here. He belonged here.

As Brax made for the delicate wrought-iron spiral staircase, Jaq looked up from a worn and ragged carpet by the window, woofing a proprietous greeting, and Ihsan glanced up with a smile.

"Ah, here's my most recalcitrant pupil," he said, his deep green eyes sparkling with humor. "I don't suppose you've come to indulge me in some advanced reading lessons?"

Trying to maneuver down the narrow stairs in full Invocation armor which included his sword, Brax smiled distractedly back at him. "I'm afraid I'd only frustrate you, Sayin. My mind's not on words today."

"Is it ever?" Spar asked without raising his head, the neutral tone of his voice showing plainly that he was no more likely to show his grief over Elif's death here than anywhere else.

"No."

"Battle-Seer Elif's joining has driven more prosaic matters from the minds of even the most dedicated of scholars today," Ihsan interjected smoothly. "Case in point," he added, gesturing at the pile of papers, "I've been trying to compile the details of her many years of temple service, but I'm afraid the work has degenerated into a series of nostalgic memories revolving around some of her more colorful exploits."

"Sounds more interesting," Brax noted. Finally reaching the bottom of the stairs in safety, he made an apologetic gesture as Spar shot him a disapproving glare. "I mean, for some people, Sayin. For warriors."

"For others, too, I'd imagine," Ihsan admitted easily. "Spar's promised me a story or two. Perhaps you might also gift me with one of your own if you can find the time before you return south."

"I will, Sayin."

"When do you leave?"

"Our ship departs for Alev-Hisar the morning after the funeral."

"Ah, Kaptin Majin's command. I remember her well from Sapphire Company. I take it, then, with such a tight schedule that it is, in fact, my young colleague here that you've actually come to see?"

Unable to ask the question he'd come about with Spar in the room, Brax just nodded.

"I shall hold you to your promise," Ihsan warned, recognizing his expression. "But I suppose I can be convinced to postpone it until you return." He rose with a faint groan. "It's time for my walk anyway. My physician insists that I break up my morning study with some small exercise to keep the blood flowing properly." Catching up a book from the table, he smiled at Spar. "But she never said I couldn't study while I was doing it," he added.

"Try not to bump into anything, Sayin," Spar murmured absently, his eyes still locked on the parchment before him.

"If I do, you'll be the first one sent to fetch bandages."

"As always." Spar continued to read as Ihsan took his leave.

Brax unhooked his sword belt and set it and his helmet to one side before he dropped down beside the youth to sit, chin on fists, staring at his left ear until Spar looked up with an irritable expression.

"What?"

"Why didn't you tell me you'd written to Brin and Bazmin?"

"What? Oh, that." Spar met Brax's gaze evenly. "How was I supposed to? By writing to you? You'd have only had one of them read the letter out loud, and they'd have found that far too funny."

"They found it pretty funny that you hadn't told me when I got back to Anavatan."

"So learn to read your own letters in private and you'll know things sooner."

"Why didn't you tell me when we went into the city yesterday?"

"I had other things on my mind."

"And now?"

"Now you already know. And I still have other things on my mind."

He met the older man's eye, and Brax nodded in silent agreement. They wouldn't talk about Elif until Spar was ready to.

"On your mind or in your vision?" he asked instead.

"The one comes from the other."

"Do they include the increased Petchan raids and this runaway cart you were talking about last night?"

"Possibly."

"Possibly?"

"Probably."

Brax leaned his good elbow on the table. "So which is it?"

Spar shot him an impatient scowl of his own. "Possibly," he repeated, jerking a pile of papers out from under the other man. "And probably. Visioning's not an exact map of the future; you know that. I get feelings, images, a sense of approaching danger maybe. When I do, I tell you. Now I've told you."

"You seem to have told a lot of people this time."

"What of it?" Spar's tone was challenging, but Brax just shrugged.

"Nothing of it," he answered. "I just thought that seers liked to keep all their little prophecies to themselves."

"You mean the *Sable Company* seers like to keep all their little prophecies to themselves."

"Maybe."

"I'm *not* a Sable Company seer. I choose who I tell, not them."

Brax raised his hands in surrender. "And so you told Kemal and Yashar," he observed mildly.

Spar just snorted. "They were fussing; I had to tell them something. They worry about you."

"I think they're getting old."

"You need to write to them more often."

"I suppose. You need to spend time with them today so they can give you your fortune for fifteen gift."

"I'll see them at noontime."

Brax nodded. The two of them fell silent, but when Jaq came over to stuff his head under Spar's hand, the youth forced the corners of his mouth up into a sour smile.

"Thanks for your gift," he said shortly.

Brax acknowledged his words with an equally uncomfortable shrug. They'd never had to talk about that sort of thing before. Brax took care of Spar. That was what he did. But Spar would soon be an adult in his own right, capable of taking care of himself, maybe even of making his own way in the world without Brax beside him. The formalities would have to be observed from now on.

"You know Elif gave me one," Spar continued in a falsely casual tone.

"Yeah?"

"Yeah, just before she died." He opened his hand to reveal a heavy golden soldis. The watchtower etched into its surface gleamed richly, and Brax's mouth dropped open.

"That's ... a buggerin' big coin," he breathed.

Spar scowled down at it. "Too big," he groused. "She

knew it would make me think, make me move along a path she thought up first. But once I've started up her stupid path, what am I supposed to do with an actual coin this big?"

Brax shrugged. "The same thing you're supposed to do with an actual coin much smaller. Spend it or save it."

Spar raised a sarcastic eyebrow at him. "Really?" he sneered, "And here I was thinking I should eat it."

"Just give it to Tanay to keep for you. That's what I did." Brax grinned suddenly remembering his lie to Yashar at breakfast. He just hadn't been able to resist giving the older man the answer he was expecting.

"So you just banked yours away?" Spar pressed.

"Sure. What else was I going to do with it? The temple provides me with everything I need. Give it to Tanay," he repeated. "It'll give you an excuse to go see her." He grinned widely at the suggestion and Spar glared at him.

"Don't be an idiot," he snapped. "She doesn't think of me that way."

"But you think of her that way."

Spar opened his mouth to deny Brax's words, then shrugged. "It doesn't matter," he muttered. "She thinks I'm too young."

"You won't always be."

The youth gave him a shy half smile, pleased by the encouragement despite himself. Stuffing the coin into the small hide purse at his belt, he straightened. "I'll go see her tonight," he agreed.

Brax gave him a puzzled look. "Why wait that long?"

Spar frowned. "There'll be ... other people there until late," he replied in a defensive mutter. "I don't like people ... looking at me."

"Then we sure came to the wrong place," Brax observed.

"I've been saying that for five years," Spar retorted,

but smiled to show Brax that he was only joking before growing serious once again.

"Everyone expects me to do the things they think I should," he continued in a resentful tone. "Make the choices they want me to make; make the choices *they'd* make. Even Elif," he added quietly.

"She said something to you before she died," Brax hazarded.

"She warned me against seeding my own desires into my interpretation of prophecy."

Brax frowned thoughtfully. "Do you ever?"

"No, it was probably just some last little bit of old abayos advice. *Make that your fortune for fifteen,*" he echoed in a passing imitation of Elif's voice.

"So that's not what she said that's got your nose all out of joint."

Spar shot him a jaundiced look, but when Brax simply waited for an answer, he gave his careless, one-shouldered shrug. "She said that I was going to *have* to make a choice some day soon," he replied with a sour grimace.

Brax snorted in amusement. "And it took a seer of her renowned abilities to tell you that? You're a year from adulthood today. If nothing else, you're gonna have to decide how you're gonna make a living."

"That's not all she said, butt-head. She told me to make a strong choice," Spar snarled back. "And what's *that* supposed to mean, anyway?" he added in a sullen mutter.

"You know what it means: it means make a choice that will keep you safe and whole, a choice that'll strengthen you, not weaken you."

"I've been *trying* to do that since we got here," Spar retorted hotly.

"No, you've been *trying* to avoid making any choices at all," Brax countered. "And doing a great job so far. It's just not gonna last. It's gonna come to an end in one full year. *Face* it."

Jaq began to growl at Brax's tone, and Spar scratched him behind one flopping red ear with an indulgent smile.

"Don't pick on me," he said with a smug expression. "Or my dog will bite you."

"I'll bite him back," Brax answered mildly. "It'll be good practice for when we finally run the Petchans to ground."

"Yeah, you said you were going back to Alev-Hisar right after the funeral?" Spar asked in a thoughtful voice, rubbing the coin between finger and thumb.

Brax nodded. "Ekmir-Koy's asked for an increased military presence this season because they're so close to the Gurney-Dag foothills."

"It's possible that I might be joining you there before too long."

"Why?"

"Kaptin Liel wants a full complement of battle-seers along the western God-Wall. I'm supposed to be accompanying them. To *hone* my skills," he added with a deeply sarcastic sneer.

"Because of the Petchan raids or to keep you away from First Oracle Bessic?"

"Both and because of Elif's deathbed prophecy."

"Ah. The twins were fishing around for that this morning."

"They'll know it soon enough. Kaptin Liel will be sending the official word out tomorrow after the seers have had a chance to chew on it for a while."

"Did she say anything that you and I need to worry about now?"

Spar's pale brows drew down. "I'm not sure. She repeated the prophecy about Hisar's birth. And no—Hisar isn't here," he added, as Brax cast an apprehensive glance about the room. "The last I saw It, It was hovering over the central courtyard."

Brax frowned. "I thought spirits couldn't get onto temple grounds?" he said remembering the feel of buzzing wings by his ear.

"Hisar's not a spirit. Not exactly. And It isn't exactly on the grounds either, It's more ... sideways of the grounds."

"Sideways?"

"Sideways, halfways, whatever. The point is that It's not truly in the world, not yet. Elif," Spar said emphatically, returning to the earlier subject, "mentioned a vision she'd had when she was young about a child and a tower standing before a crimson-covered mountain." He opened his mouth to add something, then seemed to think better of it, shaking his head with a frown. "Four years ago she told me she thought that the child was me," he said finally, giving an indignant sniff. "Even though I'm not a child anymore."

"And the tower would be your 'halfways not exactly a spirit,' Hisar?" Brax asked through gritted teeth.

"If it is, both Hisar and I are going to need your help."

Brax's mouth dropped open again. "Your ... my ..." he stammered. "You know I'll always be there if you need me," he managed after a moment.

"Yes, but I need you to be there for Hisar, too," Spar pressed.

"Why?"

"Because Hisar's young and doesn't understand how easy it is to get taken in by lifters and tricksters, Especially," he added, eyes narrowed, "God-lifters and tricksters."

"But isn't Hisar a God, too?"

"Not exactly." When Brax gave him a disbelieving look, Spar shrugged. "Not yet."

"Sideways, halfways?"

"Something like that. Either way, I don't want It pressured into making a decision It doesn't want to make."

"So, what good will my help be for that?"

"I don't know yet, I just need you to agree to it."

"Well, I can't see what use my help could be, but if you need me to, I'll help," Brax promised reluctantly. "Both you and Hisar."

"Good."

"As long as It doesn't get too close."

"Fine."

"Or actually talk to me."

"Brax . . ."

"All right." He held his hands up with a faint smile. "So, was that all there was to Elif's vision?"

"What? Oh, right." Spar frowned. "I'm the child—supposedly—Hisar is the tower, and Kaptin Liel believes the mountains are the Gurney-Dag Range."

Brax nodded. "Crimson mountains, mountains to the west, it makes sense."

"Except that the Gurney-Dag Mountains are to the south," Spar pointed out.

"Southwest," Brax argued. "Whatever. Apparently, the command council's gonna be discussing a more aggressive response to the Petchan raids tomorrow."

"Yeah, Sable Company will be there in full force to push their own agenda."

"Which is?"

"The same as it always is," Spar sneered. "Seers hate competition. Most of them have been having a lot of disturbing and confusing visions about mountains and death all season, and Elif's vision will just confirm their interpretation: the Petchan seers are a danger that needs to be met head-on and eliminated."

"Brin and Bazmin seem to think it means that the Petchans have a new leader," Brax began.

Spar shrugged. "It might, or it might mean that they're moving in a new direction and moving fast. The Sable Company seers aren't sure, and they're not used to being . . . not sure." He showed his teeth in disdain. "They're being blocked, probably by the Petchan seers themselves. Not much has ever been known about them, and seers hate secrets as much as they hate competition."

"I guess they see it as a professional insult," Brax added in a mild tone.

Spar gave a derisive snort. "The Anavatanon seers can't see anything outside their own tiny little world," he sneered. "They can't see that they're being blocked, and they're so arrogant that they don't even suspect it. After all, no one could possibly be as powerful as them, could they, never mind be *more* powerful? And you want me to join *their* ranks?" he added. "They're not worthy to join *my* ranks."

"So you're not being blocked?"

Spar's eyes suddenly went very black. "I don't get blocked," he said bluntly.

"You sure?"

Brax's voice was both serious and amused without a hint of concern over Spar's implied threat, and the youth gave him a jaundiced look before cracking an equally sour smile. "Point," he acknowledged. "I'll keep an eye on it."

Outside, the temple bell tolled the hour, and Brax stood. "Fair enough." Catching up his sword belt and helmet, he made for the stairs. "But in the meantime, I have a pack of delinkon to ride herd on. If you need me ... or if Hisar does," he added sardonically, "I'll be in the central courtyard preparing for runaway carts being driven by Petchan raiders. *You* go see Kemal and Yashar," he ordered, "and then go see Tanay."

Spar's eyes returned to their usual blue as his expression relaxed. "Yes, *Kardos,*" he said with heavy sarcasm.

"And do something about Jaq, will you?" Brax added, refusing to rise to the bait. "He smells ... unique. I think he's been rolling in something."

Returning his attention to the pile of parchments, Spar just waved a dismissive hand at him, but as Brax took his leave, he leaned over to sniff suspiciously at the dog's pelt and Brax chuckled. Spar also paid attention. They'd be all right. They'd avoided plenty of carts in the past; this one would be no different.

Tucking his helmet into the crook of his arm, Brax

took the stairs as quickly as his armor would allow, then paused at the top as he realized he'd forgotten to talk to Spar about Graize. As he glanced down, the air above Spar's head suddenly shimmered with a metallic gleam. As the youth began to speak to something only he could see, Brax's jaw tightened. Whatever Spar said, he didn't like that Hisar could come and go so easily within the confines of Estavia's temple. Hisar and Graize had been allies before, and the creature's timing was suspicious.

"We've avoided runaway carts driven by Graize and by spirits before," he warned the Godling silently. *"And promise or no promise, I won't let you or your kind put Spar in danger again. Not ever again, so you just watch your step."*

✦

As Brax took his leave, Hisar stared up at him, Its eyes tinged with metallic fire. Then, taking Its dragonfly-seeming, It spun out the window, heading east over the temple walls. Circling Lazim-Hisar, the huge watch-tower which guarded the city's Western Trisect, Its immature emotions swirled inside Its chest in confusion. It had touched Brax's spirit on the battlements of Estavia-Sarayi. Although the unwavering passion with which Brax offered up both his loyalty and his hostility were a tantalizing mixture, Hisar did not understand how Spar could believe that Brax could be made to bring these qualities to Its assistance. Whenever he spoke about It—or spoke to It as he'd just done—it was only to issue warnings and threats.

No, It decided, It would go back to Graize where It understood what was expected of It, even if Graize didn't talk to It.

It made for the clouds above, then paused as a flurry of movement caught Its attention. Far below, people scurried about, setting torches bound with white silk ribbons along the temple walls.

No, after the funeral, It determined; It would go after

the old seer's funeral. Spar would be there, his mind bright with pain and grief, and Hisar wanted to see if he could keep all those people from getting inside him and seeing it.

Settling on the watchtower's tall bronze flagpole, Hisar folded Its wings around It like a bird's and waited for night.

✦

The day passed in somber reflection, the temple's mood echoed by the cold rain that began to fall shortly after noon. Spar spent the entire day closeted in the library, emerging only when Kemal came to fetch him after Evening Invocation, insisting that he join him and Yashar for a quiet supper in their rooms. He ate in silence, then withdrew to the delin-alcove, drawing Jaq in beside him. His abayon let him be, knowing the only comfort they could offer him was to leave him to himself. As Kemal closed the latticed shutters, Yashar doused the lamps and the two of them retired for an early night as well.

✦

The armory bell had just tolled four when Yashar touched Kemal lightly on the shoulder. The younger man stirred, then opened his eyes. The light from Yashar's lamp cast a faint yellow glow across his arkados' face, leaving the rest of the room in shadow.

"It's time."

Kemal nodded. Rising, he glanced over at the delin-alcove where Spar lay, shoved protectively against the wall by Jaq's heavy frame, and Yashar shook his head at his questioning expression.

"Leave him to sleep for a few moments longer."

The two men dressed quietly in tunic and sandals. Estavia's First Day was the temple's traditional Memorial Day. At that time the eight companies would stand in full ceremonial armor in the central courtyard, listening to an account of the year's dead. Battle-Seer Elif, late of Sable Company, would be remembered then. This was a private good-bye.

"It'll be hard for him today," Yashar said, reaching for his training sword in its old, worn scabbard. "Back in the public eye again. You know how he hates being looked at."

Kemal nodded. "We'll keep him between us, and you can glare at anyone who gets too close."

"Hm." The older man turned. "I was thinking, maybe we should request a posting to Anahtar-Hisar this season. Get him away from all these seers. The sea air would do him good, and we'd be close enough to Brax so that they could see each other more often. Spar misses him more than he admits to."

As one, they glanced at the delin-alcove again, but neither Spar nor Jaq stirred at the sound of his name.

"It's a thought, but I imagine Liel will want to take over his training now that Elif's gone," Kemal noted.

Yashar's dark eyes flashed dangerously. "Then it's best we put our own oar in and soon," he growled. "Before Sable Company's kaptin forgets who Spar's actual abayon are."

"Maybe. But he is a seer, Yash," Kemal reminded him gently. "There's no hiding from it."

"He's a delos, Kem," Yashar shot back. "For one more year. And I won't have him pressured into growing up too fast. He's had too much of that already."

Kemal just shook his head with a fond expression then turned as a soft knock at the door interrupted their conversation. "I expect that will be Brax," he said. "Come on, Yash, wake him up. As you said, it's time."

✦

The cool spring air smelled sharply of cinar and plane trees in bloom as they joined the rest of Cyan Company already gathered in the main training yard. Torches led off into the darkness, marking their route. As they passed under a plain stone archway, Kemal saw Spar shiver. Brax reached over at once to lay a reassuring hand on his shoulder, and Kemal echoed the motion. In the last four years, Spar had made his way into nearly every room, garden, and hall at Estavia-Sarayi, but there was one place he'd never been found: the Pavilion of Silence, where the Warriors of Estavia gathered to say farewell to their dead.

One by one, the eight companies slowly filed into the pavilion's wide crescent-shaped courtyard. The pavilion itself stood at the far northeastern corner of the temple, guarded by the great bulk of Lazim-Hisar. Made of intricately carved white marble, it shone in the torchlight like a beacon, but it was the stone pyre in the center of the courtyard which drew their gaze tonight. The priests of Usara had surrounded it in oil-soaked sheaves of cedar in readiness for Elif's body, and a hush fell over the courtyard as the gathered surrounded it in a tightly packed semicircle. In the distance they heard the quiet sound of footsteps.

Kemal stilled a shiver of his own, feeling rather than seeing the six black-clad seers enter the courtyard, carrying a simple wooden litter between them. As one, the warriors opened a path for them as they would for their seers on the battlefield, and as Elif's body passed, he made himself turn and look at her.

Wrapped in a white silk shroud, she seemed smaller than she had in life, stripped of her sharp, domineering personality. As was Anavatan's tradition, the priests of Ystazia had painted representations of her trade on the silk: black cuirass with Estavia's crimson eyes shining from the center on her chest, sword down the length of her right arm, and shield down the length of her left, a closed helm with the white raven's eyes of Sable Company covering her head.

Her real sword, a finely-crafted hand-and-a-half weapon she hadn't carried for years, was already on display in the armory tower, lying in a place of honor beside the heavily bejeweled weapons that were said to have been carried by Kaptin Haldin, Estavia's earliest Champion.

Almost unwillingly, Kemal turned to glance at Brax. Estavia's newest Champion stood just behind Spar, hands resting lightly on his shoulders, his attention more on his kardos than on the litter passing before him. As the seers set Elif's body on the pyre and backed away, Kemal saw him still the urge to melt them both into the crowd and nodded his understanding. Brax would do his duty by Elif and by the Warriors of Estavia. He would ensure that he and Spar remained as the flames took her body, reducing it to ash that would be gathered up and placed in the urn Spar had chosen for her. But after that, they would vanish, seeking their own comfort in some high, lonely place until duty once again called him away.

Above their heads, a metallic shimmer betrayed the presence of the Godling, and Kemal stilled a sudden sense of disquiet. Elif had made a deathbed prophecy tying Spar and the creature to a future of danger and death, and Kemal was suddenly afraid that he and Yashar would not be enough to shield him from it.

He turned to his arkados and, as if he could sense his thoughts, the older man met his eyes. As one, they moved closer, covering both their delon with the same promise of protection; whatever it took, they would be there when they needed them. Between them, Brax and Spar visibly relaxed and, as they returned their attention to the pyre, the metallic shimmer disappeared.

✦

Hovering above the pavilion's white-tiled roof, Hisar stilled Its own sudden sense of disquiet. It had Its answer. Spar had maintained an iron-clad control over his mind and body until that final moment when something Kemal and Yashar had done had made that control vanish like the morning mist. But rather than allow them inside, his mind had seemed to move out to meet theirs instead. It made the Godling feel uneasy and unhappy at the same time, and It didn't know why.

With a whir of Its shimmering wings, It shot into the clouds. Graize never made It feel like that, It thought resentfully. It would return to Graize. Even if he didn't talk to It, even if he didn't think of it like a ... like a person. Even if he thought of It like some kind of ... half spirit, half animal.

It shook Its wings at the sudden sense of unhappiness the thought evoked. Why should Graize think of It like anything else? It had never appeared to him as anything else.

"Why not?" Spar's voice whispered in Its memory and It forced Itself to shrug again.

"Just leave it," It repeated with little confidence, then straightened Its wings. No, It would return to Graize whatever he thought of It. It still understood what Graize expected of It.

"Even if Graize's expectations are more demanding than they used to be?"

"Yes, even then," It snapped. Spar had said It didn't have to listen to anyone if It didn't want to, and that included Itself.

Still unsure, but determined to do things Its own way just as It had been taught, It made for the distant mountains and the other seer in Its life.

4

Graize

STRETCHED OUT ON A ragged jut of rock a hundred feet above a cascading waterfall, Graize drew in a breath of limitless vision, his gray eyes wide and fathomless. The Gurney-Dag Mountains seemed to breathe with him, exhaling all doubt and distraction, then inhaling an intoxicating mixture of mental and physical clarity he hadn't experienced since the spirits of the wild lands had torn him from a life on the streets of Anavatan and thrown him headfirst into the arms of destiny.

Destiny, he observed, was rarely clear, but it was always intoxicating.

Above him, the mountains reached up to snatch an errant cloud from the sky, hurling it down the chasm to mix with the waterfall below. Tiny rainbows of power scattered in its wake, filling his mind with images of crystal prophecy, and he smiled in pleasure.

Yesterday, he'd seen an ancient, gray-beaked raven dive into a mountain pool, emerging a moment later with its back and wings covered in a shimmering silver patina. He'd found its body an hour later, lying beneath a tangled juniper bush, stiff and cold, but still tingling with the power of the mountain spirits. The setting sun had etched a finely detailed pattern of silver symbols across its feathers, and he'd known: one of the Battle God's seers had gone to Gol-Beyaz.

The raven had entered his dreams that night, flying high above a tall tower that had turned from black to silver to gray to gold before finally disappearing into a sea of gray mist. Graize had awakened to the sound of a raven's cry and the feel of the early morning wind dancing across his cheeks.

Now, sitting up on the mountain ledge, he lifted his face to that wind, allowing its intimate caress to whisper through his hair. He'd traveled the length and breadth of the knowable world in five short years; from narrow city streets to endless plains, from salt-sprayed shores to mountain crags, but the wind was always the same. Cloaked in the hot and dusty air of Anavatan, it had swirled about him as he'd fleeced the Dockside delinkon, built itself into the high and keening gales of the Berbat-Dunya where he'd been sheltered by the Rus-Yuruk nomads in exchange for his prophetic gifts, driven him across the Deniz-Siyah Sea and battered against the walls of Cvet Tower in faraway Volinsk while he'd learned a more subtle but no more effective way to prophesize, and finally it had brought him south once more, creeping along the western ridge, hidden from Gods and seers, to the Petchan village of Chalash in the Gurney-Dag Mountains, where spinning and swirling amidst the rocky tors, it plaited his hair with secrets like a lover might plait favored bits of cloth or a length of beads.

Always the same wind.

But was he always the same man? He'd changed in those years, grown; his brown hair—worn long and braided in the Yuruk fashion—had lightened, and the line of beard across his cheeks had darkened. His appetites had matured, but his desires had remained the same. So—was he the same?

Far below, he heard the sound of tinkling bells and set the question aside as his thoughts turned to his adopted kardos, Danjel of the Rus-Yuruk, come seeking him before the sun's rapid descent played too much havoc with the limited visioning the encircling mountains allowed. An accomplished wyrdin-kazak, Danjel was more used to the freedom granted by the Berbat-Dunya's open plains where both an enemy and a prophecy could be discerned from miles away, rather than the tightly controlled safety and security of the Gurney-Dag's narrow, winding paths and hidden grottoes. Here the Petchan seers hunted their visions as an eagle might hunt a hare: hovering patiently above its den rather than snatching a meal from the air like a hungry swallow.

So, he thought, was a Yuruk swallow transported to the land of Petchan eagles still a swallow?

The conflicting images made his mind list lazily to one side like a leaky boat laden with too many fish, and he brought it back to the present with an impatient shake of his head, the beads woven into one side of his hair in the Petchan style clinking against each other. He could not afford to disappear into the murky depths of metaphor right now, he told himself sternly. He had too many other things to think about. Reaching into the hide pouch at his belt, he drew out a small, smooth turtle shell, holding it in the air so that it covered the distant sun like a shield.

Three such shells had made the journey with him from the Yuruk encampment on the shores of Gol-Bardak Lake. At Cvet Tower he'd used them to keep his focus much as he'd used his precious dead stag beetle from the streets of Anavatan as a focus among the Yuruk.

Of course, he mused, focus was a much more illusive commodity at Cvet Tower.

✦

"Nothing exists independent and alone. All things, physical and metaphysical, are entwined like lovers clasped in a fiery embrace."

Panos of Amatus, mysterious oracle of a mysterious people from across the Deniz-Hadi Sea far to the south of Gol-Beyaz, had said that. Her sweeping golden hair echoed her sire's, the powerful King Pyrros of the maritime empire of Skiros and her fathomless, black eyes revealed a prophetic ability that was said to rival that of the Gods Themselves. Panos would not say if either were true, but then Panos rarely concerned herself with anything so trivial as physical truth. She existed in a world of fluid and ever-changing sensations that broke against her mind like the tide against the shore, leading her in whatever direction her visioning demanded.

It had led her to the foot of Dovek-Hisar four years ago, one of three great watchtowers that guarded the Bogazi-Isik Strait north of Anavatan on the night the Godling had been truly born into the world. There she'd plucked Graize from the icy waters beneath the battlements of Estavia-Sarayi and spirited him across the northern sea to Prince Illan Dmitriviz Volinsk. Graize had spent those years in their company, negotiating between their two very different approaches to prophecy and power.

Illan had set all his formidable abilities to the question of undermining the strength of the Anavatanon seers so that Volinsk might someday sweep in and take control of Gol-Beyaz. He'd made a thorough study of both his enemies and his potential allies, recording their strengths and weaknesses as a quartermaster might record the contents of a storehouse. Each one was carefully assigned a place in his vision and each one was watched just as carefully to ensure they did not stray from that assigned position. He was both patient and pragmatic. He had envisioned Anavatan's downfall, and he would bring it about in both prophetic vision and reality if it took a lifetime. To this end he'd invited Panos, emissary of King Pyrros, to join him at Cvet Tower and later had groomed Graize as his own personal emissary among the Petchans.

"They come and go unhindered by the prophetic scrutiny of others, drawing a cloak about their movements

so thick that the very act of cloaking goes unremarked. Find this secret and you may be able to use it to our own advantage."

For his part, Graize was willing enough. He had his own vision to bring into being, the growth of his Godling into a force to be feared; a force under his command, and any advantage which aided this vision was worth seeking. The destruction of Anavatan was secondary, but as long as it followed a parallel path to his own ambitions, he'd happily see it burn. There was nothing but ghosts and the memories of blood and pain left for him in the City of the Gods.

That and one, final, loose end he intended to see to soon enough.

✦

On the day of Panos' pronouncement a violent autumn storm had driven all three of them to seek the warmth of Illan's sitting room. Dancing to a music only she could hear, the southern oracle had paused to stare, almost mesmerized, at the intricately carved detailing on the oaken fireplace mantel, her words emerging like water bubbling from an underground spring. Used to her sensual, many-layered analogies that often came out of nowhere, Illan had not turned from his atlas table where he was studying the pieces he'd set out to represent the growing armada of Skiros, but seated by the hearth, Graize had looked up, the expression in his gray eyes hooded.

"Independence and fire are single-faceted," he replied. "Simplistic and clean. Strong."

Running her fingers along imaginary harp strings, Panos smiled dreamily. "No, my little tortoise," she murmured. "Independence is the illusion of simplicity as fire is the illusion of life. It does not exist at all. It is the absence of existence."

Crouching down beside him, she stared into the glowing coals, her black eyes fixed on a single spike of flame. "Fire is complex," she continued. "It dances, it sings, and it makes love, consuming its lover even as it embraces it, and yet it cannot live without it and so it eventually dies. Poor little fire." She turned to stare at him with her usual intensity. "Fire is a paradox, and you are a paradox, my fiery wisp of smoke. You desire independence because you think it makes you strong, but you know that's untrue even as you fashion the very thought. Without your Yuruk, without your Godling, and without us, how strong can you really be?" She leaned forward until her hair tickled against his cheek. "You are smoke," she breathed. "All swirly and fine, but without fire . . ." she snapped her fingers. "You're whisked up the chimney."

✦

On the mountainside, Graize gave a sudden, piercing whistle, and the Godling immediately swooped down from the clouds to smack irritably at the beads in his hair. With a smile, Graize stroked his fingers along Its essence in a sympathetic but unrepentant gesture. Smoke or not, he controlled the fire, and one of the ways was to control its reactions.

The Petchan seers, known as sayers, fashioned warding-beads from clay drawn from special streams hidden deep in the mountains' glacial crags. Each color was infused with a distinctive power over the spirits of the Gurney-Dag; known to be far more hostile and unpredictable than those of the Berbat-Dunya. Shepherds and hunters wove dark brown beads into the collars of their animals and the hair of their children for protection. Sayers wore blue, which controlled the spirits themselves, or green to ensnare their dreams and so strengthen the sayer's prophecy. Chiefs and the most senior sayers carried the rarest of all, the deep red-and-silver-speckled beads made from clay found only in the highest glacier pools, believed to have been colored by the blood of the spirits themselves as the mountains were being born. Haz, the chief of the Petchan village of Chalash, had gifted Graize and Danjel with beads of blue, brown, and green as befitting their status as foreign seers.

The Godling hated them. Graize had woven his into a single thin braid worn behind his left ear to give his ethereal creature as much access to his body as possible—despite the deep misgivings of his Petchan hosts—but It still made Its displeasure known whenever It approached him.

Now, however, It froze a few inches above his head, waiting as eagerly as a dog waited for a bone while Graize raised one hand, a tiny silver seed of power clutched tightly in his fist in the Yuruk way. Graize held his position for a single breath, then flung the seed into the air, watching as the Godling dove for it, in aspect now more like a seagull than a dog.

Like Panos' visioning, the Godling was fluid, untroubled by form, but unlike her visioning It kept to one form at a time. Graize had fashioned It to be that way from a thousand spirits. The Godling was his, but It no more made him strong than his association with Illan and Panos made him strong. It, and they, were merely pieces in a game much like the pieces on Illan's atlas table. They were useful but not irreplaceable. If they proved unwilling to be manipulated, there were always new pieces to be found. Smoke was not bound to a single flame.

Now, as Danjel's lean, dark-haired form appeared around the path, Graize bared his teeth in the parody of a smile. New flames could always be found. Banishing the Godling back to Its nest of clouds, he turned a mock, wide-eyed look on the bi-gender wyrdin.

"Good morrow, Swallow-Kardos," he said, using Danjel's birth fetish creature as a form of greeting. "I see you're a bearded bird today."

Dismounting from his small mountain pony, the tiny bells in its tack chiming gently, Danjel shrugged. Able to move from male to female to both genders with ease, he rarely kept to one form for too long, sometimes changing half a dozen times a day as he saw fit. This time he'd remained in the male form long enough for a fine growth of black hair to grace his jawline. Taking a seat well back from Graize's rocky outcropping, he pulled a clay pipe and pouch from his belt before glancing at the shell in Graize's hand.

"Turtle augury again, Beetle-Kardos?" he replied, his almond-shaped, green eyes glittering as bright as the beads in his own hair.

Graize nodded sagely. "The beetle and the turtle know that the Petchan Hukumet Council convenes today. It's only been waiting for its senior chieftain, and his messenger arrived this morning with word of his coming. Haz-Chief's eldest, Tak and her kardon have gone down the mountain to escort him in." He held the shell up into the air once more. "And my turtle augury tells my beetle that he'll arrive when that far-off cloud covers the sun. An hour from now maybe, no more."

Danjel squinted at the shell. "Is that the cracked one?" he asked suspiciously.

Graize shook his head.

"Good. I'm never comfortable when you pull that one; it's a disturbing omen."

"So you've said before. It's only disturbing if I pull it during prophecy."

"Everything you do is done in prophecy, Kardos."

"Then I guess you're right to be disturbed." Removing the other two shells, Graize lined them up on the rock before him. The cracked shell gleamed in the sun with a reproachful air, reminding him of an earlier conversation on the shores of Gol-Bardak.

After a four-year absence, Graize had returned to the Rus-Yuruk that spring under Illan's direction to travel to the Gurney-Dag Mountains and convince the Petchan chiefs to increase their attacks on the villages clustered about the southwestern shore of Gol-Beyaz.

Unable to sail openly down the silvery Gol-Beyaz Lake itself where far too many Gods and mortals might mark his passage, he'd needed Danjel to guide him along the wild land's western ridge which paralleled the Gods' shining home. Born out on the Berbat-Dunya, only the bi-gender wyrdin-kazak had the skills to hide him from the Anavatanon seers. Danjel had taken some convincing, but he'd finally agreed to accompany his kardos with the understanding that they would remain no longer than a single season away from the Yuruk. Graize had agreed. It would take less time than that for his plans to take root. Illan's might take longer, but that was not his concern. Illan and his intrigues were only another piece in the game after all.

✦

On the day they were to leave, Danjel took a female form and went out onto the wild lands to gather omens for the journey. When she returned, she found Graize seated, cross-legged on the sandy shore of Gol-Bardak.

Squatting down beside him, she glanced at the three shells lined up on the ground before him. "Turtle augury again?" she asked.

"Turtle augury brings the best clarity," he answered simply.

"And their meat makes the best stew."

Graize ignored her. Lifting the middle shell with his left hand, he made a point of opening his right to show the dried pea in his palm before setting it on the ground and covering it with the shell. After moving the three in a complicated dance, he lifted the center one to reveal the pea, then covered it up again and repeated the weaving pattern.

"Which one, which one, which one has the pea beneath it, place your shine, place your shine," he murmured in a singsong voice. When he paused, he glanced up, his gray eyes bright with anticipation. "So where 's the pea, Kardos?" he asked in an innocent voice.

Danjel pointed and, with a nod, Graize lifted the left-hand shell to show her that her guess had been correct, then began again.

"Do you know what the trick to this game is?" he asked conversationally, moving the shells in a faster pattern now.

"To guess where the pea is?" Danjel asked in a sarcastic voice.

"No, that's the *point* of the game from the mark's perspective." Graize paused once more, indicating that Danjel should choose again. The wyrdin pointed at the right-hand shell and Graize lifted it to show her that, this time, she'd chosen wrong. He then lifted the left-hand shell, and then the middle one, revealing empty ground beneath them both. He then opened his right hand where the pea sat neatly tucked between his first two fingers.

"So the trick is to cheat?" Danjel asked dryly.

"No," Graize replied. "What you have to keep in mind is the actual point of the game, the point from the gamester's perspective."

"Which is?"

"To take the marks' money. Nothing else. The trick is to make the marks believe the point is the competition between them and the gamester, that victory is possible only if they pay strict attention to the shells. So they do pay strict attention to the shells, and not to the gamester's fingers. And potentially, of course," he added, scooping the shells into one fist, "not to a pickpocket's fingers either. Misdirection is the most ancient trick in the world. To beat a mark you must misdirect, that is, you must *direct* their gaze to something other than your objective.

"It's the same with seers."

"Ah," Danjel said. "I was wondering when this lesson was going to arrive at your favorite subject. You know, I *am* skilled in the ways of avoiding the Anavatanon.

That's why you asked me to come with you in the first place."

"Yes, you're very skilled at hiding under a shell like a cunning little pea," Graize allowed in a condescending tone.

"And why is it that your lessons always seem to turn into insults?" Danjel asked, her green eyes flashing dangerously.

"Because I was raised by priests too arrogant to know better," Graize replied carelessly. "Hiding behind the ridge is a fine trick, Kardos," he allowed graciously, "but one we've used before and one they may be expecting. The trick to beating seers—and, to that end, beating their Gods—when they're expecting a trick is the same as beating any mark: misdirection. You need to remember the point of the game is to take their money."

He waved a dismissive hand before Danjel could say anything else, "Or whatever the valuable object is that you want and they have. Like a pretty little solid silver statue of Incasa, once upon a time," he added, his right pupil widening perceptively.

He shook himself abruptly and his eye snapped back to its proper size as his thoughts returned to the present. "On the streets of Anavatan that object is called the shine," he continued as if the pause had never occurred. "The game is called the set, the shells are the gear, the pea is the draw, the one being drawn into the set is the mark, and the misdirection is called the jack."

"The jack?"

"It's a kind of small club."

Danjel gave him a perplexed look and Graize sighed.

"A jack comes at you when you're not looking," he explained, miming a blow from above. "It bashes your brains in so the unimaginative lifter—that's a thief, usually a pickpocket—can rob the shine from your corpse."

"Oh. The Anavatanon criminals seem to use a lot of different words," Danjel observed.

"They live in a world of prophets; what do you expect? You never know who might be listening."

Danjel made a face. "Makes sense, I suppose."

With another dismissive gesture, Graize laid the shells, one by one, onto the ground again. "Now pay attention," he ordered. "The gear is several equally possible actions; the Anavatanon seers call these streams because they're a lakeside people. You and the rest of the Yuruk wyrdin might call them—oh, I don't know—winds maybe, if you thought that way."

Danjel just rolled her eyes but said nothing.

"Seers look into the future to assess both threat and opportunity and then plot the best course of action for their people in response," Graize continued. "In this case for their defenders, the Warriors of Estavia. So we create three or more gear specifically designed to lure these marks to the set.

"Draw the attention of the Anavatanon seers in the direction we want them to look," he explained as Danjel showed signs of impatient puzzlement once again. "We show them a number of possible actions we might put into effect, all of them changing and moving around as the present puts pressure on the future, much as these three turtle shells move around as my fingers put pressure on their position," he added, beginning the weaving pattern once more. "The marks, that is the seers, choose the action they think we're most likely to put into effect—the one most likely to have the pea under it—and they do that by paying strict attention to the gear—as we want them to."

Danjel nodded. "We did that with the attacks against Yildiz and Serin-Koy five years ago," she noted. "Yildiz-Koy was the feint meant to draw the bulk of their forces away from Serin-Koy."

"Exactly. The shine that time was cattle. And pride."

"And so that your little Godling could drink from

the waters of Gol-Beyaz and be born into the physical world," Danjel pointed out.

"That, too," Graize agreed. That the Godling had drunk from Brax's essence instead was not something he'd been inclined to tell the Yuruk wyrdin.

"You needed our help to win your shine then, to breach the God-Wall around the silver lake and keep your Godling hidden from them," Danjel continued. "What shine do you need the Petchans' help to win this time?"

"This time, it's something much harder to see," Graize answered. "It's more like another bit of gear right now than actual shine; a possibility hardly even begun." He glanced over to where the Godling was spinning in wide, lazy circles above their tent pole. "It looks like a turtle shell," he continued. "Sort of. But maybe, just maybe, It's a special kind of turtle shell that just might turn into special kind of shine some day; a tower, but not a silver one." His voice trailed off, and Danjel frowned at him.

"Kardos," she said sharply, snapping her fingers in front of Graize's face. "To me."

"They can't see Its real potential yet," Graize continued, catching the fingers in front of his face and brushing them with his lips. "Even though It's already shimmering all pretty right in front of them. It started so opaque, so formless, but not anymore. Now It's grown. They won't see It because they're blinded by their own idea of what color shine It's supposed to be. It's supposed to be silver just like the kind they see all around them every day. That's the misdirection, the trick to this game of chance."

Danjel frowned. "But isn't that God of Prophecy of theirs, Incasa, isn't he also the *God* of Chance?"

Graize nodded without taking his eyes off the turtle shells.

"And so isn't He also the God of *games of chance*, and therefore the God of this particular game of yours?" Danjel persisted.

Graize frowned. "What of it?" he asked impatiently.

"Wouldn't He'd know all about this misdirection jack?"

Graize shrugged. "Of course He would."

"But what if He's using His own jack on you to draw you into some sort of set of His own and then bash *your* brains in?"

Graize chuckled. "Always the cautious one, kardos," he allowed. "Of course He *might* be; Incasa's a wily old gamester after all, but He's missing one very important part of the set."

"Oh? What's that?"

"The shine, Kardos. He doesn't know what *my* shine is. He's just as blind as the rest of them."

Danjel gave him a skeptical look. "Do *you* know, Kardos?" she asked doubtfully.

"That's the beauty of it," Graize answered, a strange, half-mad light growing in his eyes. "I know what It is now; It's a delos, my delos; and I know what It will be in the future."

"An adult?" Danjel asked dryly.

"Yes, but what kind of adult, Kardos? What will It turn Its hand to, what kind of gainful employment will It seek out when It's fully grown?"

"Silversmith?" Danjel hazarded in a sarcastic voice.

Graize's eyes glowed brighter. "I very much doubt it. How about mountain raider?"

"Wild lands raider wasn't good enough for you?"

He waved an impatient hand at her. "Of course it was, that's not the point. My delos was conceived of the wild lands, born of the city streets, and now must be seasoned by the mountains to grow strong enough to resist the Gods of Gol-Beyaz. All the world must be Its abayos."

"You've *seen* this?"

"I've fashioned it. From the very beginning when I formed Its most basic shape from the spirits that would have destroyed me."

"So that's your purpose in going south then, is it. Your gear? To season your Godling?"

"It's part of my gear. There's also Illan's ambitious little plot to destroy the Anavatanon, remember, his plot to close in on them from all sides? Misdirection, Kardos. The Gods and their seers will see the increased activity among the Petchans. They'll seek to know why. They'll see the threat—Illan's crafted threat—and think it's the only threat, but it's not *my* threat. That'll confuse them."

"I'm not surprised; it's confusing me."

"It doesn't matter. All you need to understand is the jack. I point . . ." Graize poked the middle shell with his finger. "They look, I pocket the pea, and I win the shine. Simple."

His expression darkened. "And it will be my shine or it won't be anyone's at all," he growled suddenly. With a savage gesture he brought his fist down on the middle shell hard enough to crack it and send the other two skittering off into the water.

Both Graize and Danjel stared down at the broken shell, equally surprised by the uncharacteristic violence.

"A disturbing omen," the Yuruk wyrdin noted dryly.

Graize narrowed his eyes. "Turtle augury again," he whispered. "One will be broken; two will be scattered." He cocked his head to one side. "I wonder which ones will be which?"

"Why don't you ask your stag beetle fetish for a change?" Danjel suggested in an impatient tone. "It seems to be less enigmatic."

"Yes, it does," Graize allowed, stroking the small hide bag that held the only possession that had survived his fight with the spirits of the wild land five years ago. "But I need enigmatic these days. That's the other trick to beating seers." Staring up at the sky, he watched as the Godling shot high into the air, only to disappear into a mass of gathering rain clouds.

"It's going to storm over Gol-Bardak, Kardos," he said quietly. "And all the way down the Halic-Salmanak to Gol-Beyaz itself. The storm will cause our misdirection. It will make the Anavatanon seers uneasy, and they will look to the north rather than to the south."

Danjel nodded. "Yes, it's time we were going, Kardos. Collect your turtle fetishes and come and say good-bye to Rayne and the others."

✦

"Kardos, to me."

Graize came back to himself on the mountainside to see Danjel snapping his fingers in front of his face. His eyes refocused calmly.

"You're farther out on the ledge than you usually like to be," he observed.

Danjel gave him a rueful smile. "I usually am when I'm with you," he replied. Returning to his spot, he leaned back against the rock face. "You know, you're going to lose all three shells to the wind if you let your attention wander off like that too often," he warned.

Tucking the shell back into his belt pouch, Graize just shrugged. "They're only little pieces of gear," he said carelessly. "Easily replaced if the wind wants to take them."

Danjel frowned. "You shouldn't be so glib," he cautioned. "When nature gifts you with a fetish, you should treat it with respect."

"Nature didn't gift me with these fetishes, Kardos. Caleb did."

"All the more reason."

"I suppose." Graize laid down again, hands behind his head. "And what fetish did you treat with respect this morning?" he asked curiously. "You rose very early; before the sun even peeked above the mountaintops."

Lighting his pipe, Danjel blew a small, puff of bluish-gray smoke into the air before answering. "I climbed the eastern bluff to see if I might espy the plains when the sun rose."

"And could you?"

"No." The Yuruk wyrdin made a disgusted face. "There's always more mountains in the way."

"I'm not surprised; you're a plains swallow, not a cliff swallow after all, and plains swallows fly far, not high. You needed to fly higher."

"So I asked the spirits for tidings," Danjel continued in a firm tone, "and they led me to a meadow flower in bloom." He held the small, yellow plant, twined in grasses to make a weather fetish, up as evidence. "The day will be both clear and open on the wild lands today. A good day for hunting and for prophecy." After tucking the fetish behind one ear, he sucked in a drag of smoke with a resentful expression. "But here, there will be rain and fog and everything will be obscured."

"Not everything." Graize closed his eyes with a contented sigh. "Just the vision of our enemies. They'll never see the pretty little flower fetish and that will lead to their destruction."

Danjel raised an eyebrow. "That's asking a lot from a single blossom," he noted.

Graize yawned at him. "They're blinded here," he continued. "Blinded by the mountains and the power of the Petchans, especially with so many of their own seers gathered in one place. That's the strength of the Petchans, their illusive ability to blind their enemies—and in this case, our enemies," he added with a predatory smile, "to their designs. All these enemies will be able to vision is your rain and your fog, but their arrogance will drive them here anyway because they're blinded by that, too. They've seeded their own desires into their interpretation of prophecy.

"Now where did I hear that before?" He giggled suddenly. "Oh, yes, the raven said it in my dream last night. Wise old raven." He turned. "That was *my* vision this morning, Kardos."

"Then it was yours alone," Danjel groused. "And I'm surprised you can vision anything clearly in this great jumble of blinding rock and water. You're no more used to it than I am."

Graize cast him a sly glance from under his lashes. "I'm not blinded anywhere," he murmured. "And I'm surprised that you'd admit that you are."

Danjel just gave an unaffected sniff. "I'm a wyrdin-kazak of the Berbat-Dunya, not a mountain goat. My augury is crafted by the open plains. It's hard to even breathe up here, never mind prophesize."

"Rayne would say that was a weakness," Graize pointed out, using their kardos' notoriously outspoken opinions as a prod.

Danjel refused to take the bait. "Rayne would say that we had no business leaving the plains at all," he replied. "In fact, if you'll remember, she said just that the day we left. If you're not careful, you'll be absent when she chooses a sire for her delon.

"We should go home, Kardos," he added quietly. "This is not our place, and you've been gone far too long already."

"I know." The sudden longing for the warm sheepskin-filled hide tents of the Yuruk encampments caused Graize's thoughts to scatter like the rainbow fish, and the dark-haired, dark-eyed youth now grown to manhood who always appeared in his mind when doubts obscured his vision rose up with greater force; a man who was no more a part of his life among the Yuruk than he was a part of his life among the Petchans.

"We'll return just as soon as my vision allows," Graize replied with a peevish shake of his head to clear it. "But not before. The turtle shell hasn't turned to shine yet. When it does, I'll be the first to fly back to the open plains with you."

He turned a challenging stare on Danjel's face. "And surely a wyrdin of your abilities would not be so blinded by rock and water as to miss the omens I saw on the wind this morning," he said with a faint sneer. "Flower fetish or no flower fetish to distract you."

Danjel gave him a flat, narrow-eyed glance in response. "I saw a flock of blackbirds wheeling in great agitation over the distant peaks," he replied. "Clearly something's happening to the east."

"Well done. Yes, it's the Anavatanon seers. They lost one of their number last night. An old and wise raven that dove headfirst into the silver embrace of her God."

"Ah." Danjel sucked on his pipe with renewed vigor. "Then that should blind them even further and so weaken them," he said amidst a cloud of smoke.

Graize gave a dismissive shrug. "Not overly," he argued. "It will bring them some confusion in the coming days but little else. Their augury comes from their Gods and it will take a lot more than a single death to truly weaken Them."

"And again, that's nominally why we're here, yes?" Danjel pressed. "To gain allies among the Petchans so that we might cause a greater number of deaths among the Gods' Anavatanon worshipers and so *truly* weaken Them?"

"Yes."

"The Yuruk kazak used to cause enough deaths to suit you," Danjel said with just a hint of admonishment in his voice.

"The Yuruk kazak made raids against the villages of the northwest shore and the Warriors of Estavia came out from behind their God-Wall to bring them to battle, yes," Graize agreed. "But the Yuruk have the disadvantage of flat and open ground to fight on. They're easily seen. The Petchans have the mountains and the foothills to hide behind. They're *not* easily seen and that's the advantage my vision needs this season. The advantage of the misdirection we spoke of."

"And so you abandon us to woo them," Danjel said pointedly.

This time it was Graize who refused to rise to the bait. "No, but they have a part to play in our set, Kardos, as I told you before. Don't be selfish, there'll be plenty of deaths to go around; you'll see. Your little flower fetish will be coated in blood by the time this year is done, and the Yuruk will cause as many deaths as we both could hope for in the days to come."

Standing, he exhaled a deep breath into the clear mountain air. "Almost all the gear's in place," he stated. "And soon the marks will flock to our set, and we'll snatch their shine right out from under their noses." Tossing another small seed of power into the air with a casual gesture, he watched as the Godling swooped down to catch it as gracefully as a hawk might catch a sparrow.

"Right under their noses," he repeated. "And then we'll see who comes out from behind their God-Wall to do battle this time.

"But in the meantime," he continued, turning a predatory smile on Danjel. "If that flock of cliff swallows above your head is the omen I think it is, we'll soon have a full Petchan Hukumet to attend. Your swallow cousins call you to work, Kardos. Think you can charm a hut full of fiercely independent old mountain chiefs and seers into waging a war for us?"

Danjel swept his thick black hair from his face in a dismissive gesture. "If they're anything like the ones back home," he observed, "we won't have to. The only difficulty will be sorting out who'll lead them."

"Yes," Graize agreed softly, showing his teeth at the flock of cliff swallows. "There's always that difficulty, isn't there? Who will lead, who will follow; who will be subordinate to whom." Looking up, he watched as the Godling perched amongst the cliff swallows without causing so much as a ripple in their demeanor. "And who will not be," he added meaningfully.

"Find this secret and you may be able to use it to our own advantage."

"Be patient, my little Volinski prince," he whispered to the northern wind. "I'll bring you all the power you desire, and then we'll see to whose advantage it will truly be." Calling the Godling to him, he waited until It had wrapped Itself firmly about his neck like a scarf, then headed down the mountain path, his uneven gaze fixed on the future.

5

Chalash

AS THE SUN BEGAN its slow descent toward the mountain peaks, Graize and Danjel made their way along the narrow trail, allowing their ponies to pick their way down. Below them, the mountains opened up to reveal a wide green vale, dotted with tawny-colored goats grazing placidly among a scattering of daisies and buttercups. A tangle-coated dog standing on an out-cropping of rock barked a challenge, and in the distance they could hear the high tenor of a goatherd's bell that warned of a stranger's approach. Moments later, as they drew closer, the tone changed to the deeper bass of the known bell. Returning the goatherd's wave, they skirted the edge of the vale and soon reached a deep-cut ravine with a slender rope-and-wood bridge stretched across it. Beyond lay the village of Chalash.

Of moderate size for a Petchan settlement, Chalash housed some three hundred related families during the summer months with twice that number in winter as herders and hunters swelled its ranks. As the closest village to Gol-Beyaz—no more than four days' travel—Chalash had been a staging ground for raids against the southern lake villages for centuries and, as such, was well defended; approached by a single, winding path, hard-packed from years of herds and carts, and guarded by a high, clay shield-wall that ran the length of a narrow entrance pass. A stout, iron-strapped wooden gate carved with rough, geometric images was the shield-wall's only entrance, overseen by half a dozen hidden sentinels armed with long-range bows and spears.

Chalash was key in Illan's designs against Anavatan. He'd spent the last four years building an alliance with Haz, its chief, pouring gold and gifts of northern furs and southern silks into the village like a river. With Graize and Danjel's arrival, Haz had sent messengers out across the mountains with word of a Hukumet—a great gathering—to decide on the final details of leadership, payment, and battle. Now Chalash was filled to bursting with chiefs, sayers, and their attending families.

As the two foreign wyrdins reached the bridge, an eagle soaring high above their heads screamed out its challenge, and Graize watched as the Godling broke from the clouds and streaked toward it, ethereal claws outstretched in rage. He gave a sharp whistle, and It broke off reluctantly.

Danjel squinted at the bird as it dropped out of sight on the far side of the ravine.

"That will be Maf's hunter," he observed. "Best keep your own creature tethered, Kardos. The Petchans are suspicious enough of Its presence as it is."

"It doesn't like being called names," Graize answered mildly. He snapped his fingers, and the Godling dropped, much like the eagle, into a sulky heap of half-formed feathers on his right shoulder, rippling across his throat in agitation as It sensed the bird returning to its archer-sentinel beyond the bridge.

"And I don't like being shot at," Danjel replied, sensing the same thing in the faintest wavering of the spirits on the breeze. "Be wary; Maf is old and capricious and treats that hunter like her delos."

Graize made a dismissive gesture. "Maf won't waste the arrows. We're known. You heard the bell. All she may do is curse at us."

"She could loosen the bridge ropes," Danjel muttered. "Just for a laugh. She threatened to do that yesterday."

Graize rolled his eyes. "Show some courage, will you please, my heroic wyrdin-kazak? The aged are no different than any other predator. They can smell your fear." He made a hideous face. "And so can the bridge itself, yes? Remain calm and it will remain strong. Otherwise . . ." He mimed them plunging into the ravine below, and Danjel just glared at him.

"Shut up," he growled.

Graize just shrugged. Urging his pony onto the first of the smooth wooden planks, he leaned back in the saddle, an expression of sleepy disinterest on his face. Danjel followed a moment later, his eyes narrowed in concentration.

When they reached the far side in safety, the archer-sentinel stood up from her nest of rocks, the orange and green of her felt tunic a splash of contrasting colors against the gray stone. An evil grin splitting her wrinkled, nut-brown face, Maf returned Graize's cool nod before turning a speculative eye on Danjel's slightly ashen features.

"How's your stomach today, Danjel-Sayer?" she asked, her blue eyes sparkling wickedly.

"Better, Maf-Teyos," he answered in a stiff voice, using the formal word for an older relation as the Petchans did. "Yal gave me some of last year's dried mulberries for it. She said they would help me grow used to the altitude."

"The best way to grow used to the altitude is to dance upon yonder bridge until you conquer your fear of it," Maf pointed out.

"No doubt. But fear is the body's way of telling the mind that it's about to do something truly stupid. I'd hate to dull its senses on the eve of battle."

Maf scowled at him. "Don't be so swift to bury your enemies, young one. Battle waits on the word of Haz-Chief and the Hukumet." She shook an admonishing finger at him, and the brown beads woven into her gray-and-straw-colored hair flashed a warning in the sunlight.

Upset by the motion, the eagle beat the air between them with its wings, its talons gripping the vambrace on her wrist tightly enough to dimple the leather.

The Godling hissed back at it, and Graize ran a hand over Its shimmering flank before glancing up the path, noting the fine patterns of newly thrown dust coating the open shield-wall gate. "Nur-Chief of Chavan has arrived," he stated. "The Hukumet will be tonight."

"There will be many Hukumets tonight, my little Volinski sayer," Maf retorted, unimpressed by his insight.

"Oh?" he inquired politely.

"Oh, indeed. There was a flock of starlings flying in great distress over the eastern foothills this morning. Their beating wings brought news of whispering on the wind. Jen-sayer has foreseen that there will be much whispering all across the land tonight."

"I'm sure there will be, Maf-Teyos," he replied easily. Urging his pony up the path, Graize craned his neck around to show his teeth at her in a predatory smile, the pupil of his right eye wide and dark. "In fact, I'm counting on it," he added.

Frowning at his back, Maf dug a small kidskin bag from the magenta sash about her waist and tossed it to Danjel. "Here," she growled. "A mouthful of arak works greater wonders than a handful of dried mulberries."

He caught it with a forced smile. "Are you trying to get me drunk, Maf-Teyos?" he asked.

She grimaced at him, all trace of her earlier humor gone. "When the fighting's all done, Yuruk-Delin, you and I will get drunk together and dance in the moonlight on yonder bridge until the sun comes up. And then maybe, just maybe, I'll give you leave to woo my Yal with exotic tales of the flat lands you come from. In the meantime, take heed of your stomach. And watch him." She jerked her chin at Graize. "A little madness is expected in a sayer. Too much and . . ." She repeated Graize's earlier gesture of plummeting into the ravine, then before Danjel could answer, she dropped back into her nest of rocks, the eagle tucked protectively at her side, the conversation at an end.

Holding the kidskin bag as gingerly as one might hold a snake, Danjel followed Graize, suddenly feeling a trepidation that had nothing to do with heights or bridges.

A moment later, the gate-sentinels admitted the two of them and, once they were clear of the tall, wooden portal, Chalash came into full view.

Flat-roofed, gray-stone-and-timber houses, their lintels covered with ornate carvings of flowers and vines, climbed, terracelike, up the sides of the mountain with the mill, forge, storehouses, trading house, and market stalls encircling the bowllike vale below. In the very center, a stand of carob trees threw a dappling of shade across a flock of ducks swimming in a shallow, blue-tiled pool, fed by an underground spring that no doubt also fed the village well. Large glazed pots of carnations and begonias stood guard at every doorway while pale gray-green juniper bushes and pink-spotted wild roses marched up the mountains alongside the rough-hewn log steps between each dwelling.

Most of the villagers and their guests were sitting outside in the vale drinking arak and sharpening their weapons in the warm summer breeze. Few looked up from their labors as Graize and Danjel dismounted, but the air of barely suppressed excitement was as tangible as a summer storm. The last of the mountain chiefs had arrived. Soon there would be feasting and fighting. The brightly-clad boy who came running out to collect their ponies was grinning from ear to ear in anticipation.

Graize gave him a formal nod. "Good afternoon, Las-Delin," he said solemnly.

Las bowed, his expression turned suddenly equally serious. "Good afternoon, Teyon-Sayers," he replied, wiping what looked like red mulberry juice off his hands and onto his dark green trousers. "How did you find the morning?"

"The air was filled with butterflies," Graize answered.

Las cocked his head to one side, the blue-and-brown beads woven into his pale blond hair swaying gently with the motion.

"What color were they?" he asked.

"Most were a soft dove gray, but here and there, I saw a yellow one in their midst."

"That means the elderberries will be ready soon," Las pronounced with almost pompous dignity.

"I'm pleased to hear it."

Accepting his reins, Las bowed in turn to Danjel, giving him an expectant look.

"I found the morning chill and covered in dew," the Yuruk wyrdin replied, trying to keep his encounter with Maf from tingeing his voice with peevishness. "But I did see an owl with a rodent in its claws. Will that suffice?"

Las narrowed his bright, blue eyes. "Were they a real owl and a real rodent?" he asked, trying in turn to keep his own voice from registering his suspicion. The Petchan sayers did not approach the spirits of the Gurney-Dag, believing the Yuruk's casual interaction with those on the plains to be both dangerous and foolhardy. When Danjel answered in the affirmative, relief showed in the boy's eyes.

"Then it will rain tonight," he stated. "Of course, Jen-Sayer told Haz-Chief that already," he confessed.

Graize gave an eloquent shrug. "Wise prophets seek out their own visions regardless of who else may be hunting the same game," he said in a passable imitation of the boy's seer-abayos, and Las snickered. "But the rain will not interfere with the Hukumet," Graize continued, glancing up at the sky already clouding over as if to prove the boy's prophecy correct.

Las shook his head. "The sayers are already gathering in the vision-house." He jerked his head toward the largest structure in the village, a long, low building dominating the eastern side of the vale. Its ornately carved timbers were festooned with strings of beads and sprigs of juniper in anticipation of the coming Hukumet, reminding Graize more of a Dockside Ystazia-Cami on the first day of Low Summer than a place of prophecy and respite for Chalash's oldest sayers.

As sayers themselves, Graize and Danjel had been gifted with one of the vision-house's spacious guest suite apartments in the south wing. The Yuruk wyrdin had immediately pitched his goat's hide traveling tent in its tiny enclosed courtyard, but Graize had gleefully settled into the richly furnished bedchamber. Predominantly blond-haired and blue-eyed, their Petchan hosts had believed light-brown-haired, gray-eyed Graize to be a princely emissary sent by the royal family of Volinsk who tended to that coloring, and he had no intention of gainsaying them. Not when such luxuries as woolen blankets and fresh bread with fruit and honey brought to his door every morning came with the title.

"Will you be joining them now, Teyon-Sayers? I'll bring your supper to you there if you're hungry," Las asked as if reading his thoughts.

"We will." Graize headed for the vision-house at once.

Danjel made to follow but paused as the boy caught his sleeve. "Yal wants to know if you're going to change gender-forms for the Hukumet," Las said. "If you are, she'll sit with you."

"And if I'm not?" Danjel asked, amused.

Las shrugged. "Then she's not," he answered, his tone making his opinion of the question obvious. "My kardos likes you, Danjel-Teyos, but she doesn't like beards," he added by way of explanation.

"I could shave."

The boy gave him such a look of withering disdain from beneath one pale, raised eyebrow that Danjel chuckled.

"Tell her I'll change."

Las nodded. As he took their ponies into the stables,

Danjel hurried to catch up with his fellow seer. "Butterflies?" he asked pointedly.

Graize shrugged. "I saw them just after dawn."

"You didn't mention them to me."

"That's because they wouldn't have mattered to you. You didn't mention an owl to me."

"Because it was just an owl."

"These were just butterflies. To us. But they represented something more to the Petchans."

"So, is this part of your *set*, then? To only tell people the things you think represent more to them than to others?"

Graize returned Danjel's suspicious look with one of bland condescension. "No, Kardos," he answered. "It's part of being *polite.*"

Danjel snorted. As Graize reached for the large, iron handle of the vision-house, the wyrdin-yuruk jerked his chin toward the Godling, still wrapped about the other's throat. "You know, you can't take a spirit inside with you," he pointed out. "Even a delos-Godling-spirit. It wouldn't be *polite*. The older sayers would throw a fit."

"Too true. A pity." Weaving his fingers through the Godling's sinuous lengths, Graize lifted It gently, more with his mind than with his hands, then threw It in the air much as Maf might have thrown her eagle. It took wing in much the same way, scattering a nearby flock of starlings and disappearing behind the gathering clouds in a sudden shower of golden light.

Graize frowned. "Many Hukumets tonight," he whispered, turning, as most of the villagers did, to watch the birds disappear over the eastern hills. "Many whispering Hukumets. But what color will they be? That's the question."

"Will that many seers be a problem?" Danjel asked, ignoring the rest of Graize's words. "With so many prophets engaged in vision, are the Anavatanon seers likely to catch a glimpse of what we're doing?"

Graize shook his head. "The rain will dampen their

sight and you know how much seers hate damp sight; they're worse then cats that way. But ..." He held up one cautioning finger. "All the same, you're right, we should be on our guard." His expression grew sly. "You never know when some tricksy little Anavatanon kitten might try to steal our dinner. Of course, I've blocked the way to the dish, but it just might try to dig its way underneath like a mole. A stealthy little kitten-mole."

"Can't you ever make sense, just for once, Kardos?" Danjel asked with a sigh.

"Only for you, Kardos," Graize answered graciously. "Remember what I told you on the mountainside; the Anavatanon seers are blinded by the Petchan seers, and so we are hidden from their view because so many of them are gathered together in one place. Is that clear enough for you?"

"Yes. One wonders why you couldn't have said that in the first place."

"One also wonders why you couldn't have remembered my words. I think Yal's tender attentions have softened your brain. You need to go home and be mistreated by Rayne to bring you back to yourself." Pulling the door open, he answered Danjel's glare with a falsely sweet smile of his own before slipping inside the vision-house.

✦

The air within was warm and smelled of aromatic smoke. Unfamiliar with the central wing, Graize and Danjel paused a moment in the entranceway to allow their eyes to adjust to the low light and glance about with undisguised curiosity.

A dozen wooden pillars marched along the east and west walls, creating two shadowy arcades, punctuated by six ornately decorated meditation alcoves. To either side, the white-plastered north and south walls contained an arched doorway each, leading to the residential wings. Small bits of glass and pottery were pressed into the plaster to form the traditional Petchan imagery of flowers, while brightly painted leaves chased themselves along the wooden beams and lintels.

In the center, the auditory room was wide and spacious enough for several hundred people to congregate comfortably. The ceiling was of gray stone illuminated by several hanging lamps, and the floor was hard-packed earth covered with brightly woven blue-and-orange rugs thrown over a felt under carpet. A low fire burned in the square, stone-lined fire pit cut into the very center of the room with three young sayer-delinkon crouched about it, feeding the coals with juniper twigs and handfuls of sharp-smelling pine needles meant to keep them smoldering. Beside it, Haz-Chief stood, speaking quietly with the chiefs of the five nearest villages that had joined them in the Hukumet.

A tall and lean man with a commanding eye, Haz-Chief had led both raids and trade excursions east and west since he'd won the leadership of Chalash at age fifteen. Now in his late forties, his face was deeply lined from a lifetime facing the harsh mountain winds, and his blond hair, bleached almost white from the sun, was braided with a dozen red-and-brown ceramic beads. He was dressed in green felt trousers stuffed into soft, goat's hide boots and a blue tunic embroidered with flowers. A yellow sash around his waist held a long dagger, its handle wrapped in silver wire and encased in an ornate leather sheath. Noting Graize and Danjel's entrance, he inclined his head in a reserved nod as they bowed, then returned to his conversation.

The two settled themselves on a tawny-colored sheepskin by the south door, noting the twenty-odd elder sayers already ensconced on the low, hide-cushioned chairs nearest the fire. Sayer-delinkon bustled about them, fetching food and drink and settling warm felt blankets over their elders' knees while cats, dogs, and even a few tame ferrets wove about their feet, accepting tidbits of meat and trading suspicious looks with the half dozen tethered hawks and eagles perched on wooden stands about the room. Even in the dim lamplight, the auditory was a riot of colors, odors, and underlying emotional currents. As Las appeared at his elbow with a bowl of wine and a platter of tripe and bread stuffed with goat cheese and crushed walnuts, Graize felt his focus list sideways once again.

Beside him, Danjel had already relaxed into the comfortingly familiar communal atmosphere, his eyes closed and his smooth features flowing, almost imperceptibly, from male to female, the whiskers on her face fluttering down to lie on the sheepskin at her feet. As the elder sayers began to mutter and chant, weaving the small hunting bows they used in their prophecy in a slow, hypnotic dance back and forth, Graize felt his kardos struggle against the unfamiliar sensations before sinking into vision as her wild lands blood came into play. He narrowed his own eyes, blocking out as many of the same sensations as possible, then released his mind to wander where it would.

The room dimmed. The sayers' muttering grew louder and the air heavier with the muting mixture of smoke and incense. People began to make their way inside, filling up the corners of his being with their own thoughts and expectations as they filled up the corners of the auditory. His eyes closed almost of their own volition, and far away, he heard the somber tolling of a bell. It rang eighty-one times, then stilled, the silence ringing louder than the bell had done. He felt something shift beneath him like a storm brewing in the very center of the earth and then he saw the Godling.

It sailed over the roof of the vision-house, the setting sun spraying its shimmering wings with a shower of golden fire, and the deep, translucent, blue sky casting a mantle of power across Its ethereal features. Without another thought, Graize flung his mind out to meet It.

Together, they streaked away, past the shield-wall and the bridge, scattering birds and insects in their wake. Following the Terv River as it cut its winding path through the foothills, they skimmed the waves, upsetting a host of spirits hovering just below the surface like a pair of hawks might upset a school of fish. The spirits glimmered invitingly in the afternoon light, but as thunder began to rumble far above them, the tiny, shimmering creatures suddenly turned and fled to the very bottom of the river. Graize paused, staring down at them with a new understanding.

The spirits of the plains were drawn in great, shining flocks by such weather, gaining power from the vast and sweeping storms in which they were born. But the mountain spirits had been birthed in a thousand underground springs high up in the crags and peaks. They were collected by rivers and streams and washed down through the foothills, the marshlands, and the plains until they finally trickled into Gol-Beyaz to deliver their load of pure mountain prophecy through the filter of the great wall of power to strengthen the Gods. They did not gain power in the same way, but power was power, and the spirits of the mountains were no different than the spirits of the plains, they could be used to the same ends.

Far to the east, the bending curve of the Terv sparkled with a dark indigo brightness, and Graize bared his teeth at it. Both Gods and seers would dip into those prophetic waters tonight, scooping up their catch of visions and hanging them out to dry on lines of possibility that stretched all the way from Anavatan in the north to Anahtar-Hisar in the south; seeking, always seeking the newly-spawned strategies of their enemies.

Many whispering Hukumets.

The words echoed through his mind, and he acknowledged them with a sneer. The Anavatanon seers might be many, but they were still far too few to catch him and his little Godling in their nets of intrigue and subtlety. And one day they would find themselves tangled in a net of his own weaving and then they'd see just how limited their visions really were.

The thought made him growl with precognitive hunger, and he gave in to it, feeling the Godling's own hunger rise in response. Together, they dove into the river, sucking in as many of the icy water spirits as they could hold and then soaring out again, trailing a line of silver power behind them like a tail. They shot into the clouds just as the sun broke free to paint the mountaintops with fire, and far away Graize could feel the Petchan sayers begin the ritual that would seal the vision-house. As their wards tickled against the back of his mind, he opened his eyes, leaving the river and the Godling behind.

✦

He found Las staring at him, a concerned frown marring his youthful features.

"You shouldn't touch the spirits that way, Graize-Sayer," he admonished, the seriousness of his tone incongruent with his age. "Or they'll use the gateway in your mind to suck out your life's power while you're sleeping."

His vision still swimming with the sparkling, silver light of the river spirits' power, Graize smiled at him. "Stronger spirits than those have already tried, Las-Delin," he replied. "And have found their own life's power consumed instead."

"Still." The boy stood as an older sayer-delinkos came forward with a shallow bowl of goat's blood in her hands. Dipping his finger in the dark red liquid, Las reached out to touch Graize on the forehead, leaving a small, red mark that tingled all the way down his limbs.

"This will create a barrier that will protect you from the spirits while you vision-hunt," he explained, doing the same to Danjel and then to Yal who had just joined them, twirling Danjel's flower fetish between her fingers.

"I can feel that it will, Las-Sayer-Delinkos," Graize answered formally. Far above the village, he could sense the Godling's miffed reaction and, reaching out with his thoughts, he stroked Its ruffled features, reminding It that no tiny, goat's-blood warding could keep them separated if either of them desired to come together. It was a God, not a spirit.

Mollified, It turned and disappeared back into the clouds. As the Petchan sayers finished laying their protections, Graize turned his mind inward to the place where his battle with the wild lands spirits and Incasa's response had shredded the muffling caul about his sight five years ago. Let the Gods and Their seers do what they may, he sneered. He and his Godling would triumph and then they would see who commanded the most powerful vision.

As the predicted storm finally broke above the vision-house, Graize bent all his formidable abilities to the task of reading the future.

6

Freyiz

MANY MILES TO THE south, the final note of the Evening Invocations faded with the setting sun. As Anavatan's streets emptied and the lights from a thousand hearths sparkled across the city, Incasa, God of Prophecy and Probability, rose like a vast white swan from the mirrorlike surface of Gol-Beyaz. The warm summer breeze whispered through His hair, sending it spinning about His face like a cloud and He caught hold of it with a languid motion, pressing its allotment of power against His pale lips. The wind tasted of intrigue and of opportunity.

Raising His left hand, Incasa breathed across the pair of opalescent dice nestled in His palm. Each surface reflected a different future back to Him, and His snow-white eyes narrowed thoughtfully as He considered them.

The simplest were represented by both the highest and the lowest possible scores. A pair of sixes would see the newest member of Anavatan's pantheon joined with the Gods in controllable subservience; a pair of ones would herald Its destruction. Neither future would occasion any particular danger, but neither would they offer up any particular reward. The most flexible possibility, a score of seven, carried the greatest of both.

And so it should, Incasa allowed. A score of seven could yield up seven Gods in as perfect an equality as

He, the oldest of Them, might allow. This equality would afford Their worshipers the greatest freedom and thus the greatest possibility for strength and prosperity, and the Gods needed Their worshipers to be both strong and prosperous. But a score of seven could be reached by six distinctive combinations; each embodied with a symbolic significance far beyond the addition of a single new Deity and each with its own mixture of risk and reward.

A score of six and one would allow the six established Gods of Gol-Beyaz to aid in raising the one—Hisar—molding Its developing abilities while maintaining unity within Their own ranks. However, a score of one and six would see Hisar not only fully developed, but also uncontrollable, hostile, aggressive, and worst of all, independent. The four remaining combinations would set Hisar against Incasa's dominion and split the loyalties of Havo, Ystazia, Usara, Oristo, and Estavia to a different degree from slight to catastrophic. Either way, Anavatan's security would be compromised to Their enemies' advantage.

Incasa raised His head, allowing two fleets of ghostly ships to pass across His inward gaze. Two enemies lay poised to move against Them: the Volinski to the north and the Skirosians to the south. Years of subtle intrigue had kept them apart; years spent manipulating the power of the spirits until a new God could be raised up to strengthen Their numbers. So far the Godling and Its young seer-abayon, Spar and Graize, had been allowed to play and grow as children, untroubled by this danger, but no longer. It was time for Hisar to grow up and take Its place as the bastion of defense Incasa had foreseen.

The dice clinked in His palm, and a frown marred the smooth perfection of Incasa's features. The dice had begun to roll with Hisar's birth, but the outcome had never been uncertain. The odds always favored the House, and the God of Chance controlled the House. It was not yet time to roll six and one, but it was time to show the stripling God of Creation and Destruction and Its two junior priests just how great the odds of that combination really were.

Stretching a hundred feet into the air, Incasa fashioned a complex new prophecy, then reached out for the mind of His most favored seer.

✦

Taking her ease in a delicate wrought-iron pavilion in the temple gardens, Freyiz, once First Oracle of Incasa-Sarayi, sipped a glass of salap and swatted irritably at an overly curious moth that fluttered about her face.

All around her, she could hear the lamplighters moving about the temple's formal herbariums, illuminating the white-gravel paths so that the legion of delinkon sent to harvest the night's first crop of prophetic botanicals might see to work. The air was filled with their rustling movements punctuated by the occasional sneeze, and Freyiz grimaced in sympathy. Incasa had gifted the most heavily scented of plants with the elements of augury and the olfactory assault of datura, artemisia, calamus, and lily had always made her head ache. As a consequence, her own small gardens at Incasa-Cami in Adasi-Koy contained mostly unscented, and therefore purely ornamental, plants. Their power signatures hardly registered on her inward vision at all and were therefore both quiet and peaceful, unlike the riot of prophetic imagery that battered against her inward sight in the gardens here.

"And I'd be in my own gardens right now," she grumbled to herself. Or rather, she admitted silently, she'd be in her sitting room overlooking her gardens, drinking a glass of raki and listening to Sanni, her youngest relative, practice the quintara, if a pompous yet supplicate message from First Oracle Bessic had not summoned her back to Anavatan.

✦

"Battle-Seer Elif of Estavia-Sarayi is dying. Her last words will be of great significance, and your presence would lend a valuable store of experience to our study of the matter if you would do us the honor of your insight."

Freyiz gave an unimpressed snort. Bessic was far too astute to allow his actual request to be written down, but she'd known him since he was child, and his meaning had been as clear as if he'd shouted it at her from across the water.

"Please come and untangle the final mutterings of an inscrutable old woman, much like yourself, so that Incasa-Sarayi might glean whatever tiny advantage possible in the murky world of temple politics."

✦

Tipping her head to one side, Freyiz drank in the sensations spilling over the temple wall from the city beyond. The air smelled of restfulness and peace, of the day's labors being set aside for the night's repose. Those at Estavia-Sarayi who had known Battle-Seer Elif would feel her absence like a rent torn in the tapestry of their lives, but for most people—those content to let the future unfold without the aid of prophecy—life would go on as seamlessly as it had before her death, whatever her final words might have been.

Of course, Freyiz considered pragmatically, by the very nature of their vocation, the priests of Incasa had never been content to let the future unfold without the aid of prophecy and, subsequently, without the intervention of its prophets.

And once a prophet always a prophet, she sniffed. Smoothing a wrinkle in the fabric of her robes, she considered Bessic's unspoken request.

Elif had been eighty-one years old, a full six years

older than her own seventy-five, but to anyone younger than sixty, they were of an age. And she supposed that in many ways they were. They'd both been born with the advent of the new century and had both seen it through very nearly to its end. Of different—often competitive—temples, they'd not been friends, nor even acquaintances, but Freyiz had attended Elif's sickbed two days ago at Bessic's request. He'd hoped of course, that the old battle-seer would share some dying insight with Freyiz alone.

The two old women had shared a joke at their juniors' expense, drunk some raki Freyiz had smuggled in past Elif's ever-watchful attendant, and reminisced about past prophecies, trading outrageous lies meant to scandalize those listening until, finally, Elif had pulled the other woman close.

"Look after my Spar," she'd rasped in a hoarse whisper. The image of the blond-haired youth had swum between them, generated by the power of both their abilities. "He's a prickly little bugger," she'd continued, "and he won't thank you for any interference. He'd ..."

A thick, ropy cough had interrupted her words, and her attendant had leaped between them with a silken cloth that smelled of lilac. For a moment Freyiz had feared that this would spell the end of the old seer as well as their conversation, but eventually Elif had caught her breath, waving her attendant away with an impatient gesture. Her face noticeably paler, she'd gestured Freyiz to her once again.

"He'd rather stand out in a thunderstorm than accept the offer of an awning," she'd continued. "But he'll need all the help he can get. He's so very ... young," she'd added with a fond but exasperated sigh, then shook herself, her expression returning to one of business. "He's important," she'd continued. "He's ..." She'd paused a moment as if trying to decide how much to reveal to a rival seer, then had shrugged her frail shoulders in irritable resignation. "He's the key to controlling the new God," she'd said finally, her words so quiet Freyiz had to press her ear to the other woman's lips just to hear them. "The key to the tower's heart."

✦

"The key to the tower's heart," Freyiz now repeated. "A cryptic and powerful deathbed vision or simply a bloody-minded bit of poetry from a cantankerous old abayos who wants me to take on the responsibility of yet another delos at my age?"

The moth alighted on her knee and she stared down at its tiny allotment of power illuminating the fabric of her robe. "It could be either, you know," she told it sternly. "Clarity's not a common characteristic of prophecy or prophets."

And the older she grew, the more that lack of clarity was starting to annoy her.

The moth fluttered away, and she frowned at the erratic streaks of pale light that marked its passage. Still awaiting the official news of Elif's final words from Estavia-Sarayi, Bessic and the others on the temple's Seeking Council had behaved just as erratically. She'd given them Elif's words and her insight and left them to argue over their meaning, but it had seemed crystal clear to her. The old battle-seer had been worried about Spar, afraid that fate had handed him a role he wasn't old enough to shoulder but was too stubborn to relinquish. Hisar, the new and still-unbound Deity of Creation and Destruction must be brought safely to Gol-Beyaz. Obviously, this would be the task of the Gods and their temples, but Spar was involved despite his youth. Deathbed words—no matter how bloody-minded or manipulative—could not be ignored. He was the key.

Freyiz sighed deeply. A half-grown suspicious and resentful key that would require some very delicate handling, she noted with an egregious frown. Handling she was far too old to bother with anymore, but if she didn't, Bessic would. With disastrous results. He'd already trundled out the four-year-old argument that Spar should be removed from Estavia-Sarayi and trained as an Oracle of Incasa. Many of the more conservative temple elders—believing that the gift of prophecy came from the God of Prophecy alone—were in agreement, but now—as then—Freyiz had spoken up sharply against any such action. An unwilling follower brought the Gods no strength; this was the oldest tenet of their relationship with Gol-Beyaz. Spar could not be coerced. To attempt to do so would only drive the delos into making the kind of defiant decision they could not afford to have him make and create a schism between themselves and Estavia-Sarayi that would weaken both their temples and ultimately their Deities.

"And anyone who can't see that is a complete fool," she growled.

But Elif had laid the problem squarely in her lap, and so Incasa's temple must be involved in Spar's decision making, regardless. The question was how?

A loud sneeze interrupted her deliberations, and she gave a weary sigh. There were days when she felt as young as the delinkon in the gardens and days when every single one of her seventy-five years weighed heavily on her joints and on her patience.

Today was one of the latter days.

She'd retired from temple life four years ago after seeing *the new God* onto the path toward Gol-Beyaz as Incasa had required, then handed over temple authority—and all the worldly visions and endless politicking that went with it—to Bessic, without a flicker of regret and had gone home to sit by the hearth like an old cat. But some habits were hard to break and the temple knew that if they called, she'd answer.

"Your presence would lend a valuable store of experience to our study of the matter if you would so honor us with your insight."

"Do the work for us, you mean," she muttered. "One day I'm going to say no, and wouldn't that just surprise all of you.

"Yes, and that includes you, too," she added as Incasa's sudden touch, softer than the moth's gossamer wings, caressed her cheek.

But clearly that day had not yet arrived. Laying her hands in her lap, Freyiz stilled her thoughts, waiting for the God to speak His piece, knowing that His words would be just as cryptic and yet just as demanding as Elif's had been.

And feeling just as annoyed by it.

Incasa's response was immediate. A blaze of prophetic light burst across her inward sight with such force that it snapped her head back. Decades of practice kept her from spitting out a curse of surprise; instead, she absorbed the brunt of the vision's power, channeling it down the path of her formidable interpretive abilities before spinning it out in strands of visual imagery that might be more easily seen and understood, then opened her sight to its message.

A shimmering tower, blazing as bright as the noonday sun, first gold then silver then gold again, rose up before her. Behind it, a range of mountains burned with a crimson fire that threatened to set the entire world aflame while above, the sky roiled with angry clouds. Three figures; the first consumed in silver light, the second holding darkness like a shield, and the third wearing a mantel of gray mist as heavy as an ocean fog, stood before the tower's gate. She bent her attention to these three, trying to bring their features into sharper focus. The vision wavered, grew faint, and she bore down, then, with a snort of impatience, sent out one simple thread of supplication.

It was all the invitation Incasa required. With an explosion of sleet and ice that shattered the garden's delicate hanging lanterns, the God of Prophecy burst into being above the pavilion. His white-marble features

were drawn into a grimace of feral adoration and, as He
caught Freyiz up in His arms, the intensity of His embrace nearly froze her mind as well as her body. A vast
blizzard rose up all around her, blinding her to all but a
single silver flame that burned in the very center of His
regard. As it filled her with a strength she hadn't known
for years, Incasa stripped away the superfluous outer
symbolism of His vision with a savage jerk, then flung
out one fine-boned hand to snatch a creature from the
wind and thrust It toward her.

✦

High above the southern mountains, Hisar suddenly
felt Its essence caught and crushed by a power stronger than any It had experienced before. A force like
a great hand squeezed Its being until It became the
tower-shaped form of prophecy and, blazing with both
silver and golden fire, It stared into the freezing-cold
eyes of a potent old woman a thousand times stronger
than Elif had been. Her gaze shattered Its immature
defenses, stabbing through to Its very heart. Screaming
in pain and fear, It fought against Its bonds in rising
panic before the years of Graize's teachings came to Its
aid. It forced Itself to still, the power relaxed Its grip,
and changing suddenly to Danjel's birth fetish swallow
form, It squirmed between the power's fingers and shot
away.

Its distress sent shock waves slamming through Gol-
Beyaz like a typhoon. Estavia shot from the waters,
weapons drawn. Oristo followed almost at once and the
movement behind Her spun the Battle God about with
a scream as high-pitched as an angry cat's. Her twin
swords streaked down to crack against the waters at the
Hearth God's feet. This brought Havo into the fray at
once, leaping between them, with scythe and flail spinning so fast the air began to spark. Ystazia followed,
throwing Her cloak before the Hearth God while
Usara rose up before Estavia, demanding She lower

Her weapons. Incasa turned on Them all, eyes blazing and, as He leaped forward, He released His vision with a crack of displaced air that shattered windows across Anavatan.

A new future stream spewed up in its wake like a water spout, spreading out until it flooded into His seer's mind, still burning from the vision's passage, with a hiss of power.

✦

Freyiz came back to herself lying on the gravel path, the vision still blazing across her mind. She tried to speak, but the words came out in a cough of pain as a great weight suddenly pressed against her chest. It was all she could do to gasp out one word to the delinkon clustered about her.

"Bessic."

They ran.

✦

At Chalash, Hisar smashed through the vision-house's protective wards like a charging bull, slamming into Graize with a force that cracked his head against the wall. As a spray of blood issued from his lips, the Hukumet erupted in chaos.

Somehow, Danjel managed to get them both out of the building in one piece. Clutching the shrieking, half-physical Godling in his arms, Graize stumbled across the rain-drenched square, keeping up a constant flow of comforting words and snatches of half-remembered lullabies, until he sank to his knees beside the tiled pool. When the Godling finally stilled, Graize raised his uneven gaze to Danjel's face.

"Get them calmed down in there if you can," he shouted over the wind, jerking his bloodied chin toward the vision-house. "Get the protections back in place, get back into vision, and finish the Hukumet."

Shielding her eyes from the driving rain with one

hand, Danjel shook her head in disbelief. "I could just as easily fly home with the storm clouds, Kardos," she shouted back. "What am I supposed to tell them just happened?"

Struggling to keep the waves of hysteria still emanating from the Godling from overwhelming his mind, Graize waved a hand at her. "Tell them the truth," he spat. "That simple blood wards may be effective against mountain spirits, but against the Gods they might as well leave the front door wide open. If this is the vaunted, blinding power of the Petchan sayers, I'm not so impressed."

"I say that and we'll be lucky to keep the Petchan alliance intact," Danjel objected.

"If you don't say it, we'll be lucky if there's a Petchan alliance left to keep. The Gods know we're here now. They know my Godling's here. It'll be easy enough for Them to figure out why. We can't hide, but we can still misdirect; we can still lie; we can still make Them think the pea is under one of our own three turtle shells."

"And is it?"

"No. It never was. How could it be? It's far too valuable to risk like that, but They have to think that it is or the game is lost."

Pushing her sopping wet hair aside, Danjel brought her face close to his. "I don't like this game of yours," she hissed, green eyes dark. "Play whatever games you want, Kardos, but if I ever find you playing the Yuruk, you'll have a lot more to worry about than the Anavatanon Gods."

She turned and made her way back to the vision-house, leaving Graize crouched in the rain, blood trickling down his chin to patter against the Godling still wrapped in his arms.

His own eyes narrowed. "You won't, Kardos," he whispered. "And neither will the Gods. The rules have changed; the rules always change to suit the game."

Opening his mind, he teased Incasa's attack from the

Godling's memory like one might tease a reticent fish from a pool of water. The three figures from His vision rose up before him, and he nodded.

"It always comes down to us, doesn't it?" he whispered. "Three little street lifters . . ." He felt the Godling shudder and began to rock It back and forth. "Tied together by pain and blood," he continued, "determining the fate of an entire people." He grimaced in disgust. "How pathetic is that?"

Lifting his face to the rain, he watched as a streak of lightning lit up the sky.

"Silver, black, and gray," he mused, his right pupil opening almost painfully wide. "Silver for Brax," he said, and the Godling twitched in his arms as he spoke. "Petty thief turned subservient lapdog champion of the Gods and keeper of the path They want my delos to walk.

"Black for Spar . . ." His tone became suddenly so deeply scornful that it made the Godling shiver. "Little street-rat seer-child cloaked in Sable Company ebony and thinking he has the skills and the power to destroy what I've spent five years building.

"And finally, gray for me; gray like the mist; gray like the sea; uncontrollable, unpredictable, comforting gray." He tightened his grip and, under the pressure of his mental handling, the Godling wove about his neck with an audible sigh.

Closing his eyes, Graize envisioned the three of them standing on Illan's atlas table and bared his teeth in a snarl. "The silver and the black pieces are far too close to my tower," he growled. "I think it's time to give them both a good shove." In his mind's eye, Brax and Spar were hurled out Cvet Tower's highest window to dash themselves on the rocks below.

"But how to accomplish it," he mused. "Silver and black never stray too far from their shield-wall, do they? So they'll have to be lured."

The image of a group of figures crossing the grasslands

to the east whispered across his prophecy like a mirage in the distance. One sparkled like silver in the sunlight, and he showed his teeth triumphantly. "Too easy," he chuckled.

As the figures faded, his pupil snapped back to its regular size so fast it made him blink, and he nodded to himself as he ran one hand along the Godling's shimmering flank. "The silver one'll come to me, the black one'll follow, an' we'll crush 'em both, yeah?" he said, allowing the slurred accent of Anavatan's dockside poor to creep back into his voice. "An' no one'll stand in our way then, an' everything'll be mine."

As the image of the dark-haired man drifted through his mind like the smoke from a signal fire, Graize settled down beneath the carob trees, ignoring the rain that drizzled down his hair and under his collar. The Godling poured into his lap, and he closed his eyes, sending a single tendril of ambition stretching out to the northeast. It touched the mind of his oldest rival with a shiver of warning; the first move in his newest campaign. *"Feel the danger,"* he whispered, sending his words out onto the wind where Spar would be sure to perceive them, *"And know that you can't stop me.*

"And you," he added darkly toward the Gods of Gol-Beyaz as the Godling continued to shiver in his arms. *"Know that you never should have harmed my delos. You'll pay for that."*

The storm rumbled its agreement. As the night settled in, it rolled down the mountains and across the plains to batter against the walls of Anavatan.

✦

At Incasa-Sarayi the white marble halls were quiet, muffling the sounds of rain and wind. The rapid footfalls that had followed Freyiz-Sayin's unexpected collapse, were equally quiet. Priests and delinkon clustered in the temple's inner hall while their seniors hovered about the High Seeking arzhane's antechamber. No one spoke. There was little to say. Every one of them had felt the great, squeezing pain that had gripped their elder's heart like a vise. And every one of them had felt it when it stopped.

Within the arzhane, First Oracle Bessic sat holding the body of the woman who'd taught him to be a seer cradled in his arms. He felt numb.

Incasa's manifestation had taken an entire temple of seers by surprise. Bessic had been in his study, struggling to draft yet another useless missive to Marshal Brayazi, when the explosion had knocked him off his feet. A single, desperate image had got him up and running for the garden so that he'd nearly collided with the delinkos sent to fetch him. Skidding to his knees on the ruined path, he'd caught Freyiz up in his arms.

The physical contact had slammed their minds together. Incasa's vision had crashed over him like a typhoon, and he'd gasped in shared pain as his heart had fought to maintain its own, steady beat against Freyiz's faltering rhythm. Only when it had threatened to reach out and ensnare the youths clustered about them was he able to bring his own strength to bear against it. He'd lifted her like a child, pressing her to his chest, willing her heartbeat to follow his, as he'd run for the serene calm of the arzhane. But even after he'd stumbled inside, Incasa's vision had continued to overwhelm his Sight. Only when the God had caught up His favorite in His icy embrace, leaving Bessic clutching the empty shell of his first teacher, had the maelstrom ebbed.

Now Bessic sat, feeling the cold of the arzhane's stone floor seep into his body as the cold of Freyiz's still form seeped into his spirit. Always practical to the point of pedantic, his mind took advantage of the silence to begin reeling out a litany of unwanted priorities: prepare the body, prepare the temple, prepare the priests, the worshipers, the city. Arrange the funeral, make a formal announcement, still the rumors and the fears that were bound to emerge, show a strong and confident front to the other five temples and their people. This must not weaken Incasa-Sarayi's position. It must strengthen it. Somehow.

He listened in unwilling obedience, knowing it had to be done, knowing he had to do it; wishing for the first time in his life that he'd never become a seer at all. Arranging Freyiz-Sayin more comfortably in his arms, he rose and made for the door, her last gasping words echoing in his mind.

"Look after Spar. He's the key to the tower's heart. But don't be a fool and try to force him, or all will be lost."

✦

An hour later, messengers from Incasa-Sarayi visited each of the other five temples, and one hour after that, the Temple Chamberlains were summoned to an emergency meeting at Oristo-Sarayi.

✦

Evening at the Hearth God's temple was traditionally a time for quiet contemplation; to reflect upon the past day's labors and plan for the next day's labors to come. It was especially important to Oristo that the abayos-priests be seen to practice this ritual as an example to each and every home in their charge, from the grand palaces of the city's Central Precinct to the simple one-room village dwellings on the far banks of Gol-Beyaz.

Tonight, however, the temple bustled with activity. As she settled herself on her divan, Senior Abayos-Priest Neclan scanned her private audience chamber with a stern expression. Everything was in place as it should be. Order would be maintained. There would be no question about that.

Breathing in the calming scents of rain and lavender that wafted in through the latticed windows, she inclined her head as her delinkos placed a small glass of raki at her elbow. She did not like to call impromptu meetings; the official Weekly Consultations were usually enough to keep the city running smoothly; however, tonight's events had made it necessary.

Events had a habit of doing that, she thought with a disapproving frown. On the best of days Senior Abayos-Priest Neclan did not approve of *events*. Something had so disrupted the Gods tonight that it had set Them at each other's throats. Chaos had erupted across the city. Despite the rising storm, people had flocked to their abayos-priests, looking for answers. They'd been told to return to their homes; most of them had obeyed, but come morning they would expect a proper response.

And they would have one, she thought firmly, but first Oristo must be calmed. The Hearth God was so agitated that the temple was filled with the smell of burned toast. Even Neclan had been unable to penetrate it. The firm, confident tone of this meeting would have a direct influence over the God's demeanor, after which things *would* return to normal across the city.

As the small porcelain clock above the door chimed the hour, she heard voices in the outer hall. After smoothing an invisible crease in her robe, Neclan drained the raki in one swift swallow.

"Tea and light confectionaries, Manilik," she said, handing him the glass.

The delinkos bowed. "Of course, Sayin."

The chamberlains entered the room, shaking out their cloaks and talking quietly as their individual friendships or alliances dictated. As they bowed to their superior and took their seats, only a trained observer could have seen the lines of tension between them. Neclan swept her gaze over them approvingly.

Seated side by side, Chamberlain Rakeed and Chamberlain Tanay of Usara's and Estavia's temples respectively resembled a pair of statues carved to represent the concept of equal but opposite. Dark-eyed, amber-skinned Rakeed of Calmak-Koy was an easygoing man with a quick smile and a flair for the dramatic. He suited his position well as Usara's hospital-cum-temple was not political, preferring to concentrate on the city's physical well-being to the exclusion of all else.

Pale-skinned, blonde-haired Tanay of Ekmir-Koy, on the other hand, was pragmatic and serious, gifted with just enough *Sight* to navigate the murky waters of Estavia-Sarayi's very unsubtle temple politics without it interfering with day-to-day matters. Responsible as she was for a large contingent of seers as well as soldiers, this was an important ability.

Beside them, Kadar, Oristo-Sarayi's own chamberlain, frowned at Rakeed, silently daring him to make an inappropriate remark. Fussy and bad-tempered, the bi-gender abayos-priest was particularly agitated over Oristo's consternation tonight. Rakeed would do well to heed the warning.

As Manilik and a younger delinkos entered with the tea and confectionaries, Chamberlain Penir of Havo-Sarayi snatched up a date simit. As sighted on the present as the God of the Seasons whose temple she oversaw, Penir was getting a little round about the middle. The bi-gender chamberlain regularly petitioned Oristo for a gender change and, living as a woman this year, preferred her female form to be on the voluptuous side.

They were all getting older and less able to eat the way they used to, Neclan noted sourly. In a year or two they'd find plain biscuits and orange slices on the tray. But for now, she accepted a simit ring of her own, before returning her attention to her people.

As if to illustrate her superior's thinking, Chamberlain Isabet poked Penir in the side with one finely-manicured finger before accepting a cup of tea from Manilik. Although small and delicate in stature, it was said that Ystazia-Sarayi's chamberlain ran her temple with an iron fist clad in a silken glove.

Neclan wholeheartedly approved. As far as the senior abayos-priest was concerned, musicians, poets, and artists were absent-minded at best and irresponsible at worst, and needed looking after.

To the other side of her, Chamberlain Farok waved off the offer of tea with a composed expression. The oldest of the chamberlains, he was also the most subtle, a thoughtful choice of Neclan's predecessor for a thoughtful position. On the surface, the duties involved in managing Incasa-Sarayi were the same as at any other temple; ensure that everyone was properly fed and clothed, the laundry done, and the carpets freshened; essentially that all aspects of life that did not involve the temple's own God moved as smoothly and as invisibly as the undercurrent of Gol-Beyaz.

However, Farok had a second, underlying duty that must run equally smoothly and invisibly: Oristo-Sarayi must be kept informed of anything that might threaten the security of the people and that included any foreknowledge of such a threat. Incasa's seer-priests were both subtle and political, and they no more liked sharing knowledge than a miser liked sharing gold and silver. Maintaining the trust of both temples was an extremely delicate balancing act of craft and discretion and one which Farok practiced extremely well.

He would need this skill in the days to come, Neclan mused. They all would. *Events* had seen to that.

Now as each of the chamberlains turned their attention to their superior, she inclined her head.

"This Consultation will not take long," she said without preamble. " We are met here to craft Oristo-Sarayi's official response to the Gods' manifestations this evening. First of all, it's important to remember that the Gods are like any family; They've squabbled in the past and will squabble in the future. It is, of course, upsetting for Their followers, but it does not have to herald an echoing argument among Their respective temples.

"And it *will* not," she stressed, fixing the gathered with a stern expression. "It's up to us to impress this upon our various charges in the days to come.

"Now, as to the reason for the Gods' disquiet, I believe Farok may be able to shed some light upon that."

She turned to Incasa-Sarayi's chamberlain and, running his fingers through his short length of steel-gray beard, he nodded.

"As you may have already heard," he began, "Freyiz-Sayin joined with Incasa tonight after suffering a massive heart attack. First Oracle Bessic immediately called a Senior Seeking Council, after which he requested my presence in his private audience room."

This announcement had the desired effect as every person in the room sat up with renewed interest.

"The official word from Incasa-Sarayi is that Freyiz-Sayin died in vision due to advanced age," he continued. "Bessic would neither confirm nor deny that the vision was both sudden and unexpected, but the temple is abuzz with rumor. It's believed that Freyiz-Sayin received this vision directly from the mind of the God Himself and that it was so dire and violent that the repercussions swept down into Gol-Beyaz itself, throwing the Gods into an uproar.

"Again, First Oracle Bessic will neither confirm nor deny this, nor would he share the vision's particulars. Incasa-Sarayi's official response is, as always, that everything is under control."

"Under *their* control," Kadar sniffed.

"As always," Isabet agreed dryly.

"What does Ystazia-Sarayi say?" Farok asked.

Isabet studied the nails on her right hand with a peevish expression. "Ystazia-Sarayi has begun its Last Day revelry and barely noticed. Subsequently, the Arts God was the first to return to normal."

"Perfectly understandable," Penir noted, finishing her tea. "A party is always a fine distraction. For its part, Havo-Sarayi was very unsettled by Havo's uncharacteristic violence, but is unwilling to commit to any explanation as yet. Their official stance is to wait and see what develops."

"Spoken like a true gardener," Rakeed observed, popping a date ring into his mouth. "Usara's official stance is, of course, spleen."

"Spleen?" Penir asked with a frown.

"Spleen. Too much or too little. That's always a physician's answer."

"That doesn't make any sense."

Rakeed just shrugged.

"And the Battle God's warriors? What of them?" As Neclan turned to Tanay, the room grew quiet.

Tanay pursed her lips thoughtfully. "There was no official word when I left," she said finally. "But Marshal Brayazi had already sent word to the watchtowers to be extra vigilant. When Estavia's unsettled, they fear the worst. Sable Company will have gone into vision by now and will have received some kind of an answer to give the people. I'll send word when I learn of it."

Neclan nodded. "Good. We will do the same." She sniffed the air with a thoughtful expression. "The smell seems to have cleared somewhat," she noted. "We will petition Oristo for answers, after which you may return to your temples with word that Oristo-Sarayi has every confidence that the Gods are as one and so are Their people."

She stood, her expression firm. The Gods *were* as one, Their people *would* be also, and no amount of visioning nonsense was going to disrupt that.

As she swept from the room, Kadar and Tanay shared a glance, but kept their doubts to themselves as the gathered followed in their superior's confident wake.

In the depths of Gol-Beyaz, the Gods continued to rumble in disquiet until Incasa, dice held up to reveal a six and one, swept an ice-clear prophecy from the lake bed to parade in front of Them.

7

The Silver Champion

"THE KEY TO COMMUNING with Estavia on the battlefield is to cultivate stillness while remaining fully alert. Even non-seers can receive Her messages clearly if they focus on these abilities."

The next morning, standing in first attack position in the central training yard, Brax snapped his teeth together in irritation as Kaptin Liel's voice, tight with the strain of Estavia's earlier anger, broke through his concentration like a stone thrown into a puddle of water. Behind him, the other members of his troop stirred and Brax resisted the urge to turn his head, remaining motionless until, taking their cue from him, they brought their attention back to the morning's purpose.

Cultivating stillness.

Non-seers would do better to cultivate the absence of seers if they wanted to receive anything besides a pain in the arse, he noted sourly then, biting back a curse, he struggled to block out the rush of sensations that took advantage of the distraction to sweep over him again: the smell of cooking from the kitchens; the sounds of shouted orders and the clash of weapons from the dozen other training circles; the sight of Spar on the archery range practicing with the Verdant Company delinkon, loosing shaft after shaft with all the stillness that Brax was finding so illusive; the pain in his body, too long held in one position and the knowledge that his people were feeling the same. With a growl, he pushed them all to one side and concentrated on stillness.

He'd been standing in the same position for what had seemed like hours but had probably been no more than a few moments. Right arm raised above his head, sword held high and parallel to the ground, left arm with his shield held at chest height, left leg forward, right leg back, equal weight on both, and knees slightly bent. The need to move had passed eventually, taking with it the burning sensations in his arms and shoulders, the stabbing in his neck, and the throbbing of the old injury in his left elbow, leaving a numbness in his body that soothed the scorched feeling in his mind.

Estavia's explosive appearance last night had caught Her warriors completely by surprise. Seated in the Cyan Company dining hall with Kemal and Yashar, the force of it had snapped Brax's head back as if he'd been slapped. The overwhelming sense of danger that had followed had triggered a mass exodus for the battlements, checked only by the swift response of Kaptin Liel. Sable Company's commander had screamed out the order for battle formation, and the temple ghazi had found themselves obeying without thinking.

Standing in the midst of his own troop, Brax had fought to maintain his sense of self throughout the maelstrom of Estavia's rage. Skidding into place at their head, Marshal Brayazi had sung out the first, ragged note used to bond with the God during combat. One by one, the commanders had added their voices to hers, throwing their strength behind their God in a single, disciplined stream, and slowly, as they'd calmed, so had the God. Rising above them, Her swords whipping back and forth like an angry cat's tail, She'd screamed out one last challenge before hurtling back into Gol-Beyaz.

The release of energy had almost knocked Brax off his feet.

Later that night, as Sable Company had barricaded themselves in the central shrine, Brax'd found Spar seated on the eastern battlements. The youth had mouthed the words "runaway cart" at him before returning his gaze to the dark waters below. He'd refused to say more, and finally Brax had allowed himself to be pulled away by Brin and Bazmin come in search of more physical comfort.

The next morning, frustrated in their attempt to get a clear answer from the God, the order had gone out from Marshal Brayazi. All temple ghazi were to receive the basic training of the battle-seers, beginning with Her Champion and favorite. Eventually, She was bound to tell someone what the danger was and clearly the marshal was hoping that someone would be Brax.

He'd had just shaken his head in disbelief. He was no seer. He could no more reach into the misty place where Spar and Sable Company drew up their intangible images of the future than he could reach into Gol-Beyaz for the temple's yearly catch of fish. And he didn't want to. Hearing Estavia's words, feeling Her presence, was all he needed. The present was difficult enough to understand, the past even harder. Adding the cryptic symbols of events that hadn't happened yet—or might never happen—just made it worse. The idea alone was enough to give him a splitting headache. But he'd sworn to serve Estavia and he would do whatever it took to be Her Champion, and so when Kaptin Liel had summoned him, he'd obeyed.

Now, breathing deeply, concentrating on each breath, ignoring the need to do anything but breathe, he focused on Estavia's ever-constant lien. As his mind stilled, Her presence flooded through him, bringing a renewed strength of purpose and belonging. He relaxed into the sensation, relieved that She was no longer in a slapping mood. Only when he felt himself about to lose track of his body altogether, did he begin to complete the attack move; slowly, very slowly, so slowly that the move itself was not the purpose of the act. Weight taken by the left leg, right leg thrust forward, left arm drawn in, and right arm swinging wide to slash at an imaginary opponent, but again so very slowly, all the while concentrating on nothing but the sacrament of battlefield technique as sanctified by the God of War.

Behind him, his people copied his motion with perfect symmetry and he stilled the urge to nod his approval. When the move was complete, he froze once again, struggling to hold the second attack position with the same focus as before.

He was still, but stillness of body was not stillness of mind. His mind continued to babble at him, commenting on the tiniest sensation. If he wanted to commune fully with Estavia in the way the battle-seers taught, he'd have to have stillness of mind.

The warm summer breeze flitted playfully through his hair, whispering of more pleasant pursuits, Brin and Bazmin behind him, the server of Oristo who'd smiled at him that morning—who smiled at him every morning. The thought of the four of them together . . .

He pushed the images aside. Now was not the time. Later, when the setting sun brought peace and shade and an end to the day's training, he might seek them out, but not now. Now he had to be still.

A bee buzzed past his face, trailing thoughts of bread and honey in its wake, making him hungry and thirsty at the same time. He ignored it. A dozen itches chased themselves across his back, each one making the absurd suggestion that spiders, lice, or maybe even rats might be causing the discomfort, and he shrugged each one aside with a frown of concentration; but when a toss of Spar's blond hair flashed in the corner of his eye, his thoughts went tumbling into the past and, with a resigned sigh, he followed them.

✦

The Winter of his tenth year had been a cold one, the chill, damp air blowing off Gol-Beyaz keeping the city in its grip even three days past the advent of Low

Spring. As Brax pulled the collar of his threadbare jacket up over his ears, he peered out the doorway he and Spar were hiding in and grimaced. Down the street, a wooden sign swung back and forth, the light spilling out from the small shop window illuminating the twin brooms painted on its surface.

He spat irritably at the cobblestones. "Dusk, and the old fart's still workin'," he muttered. "When's he gonna bugger off to his supper?"

Beside him, five-year-old Spar shivered. Brax put an arm around the younger boy's shoulders. "Won't be long now," he promised. "Soon as Karok locks up, we go in. It'll be warm inside an' we can catch some sleep till Cindar gets here at full dark, yeah? After that, we'll have all the shine we need for a good supper of our own, thanks to that carking old brogger."

Spar glanced up, his expression dull from the cold. "Thought he were a brushmaker," he said.

"He is. He's also a brogger." Brax's brows drew down. "A goodsmonger, a merchant, you know?"

"Like Maklin, the bookbinder?"

"Yeah, like her, sorta. But ... not really. Cindar sells what we lift to him, an' he sells it to ... well, to everyone else. Cindar says he cheated us last time, so we're just gonna take what's ours." Brax searched through his clothes until he found a couple of dried dates tucked in a fold. "You hungry?"

Spar nodded.

Brax passed the fruit over, then peered around the doorway again as Spar stuffed both dates into his mouth at once. When his mouth was finally empty again, the younger boy glanced up, his expression troubled.

"Brax?"

"What?"

"Is this wrong?"

"Is what wrong?"

"This. Liftin'. Is it wrong?"

Brax glanced down at Spar with a frown. They'd been

together for nearly a year now. At first, Cindar had just used the younger boy as a lookout or a "pother," a diversion—there was nothing better than a crying child to keep a mark's attention off their shine—but he'd quickly moved up to "drawing," picking pockets, and "cubbing," squeezing into the narrow shop windows that Brax had grown too big to fit through. Spar could climb any wall and squirm into any opening, no matter how tiny, and because of this, they'd pulled off a dozen good lifts last Winter that would have been beyond their reach otherwise. It had put shoes on their feet and food in their bellies.

But was it wrong?

Brax shrugged inwardly. It's what they did. Cindar was a lifter, Brax and Spar were his delinkon, like other children were delinkon to the fishmongers, carters, and laborers that plied their own trades on the western docks. Brax had never bothered to question the ethics of their life, but if Spar was already having doubts, it would make him hesitate, and hesitation would get them snatched by the garrison guards of Estavia. Cindar would go to prison, Brax might also, and Spar . . . Spar would be alone. He made a swift decision.

"No," he answered firmly. "Everyone's gotta eat, yeah? So everyone needs shine. This is how we get ours."

Spar frowned, the bright blue eyes that could convince a hardened beggar to give up his only piece of bread, narrowed in concern. "But that priest this morning said it were wrong," he pointed out.

Brax cursed under his breath. He'd hoped that— distracted by a passing pastry seller—Spar had not heard the argument between Cindar and one of those nose-in-the-air abayos-priests from Oristo-Cami.

Crouching down so that he and Spar were eye-to-eye, he caught the other boy by the arm. "That priest is fed by her cami," he said sternly. "We're fed by Cindar. Cindar's a lifter. That's the way it is."

"So *you* don't think it's wrong?"

The emphasis was obvious; the eyes staring hypnotically into his far too trusting. For nearly twelve months Brax had kept Spar warm, safe, and fed, had taught him how to survive on the docks and shielded him from Cindar's temper, the priests' interference, and the garrison guards' notice. In all that time he'd never lied to him. He'd never had to.

So did he think lifting was wrong?

He pushed the question aside. It didn't matter. A lifter who hesitated got snatched. That's all that mattered.

"No," he repeated. "I don't think it's wrong. Now, come on, Karok's just left."

Spar nodded, following obediently behind Brax as he always did.

But that had not been the end of it.

✦

In the training yard, the itch traveled across Brax's back and lodged between his shoulder blades, but the sound of Spar's arrows rhythmically thunking into straw kept his mind in the past.

✦

It was High Spring; three months before the injury that would see Spar limping to this day whenever he grew tired; three months before Cindar's brush with the garrison guards—caused because Spar had been too ill from his injury to *see* them coming—put an end to their precarious grip on peace and security. But this day the warm, fragrant breeze blowing off the Halic-Salmanak Strait smelled of fish and water weeds, and the bustling wharfs, crowded with local and foreign shipping, offered the prospect of a prosperous Low Summer to come.

Sitting with his back against a pier, fourteen-year-old Brax watched a squawking flock of lake gulls fighting over a school of immature tchiros in the shallows while eight-year-old Spar poked about in the sand with a thin piece of driftwood. Squinting in the noonday sun, Brax watched him in bemusement.

"What're you doin'?" he demanded finally.

Spar didn't bother to glance up from his task. "Lookin' for crabs," he answered.

"You'll never find any. This time of day they've all gone too deep."

"Will, too," Spar retorted, pulling a tiny creature from the sand by one leg in proof. "An' if I find enough, we won't have to lift today," he added in a carefully crafted tone of indifference.

Brax shook his head. "You know we will," he said, not unkindly. "It doesn't matter how many you find. Crabs won't buy raki, an' as soon as the afternoon trade starts, Cindar'll want us out earnin' our shine."

"We could earn it doin' somethin' else," the younger boy replied stubbornly.

"Like what?"

Spar gave his characteristic one-shouldered shrug. "I dunno, carryin' stuff or cleanin' stuff."

"Why would we wanna do that?"

Spar gave another shrug and, rising, Brax took the wood from the younger boy's hand and led him back into the shade beneath the pier. "What's goin' on, Spar?" he asked.

"Nuthin'."

"Come on."

"No, nuthin', just . . ." The younger boy glared down at his bare toes. "Graize says I'm no good at liftin'," he admitted in a sullen voice.

"Graize?"

"Yeah, he's the . . ."

"I know who he is," Brax said coldly. Twelve-year-old Graize led a gang of lifters—all around Brax's own age or older—who ran dice rings and shell games on the docks besides picking pockets and "curbing" small items from open shop windows. It was whispered that he was a seer, and he traded on that reputation. His gang always did seem to find the best pickings and had the uncanny ability to know just when to cut and run, but Brax had always found him to be a puffed-up, arrogant little fart.

And there was no good reason for him to be talking to Spar. Especially without Brax.

"When were you talking to Graize?" he demanded harshly.

Spar scowled at the water. "Yesterday, when you an' Cindar were liftin' spice from that warehouse. He found my lookout sight; I didn't call him over," he added defensively. "An' he said I was holding you back."

"The little arsehole," Brax snarled.

"*Am* I holding you back?"

" 'Course you're not. Don't you ever think that. We need you. You know things, you *see* things, yeah?"

When the younger boy didn't answer right away, Brax shook his arm gently. "Yeah?"

Spar shrugged. "Yeah."

"An' your seein' things keeps us outta the hands of the garrison guards, so don't ever think you're holdin' us back," Brax continued forcefully. "You're the makin' of us. Without you, we'd be nuthin."

"But Graize said . . ."

"Bollocks to what Graize said. Don't you listen to him. An' don't go near him either, you hear? He's a poisonous little shite, an' he's crazy to boot. I tell you what it is, he's jealous 'cause you're a real seer, not a conniving little pizzle like he is. He comes near you, you scream your head off, all right? He's just as likely to pitch you in the strait as look at you. An' he'll always lie to you. You can't believe a word he says."

When Spar still looked doubtful, Brax knelt down so that they were eye to eye again. "He's just trying to make us weak, Spar, 'cause we're better at liftin' than he is, all right?"

"I s'pose."

"You s'pose?" Brax stared into the other boy's troubled blue eyes until he nodded.

"We are," Spar agreed.

"You bet we are, an' we'll always be as long as we stick together," Brax reiterated. "We're a family, we're kardon, you an' me, that's what kardon do, we stick together and together we're strong an' nobody can ever defeat us, yeah?"

"Yeah."

"All right, then. Go back to your crab huntin'," Brax said, gesturing at the struggling creature still clutched in Spar's small fist. "At least, if you find enough, we won't have to lift our supper."

Leaning back against the pier, Brax watched as Spar returned to his task, trying to recapture the sense of cautious optimism that the warm High Spring day had conjured, but finding it almost impossible now. The next time he saw Graize, he vowed, he was going to pitch him in the strait and good riddance.

✦

"When are you gonna walk away from that fat piss-pot and the little cripple and make some real shine?"

The next Winter had been an unusually harsh one; an icy wind sweeping down from the eastern Degisken Dag Mountains covering the streets in sleet. Now, two days before the three nights of storms known as Havo's Dance that heralded the coming of Spring, the air still smelled of frost. Coming out of an apothecary's where he'd spent their last few aspers on a salve for Spar's leg, Brax almost collided with Graize leaning against the shop wall. The other boy was warmly dressed in a thick goat's hide jacket and cap with heavy cloth breeches tucked into a pair of stout leather boots. He looked healthy and well fed, and Brax pushed past him, suppressing a stab of jealousy.

"Go drown yourself," he growled in response.

"It'll never really heal, you know," the other boy said in a patently false tone of concern. "Spar's just not strong enough." His knife suddenly appeared in his hand, and he studied it intently before paring his left thumbnail. "It'll slow him down one day when he needs to be fast, and that'll be the end of him.

"An' your drunken excuse of an abayos won't last much longer either. He'll drink himself into the strait, or the spirits'll suck out his brains on the streets one night; maybe this Havo's First Night, maybe the Second—they love the taste of the unsworn, don't they; we all know that—an' then where'll you be, Braxy?" Graize turned his pale gray eyes on the other's face. "You wanna know?"

Despite himself, Brax hesitated. "Get stiffed," he retorted, but both boys could hear the lack of conviction in his tone.

"You think I'm lying? I've *seen* it," Graize continued carelessly. "A long time ago in a dream. I saw the two of us ruling the streets together, but *only* the two of us." He cocked his head to one side. "Spar's supposed to see things, too, yeah?' he asked. "But I'll bet he hasn't told you anything like this. An' he wouldn't even if he has. He doesn't dare. He knows that one day I'm gonna be all you've got."

"Yeah, an' what about Drove?" Brax threw back at him. "You just gonna dump him in the strait when we get to be these great street rulers?"

Graize shrugged with careless élan. "Drove won't need me by then, but *you* will. You can't make it on your own, an' we both know it.

"So don't go too far," he added with a harsh laugh, as Brax turned his back on him. "I'll only have to come and find you."

Spinning about, Brax pulled his own knife from his belt. "Come within arm's reach again and you'll find my blade in your guts," he snarled. "So you jus' keep away from us—from all of us—d'you hear me?"

Graize straightened, his eyes suddenly glittering like chips of polished gray marble. "Why don't'cha go ask him?" he said in a challenging voice. "Ask the baby-seer an' see what he says, yeah? Or are you too scared, Braxy? Too scared of what he'll say? It takes strength to face the future; more strength than he's got. Is it more than you've got?"

Brax took one menacing step forward, but as Drove came around the corner of the nearby alehouse, he turned. "Why don't you just piss off," he said over his shoulder. Holding the jar of salve like a weapon, he stalked off, the other boy's mocking laughter echoing in his ears.

✦

Spar was waiting for him, sitting by the window of the dingy, second-floor room they shared with Cindar when he returned from the apothecary's. The light filtering in through the broken shutters cast a mottled pattern of shadows across his face, making him appear even more gaunt and pale than he already was. When Brax gestured, he stretched out his leg, but as the older boy bent to examine the thin scar that twisted from his heel to halfway up his calf, his blue eyes narrowed. Staring at the top of Brax's head, he waited until the intensity of his gaze caused the other boy to growl in irritation.

"What?" Brax asked, opening the jar and sniffing at the gritty, gray paste inside with some suspicion.

Spar continued to stare at him.

"Your eyes are gonna stick like that if you don't quit it."

Spar just snorted.

Scooping out a small fingerful of salve, Brax smeared it over the scar as softly as he was able, then sat back on his heels. "So," he demanded. "We gonna play guessing games all day or what?"

Spar curled his lip at him briefly. "What's wrong?" he asked.

"How'd you mean?"

"You're mad. What's wrong?"

A dozen dismissive remarks came and went before Brax gave one of Spar's one-shouldered shrugs. "Ran into Graize," he replied, knowing the younger boy would not be put off until he got a piece of the truth anyway. "You know how the little shite is."

"Did you fight 'im?"

Spar cast an anxious glance across Brax's face, looking for blood or bruising, and the older boy glared at him. "No, I didn't fight 'im," he snapped, standing up abruptly. "I ran away, all right? I had to get this home, didn't I?"

A flash of pain came and went in the younger boy's eyes, and Brax sighed deeply. "Drove was with him," he said in a gentler tone. "I'd a got pounded, so I walked away, all right?"

Spar nodded. Touching the older boy on the arm, he looked into his eyes. "We'll get 'im," he said intensely. "One day we will."

"Yeah, I know." Turning away, Brax stared around the room, noting their few ragged belongings lying beside the two thin pallets, the damp, crumbling walls, the dirt, and the lingering smell of sickness. "Where's Cindar?" he asked woodenly, knowing the answer already.

"Out drinkin'."

"Piss-head."

"He'll drink himself into the strait. Then where'll you be?"

Graize's words echoed in his mind, as mocking as his laughter.

"You wanna know?"

"No."

"Spar's supposed to see things. Why don't you go ask him an' see what he says?"

"No."

"You scared?"

"... yes."

Spar made an inquiring noise, but Brax just shook his head. Suddenly feeling unbearably confined, he forced himself to give the younger boy a tight smile.

"You hungry?"

When Spar nodded, he gestured toward his ragged jacket. "Then let's get outta here. It's not all that cold. We could head up to the fish stalls and maybe curb a oyster or two an' then sneak into the Findik-Meyhane. It'll be so busy no one'll even notice us, an' a spell by a warm fire'll do you good, yeah?"

"Yeah."

"Come on, then."

Once out on the streets, they made a swift beeline for the western market, shivering as the wind drove its icy fingers through their worn clothing. Above their heads, the gathering storm clouds promised more bad weather to come, while about their feet, unobserved, the few, thin spirits that had managed to worm their way through the cracks in the Gods' great wall of stone and power, hunkered sullenly in the shadows, biding their time. Soon there would be far more to worry about than youthful Dockside rivalries.

✦

In the training yard, Brax's sword arm twitched as the memories from that spring flooded his mind. Three day later, Cindar was dead, just as Graize had predicted, Havo's Dance raged above the city, and the four boys faced each other, knives drawn, beneath a wooden pier on Liman-Caddesi while a maelstrom of wild lands spirits, driven mad by rage and hunger, exploded onto the streets. Drove was the first to fall, the life sucked out of him by a thousand needlelike teeth and claws; then Graize; snatched into the air, still screaming out his hatred and defiance. Swarmed by the savage creatures, Spar dropped to the blood-soaked sand, curling into a tight, defensive ball, and Brax threw himself over him, trying to protect the younger boy's small body with his own. One cheek streaming blood where Graize's knife had scored him, he cried out the oath that had saved their lives.

He hadn't seen Graize again until they'd faced each other on the field at Serin-Koy, and then again on the battlements of Estavia-Sarayi. Locked in combat, he and Graize had hurtled into the cold waters of Gol-Beyaz. As a thousand stars had exploded in his mind, he'd had his one and only vision: blood and gold strewn across a sunlit floor and the enemies of Anavatan rising up against them. And then as the cold had frozen the breath in his lungs and the God of Battles had reached out to take him into Her embrace, he'd seen Graize, older and clear-eyed, armed with steel and stone, standing by his side on a snow-capped mountain ridge.

Graize

"No."

Older and clear-eyed, armed with steel and stone stood by his side . . .

"I said, no!"

"One day I'm gonna be all you've got."

"Shut up!"

✦

"Excuse me?"

Physical sensation returned in a rush of pain, every injury he'd taken in battle and before shrieking in protest. He swayed, disoriented for half a heartbeat, then caught himself, and again, very slowly, and with great deliberation, sheathed his sword, lowered his shield, and returned Kaptin Liel's raised eyebrow with a shake of his head. "Nothing, Kaptin," he said, as behind him the troop took the opportunity to break formation as well. "Just answering a memory."

"A memory caused by a distraction or a memory sent by the God?"

"Spar's supposed to see things. Why don't you go ask him an' see what he says?"

Across the yard, Spar had paused, watching them curiously. With the past still so prevalent in his mind, the years of trusting no one but each other spoke Brax's answer for him.

"I don't know, Kaptin," he said with a deliberate shrug, playing on Sable Company's condescending opinion of non-seers the way he'd played the marks on the streets. "I'm a ghazi, not a battle-seer. I have about as much prophetic ability as a block of wood."

"Less," the bi-gender seer kaptin agreed in a dry tone.

"Right. So, if Estavia doesn't use any actual words, I'm lost."

"Then I suppose we should be thankful that She does use actual words with Her infantry ghazi so very often," Kaptin Liel answered, glaring the rest of Brax's troop into loose attention.

"Be that as it may," the kaptin added as Brax made to give a departing salute, "stillness remains an ability worth cultivating. Our control is the Battle-God's control. It strengthens our bond with Her, allowing Her strength to become one with our own, and with Her strength flowing unimpeded through our minds and bodies, we can overcome any weakness, fatigue, or injury, even when near death, as I think you've already discovered in the past, yes?"

"Yes, Kaptin."

Sable Company's commander favored the deliberately formal response with a suspicious gaze but nodded curtly when Brax's expression remained impassive.

"Good. Well, you're all free to return to more physical training for the moment. However, you will be expected to become proficient in this area. If for no other reason than to give support to Sable Company in overcoming the prophetic shielding caused by the Petchan seers this season."

"Yes, Kaptin."

"Their shielding's *not* strong," Kaptin Liel added with

unnecessary emphasis. "If we all act in concert, it should be easily overcome."

"Yes, Kaptin."

"Yes, well. You're dismissed then."

"Thank you, Kaptin." Brax turned. "A short break, everyone, then sword work until midday." As the other members of the troop immediately made for the dining hall, he headed for the eastern battlements.

✦

Spar fell into step beside him without a word as he passed the archery range. With the ever-faithful Jaq padding along behind them, they took a set of external stone stairs, two at a time, up to the granary rooftop. It wasn't until they were settled in their usual place overlooking Gol-Beyaz that Brax answered Spar's expectant look with a shrug.

"We're expected to become proficient at stillness if we're to overcome the prophetic shielding caused by the Petchan seers this season," he said in an exaggerated imitation of Kaptin Liel.

Spar raised a politely incredulous eyebrow.

"Because their shielding's *not* strong," Brax continued. "If we all work together, it can be easily overcome."

"By infantry?" Spar asked with a smirk.

"Oh, no." Brax drew his brows down in an expression of mock disapproval. "By proper Sable Company battle-seers, of course. The infantry are just supposed to ... help. The seers probably don't *really* need our help, but stillness is a good ability to *cultivate*."

"Because the Petchan shielding isn't strong."

"Right."

"Right." Spar gave a loud, unimpressed snort. "I told you they were being blocked," he sneered.

"You did."

Scratching behind Jaq's ears, Spar gave Brax a sideways grin. "And they started this *cultivating* with you?" he asked.

"Yep."

"I guess it's true, then. The Petchan shielding *isn't* strong."

"Get fleas."

Spar snickered. "How'd you do?"

Picking a bit of lichen off the top step, Brax threw it over the wall with an expression of disgust. "How'd you think I did? Every time I tried to think about not thinking all I could do was think about a hundred other things. I don't know how you do it," he added with a resentful grumble.

"By not thinking about not thinking," Spar said absently, studying a piece of lichen of his own.

Brax glared at him. "Clear as mud."

Spar just shrugged. "When you train with your sword, you think about hitting; not about *not* hitting. You imagine an enemy in front of you whose head you're whacking off, yeah?"

"Yeah."

"So, when you're *cultivating* stillness, you don't think about *not* thinking . . ."

"You think about thinking?"

"No stupid, you think about *something*. You *cultivate* a single thought about one thing, anything: a . . . sword or a word or . . ."

"A memory?"

Spar gave him a shrewd look. "What did you see?"

Brax smiled, remembering how many times he'd asked Spar that very same question. "Nuthin'," he answered, falling into their old Dockside accent with a grin of his own.

Spar snorted. "Nuthin'," he echoed. "Nuthin' at all?"

"Nuthin' worth botherin' about."

"Then why were you grinding your teeth so hard I could hear it across the training yard?"

Brax sobered. Rubbing at his left elbow, he scowled darkly. "I was just remembering a couple of days before we were attacked on Havo's Dance. I met Graize coming out of the apothecary's. He said some things."

He paused, and Spar gave him an expectant look. "It wasn't anything; just the same pissy crap he always said," he expanded.

"If it was the same pissy crap, you wouldn't be remembering it now," Spar pointed out.

"Yeah, I guess." Staring out at the silver lake's sparkling waters just visible over the battlements, Brax frowned. "It was all just lies anyway," he said almost to himself.

"Lies about what?"

"Doesn't matter."

Spar stared at him and, with a growl of annoyance, Brax cast about for an answer that would satisfy him. Nearly everything Graize had predicted had come true: Cindar's death, Drove's death, Spar's injury, so what had he actually lied about?

"He said I couldn't make it on my own. He said he was going to be all that I had. He said you knew and you didn't dare tell me. He said he was going to come find me one day . . ."

Graize, older and clear-eyed, armed with steel and stone, stood by his side on a snow-capped mountain ridge.

"No."

"He said he saw us together, him and me," he replied after a long moment.

Spar gave an unimpressed shrug. "He told me that, too. He was always pulling that game, trying to split us up."

"Like I said, lies," Brax repeated weakly.

"But a lie that stuck in your head."

Brax scowled. "It wasn't a prediction," he said so forcefully that Jaq sat up with a growl.

"No," Spar agreed. "It wasn't. Lay down, Jaq." Kicking off his sandals, the youth scratched the dog's neck with one bare toe. "Graize is a trickster," he continued once the dog had flopped back down at his feet again. "Tricksters always mingle lies with the truth. It's how they get you. It's how they turn you into a mark. You *know* this."

"He said you'd seen it, too," Brax added, staring intently at the turrets of Dovek-Hisar across the strait as he spoke the words he'd kept hidden for so long. "But that you wouldn't tell me. He said I should ask you."

"But you didn't."

"No."

"Why not?"

"Seemed stupid."

"No, it didn't."

Brax gave him a jaundiced look which Spar ignored.

"You were scared it might be true," the youth continued. "And you didn't want to know."

Brax shrugged. "Maybe."

"Maybe nothing." Shaking his head, Spar leaned back against the wall. "Remember what you told me about Graize a long time ago?" he asked. "You said he's a liar, he'll always lie to you, and he's just trying to make us weak. Now I'm telling you: he told you what you were afraid of and gave it back to you formed like a prophecy to make it sound real. He invited you to ask me for the truth, knowing that you couldn't. He made you a mark, and he won."

"Won?"

"He weakened us."

Graize, older and clear-eyed . . .

"I guess."

"Brax."

"What?"

Turning the full intensity of his Dockside stare on the other's face, Spar waited until Brax met his eyes and then spoke both clearly and slowly. "I haven't seen you and Graize together. With me or without me, I haven't seen it. If I do, I'll tell you, all right?"

"All right."

"All right. But . . ." Spar's intense stare held him in place. "That doesn't mean that what you saw wasn't important. Sable Company's been having confusing visions about the Petchans all year. I told you that before. Everything points to a new leader, and now you have a memory about Graize when you're practicing battle-seer techniques?"

Brax nodded his understanding. "Yeah. I meant to talk to you about this yesterday. The last time an enemy of Anavatan came up with a new leader ... ?"

On a snow-capped mountain ridge ...

"It was Graize."

"It was Graize. And Sable Company's never been able to see him in vision."

"And just like they couldn't see the reason behind the Yuruk attacks four years ago, they can't see the reason behind the increased Petchan activities now."

"Because the little shite's in the Gurney-Dag Mountains stirring up trouble the way he stirred it up in the wild lands. And he knows how to hide."

Spar nodded. "Especially now after Elif's death."

"And Freyiz-Sayin's. Bad timing."

"Suspicious timing."

Brax gave him a penetrating look. "Suspicious enough to figure they're connected?"

Rubbing Jaq's belly absently, Spar gave his familiar one-shouldered shrug. "Just suspicious enough to know our enemies'll take advantage of the holes in our prophecy if they can. *All* our enemies," he added.

"So what do I do?"

"About what?"

Brax scowled at him. "About this vision or memory or whatever it was, and about Graize. Do I tell Sable Company?"

Staring up at the distant clouds, Spar shook his head with a frown. "No," he answered after a moment. "They won't accept its importance, not coming from ..." he paused.

"Infantry?" Brax suggested with a sneer.

"A non-seer," Spar replied caustically. "It wouldn't

matter if it was Marshal Brayazi's own vision; they wouldn't take it seriously. No, Graize is our problem, he always has been. *We* have to deal with him."

"How?"

"I have some ideas."

"Like sticking a sword in his guts, maybe?"

Spar narrowed his eyes. "Maybe," he allowed. "Like it or not, our fates are mixed up and he knows it. He'll be ready. We'll have to be ready, too."

Unless I get a chance to gut him early," Brax added with a martial gleam in his eye. "You won't mind if I start without you, then, will you?"

"As long as I get to be there for his memorial service, you go right ahead."

"It'll wait for you even if I have to preserve his body in a barrel of pickling spices."

Spar snorted. "You wouldn't know pickling spices if they preserved you on the arse. Just burn it. I'll send you an urn."

"Done."

"Still thinkin' that his words about the two of you bein' together might be true?" Spar scoffed.

Brax's expression sobered.

"I'm going to be all you've got . . ."

"I never really did," he said quietly, giving the other a sideways look.

"Yeah, you did."

"Mostly I didn't."

"No." Turning, Spar stared across the temple rooftops to the western docks barely visible in the distance. "Mostly you didn't," he allowed.

"So we're all right?"

"Yeah." His gaze still riveted on the distance, Spar nodded absently, but when Brax didn't move, he turned. "We're all right," he repeated.

Brax jerked his chin in the direction Spar was staring. "What are you looking at, kardos?" he asked.

"What? Nuthin'."

Brax grinned. "Nuthin' at all?"

Spar shook his head impatiently. "Nothing," he said with deliberate clarity.

"So what are you not looking at, then?" Brax cocked his head to one side. "Hisar?" he hazarded. When Spar made no answer, he gave a faint bark of laughter. "It's probably off wherever It goes when It's not with you," he said. "What's the problem?"

Spar gave him an impatient look. "No problem. It's just that tonight's Estavia's First Night."

"And your little God-spirit likes parties?"

"Yes. But what It actually likes is new experiences. Especially experiences that involve the Gods. Estavia's First Night is tonight, Freyiz-Sayin's funeral will probably be tomorrow. That should draw It here."

"You think maybe something's happened to It?"

"I don't know."

"*Can* something happen to It?"

"*I don't know.* Look, it doesn't matter right now. I hear Brin and Bazmin down in the courtyard. Go get laid or something."

Brax stood. "Can't, we've got sword practice. That's probably why they're here."

"Then go hit something." Spar returned his attention to the empty sky. "Look, I'll come and get you if I need you," he grated without turning. "Go."

"Fine, I'm going, don't sic the dog on me." With a shake of his head, Brax headed down the stairs.

✦

The twins pounced on him as soon as he reached the bottom.

"Did the God of Battles tell Her favorite what She wouldn't tell Her seers while he was *cultivating stillness*," Brin asked gleefully.

"No."

"Funny, the way you were flopping around, I thought for sure She'd told you something."

"Get stiffed."

"There isn't time, lover and commander."

"Did She at least say whether we'd be going to war against the Petchans this season?" Basmin added.

Falling into step between them as they headed back to the training yard, Brax just shrugged. "We are."

Bazmin's eyes widened. "Really?"

Glancing up at the clouds turned a misty crimson in the setting sun, Brax scowled as the sporadic shimmering in the air that he was beginning to recognize as the elusive presence of Hisar finally appeared above the granary battlements. "We're going to war because it's what we do," he replied tersely. "We don't need a vision to tell us that."

"And when we do, a certain God-like spirit thing had better make up Its mind whose side It's on," he added silently. *" 'Cause in war there's no room for fence-sitters."*

"If it's not gonna be as a Sable Company seer, what's it gonna be, then?"

He shook his head. *"Sable Company seer,"* he told himself firmly. *"It has to be."*

They didn't need a vision to tell them that either.

"Come on," he added, stepping up the pace. "Or the others'll figure we've gone off to screw in a sentry box and they'll come looking for us."

"And those boxes are far too small for ten people," Bazmin agreed.

"Right." Keeping his eyes firmly off the skies, Brax shoved the afternoon's entire experience, memories, conversation and all, to the back of his mind. Spar would come and get him if he needed him. That would have to do for now.

8

The Black Champion

THE MOON HAD RISEN well above the walls of Estavia-Sarayi when Hisar appeared, flitting silently across the shrouded courtyards. Half in and half out of the physical world, It lit upon the marble stairs leading up to the Pavilion of Silence and paused. The metallic gleam of the old woman's funerary urn inside reflected in the eyes of Its dragonfly seeming as It cocked Its head to one side.

Hisar was no stranger to death. Born of the wild lands spirits and raised on the conflict between the Yuruk and the Battle God's Warriors, It had been both witness and cause in the past and It understood how fragile the physical world could be. But until recently It hadn't thought that had anything to do with It.

The memory of Incasa's attack caused a ripple of distress to mar the surface of Its seeming, and It smoothed it down quickly before it came to Estavia's notice. The Battle God's response had been even more frightening because It didn't understand why She would want to come to Its aid. Her fiery possessiveness surrounded Her temple like smoke, and the lien Her people willingly carried within them felt like a giant snake ready to strike whenever the Godling got too close.

Hisar was not part of Her temple and did not carry any such bond, but when It had cried out in pain and fear, Estavia had exploded from Gol-Beyaz ready to do battle with Its attacker. Rather than feeling comforted and grateful, it had only caused Hisar to feel confused, lonely, and unhappy. It had fled back to Graize, but even wrapped in his arms in the faraway mountains where the Gods held no sway, the memory of Her response whispered through Its newly-formed emotions, drawing it back on a silver thread of longing.

Finally the draw had become too strong, and Hisar had returned. Taking Danjel's swallow-form once more, It had lit upon the temple's granary roof, tucking Itself deep into the shadows, and watching with barely concealed fascination as the sun had set and the familiar Evening Invocations became the celebration of Estavia's First Day.

In the midst of Her warriors, Brax and Spar had stood with their abayon just as they'd done during Battle-Seer Elif's funeral. The older men had flanked them like bodyguards, and Hisar had felt the same sense of longing at the sight.

It had almost turned away then, when a line of torch-wielding delinkon filing from the armory tower had given It pause. A hush of unusually somber anticipation had fallen over the gathered, and Hisar had found Itself echoing the feeling, pulling Its chest in as tightly as It might have done if It'd had a breath to hold.

Even the singing had been different tonight. During Invocation, Her warriors called to Her as a lover might call, each note an invitation to join with them in an intimate embrace. On the battlefield they summoned Her to fight with them, their voices rising up like the drums and trumpets they used to summon each other. But on this night their singing had held such a strange mixture of joy and sadness that it had caused a thrill of disquiet to work its way through the Godling's tiny body. The urge to change and grow large enough to allow their song to fill It up completely was almost overwhelming.

Only Estavia's appearance had held it at bay. She'd risen a hundred feet into the air, staring down at Her people with a look of feral adoration that had bordered on gluttony. Marshal Brayazi had sung out the names of this year's dead; as Estavia had accepted each one, Hisar had felt Her power rush over It.

Estavia was not a God of serenity or solitude, She was a God of armies, of violence and bloodshed. Her presence invoked a need to kill the enemy—any enemy—in Her name to protect those in Her charge, and suddenly Hisar had understood why Her people accepted Her lien so completely.

And knowing that neither song nor response was for Itself had caused an even greater sense of pain to ripple through Its newly-born senses.

Now, staring into the pavilion, Hisar wondered what it must be like to join with the Gods in Gol-Beyaz and, equally, what it must be like to accept that joining as one of Them.

The memory of Brax's essence flowing through It, bringing a strength and power unlike any It had felt before or since, caused the young Godling of Creation and Destruction to rise slowly into the air, Its dragonfly-seeming growing and changing in unconscious imitation of Estavia's manifestation. The limits of Its youth pressed against It, hampering Its movements and, as It struggled to overcome them, It reached out for strength.

Estavia's response was immediate. One slap and Hisar was flung from the bounds of Her temple. Hurt and angry, It turned and sped back toward the distant mountains at once.

✦

The God of Battles watched It go, a dark expression in Her crimson eyes. Hisar's earlier distress still echoed in Her breast, mingling with Its more recent longing to create a summons similar to that of Her people, but not similar enough to open a clear channel of response. Hisar was a delos, and Estavia was not the God of delon.

She knew about loyalty and love and the demands of protection and sacrifice; She'd been formed by those selfsame pressures of dependency and obligation in the days of Kaptin Haldin and Marshal Nurcan. Her warriors called to Her and She came, granting them the strength of arms necessary to defeat their enemies in exchange for the strength of their reverence. The needs of Her soldiers were Her domain; the needs of their delon were the domain of Oristo. And the needs of the Gods, old and young, were the domain of Incasa.

A ripple of prescient warning caused the God of Battles to sweep Her crimson gaze both north and south. A growing sense of danger had been preying on Her dreams. Her seers had been unable to pierce the overlying fog that blanketed the future, but somewhere out there an enemy lurked, growing stronger with each passing day. That enemy must be found and destroyed, and if Her seers could not ferret it out, Her favorites must be made to do it. Brax was already seeking, She could sense it within him. He needed reinforcements, but She needed them first. Using the power gifted to Her by Her First Day celebrations, Estavia reached out for Incasa.

The God of Prophecy rose from the waves as if He had been waiting for Her summons, His pale eyes meeting the crimson fire of Her gaze with an inscrutable expression. The silence stretched between them, then with one, languid motion, Incasa reached down to draw two small objects from the depths and flick them toward Her temple battlements.

Together, the Gods of Prophecy and Battle returned under the waves as the two wooden dice came to rest against the wall to reveal a six and a one.

✦

On the western shore, Oristo watched until the ripples which marked Incasa and Estavia's passage disappeared, then turned and gave a single, summoning call.

When Estavia-Sarayi's chamberlain appeared on the wall with a sleepy expression, the Hearth God drew four tiny ceramic beads from the lake bed, passing them to her with a single word.

"SPAR."

Tanay nodded.

✦

The next morning, Spar stood on Estavia-Sarayi's kitchen wharf, watching a lake gull eye a barge from Caliskan-Koy being unloaded. Thick coils of hemp rope and bales of heavy canvas joined rounds of hard cheese the size of cartwheels and a dozen barrels of raki on the pier.

But no fish.

After a moment, the gull took wing, squawking indignantly, and Spar snorted. Gulls were supposed to be the birds of Incasa, renowned for their ability to sense a storm coming from miles away; you'd think this one might have sensed there was nothing for it to eat in this cargo before now.

Watching the gull wheel off to the south, Spar tried not to look for a distinctive black sail on the water. The bulk of Estavia-Sarayi's southeastern battlements blocked most of his view of Gol-Beyaz, and besides it was well past noon. The sea breeze sweeping down from the Bogazi-Isik Strait had been fast and strong this morning. The barge that had taken Brax south would be halfway to Serin-Koy by now.

Pushing his back against the cool, stone wall, he slowly dropped until he sat with his legs tucked under him on the sun-warmed wooden pier. As Jaq settled down beside him, he scratched the animal between the ears and mulled over the events of the past few days.

Elif's funeral had passed in the blink of an eye. He had stood between Kemal and Yashar, allowing himself some small comfort in their presence but holding himself as stiff and as straight as they did. Even when a junior seer-delinkon—a full year older than himself—had broken down crying, he'd refused to give anyone the satisfaction of seeing his loss. When they'd all been dismissed to the commissary hall to eat and drink their fill and remember her to each other in small, hushed groups, he'd returned to his perch on the eastern battlements, alone.

Her name had been sung out with the others who'd died in the past year at Estavia's First Day celebration, and the urn he'd chosen, holding all that was left of her physical body, sat within the Pavilion of Silence. A year from her death, it would be moved to its permanent location in the west wall beside those of Sable Company who'd joined Estavia before her. And that would be it, all that remained of a life eight decades in the making. It didn't seem worth it, somehow.

Brax had spent the night with him on the roof before his bedchamber window. After Kemal, Yashar, and especially Jaq had been convinced to leave them to their own company, they'd sat side by side, saying nothing, needing nothing but each other's presence, feeling the day's warmth slowly bleed away before the cool breeze off Gol-Beyaz, watching the temple bats hunting insects in the orchards and listening to the nightingales singing in the gardens as the moon traversed the sky. When the priests of Havo'd called the dawn, they'd gone inside. An hour later, Brax had taken ship for Alev-Hisar.

Kemal and Yashar had joined him on the Warriors' Wharf to say good-bye. The older man had taken Brax in a huge bear hug—the same as he'd done when they were younger—and refused to release him until he'd promised to write more often. With the breath squeezed out of him, Brax had promised with a gasp, much to the amusement of the rest of his troop standing nearby.

Spar snickered at the memory. The twins wouldn't let Brax forget that embarrassing moment any time soon and that was all to the good. It might be the only thing that kept him from forgetting his promise altogether; Brax hated writing almost as much as he hated reading.

Hopefully, the twins' nagging would see at least one or two letters coming north before they joined him later that season. It might also keep their abayon from fretting too much, but he doubted it. With a faint smile, he pressed his fingers against the small cloth bag that held a dozen silver aspers hanging about his neck.

✦

"Fortune for fifteen."

Spar accepted the gift from his abayon with an embarrassed smile, then tipped it open to reveal two silver aspers gleaming in the center of his palm.

"Thank you," he said awkwardly.

Yashar beamed at him. "In one year you'll be an adult, a temple-delinkos and not a delos anymore. Today starts you off on that path. Save them well."

"It's tradition that delon and their abayon spend one year saving for an apprenticeship," Kemal added.

Spar gave them both a sly smile. "But I thought temple-delinkon didn't pay for their apprenticeships, Aban," he said. "Why do I need to save these at all? Why couldn't I just spend them?"

"Again," Kemal said before Yashar could answer, "because it's tradition. And because it's prudent. You save for the future even if that future's assured. You save for fortune for fifteen and the years to come."

Spar gave them the same sly smile. "And you will save with me, Aban?" he asked.

"We'll match your savings," Yashar answered. "That's also tradition."

Spar's features shone with a sudden avarice he did nothing to hide. "You'll both match my savings equally?" he asked, his voice dripping with sly entrapment.

Both men chuckled. "Yes, Spar-Delin," Kemal assured him. "We'll both match your savings equally."

"Then I'll be sure to save every last asper I get for the next year to amass as huge a fortune for fifteen as possible."

Yashar took him in his usual bear hug. "You do that, my delos, and I'll be proud to embrace poverty in your honor. Very proud."

A momentary silence fell between them, then Kemal gave a slight cough.

"About Elif . . ." he began.

Pulling himself away from Yashar, Spar shook his head. "I'm fine."

"You're sure?"

"Yes." He turned a somber expression on them both. "People die, Aban," he said, the adult tone of his voice belying the still youthful cast of his features. "It's what they do."

"Still . . ."

"We worry," Yashar finished for him. "About you and Brax equally."

"I know." Spar gave them a faint smile. "That's why I'm saving my silver even when I don't have to."

"Well, try to get Brax to save a little also, will you?" Kemal said, playing along with the change of subject. "I know his apprenticeship's over, but it doesn't hurt to have a little money put by anyway."

"To begin saving for his own delon's fortune for fifteen," Yashar added with a wink.

"So you just banked yours away?"

"Sure. What else was I going to do with it?"

"I'll talk to him."

"Remind him to write."

"I will."

"And to stay safe."

"I *will.*"

✦

On the Warriors' Wharf, once Yashar had finished pummeling Brax good-bye, Kemal had stepped forward and, with a start, Spar had realized how much Brax had grown in the last five years. Although he would never be as tall or as broad as Yashar, he and Kemal were almost of a height now. Brax looked stronger and more capable than he ever had, the growth of dark beard along his jaw making him seem more like Kemal's younger kardos than his delinkos. Even the lack of a full night's sleep had done nothing to tire him. He looked like a man, not like a delos anymore. As Kemal'd stepped back to allow him and Brax a private moment to make their own good-byes, Spar had banished a momentary stab of jealousy.

Brax had sensed it anyway, of course, and had rightly guessed its source. Unable to resist, he'd run his fingers along one bearded cheek with a grin, and Spar had favored him with a sour look in reply.

"You still act like an idiot," he'd snapped

"And you still act like a cantankerous old man."

A wisp of cloud had covered the sun, momentarily dropping the other's face into shadow and raising the hair on the back of Spar's neck in a chill of prescient foreboding.

"That's not as likely to get you killed," he'd answered, but the distraction had leached his voice of its usual force and Brax had just shrugged.

"Maybe, but we've already been through this. You do the warning, and I do the shoving. We'll be all right. We always are, yeah?"

"Yeah." Spar'd fingered the two beads, one blue and one green tied into his hair with a frown. Along with her own gift—another silver asper—Tanay had given them and two others to him that morning with cryptic and unwanted message from Oristo.

"A fortune for fifteen gift from the Hearth God."

Tanay gave a faint shrug as Spar looked down at the beads in both confusion and suspicion.

"Isn't silver the traditional gift," he asked, her own gift already safely tucked away in his cloth bag.

"Yes," she agreed. "And don't ask me why Oristo's

gifting you or what this gift means because I have no idea." Tanay's voice was tinged with reproach as if the Hearth God should have known better. "But the last beads proved useful. These should, too."

"But the last beads were from you, weren't they?"

"Yes. I had a premonition you would need them, and I was right."

"So, do you think Oristo's having the premonitions now?"

"Maybe. The Hearth God has some small, prophetic talent just as Estavia does."

"But no seers."

"No." She laughed. "Abayos-priests are traditionally suspicious of seers. But still," she added with a wink. "It always helps to know whether it's going to rain on laundry day." Reaching out, she closed his fingers about the beads. "Do whatever you feel is most appropriate with them," she said. "I trust your judgment. So does the Hearth God."

✦

On the wharf, Spar had glanced at Brax suspiciously. "You have the other bead I gave you?" he'd demanded.

Brax'd placed his hand on his chest. "On a cord around my neck, one green bead to go with the brown one you gave me before."

"Good. Brax?"

"What?"

Spar'd jerked his head at Kemal and Yashar. "Our abayon say you have to start saving your shine to give to your own delon."

"Oh, they do, do they?"

"And to write."

Brax had just rolled his eyes.

"And to stay safe."

"You, too. And take care of them." He'd jerked his head at their abayon. "They're not as young as they once were."

"I will."

Squeezing Spar's shoulder, Brax had paused to stare up at Estavia's statue standing guard above the main temple wharf to their right, then turned and jumped the barge railing, throwing a grin over his shoulder as he went.

As the barge had cast off, Spar had set the sense of foreboding carefully to one side to be examined later. Their years of lifting on the streets had taught him many things, the most important being that bravado did not banish danger, whatever Brax might believe. If he was really going to stay safe, he was going to need help.

✦

Now, watching Tanay's servers arrive to muscle the Caliskan-Koy cargo in through the kitchen wharf's huge, iron-strapped doors, Spar turned Oristo's two remaining beads between finger and thumb, realizing that this was not the place to begin such an examination either. There were too many distractions and too many Gods perched above the walls. He needed somewhere quiet and private.

Standing, he waited for a break in the line of heavily laden servers to allow him to return inside the temple proper, but as a fresh breeze off the lake brought the sudden powerful scent of rot and . . . flowers wafting past them, Jaq raised his head with a questioning woof. Spar frowned, turning his head back and forth, unable to find the source of the smell.

"Where is it, Delin?" he asked.

Jaq stood, questing the air with his nose, his expression more eager than suspicious as he peered through the busy line of servers who cheerfully ignored him. As possibly the only temple-delinkos to even visit the kitchen wharf, never mind occasionally lend a hand unloading the boats that kept Estavia-Sarayi supplied with fish, oil, charcoal, pots, cloth, carpets, and any number of a hundred other goods that arrived daily, Spar and

Jaq were well known, so when the dog suddenly dove between the legs of two burly servers carrying a huge coil of rope between them, they did no more than call out a warning. The dog landed on the stony beach below in a spray of pebbles and Spar watched him intently as he began to scrabble at a large pile of drying lake weed thrown up against the foot of the temple wall by the tide. But when he dropped his head and began to grind his cheek into the weeds, Spar saw, too late, that what he'd actually found was a lake gull.

A very dead lake gull.

With an expression of disgust, he jumped down, catching the dog by his braided collar.

"Get outta there!" he snarled, tugging at the animal. Jaq resisted, catching the gull by one wing and pulling it free with a splattering of algae and weeds. Releasing his collar, Spar caught hold of the other wing. A tugging match ensued until finally Jaq gave it up reluctantly, watching with a deeply aggrieved expression as Spar flung the bird into the water amid the general laughter of the servers above.

"Don't give me that look!" he warned the dog. "It stank!"

The smell of rot lingered on his hands and in his nostrils. As he bent to wipe his palms on the ground, he froze as the smell of lilies and datura suddenly rose up from the disturbed pile of lake weed. His mind filled with the memory of rain and hail and a desperate gamble to deflect the will of a God, and he turned, moving as slowly as if every step had to be taken through two feet of water, approaching the temple wall with the image of what he'd find already sharp and clear in his mind.

A pair of wooden soldier's dice tangled in a nest of sodden feathers, weeds, and tiny, rotting water creatures.

A thrill of disquiet chased itself down his spine as he bent to pry the dice free, then straightened, staring at the green-stained, water-slicked objects on his palm, a deep frown drawing his pale brows down to meet at the bridge of his nose.

Yashar had given him the dice on the night Hisar had exploded into the physical realm; an innocent gesture bloated with prophetic meaning. Using them as a focus to strengthen the channel between his mind and the dark place, he'd faced Incasa—unsworn and unfettered oracle of an uncharted power and the God of Prophecy standing face-to-face, each one holding the same physical manifestation of their mental prowess high in the air, ready to cast, knowing that the outcome would be far more than symbolism on this night and in this place. The freezing cold force of Incasa's will had battered against his mind like a typhoon, threatening to overwhelm him, but the stubborn tenacity of his own character had held firm and he'd screamed his terms into the rising storm. Incasa's eyes had blazed as white as the High Summer sun, greed and rage in equal mix. His voice, booming through Spar's mind, had blotted out the howling wind, but against all odds a deal of sorts had been brokered. Together, they'd dropped their dice, Hisar had taken wing, as unfettered and unclaimed as Spar himself, and Jaq had dragged Brax from the waters of Gol-Beyaz alive.

Spar had not seen or felt Incasa's presence since then, but he'd known that wouldn't be the end of it. Gods were poor losers and equally poor winners and you didn't force a stalemate with one of Them and expect Them to accept it gracefully.

Gods are big, and They'll do you if you let Them.

The Dockside phrase, cynical but true, repeated in his head as he jiggled the dice in his palm. This would be Incasa's first move, meant to rattle him and make him uncertain, meant to make him wonder why the God had given him a warning shot.

Spar's eyes narrowed. Or it was a trap meant to lure him to Incasa-Sarayi. The Prophecy God's temple had been after him ever since he'd uncovered the Yuruk feint on Yildiz-Koy four years ago. Elif's death would make them even more determined.

A cold breeze off the water feathered through his hair, knocking the two beads together, and he pressed his back against the ancient stone wall, suddenly feeling incredibly exposed. Although both Oristo and Incasa's statues stood too far to the south to see him, Estavia's loomed above his right shoulder, the weight of Her crimson regard burning a hole through his tunic. The Gods talked to each other even when They fought. Everyone knew that.

Wrapping his fist around the dice as if to hide them from the Battle God's scrutiny, he made himself breathe deeply and evenly, bringing the sudden panic down to a more manageable level.

A paw landing on his chest with a thump brought him back to himself, and he glanced down to see Jaq looking up at him with the same aggrieved expression on his face.

"What?"

The paw hit him again.

"If you want something decent to eat, you can go beg it from one of the kitchen servers, not from me. I gave you half my breakfast."

When the dog continued to stare at him, he jerked his head at the door. "Go on."

Jaq did not budge.

"Fine."

Clambering back onto the wharf, Spar made for the door himself, only to have Jaq nose quickly past him, his toenails clicking on the floor of the wide, stone tunnel under the battlements. Rolling his eyes, Spar followed the animal into the cool darkness, squinting from the afterimage of the bright, reflected sunlight outside.

The tunnel forked almost at once, one way heading due west along the south battlements to the kitchens, the other turning north toward the smithy, granary, and secondary storehouses. When Spar turned north, Jaq paused, obviously torn, and Spar shook his head with an understanding expression. Jaq took his guard duties as seriously as he took his dead, rotting lake gulls; equally unwilling to abandon either one, but he was also hungry, the possibility of a visit to the kitchen warring with his desire to keep his charge in full view.

"Go on, then," Spar said more gently this time. "Go get a bone or a slab of tripe or something and come find me later."

The dog began to whine.

"I'm surrounded by warriors and big stone walls. I'll be fine. Go find Tanay."

At the chamberlain's name, Jaq shook himself, then headed purposefully down the western tunnel while Spar took the north. He had maybe half an hour before the dog joined him once again—ensuring that he remained on ground level instead of up on the rooftops where he preferred to be—so he'd better make the most of his solitude while he had it.

Ducking through the first archway he came to, he found himself in a small, unkempt, graveled garden filled with pigeons. It was maybe ten square feet in total with high, thick walls, cut like steps to encourage the birds to spot the many nesting sites from the air and then move inexorably to the four dovecotes built in each corner where their eggs could be gathered more easily. Feathers floated in an octagonal, dung-encrusted pool in the center and the air was filled with the sounds of wings and cooing. A dozen birds pecked about at the scruffy ground searching for the last few seeds the temple bird keeper—a retired priest of Havo—had scattered that morning. Most of the creatures' feed came from their own scavenging, but the seed encouraged them to return to the dovecotes.

As Spar stepped farther in, he spotted a pair of ravens—blatantly waiting for the opportunity to steal an egg or two—perched at the very top of the eastern wall crenellation. The birds stared challengingly back at him, and he narrowed his eyes, mistrusting the symbolism.

Ihsan had told him that birds were sacred to the Gods, each one claiming a particular kind that mirrored some particular trait of Their own: gulls, the birds of Prophecy, for Incasa; pigeons, the half-tamed, four-season-laying opportunists for Havo; and the battle-following ravens for Estavia. Of the rest, Ystazia loved peacocks for their brilliant plumage, Oristo claimed the well-domesticated chicken, and Usara's physician-priests kept canaries, believing they brought comfort and healing with their song.

"So why haven't I seen the rest of your lot," Spar demanded of the ravens.

The birds ignored him.

In his hand, the dice suddenly felt heavy and portentous, but he refused to look at them until he'd found a proper place to sit quietly. Elif had once told him that no one could see the future with a cold or itchy arse. Kaptin Liel had explained it more politely: physical discomfort interfered with one's focus. Either way, the pigeon's yard was not the best place in the temple for prophecy. It was too noisy, too filled with whirling wings, and the smug sound of birds laying eggs layered his thoughts with Oristo's concerns despite their connection to Havo. But Elif had also said that nothing happened by chance, so something in this place was be meant to either become part of his vision or enhance it.

Glancing around, his eyes followed the wall crenellations on either side of the archway, noting how they made the small enclosure look like a chicken house that'd had its roof burned off.

Or like a double set of narrow stairs.

Swiftly scaling the rough stonework, he used them as such, then leaped to the storehouse roof and tucked himself in the lea of the southeastern sentry box. Only then, after he'd ensured that he was completely concealed from both people and Gods, did he return his thought to the dice in his fist.

On the streets, casting dice was one of the few activities that carried an air of respectability. It was commonly believed to be the most reliable means of legitimate augury, with each combination capable of representing a separate outcome depending on the situation. But Spar knew it was also one of the most misused. Dice were the cheapest gear to buy and the easiest to manipulate. With a good pair of loaded dice you could make any mark believe anything you wanted them to—it was amazing how double ones thrown three times could frighten even the most hardened of skeptics.

Naturally, the priests of Incasa discouraged such unsanctioned casting, claiming that it tarnished the reputation of legitimate seers—namely themselves, but most people believed that the priests only objected because it drew shine from their temple. Either way, street-casting had always flourished; especially in times of strife or uncertainty. Spar remembered that—next to shells—it had been one of Graize's favorite methods of fleecing the unwary.

"Place your shine, place your shine . . ."

Spar himself had always disdained the use of physical objects, preferring to rely on instinct and those personal images and symbols that appeared in his mind. What you couldn't hold couldn't be stolen or misrepresented by someone else. However, a set of lost dice practically washing up at his feet was too obviously a God-created omen to ignore, so after clearing his mind of any expectation, he opened his hand.

A two and a four stared inscrutably back at him.

His lip curled in annoyance. This was why he hated using physical objects: they could mean anything or nothing on any given day, and the Gods were just as likely to jerk you around as tell you anything important.

After stuffing the dice unceremoniously into his belt pouch, he took several deep breaths to clear his mind.

God-created or not, he would get his answers in his own way. As his eyes went black, the physical world around him grew indistinct and the dark place beckoned. He paused for a moment, allowing the familiar sense of absolute silence to envelop him like a shroud, then stepped out onto the black sand beach of prophecy.

An ebony ocean stretched out before him, merging imperceptibly with a midnight sky devoid of stars or moon. The air was cool and still and had no odor. Nothing stirred, not even his own heartbeat. This was the place where he'd first seen Hisar as a tall, dark tower standing on the shore; strong and unassailable before Its entry into the physical world had taught It to be afraid of death.

Spar was not afraid of death; death was solitude and peace and the end of fear. Life was far more frightening. Life was chaos and loss and betrayal. Life diverted your attention with sensations and expectations, then lifted your shine or bashed your head in when you weren't looking. Life turned you into a mark, it couldn't help itself, that's what it was; the ultimate trickster. It made promises it couldn't keep. Death made no such promises. Here, in the dark place, death only promised the clarity of vision that came with silence. Here he could let his guard down and think without distractions; here, in this place where no one else came, he was safe.

Crouching, he caught up a handful of black sand, allowing it to drizzle slowly through his fingers. The dark place held every possibility and every path—every stream—as Kaptin Liel would call them. Here Spar could reach into the past for the words or deeds of any teacher he'd ever had, willing or unwilling, good or bad. Cindar, his first and most cynical abayos. Chian, the seer-priest kardos of Kemal who'd saved Spar's life at Serin-Koy. And Elif, the force of her personality still echoing in his mind, making his chest tight and his throat sore with the effort not to cry. Spar never cried. Except on purpose.

Catching up another handful of sand, he brought himself back under control.

He could access the present for the living here as well, for Kemal and Yashar and Tanay and Kaptin Liel. And for Brax. But the dead were so much easier; they didn't complicate his prophecy with change. The living always changed. Still, between the living and the dead, the present and the past, here in the dark place he could reach unimpeded into the future.

Turning his attention to the sand spilling through his fingers, he watched as it pooled beneath his feet, spelling out emotions and images: foreboding and confusion, loss and sadness; birds and carts. Crimson mountains looming over towers etched in gold where the more traditional metal would be silver, the metal of the Gods; Hisar, wearing Its Graize-seeming, offering choices.

And dice.

"Place your shine, place your shine . . ."

Choices, both wanted and unwanted, personal and public.

Hisar, wearing Its Brax-seeming, demanding responsibility.

"Fortune for fifteen . . ."

Choices and responsibility and danger.

"Everything's going to change after tonight. You know that, right? Everything's gonna speed up like a runaway cart from now on in."

Danger in the choices. Danger in the responsibility. Danger coming at them from all sides, affecting everyone, not just them. Danger in getting lost in the maelstrom, in becoming just another casualty. Danger in letting down your guard in a moment of weakness, or worry, or grief, and losing everything.

A fine thread of danger bringing Graize to mind again.

"Place your shine . . ."

"About Elif . . ."

"I'm fine."

"You're sure?"

"Obscurity's not found in prophecy, but in the prophets who seed their own desires into their reading of it."

"I don't get blocked."

"You sure?"

Wiping his hands on his tunic, he stared out to sea. Why did everyone keep asking him if he was sure? He was always sure. But was their asking part of the prophecy?

He frowned at the trickling sand, mulling over each element of his vision individually. Foreboding and fear of an uncertain future and the confusion of seers blocked by their own arrogance. The loss of a wise and experienced councillor and the sadness over her death causing even more confusion and uncertainty. The Gods, perched above the world like birds on a wall, watching the future unfold as fast as a runaway cart and just as dangerous for anyone standing in its path. Hisar at a crossroads in the Gurney-Dag Mountains. Brax, and dice, and Graize.

Spar's eyes narrowed. That Graize was involved was no surprise. Graize was always involved, tucked away in some hidden corner spinning webs of power and deceit, taking the seeming of Yuruk or Petchan, or anyone else who might hide his actions for him. As Spar had told Brax, Graize was their problem, he always had been, and they would have to deal with him. And they would. This season.

And birds.

He nodded to himself. All the Gods' birds would be involved, not just the ravens of Estavia. Soon they would all take flight, filling the air with the whisper of their wings. They were poised to do it; he could feel it.

Hisar wearing Its Graize-seeming.

Although the Godling rarely spoke about Graize and Spar rarely asked, he knew his rival had molded Hisar's earliest development with his own desires and probably still did, no doubt by holding his knowledge

and understanding of the world over Hisar's head like
a stick, trying to turn It into a weapon that only he
could use.

Spar had always hated that kind of game and had
decided early on not to play it. He didn't lie to Hisar,
he didn't hide knowledge from It, and the only thing
he tried to mold was caution. And that usually worked
about as well as trying to caution the wind.

Hisar wearing Its Brax-seeming.

Or trying to caution Brax, he acknowledged. That
Hisar was four and Brax was twenty didn't seem to
make any difference; if either one of them had to
choose between caution and reckless stupidity, you
could bet they'd always chose reckless stupidity.

"Place your shine, place your shine. . . ."

No, Spar didn't play that kind of game either. That
kind of game was for marks. Standing, he began to
fashion the heavy black net he'd first used to snare the
half-formed Godling on the battlements of Orzin-Hisar.
Incasa was also trying to turn Hisar into something He
could control, he thought; a nice, safe, silver tower that
did what It was told whether It wanted to or not.

Incasa and Graize and Hisar; Spar began to slowly
and methodically weave each one into the strands of
his net. The battleground would be the Gurney-Dag
Mountains and soon, the fighting between the Petchans
and the Warriors of Estavia. And Brax would be in the
middle of it as always; Kaptin Haldin reborn into the
world, Estavia's Champion armed with silver light, a
runaway cart, and Spar's only kardos.

Just another casualty.

No. Not Brax. Not again.

Four years ago, another seer had taken the field, a
northern sorcerer named Illan Volinsk, who'd stripped
away the childhood protections from around Spar's
sight, forcing him to see the future as Illan had wanted
him to see it. His visions had become chaotic and violent and filled with fire, but then Chian had brought him

to the dark place where the cool waters had quenched
the flames and Elif and Kaptin Liel had taught him how
to control the chaos and draw the symbolism from the
violence. Illan was still out there somewhere, hiding, like
Graize, behind a screen of other people's actions, waiting for his chance to bring his own designs into play. But
the next time he surfaced, he would not find an inexpe-
rienced child on the field; he would find a seer versed in
a prophecy like no other.

"*I don't get blocked.*"

"*You sure?*"

Yes, because you couldn't block something if you
didn't know it existed. That was the great advantage of
the dark place. It was a vast ocean of potential, and only
he knew how to draw that potential from its depths.

He added Illan to the strands with a certain amount
of grim satisfaction, then cast his net toward the water,
watching as it slowly sank out of sight.

When he drew it up again, its catch was not surprising: mountains and towers and birds; Brax, and Graize,
and dice, overlaid by an almost overwhelming sense of
impending danger.

"*You won't mind if I start without you, then, will
you?*"

"Yes."

Brax was going up into the Gurney-Dag Mountains
to deal with Graize once and for all.

And Graize was ready for him.

Spar opened his eyes to see the granary roof awash with
sunshine. Staring up at the bright summer sky, he allowed
his mind to slowly emerge from the dark place. Then,
pulling the dice from his pouch, he glanced down at the
five and the three looking inscrutably back at him. Dice.
Multiple paths and multiple meanings adding layers of
confusion to an already confusing prophecy, like too
many pigeons trying to nest in the same box.

Jiggling the dice in his palm, he narrowed his eyes as each possible combination was created and destroyed by the movement of his hand. Pigeons aside, dice meant choice masquerading as destiny and one choice was obvious: Brax's. He was going to choose to face Graize and the Petchans without him, maybe even without his fellow warriors.

Spar made a sour face. It didn't take a seer to figure that one out, Brax was a ghazi-warrior, he would always choose to fight. And he was the acknowledged Champion of Estavia—not to mention a bloody, great idiot; he would always choose to enter that fight alone. And the fight was going to happen soon, Spar could already sense the metallic taste of lightning and storm clouds in the air. Marshal Brayazi and Kaptin Liel were in daily consultation with messengers from the southern villages. They would be taking action any day now, maybe even today.

And so would Graize. Graize upped the stakes. Graize made it personal.

"Obscurity's not found in prophecy, but in the prophets who seed their own desires into their reading of it."

The loss of a wise and experienced councillor.

"Don't worry, Elif," he said quietly. "I'm not seeding anything. I'm just choosing what to reap and what to leave lying in the field."

A thin shaft of sunlight touched the dice in his palm, lighting up the six and one that seemed to stare up at him.

Dice.

He frowned as a new interpretation occurred to him. What dice meant was choice, but what dice were was a means of augury; a tool for piercing the future.

"I don't get blocked."

Spar had always disdained the use of physical objects.

He stood.

But that didn't mean he didn't know how.

A warning shot, a trap, or a radical new choice that would take all his skill and ability to pull off?

Choices. Choices, responsibility, and danger.

He would have to write to Brax, send him some kind of warning that would make him think, make him wait, keep him safe, until this new choice paid off.

He snorted. That was going to be harder to orchestrate than the choice itself.

Returning the dice to his pouch, he peered down at the pigeon yard where Jaq was now sitting, whining impatiently.

"Make a strong choice, that's all I ask."

"I always do, Elif."

Jumping down, he joined the dog on the ground, then headed for the armory tower already rehearsing what he was going to say to Marshal Brayazi and Kaptin Liel. The two commanders would be shocked and concerned, but because he was still a delon, because he had a choice, they would give in to his request. They would summon First Oracle Bessic.

✦

In Gol-Beyaz, Incasa held His own dice between finger and thumb with a smile. Estavia had Her reinforcements; the Silver Champion had taken the field; the Black was poised to follow. All that remained was the Gray. The Gray would take time and the subtlest of manipulations, but Incasa was the God of subtle manipulations. It was He who had invented dice. And it was He who had first loaded them.

9

The Gray Champion

A T CHALASH, THE HUKUMET had re-formed under Danjel and Haz-Chief's direction. Now, as the first of the new raiding parties slipped silently from the gates, Graize stood in a muting darkness so total that he could not even hear his own heart beating. Far away, he could sense the Godling stirring in Its own strange dreams, made all the more complex from its experience with Incasa, but he could not reach It.

For a moment he wondered if he were dead, and then very faintly he began to perceive first one sensation and then another: the feel of his fingertips against the palms of his hands, the pungent aroma of wet clay, the sound of water droplets splashing against rocks, the coppery taste of blood where his teeth had caught a dry spot in his lip, and finally, the sight of a shadowy figure seated before him. For some moments, he thought it might be his unwanted dark-haired man, but as he reached out, his fingertips touched an unfamiliar face and a voice, as clear and cold as a mountain stream, sounded in his ear.

"How did you find your journey, Graize-Sayer?"

All sensation vanished as the words echoed through his sleeping mind, taking on a greater and greater significance with each reverberation. The muting darkness swept in again, and he floated in nothingness for what seemed like an eternity while his prophetic ability cast this way and that, seeking some place for him to land, and finally set him down in the recent past.

He stood on the gravel beach below Cvet Tower, staring out to sea. The setting sun cast a hint of orange across the blue waters and slashed a dark red streak of fire across the billowing white sails of a southern ship at anchor below. The waves lapped against the rocks with a quiet, musical air, not so dramatically as they might have done during the previous night's storm, but also not so delicately as they might have done on the hot and breezeless dawn afterward. It was more like a single note from a reed pipe played by one of Panos' sailors. As a diving sea hawk added its own flash of motion to the tableau, the golden-haired oracle stepped onto the beach beside them. She raised her hands, and when she spoke, her voice whispered like a warm southern breeze across cold northern waters.

"Nothing exists independent and alone. All things, physical and metaphysical, are entwined like lovers clasped in a fiery embrace."

Graize sensed the shadowy figure waiting for an explanation and yawned with deliberate disinterest. For Panos, sound, color, movement, and metaphor all played an integral part in her prophecy, each one bringing its own individual flavor to the whole, and each one as fluid and as changeable as she was herself. But for Graize, they were virtually meaningless; they were a means to the end of having Panos believe he possessed the same abilities in equal strength to herself. A means to the end of the game. Because the game was everything.

The shadowy figure cocked its head to one side as if it could hear his thoughts as Panos spoke again.

"Without your Yuruk, without your Godling, and without us, how strong can you really be?"

Graize turned a scowl on them both, but before he could reply, the dream changed; Panos became a seagull soaring effortlessly on the wind, and Graize and the shadowy figure turned their attention to the sky. No clouds disrupted their view of the panoramic sunset except for a faint line of orange and red that dusted the horizon, caressing the high black cliffs that separated the faraway wild lands from the sea.

As if waiting their cue, memories of his earlier home flooded into his mind, and the air grew thick with the smell of wild flowers, drying lanolin, and dung. The tinkling of bells woven into the tack of Yuruk ponies sounded in the distance, and as he and the shadowy figure cocked their heads to listen, a mounted kazakin galloped into view. Kursk, Timur, and Danjel reined up before them, the sky at their backs, the brilliant blue of a High Summer's day. As one, they each threw an individual grass fetish into the air, watching intently as the wind caught them and spun them in circles above their heads.

The shadowy figure turned to Graize, but he shrugged, his expression carefully neutral. The three Rus-Yuruk wyrdin-kazak had taught him to study the ebb and flow of the natural world all around him in order to catch the faintest signs that events were beginning to unfold; the undulating grasslands below and the vast, open sky above speaking to them in a thousand different ways. For Graize, however, they rarely gave up their secrets fully. He'd not been born to their language, and the subtleties of their messages often escaped his notice. Yet he was very adept at gleaning the clues to the prophecy of others and had held his own in this vaunted company because of this ability.

Sparing a single narrow-eyed glance at the shadowy figure, Graize turned as the landscape of his dream changed again and the three wyrdin-kazakin became Illan Volinsk bent over his atlas table in his study at Cvet Tower. Graize inclined his head with a grudging gesture.

Of them all, Illan's visioning was the most similar to his own, elements of imagery and intuition suggesting multiple avenues of possibility to be exploited. But where the Volinski prince controlled and maneuvered these elements like a general, confining their development to a design already set in place by his own ambition, Graize preferred to observe their movements, choosing the most advantageous element from among them, then exploiting it before it disappeared. But once again, he'd played the game with Illan, speaking such words as the prince wanted to hear because, once again, it was the game that mattered and Graize was very good at the game.

The faintest hint of movement suggestive of a luminescent dragonfly flitted across the horizon, and Graize reached up to caress the Godling's shimmering wings as It flew past before shooting a dark and challenging glance at the shadowy figure.

All his self-professed teachers were powerful oracles in their own right, but none of them lived so intimately with the spirits that carried the purest source of prophecy within their very essence as he did, none of them were capable of drinking from that source whenever they chose to, and none of them had ever fashioned these spirits into a fully formed being in Its own right. Graize alone had earned that intimacy through madness and defiance and a hunger as insatiable as the spirits' own. No other prophet had dared so much, and no other prophet would reap so much reward for the daring, not even the most subtle and talented of the seer-priests of Incasa who touched the mind of their God when they touched the future.

As the dream-sky above them darkened toward nightfall, a host of brilliant stars appeared and Graize bared his teeth in the direction of the distant seers slumbering in the midst of their God-sent dreams. The abayon-priests of Oristo who'd raised him until the age of eight had disdained the use of prophecy and vision, believing that it interfered with the more important aspects of living. They'd taught him that dreams were often no more than shadow puppets acting out the trivial details of the day with no hidden meanings or importance for the future.

On most days he agreed with them; prophecy was only useful if it fulfilled a need or a desire. And a dream of the past, however diverting, did not fulfill either. It merely illustrated what he already knew: that a truly powerful prophet was not confined to a single venue but ranged from one to another as the game demanded. He'd had many teachers and was already more than the sum of them all.

He turned a jaundiced eye on the shadowy figure beside him. And mysterious powers, either familiar or unfamiliar, who thought to gain some inkling into his motivations through dream imagery would be no different. He had faced that before as well and had defeated it.

The shadowy figure seemed to smile serenely back at him. The stars above them dimmed, and the wind grew cold and strong, slapping his hair into his eyes. Rain splattered against his skin; far away, he saw lightning skip across the sky and heard a faint crack of thunder. A fine white mist began to gather, clinging to his feet and legs like sticky spiderwebbing, and Graize felt his heart begin to pound in remembered fear. The image of the dark-haired man rose up, and Graize snarled in sudden anger. Raising his arm, he slashed at the tableau as he had slashed at Brax five years ago on the streets of Anavatan, and the dream shattered as someone began shaking him by the shoulder.

Graize's eyes snapped open. For one confusing moment, his mind tried to incorporate this new element into his prophecy and then, with a start, he found himself staring up into Yal's bright blue eyes.

The faint starlight, spilling in through the window, lit up the heavy locks of pale blonde hair that fell across her cheeks. His mind, still half in the world of dreams and memories, saw Spar and a sudden and violent surge of jealousy welled up inside him, and then he was more fully awake but staring up at her with no less confusion.

"Danjel's in the garden," he croaked, assuming she was looking for the Yuruk.

Releasing his shoulder, Yal sat back on her heels with a laugh. "No, Graize-Sayer," she corrected with a lascivious gleam in her eyes, "Danjel's all finished in the garden. Now she's in the vale."

The breeze blowing in from the window feathered across his skin, causing him to shiver with a prescient foreboding, and he sat up, suddenly aware that the thin, silk sheet he'd gone to sleep under was now some distance away lying in a crumpled heap on the floor. Brushing away the absurd thread of embarrassment that followed, he forced himself to rise up on one elbow. "If you're wanting to compare our techniques," he said, using an air of false bravado to cover his confusion, "I should warn you that what you see is what you get; I can't change my form to suit your tastes like Danjel can."

She grinned. "Haz-Chief has received a message from Dar-Sayer," she answered instead, putting special emphasis on the second name as if he should know who she referred to. "You're to go at once."

Her words bounced off the surface of his mind like a scattering of pebbles on a frozen pool of water, refusing to sink into any kind of understanding, but again, the game was all that mattered and so he glanced past her shoulder at the night sky with a quizzical expression.

"You didn't bring breakfast," he noted dryly.

"Breakfast is also in the vale," Yal snorted. "Come, Graize-Sayer," she added, straightening. "Dar-Sayer's delinkos has been walking since before dusk to bring you to him." She leaned forward, a mocking expression in her eyes. "Dar-Sayer is the strongest of our prophets, kardos to Haz-Chief, and the keeper of the Petchans' greatest secret," she explained. "It's only because of this summons that Haz-Chief has agreed to reveal it to you. Don't you want to know what that secret is, Graize-Sayer?"

He allowed the responding flash of avarice to show on his face. "You know I do," he answered simply.

"Then arise. It's a long journey to Dar-Sayer's home; we need to leave at once." Her eyes crinkled in amusement as they tracked down the length of his body. "And dress for rain; it's going to storm," she added, "again."

✦

It was cold and damp, smelling of the promised rain when he joined Danjel in the darkened vale a few moments later. Already dressed for travel, the Yuruk wyrdin was standing beneath a small lantern tied to one of the carob trees, eating a pita stuffed with goat's cheese and apricot slices. She handed one to Graize as Yal went to fetch their ponies.

"You heard?" she asked.

Graize shrugged carelessly. "*Dar-Sayer* will see us," he said.

"Yal says it's is a great honor."

"Hm." Raising his eyes, Graize scanned the sky for signs of the Godling. Strangely, It was nowhere to be found. "It's an hour before dawn, at least," he said instead. "Good thing we'll have the ponies to pick out the path for us."

Danjel made a sour face. "Yes, let's hope they don't fall off some cliff anyway. Even a Petchan pony has its limitations."

"I imagine Yal's prepared to snatch you from harm's reach if you do fall," Graize noted, and the Yuruk brightened visibly.

"There is that," she agreed.

"Unless Maf is lying in wait around some corner with a pointy stick," he added with a malicious air, his eyes still riveted on the sky. "And then I'm afraid you might be on your own."

Danjel cast him a dark look. "Why is it that you always have to go that little bit farther, kardos?" she growled.

He shrugged. "It makes life that much spicier." Lifting the pita to his mouth, he chewed reflectively for a moment. "It needs nutmeg," he said with a sigh.

"What does, life?"

"No, breakfast." As Yal and Las emerged from the stables, leading four ponies, Graize waved the food at the other seer. "Try to make some small sense today, will you, kardos?"

"So speaks the high priest of obscurity," Danjel replied with a sarcastic expression, but as Graize headed across the darkened vale, she finished her own pita and followed him.

✦

Dar-Sayer's delinkos turned out to be Haz-Chief's youngest delos, a boy of eleven named Nir. Perched easily on his pony's back, he led the way up the steep main steps of the village, emerging onto a thin, winding mountain path, barely discernible in the faint starlight. Yal, Graize, and Danjel followed in silence until the dawn sun sent a pale wash of light to color the sky, then Danjel glanced up at the mountains rising all around them with a frown.

"How far up will we travel?" she asked Nir.

"To the cleft in yonder peaks, Danjel-Sayer," the boy answered in a formal tone. "Then we'll descend for a time."

"It's more than half a day's walk," Yal noted. "The rain may catch us up before then."

"Dar-Sayer's seen the rain fall upon Chalash but pass us by on the path, Yal-Teyos," Nir replied, and Yal gave Danjel a warning glance as the Yuruk snickered at the title usually reserved for an elder. "But he also says that there will be a rainbow of incomparable brightness," the boy continued, seemingly oblivious to her expression, "which we may pause to enjoy if you wish."

Yal nodded, her mood restored. "Rainbows carry the spirits of the plains and foothills that couple with those of the mountain streams," she explained in response to Danjel's questioning look. "Their offspring are less dangerous than either, so to see a rainbow on a seeking is considered a good omen."

"I would count it a good omen just to spend a few moments with the spirits of my homelands whatever their purpose in coming here might be," Danjel replied wistfully. "I miss their singing."

Yal frowned at her, but said nothing; Graize broke off his continued scrutiny of the sky to glance back at them. Both the Petchans and the Yuruk believed that to heed the singing of the spirits—any spirits—led to madness, but Danjel had been born deep in the Berbat-Dunya and had no fear of them.

"As an infant, our dauntless wyrdin-kazak was rocked to sleep by the crooning of the wild lands spirits," he told Yal, "and gets cranky if it's too peaceful."

"And what about yourself, Graize-Sayer?" she asked pointedly.

"I don't like it too peaceful either," he replied. As he finally caught sight of the Godling splashing joyously in a distant waterfall, he showed his teeth at Yal in a parody of a smile. "But the spirits do not rock *me* to sleep. Their singing serves a different purpose altogether." He gave a piercing whistle, and as the Godling streaked from the clouds to spin about his face, he urged his pony forward with a hungry expression that made Yal shiver.

✦

The storm finally broke an hour later, streaming down from the distant clouds in sheets of gray mist. The rainbow which followed was every bit as brilliant as Nir had predicted. The four of them dismounted and settled themselves on a shelf of mossy rock to watch it arch across the sky. Spirits cavorted along its length, lighting up each individual band with flashes of silver, and the Godling hurled

Itself at them like some shimmering, predatory fish, catching them up with greedy abandon before shooting away, trailing streamers of color behind It, only to spin about and dive into their midst once more.

Had they been alone together, Graize would have sent his mind to follow It, eager to discover whether each color lent a separate flavor to the spirits' essence, but because of the presence of the two Petchans—especially the unknown quantity, Nir, who was staring up at the rainbow with an all too knowing and far too adult smile—he contented himself with enjoying the Godling's obvious pleasure, knowing that It would share everything It had experienced with him as soon as they were alone. As the rainbow began to fade, he returned to his pony, the Godling settling about his neck like an overfed housecat.

✦

The sun was a sharp blue disk of fire high in a now cloudless sky when they finally fetched up at the base of a ragged cliff face flecked with juniper and wild rosebushes. Far above, a small, narrow opening suggested the presence of a cave. With the suddenly agitated and fretful Godling hovering over Graize's head, they dismounted.

"Dar-Sayer's home," Nir said quietly, and Graize felt the same shiver of foreboding that had chilled him that morning. The opening seemed to wink in and out of sight, and Nir nodded at his unspoken question. "It's difficult for a non-sayer to see it," he said, "and nearly impossible for an actual sayer; the more powerful you are, the more invisible it becomes." He laughed suddenly at Graize's responding frown, the somber and formal expression of a Petchan delinkos vanishing before the impish grin of a mischievous eleven year old. "Don't worry, Graize-Sayer," he said in a condescending voice. "You're powerful; the only reason you can see the entrance is because Dar-Sayer wishes you to."

A dozen replies came and went before Graize settled on inclining his head in a regal gesture. "Then Dar-Sayer has my thanks," he answered, the dry tone in his voice once more. "I'd have hated to have climbed all that way up only to have fallen into it by accident."

"Fall into it afterward." Yal called out to them from where she was laying out a quick meal of bread, hard cheese, and dried goat's meat. "Come and eat first; there'll be no time for it later."

When Graize glanced over at Nir, the boy nodded. "Dar-Sayer will be expecting me to aid him with his own meal," he agreed as he dismounted. "Yal will bring you when you're finished with yours." He turned and, nimble as a mountain goat, scrabbled up the cliff face and disappeared inside the cave without looking back.

✦

"I told you, I'm not going. Someone has to stay with the animals."

"They're Petchan ponies. They won't stray."

"Something might eat them."

"Oh, don't be absurd!"

With the meal over and the ponies tucked into a lush grassy dale nearby, Yal and Graize had made for the cliff face immediately only to find, with some surprise, that Danjel had not followed them. Now the Yuruk wyrdin stood beside his mount, arms across his chest and an expression of stubborn disapproval in his green eyes, but the evident anxiety that had shifted his form from female to male twice already belied his belligerent stance and Graize could see that Yal was getting impatient with his reasoning.

"It might be seen as impolite," he suggested before she lost her temper and said something that both she and Danjel might regret, but the Yuruk merely bared his teeth at this unusual act of civility.

"Bollocks," he spat. "Dar-Sayer sent for you, not for me, and if he's as powerful as everyone says he is, he'll have known I wasn't coming and that will be why he didn't include me in his invitation."

"So why did you come all this way in the first place?" Yal demanded.

Danjel turned a smile of calculated charm on her. "Why, to be with you, my lover," he said sweetly, "away from your abia's jaundiced eye."

She favored him with a sour expression in return. "Then you can do it just as easily from up there." She gestured sharply at the cave mouth.

"No; I told you already: I don't like heights and I don't like caves. Besides," he added, "there's something wrong about that place; I can feel it."

She sobered. "What you're feeling is its natural defenses," she explained. "It's a muting place; a place where a sayer's abilities die."

"Die?"

"Not die for real," she replied impatiently. "It's where their abilities become *muted* so that they can't see the future. It would be as if you temporarily lost the use of your eyes, nothing more."

"It sounds rather as if you suddenly lost the use of your mind," Graize observed, glancing up at the cave mouth which continued to wink impudently in and out of his sight. The Godling hovered about fifty feet above it, unwilling to get any closer, but equally unwilling to withdraw.

"And that's rather more than nothing," Danjel agreed stiffly.

Yal shrugged. "The whole of the Gurney-Dag Mountain Range has this effect to one degree or another, and so does everything born on its slopes, even the people. To drink the water from its springs and eat the fruit from its trees and the flesh of its herds every day is to absorb this muting without even knowing it. The Petchan sayers train their minds to recognize this effect within themselves and to make use of it. One of our most important adult rituals is to spend a night here where it's the strongest. Those who feel the greatest muting effect are destined to become powerful sayers, and spend much of their time here, strengthening their abilities."

"You mean you blind your most gifted delon on purpose?" Danjel asked, his eyes wide.

"It's not torture, it doesn't hurt them," she snapped. "It disciplines their minds and teaches them to use the muting effect and not be frightened by it. The strongest of them can use it to blind the prophetic sight of our enemies, which even you must admit is a skill worth mastering."

"Oh," he said, subsiding a bit. "Like the protections in the Hukumet."

"No, that's using the natural muting properties of animals and earth; this is using the muting properties of one's own mind. If I were as powerful as Dar-Sayer, I could be standing right in front of you and you'd never even see me. That's the secret of the Petchan sayers."

As the cave opening suddenly halted its winking and grew steady, Graize's uneven gaze sparkled greedily. "And Dar-Sayer's going to teach me this skill," he said, almost to himself.

The Godling began to keen in distress, and both Danjel and Yal turned to stare at Graize.

"Not necessarily," Yal cautioned. "Dar-Sayer's always been unpredictable. And so has his reason, his mind," she added. "He may only want to test you."

Graize waved a dismissive hand at her. "We've been through that already, he and I," he answered airily. "We spent the night together. His testing is over."

"That's as may be," she allowed, showing no surprise at his revelation, "but Dar-Sayer's not a teacher, he's a solitary oracle."

"A solitary oracle with a sayer-delinkos?" Danjel asked.

Yal shook her head. "He has physical limitations,"

she explained. "Nir's not a sayer-delinkos; he's a healer-delinkos."

"Regardless," Graize interrupted. "Dar-Sayer will teach me; I have seen it." He moved forward, and the Godling swooped down to wrap Itself about his neck, beating Its iridescent wings so frantically that it fluttered the hair about his face, knocking the beads against his cheek. He reached up to stroke Its flank but continued forward, moving slowly now as if he pushed his way through shallow water. "I will learn to control this muting power," he continued, "and I will use it against my enemies." He gave the Godling a comforting smile. "I will use it against the Gods of my enemies," he crooned. "And one day, you'll be the only creature of power remaining. You'd like that wouldn't you, Delin?" As It snapped Its teeth at him in agitation, he turned. "Surely you'll like that, Kardos," he added. "No nasty God-Wall to protect all those tasty Gol-Beyaz flocks and herds? But it's going to take weapons of great power to make it happen, you know; you can't just will it into being."

Danjel shot him an unimpressed look. "And three kinds of prophecy aren't enough weapons for you, Kardos?" he replied.

"If any small number of prophecies were enough weapons for me, *Kardos*, I wouldn't have sought out a bi-gender wyrdin-kazak of the Berbat-Dunya to teach me to see as the Yuruk see," Graize countered.

"And if that wyrdin-kazak had known such teaching was merely one among many, it might have been more dearly bought," Danjel shot back.

"Well, it's too late to renegotiate now; you'll have to stick with your original price. But don't worry." Graize gave him a predatory smile. "I'll always let you know which turtle shell covers the pea."

"Somehow that doesn't comfort me as much as I would like it to."

"It should." Turning back to the cliff face, Graize

lifted the Godling from his neck and tossed it gently into the air where It took flight in a panicked spray of gold-and-silver light. "The more powerful I am, the safer we'll all be when youthful innocence becomes adult desire," he added, watching as the Godling returned to hover frantically about the cave entrance, then turned. "The day's passing, Yal," he said pointedly. "Are you coming?"

"I am." With a swift look at Danjel, she started forward. "See you when we descend?" she asked.

Pulling out his pipe, the Yuruk settled himself against a tree. "I'll be here," he answered.

"Try not to grow a beard, will you? It covers too much of your beautiful face." She gave him an experimental smile which he returned.

"I'll do my best to remain clean-shaven," he promised.

With a relieved expression, she turned and followed Graize who was already halfway up the cliff face. As Danjel watched, the faint outline of the Godling beat Its iridescent wings against Graize, trying to keep him from entering the cavern, but once he and Yal disappeared from sight, It spun off into the clouds. Danjel watched It go with a pensive expression, then leaned over, pipe clenched in his teeth, and plucked several long grasses from the hillock nearby. Weaving them together to form a new fetish, he settled down to wait.

✦

Once within the cave mouth, Graize glanced carefully about. The cleft in the rocks beyond the entrance was cool and dark, the light spilling in illuminating no more than a few feet inside. It was narrow, hardly more than shoulder width wide, but high enough for both him and Yal to walk upright.

She led the way and, as he followed, he could feel the now familiar muting effect grow stronger, blocking out all sensation, not just his mental abilities. His mind strained to operate in its usual chaotic fashion and then dropped into a hesitant stillness, throwing up the occasional random image, much as a butterfly might open and close its wings from time to time to cool itself on a hot day. Outside, he could feel the Godling begin to whine as their bond grew tenuous, but when it did not disappear completely, It calmed somewhat. With a measure of relief he hadn't wanted to admit to, Graize carried on.

Slowly it grew darker, colder, and quieter, until even the sound of his heartbeat faded and he bunched his hands into fists, slowly rubbing his thumbs against the base of his fingers, using the scrape of skin against skin to focus his thoughts. As the floor began to descend, Yal turned to peer back at him, and he gave her a baleful stare in return.

"Are you expecting me to grow so frightened I'll run away?" he demanded.

She shrugged. "No sayer's comfortable in here," she said. "A child with the gift of Sight still unformed can manage well enough, but it's much harder for an adult. It's like being a fully grown eagle in a cage."

"I'm flattered by the comparison, but I'm fine."

"It gets worse."

"I said, I'm fine."

She pressed on and Graize followed, deliberately ignoring the growing sense of oppression as the cleft narrowed. Rock brushed against his shoulders, then caught against his jacket, and he was forced to twist his body slightly to continue forward. When he lost all sense of Yal a moment later, he nearly stopped, but he forced himself to continue, lips pulled back from his teeth in a snarl.

Images of cave-ins, tons of rock and dust crashing down all around him, overwhelmed his thoughts, and his mind, precarious at the best of times, began its familiar list to one side, taking the form of a leaking boat as it always did. With a deliberate gesture, he allowed the

boat to fill with water, watching as it slowly sank out of
sight with a gurgle. When it touched bottom, his mind
grew still again. He understood water imagery; what
had been sunk could always be raised.

He made himself keep walking, moving with a kind
of jerky imprecision now as if he'd always relied on
prophecy to guide his footsteps. Yal's disembodied
voice floated back to him and it was some moments before her words penetrated the shield of his self-imposed
control.

"Not far now, Graize-Sayer."

He made no answer.

After what seemed like hours, but was probably no
more than a few minutes, the narrow cleft suddenly
opened. Yal moved aside, and the sense of oppression
eased. Graize stepped inside a large cavern lit by half
a dozen oil lamps and divided by long spikes of rock
climbing up to meet longer spikes of rock coming down
with thin shafts of sunlight and wafts of fresh air betraying the presence of a number of overheard vents.
The smell of damp clay and the sound of splashing
made him think he might be dreaming again, and then
his attention was drawn to a series of earthenware jars
lined up to catch small rivulets of water trickling down
the cavern walls. Another set of smaller jars, sealed, no
doubt to keep water and rodents from their contents,
stood a short distance away. In the center of the cavern,
the shadowy figure from his dream sat on a thick tawny
sheepskin before a steaming pool, smoking a pipe.

As Yal advanced and bowed, Graize studied the figure intently, seeing for the first time in his life nothing
but what the physical revealed.

The figure was a tall man, thin to the point of ema-
ciation and surprisingly young, seemingly no more than
a year or two older than Graize himself, wearing a
simple woolen tunic of brown and green with a red bead
flecked with silver on a strip of hide about his neck. Pale
lines of smoke, like fine strands of ivy, trailed through

his braided blond hair, and his eyes, as blue as Yal's own, held no hint of the misty white that covered the eyes of the Anavatanon seers. Beside him, Nir held a spoon and a bowl, and Graize noticed that the figure's hands were unnaturally twisted into wizened fists. As the figure reached up and caught the pipe stem deftly between two curled fingers, pulling it free from his lips, he smiled at them, showing a mouthful of straight, white teeth.

"How did you find your journey, Yal-Kardelin?" he said, his voice a high, fluting tenor.

"Very clear, Dar-Teyos," she replied. "The family sends their love and my abia sends a pie." Nir set the bowl and spoon to one side and came forward to accept the cloth-wrapped bundle she held out.

"Give her my thanks," Dar-Sayer acknowledged. "Nir and I will share it for our supper." He turned his bright, blue eyes on Graize, and they seemed to sparkle with either amusement or speculation, he couldn't tell which.

"And how did you find your journey, Graize-Sayer?" he asked, his voice echoing in the vast space.

Graize cocked his head to one side, ignoring the chill that worked its way up his spine. "Pleasant enough with pleasant company," he said in a noncommittal tone, taking the question at its physical face value.

Dar-Sayer smiled. "And you could not prevail upon Danjel-Sayer to accompany you to your journey's end?"

"Danjel-Sayer doesn't like heights," Yal supplied. "Or caves."

"Or mysterious summonses from unknown oracles?" Dar-Sayer included, his eyes twinkling.

"Nor that either," she agreed.

Dar-Sayer chuckled, then turned to Nir, who rose fluidly. "Will you take some refreshments?" he asked as the boy came forward holding a tray.

Yal glanced sidelong at Graize who nodded. "That would be a kindness, thank you," she said.

✦

After they'd shared a bowl of goat's milk and a handful of dried dates, Dar-Sayer fixed Graize with a penetrating look. "The Volinski negotiations with Haz-Chief have gone on for some years," he said without preamble, all hint of his earlier ethereal attitude vanished. "But things have now come to a head. There's to be war with the people of Gol-Beyaz for spoils, trade, and free access to the waters of the silver lake. The Volinski purpose is clear, but your own purpose is shrouded. You're not Volinski, you're Anavatanon, yet you hold no love for your own people; indeed, you actively seek their downfall."

Although he'd not asked an actual question, Graize shrugged. "They're my enemies," he said just as bluntly, "and the enemies of the God I have fashioned. They did not protect me, and they will not protect It, so they have no right to expect such protections from either of us."

"And to what purpose will you put the protection of our secrets should I choose to reveal them to you?" Dar-Sayer asked.

Graize met his eyes with a neutral expression. "I will use them to defeat my enemies," he answered. "To what purpose would you give me these secrets of your protection should I choose to embrace them?"

Accepting a new pipe from Nir, Dar-Sayer grinned widely. "To the purpose of holding a God and that God's first priest in my debt and in the debt of my people," he replied, blowing a ring of blue smoke into the air. "So that they and we may defeat our own enemies in turn."

"And how do you know we will honor that debt?"

"The same way you know the debt will be worth honoring."

"And when we are free of enemies, what will we do then?"

Dar-Sayer shrugged. "We will die."

"No doubt." A shadow flitted across Graize's face. "But at least then there will be no one left to whisper little songs of love and betrayal on the wind or in our dreams, will there?"

Dar-Sayer pursed his lips. "There may still be," he replied. "Even death has a melody, however low."

Graize shrugged, the mask of neutrality in place once again. "Then spilling their blood will have to be enough," he answered. "Maybe their song will change into something more accommodating." He met Dar-Sayer's gaze. "Let's conclude our negotiations, shall we; Yal is eager to return to Danjel's company. If you'll teach, I'll learn, and we'll let the debt play out in whatever way it will whatever may be whispering on the wind and in our dreams."

Dar-Sayer inclined his head. "Done." He turned. "Graize-Sayer will return to Chalash when we're finished, Yal-Kardelin; you needn't wait."

She rose and bowed. "Thank you, Dar-Teyos. What shall I tell Haz-Chief and the Hukumet?"

The oracle considered the question with a serious expression for a moment. "You may tell my kardos to look to the northeast corner of the building for a crack in the wall that may let the rain in to ruin the carpets," he answered with a smile. "But as for the Hukumet, ask them to be patient. I will send my thoughts on the matter with Nir when Graize-Sayer and I have completed our purpose."

She chuckled. "They will be patient only because it's you who requests it," she observed. "But I have no doubt that they'll do as you ask."

She made her good-byes with as much formality as courtesy demanded, but with an eagerness that belied her pace. When she'd disappeared through the cleft once more, Dar-Sayer gestured at the pool behind him. "The spirits of the mountains are born of cold water," he said to Graize. "They cannot tolerate my hot springs and so they cannot deceive or distract you with visions that conceal your real motivations and desires. In these waters you will see what truly lies behind your actions, and without such shadowy motivations muting your decisions you will be able to use the power of the Petchans against your enemies instead of your own mind using it against yourself." He leaned forward. "If you have the courage to face them," he added in a challenging tone. With Nir's assistance, he stood, shrugging out of his tunic before holding out one gnarled hand. "Do you have the courage to confront yourself unmasked, Graize-Sayer?"

Graize showed his teeth at him. "How could I answer that question with anything but yes?" he replied.

Dar-Sayer laughed. "You couldn't. So, then come, my indomitable Anavatanon eagle; let the secret of the Petchans be your latest teacher, and we'll see if you can live without the sight and, by doing so, learn whether you really do fly as freely as you think you do or whether you're actually in a cage of your own making as I suspect you might be."

Eyes narrowed, Graize tossed off his own clothes, and then moved forward, deliberately returning the oracle's challenging smile with one of his own. He'd fought Gods and spirits and the frigid waters of Gol-Beyaz and emerged victorious. This would be no different.

10

Dar-Sayer

STEPPING INTO THE HOT springs felt as if he'd been plunged into an icy cold river despite the heat rising from its surface. Startled, Graize fell forward, his limbs suddenly heavy and frozen, and might have gone under if Dar-Sayer hadn't kept one arm wrapped tightly about his chest. With Nir's help, the two of them settled into the water and, his eyes painfully wide, Graize pressed himself against the oracle's body, unable to accept the vast emptiness that swept across his mind like a sandstorm. His head felt like it was going to split open from the pressure; he opened his mouth to scream, and then suddenly the world seemed to take on a terrible focus, every cleft and crevasse in the surrounding rocks standing out in stark individuality. For a heartbeat, his mind teetered on true madness, and then he was jerked into the past.

✦

He was three and he was cold, so very cold. He could hardly feel his hands and feet, could hardly see through the mist that had grown since the sun had begun to set. It was dark and he was hungry and tired, and so very cold. Crouched in a doorway out of the driving rain, he wrapped his arms about his chest trying to hold on to what little warmth he had and closed his eyes. He would only sleep for a moment, and then he would keep going, keep looking for ... The knowledge swept away on the wind, and he was left unsure of who or what he was looking for. But he knew he had to find them before the things in the mist found him. It was cold and growing dark and the things in the mist waited for you when it was cold and dark; he knew that already. He'd seen them.

He heard a sound, opened his eyes, and saw a boy, a little older than himself, dark-haired and dark-eyed, suddenly staring back at him. Graize made to speak, but then he was being lifted by a man in yellow and borne away out of the cold and the rain, away before the things in the mist could get him. His last sight was of the boy, a line of misty red blood—future blood—appearing across his cheek, watching him from the doorway before he disappeared inside.

✦

In the cavern he could feel Dar-Sayer's interest, but before he could react to the oracle's presence, the past rolled over him again and he was five and the mist lay thick upon the ground outside the temple walls. But not inside; the things in the mist, the spirits in the mist, could not get him inside.

He'd dreamed about the spirits last night and about the dark-haired boy who'd saved his life two years before. His dream had shown him this tiny landing at the very top of the temple's single minaret, and he'd climbed up here after everyone else had gone to bed, to stand on tiptoe, staring out at the rain-drenched city. The spring storms of Havo's Dance had shrouded the moon, making it hard to see the spirits in the mist, but he knew they were there. If he squinted, he could just make them out, weaving this way and that like tiny silver snakes, their mouths agape, their rows of silver teeth gleaming in the mist.

Leaning out the minaret's small window, he rested his chest against the sill, feeling the cold seep through the thin cloth of his yellow tunic. If the spirits ever got him, they would make him cold like that all over, but they couldn't get him here; he was safe here; as long as the dark-haired boy came to him in his dreams. He knew the boy would keep the spirits away, but he still dreamed about them because they still wanted him. They always wanted him. They knew he could *see* things.

Graize had the Sight. It had come on him so slowly that, at first, he'd thought that everybody knew what other people were going to say and do before they did it. When he'd realized that they didn't, he'd finally understood why everyone had always acted so strangely around him.

Laying his chin on his arms, he stared down at the temple's tiny orchard below, seeing the cherries and lemons that would soon grow fat and juicy on the trees ripen before his mind's eye.

He'd lived here at the Tannery Precinct's Oristo-Cami since that night when the dark-haired boy had led one of Oristo's priests to him in the doorway. The adult protectorates and abayos-priests who taught him his chores and his temple duties were kind but cold, and the dozen other abayonless children who lived with him in the west wing dormitory were afraid of him. Full of energy one moment, moody and angry the next, always distracted by the constant flood of images that paraded in front of his eyes, it was hard for him to make friends.

Yesterday, the old priest of Ystazia who taught him his letters had shown him a map of the northern sea. She'd pointed out a country called Volinsk and told him that his abayon had probably come from that faraway land because he had the look of the Volinski sailors who brought goods to the city. She'd said that Anavatan and Volinsk had been at war a long time ago and that many of the protectorates who served at Oristo's camis had been orphaned in that war.

Graize had stared at the map in confusion, wondering how anyone could possibly have come such a long way only to leave him behind. And then he'd decided that he didn't care. He'd torn the map in half and then run away when it seemed to mend itself right in front of his eyes. He hadn't even heard the priest shouting after him or the protectorates sent to find him.

That night, he'd dreamed that he and the dark-haired boy had stood together in the temple minaret looking down at the city, and he'd known that, one day, maps, priests, absent abayon, and even the hungry spirits that waited for him in the mist wouldn't matter anymore. All he had to do was find that boy and everything would be all right, forever.

A voice drifted through his mind, and it was a moment before he understood the words.

"And did you find him?"

✦

Graize shrugged off the question and suddenly he was eight, standing in Oristo-Cami's unadorned central hallway in the middle of a High Summer night, staring down at the future: a scrap of tattered, yellow cloth holding seven aspers; all the money he'd managed to collect in three long years of planning and waiting. His mind, ever busy, flitted from one thought to another, moving to the same rhythm as the fingers of his left hand which kept up a constant, focusing tapping motion against his thigh.

During the day he had to struggle to ignore this barrage of images, but here, in the hours before dawn, the temple was dark and quiet. Here, the outside world made no demands on his attention. Here, he could allow his thoughts to go wherever they wanted to go, knowing that they would eventually throw up everything he needed to make his dreams a reality.

Reaching out, he drew a single object from the swirl of imagery that danced before his eyes. A key.

Graize smiled. Glancing behind him, his pale gaze focused on the line of doors which led to the dormitory wings, the kitchen, and the cami's one public and one private shrine. In less than an hour the temple would be bustling with life: bakers, launderers, cooks, protectorate laborers, and priests all scurrying about to the heavy rhythm of the Hearth God's throbbing heartbeat, but he'd be gone by then. It was time.

His gaze returned to the seven copper coins in his hand again, wishing they were more, knowing that they soon would be because he'd seen it. In his dreams they were seven times seven hundred and more, many more. The dark-haired boy had shown him the way.

His gaze tracked to the line of doors again and the route he'd gone over in his head a hundred times. The fourth door on the left-hand side of the central hall led to a small corridor used by the gardeners and kitchen servers to reach the few meager vegetable plots which kept the temple supplied with food. It was fifteen steps to that corridor, then thirty-two along its length to the outside door, forty-five to the lemon tree growing by the back wall, and two hundred and twenty to the market street beyond. He'd seen it; he'd dreamed it; all he had to do now was walk it, counting out all those steps for real, and his new life would begin. But somehow, now that he'd decided to go, he hesitated.

Reluctantly, his gaze turned to the last door on the right; the door that led back to the dormitories. Of the children raised with him who had not already been placed with families or sent into the trades, one or two would grow up to become priests of Oristo, but most would remain protectorates forever, raising the next generation of abayonless poor who would do the same. They had no ambition and no drive and did not encourage it in their charges.

Graize had both.

His gray eyes darkened with anger as the future Oristo-Cami had planned for him washed over his mind.

The abayos-priests had talked it over and it had been

decided that, when he turned eleven, he would be sent
to a retired priest of Incasa in preparation for a life as a
seer-priest at Incasa-Cami in the Dockside Precinct. But
Graize had seen his future with this woman and knew
that she was a drunkard who could teach him nothing
and would treat him as little more than a glorified protectorate. Whatever his abilities, Graize did not have money
enough to buy the respect his birth had denied him.

Life at Incasa-Cami would be no better. Although
they would teach him to develop his talents, the seer-
priests who served in Dockside spent most of their time
predicting weather patterns and trade opportunities for
the local shipping merchants who paid the subtemple,
not the seer. Graize had no intention of using his abilities to make money for other people.

Deep within his mind, the image of the dark-haired
boy stirred impatiently and Graize nodded, more to
himself than to his silent companion. There was nothing for him here, there never had been; it was time. He
began to walk toward the door, his bare feet slapping
against the worn, wooden floor, counting off each step
until he reached fifteen, using the numbers as a focus to
keep his mind on the task at hand.

The door was right where it should be and he pushed
it open, peering down the long, dark corridor. Nothing
stirred as he slipped inside, beginning his count again.
When he reached thirty-two, he put his hand out in the
dark and clasped the key to the garden door. Lifting it
free from its peg, he thrust it into the lock, turning it
carefully so it would not make a sound, then pulled the
door open just enough to peer outside.

Moonlight poured through the opening. The night
air was cool and clean, and all doubts vanished as he
slipped through and closed the door softly behind
him. He took a deep breath and then broke into a run,
headed down the graveled path to the lemon tree. He
scrambled up its branches, sat poised on the wall for the
space of a single breath, then jumped.

A few moments later he vanished into the maze of stalls and tents that made up the Tannery Precinct's shabby marketplace, the image of the dark-haired boy leading him on into the night.

✦

The voice spoke in his head again. *"So you went to find him after all. Did you succeed?"*

"What?"

Graize blinked as the past receded and the muting effect reasserted itself; easier to bear now that he'd had some respite from it. The smell of damp clay filled his nostrils, the warm water lapped against his belly, and he looked down to see Dar-Sayer's arm still wrapped about him, gnarled fingers pressed into the pale hair on his chest.

"The dark-haired boy?" the oracle repeated. "Did you find him?"

Graize shrugged.

"Who was he?"

A dozen glib answers came and went, but somehow, in this place, the truth seemed the only answer to make. "Someone who's haunted my dreams since before I can remember," he said quietly. "I used to think he was a protective spirit or maybe just a statue that I gave life to in the mist, but then ..." He paused.

"But then?"

Graize chewed at a dry spot on his lower lip, tasting blood where his teeth had caught and torn the skin. "But then I met him," he said finally.

"And?"

"And then he became my enemy. That's all."

"How?"

"It doesn't matter."

"It does."

And the cavern receded as the past rose up again.

✦

"Think I can hit that pier from 'ere?"

Eleven-year-old Drove hefted a rock in one hand, waiting for some encouragement from the younger boy at his side, and ten-year-old Graize gave him a smile, calculated to mean whatever the older boy wanted it to mean.

He'd been on the Dockside streets for two years, running with a gang of young lifters as one of their most gifted planners. The largest by far, Drove served the gang as muscle and the two of them had formed an immediate friendship, because Graize immediately recognized the usefulness of muscle for his own personal well-being and encouraged the larger boy to use it.

Now he leaned back with a self-possessed air, keeping his left fist tightly clenched so that he wouldn't begin tapping it.

"Yes," he stated, and Drove grinned in pleasure.

Cocking his arm back, the older boy let the rock fly, hitting the wooden pier just above the waterline. As he picked up another one, Graize sent his pale-eyed vision tracking across the wharfs.

It was High Summer and Dockside was crowded with sailors, porters, dockworkers, merchants, and delinkon. Ordinarily, Graize would be working the wharfs, picking pockets with Drove on lookout with two others, a pair of siblings named Gilin and Ephan, acting as decoys. They made a good team, but Graize had known it wouldn't last. In fact he'd known it wouldn't last beyond today. The Dockside factor—a kind of thief's foreman—jealous of the gang's success since Graize had joined them, had spent all that High Spring trying to bring them into his own organization and, when that had failed, had stooped to involving the garrison guards of Estavia who patrolled the Dockside streets. By noontime, most of the lifters, including Gilin and Ephan, would be in custody.

Most of them except Graize and Drove. Graize had seen it unfold last night as if it had already happened and had pulled the larger boy from his bed early that morning. By the time the priests of Havo had sung the dawn, they were long gone. With the shine he'd stashed away—far more than the seven aspers he'd begun with—he'd taken rooms for themselves and an imaginary abayos at the Kedi-Mayhalle Inn on the east-ernmost wharf, then ambled out to collect Drove and spend the day watching the tide come in and planning for the future.

Graize grinned as he remembered the curtsey with which the owner of the Kedi-Mayhalle had greeted the transaction. On Dockside, imaginary people were all the more welcome when they paid for their rooms with real silver.

Now, catching Drove's arm, he drew the two of them into the shadows of a potter's workshop just as the expected troop of garrison guards went by, their black leather breastplates embossed with the ruby-eyed image of Estavia gleaming in the morning sun. The gang's future arrests trailed after them like smoke, and Graize nodded to himself with a satisfied air. He made to step out once they'd passed, then froze, one foot al-ready in the act of moving forward.

Across the road, a dark-haired boy crouched beneath a fishmonger's awning, also watching the guards pass by with a wary expression in his dark eyes.

Graize's own eyes widened in shock.

For weeks after leaving Oristo-Cami he'd searched the Dockside streets, certain that the boy from his dreams would appear now that he was free of the Hearth God's abayos-priests. But as each day brought no sign of him, he'd finally given up, hurt, disappointed, and angry that for the first time in his life his prophetic abilities had failed him. The boy continued to haunt his dreams, but now his form seemed hazy, as if since Graize could no longer rely on his presence to guide him, he could no longer manifest him fully in his mind.

And now, unbelievably, Graize's abilities had failed

him again. All his life he'd never been surprised, never been caught off guard, not once, until now when the one person he'd sought for so long had suddenly appeared before him out of nowhere. As he stared, the dark-haired boy turned and, with an unmistakably protective air, drew a scrawny, blond-haired boy of maybe five or six years old out from behind him. He bent to speak a few words in the younger boy's ear, and Graize felt a rush of overwhelming jealousy. Breathing heavily through his teeth, he forced his expression to one of mild curiosity, and turned a quizzical look on Drove, jerking his head toward the two strange boys.

"Who?" he mouthed.

Pulling his knife, Drove began to pare one fingernail with a disdainful air. "Jus' a couple of wharf rats," he said with heavy scorn. "Brax an' Spar, I think they're called. They lift for Cindar what used to be a porter for the Kabak-Mahalle till he got into a fight with the cook an' busted up the place. They called the guard, but he ran for it before they got there."

"I never saw them before," Graize allowed casually.

"They used to lift a bit north a here. Guess Cindar cocked that up somehow, too, so they've come more south." Drove's eyes narrowed. "You figure they might crowd our trade?" he asked, cracking his knuckles to show his response to this possibility.

Graize made himself laugh with a derision he didn't feel. "No, they're heading down, not up," he replied, feeling a cold chill work its way across his shoulder blades. "You can see it."

As the other boys emerged from their hiding place, the shabbiness of their clothes was revealed and Drove nodded happily. He left his own place and swaggered by, throwing them a contemptuous look as he passed. Graize remained hidden, watching as anger flashed in the dark-haired boy's eyes and the familiar calculation of a seer flashed in the blond-haired boy's, and he felt another rush of jealousy before they turned and headed off in the opposite direction.

A few moments later, he emerged as well, to stand in the middle of the street, watching them disappear into the Dockside crowds, his eyes sparkling with furious tears. This was not how it was supposed to be, this was not the future he had seen, and he would not allow it to be.

✦

"He had someone with him."

Still locked in the memory, Graize brushed Dar-Sayer's words aside with an angry shake of his head.

"And you couldn't approach him with another in your place," the oracle continued.

Graize gave a bark of laughter that rippled the waters of the pool away from them. "Who says I didn't?" he demanded.

"And?"

"And he turned out to be no one worth approaching," he spat. "A petty lifter, a wharf rat just like Drove said he was; driftwood, nothing more."

"And yet he still appears in your dreams to this day, growing older just as you do."

"He appears as the symbol that was pressed into my prophetic interpretation before I was old enough to choose a better one," Graize retorted.

"An interesting symbol. One that speaks to the dangers of unfulfilled egotism, don't you think?"

"No, one that speaks to the dangers of relying on others for salvation and security."

✦

And once again the cavern receded and thirteen-year-old Graize faced the dark-haired boy on the streets of Anavatan while the spirits of the mist rose with the setting of the sun on Havo's Dance. But this time there was no intervening priest of Oristo, only four young lifters desperate for the shelter of an upturned fishing boat that could only protect two of them. It should have been him and Brax; every ounce of prophetic vision he possessed screamed this truth in his ears, louder than the rising wind.

But Brax had chosen Spar, and as Graize lunged toward his younger rival, hatred etched across his face, Brax flung himself between them. Graize almost screamed at him to run, to save himself for the future he was certain they shared, but then the streets were filled with a blood-flecked mist and it was too late. The spirits of his dreams streaked toward them, knifelike teeth and claws outstretched in terrifying hunger. Hundreds of them snatched Drove into the air, savaged his body, and then tossed him aside. Rage and fear giving him a strength he'd never possessed before, Graize caught Spar by the jacket and flung him toward the creatures, then jerked the fishing boat upright.

The world seemed to slow as, before his disbelieving eyes, Brax leaped forward and caught Graize around the middle. The other boy's touch seemed to burn right through the cloth of his jacket, and then he threw him directly into the path of the very spirits he'd saved him from ten years before. Graize's knife scored across Brax's cheek and the line of misty, red blood that appeared sent a shock of prophecy sizzling through him before he was jerked into the air.

Once again he fought the spirits of the wild lands, screaming out his rage and defiance as a thousand ravaging teeth and claws tore at his mind and body. Once again, he caught up the largest of their number, driving his own teeth into its misty face and feeling the icy slap of pure prophecy as its essence poured down his throat. And, once again, they flung him to the hard ground of the wild lands, cold and still but alive, as the rising sun brought an end to their struggle.

As the past vanished and Dar-Sayer's cavern reap-

peared, Graize jerked himself from the oracle's arms
and pulled himself from the pool.

✦

"We often give so much thought and energy to our
enemies that we gift them with more power to injure us
than we gift even to our lovers. In this way we become
caged by hatred and thwarted desires."

"I'm not caged by anything."

"No? Do you fly free, acting only in self-interest or
selfless altruism?"

Graize frowned.

An hour had passed since he'd pulled himself from
the hot springs, unwilling to relive any more of his past.
Now, he and the oracle sat together on Dar-Sayer's
sheepskin, wrapped in woolen blankets, the remains of
Yal's pie scattered on three plates before them. As Nir
passed Graize a flagon of wine, he took a long, shudder-
ing drink before answering.

"I act on self-interest," he replied. "Altruism is for
priests."

"And you're not driven by revenge?"

"What if I am?"

"If you are, you'll have nothing left when you attain
your goal. The very act of realizing your revenge will
tear a great hole in your focus, and that's when the spirits will finally defeat you."

Clutching his pipe between two knuckles, Dar-Sayer
waited until Nir had lit it for him before continuing.
"All spirits hunger after the power of physical, living
creatures, even the half-grown God-child you fashioned from the ones who attacked you above the wild
lands," he said, puffing on the pipe until a wreath of
smoke curled about his head. "But the spirits of the
Gurney-Dag are much wilder than even those whose
terrible need you've already experienced. They cannot be bribed with small seeds of power such as your
Yuruk wyrdin wield to gain their cooperation because

they have access to as much power as they need in the mountain streams and springs where they were born. Neither can they be compelled, for unlike your God-child, there's nothing you can withhold from them that you would willingly give them. All you can do is protect yourself from them. The creatures and the people of the mountain slopes have developed a natural latent muting in the blood that accomplishes this, but when our sayers reach into the future, they have to reach beyond that muting, and that's when they're at their most vulnerable."

"So, why haven't I been at *my* most vulnerable since the first time I stepped into their territory?" Graize demanded.

"Because you wear the clay protections given to you by Haz-Chief," Dar-Sayer shot back. "And because, I imagine, your God-child keeps the other spirits at bay. It's a creature of tremendous potential, after all: a single entity created by the merging of many and capable of gaining power by consuming those of its own kind that are weaker than Itself.

"And you're powerfully focused, despite your seeming lack of it," Dar-Sayer continued. "That unswerving desire for revenge which drives you acts as a protective wall for your mind, much as the infamous God-Wall around Gol-Beyaz protects the city you were born in. But that's exactly why you'll become vulnerable if you ever attain your revenge without first setting new protections in place."

He waved one twisted fist at the cavern walls. "As I've told you, the spirits cannot tolerate my hot springs, and the strength of its natural muting effect has so permeated this place that it makes them loath to venture closer than the cave mouth you entered through. That's why the Petchan sayers practice their prophetic skills here where they can unfocus their minds in safety. By the time they return home to speak prophecy in their own villages, they've learned to recognize and wield the latent muting effect inherent in their own blood to protect themselves. But it takes patience and discipline to master this ability, never mind to make use of it to blind the prophetic ability of others."

The oracle gave Graize a penetrating look, made all the more disturbing by the brightness of his eyes in the flickering lamplight and swirling pipe smoke. "But you're neither patient nor disciplined, Graize-Sayer," he said bluntly. "You pass from moment to moment, ally to ally, cause to cause, Anavatan lifters, Yuruk nomads, Volinski princes, and Petchan sayers, none of whom mean anything to you. You leap from one path to another like a drunken mountain goat. What is it that you truly want; what motivates your blood to stir in your veins? If it is truly nothing more than revenge, what will you do when that goal is achieved? Die? There may well be someone left to whisper songs of love and betrayal on the wind and in your dreams, but you won't be there to know it. It seems a poor use of a sayer's life to me."

Graize remained stonily silent, and after a moment, Dar-Sayer sighed. "Sleep for a time," he said. "When you're rested, we'll return to the pool and see if you can find an answer that will satisfy you. After that, I'll decide if you have what it takes to learn the muting ways of your latest allies."

✦

Hours later, the landscape within his mind was vast and empty but filled with voices and images he couldn't understand. Nothing seemed to make any sense to him, so he merely drifted, feeling as if the connection between his mind and his body had been severed and not caring. One by one, the voices silenced and the images faded. When there was nothing left but a peace and a stillness he'd never experienced before, he turned to face the single question that remained.

What did he want?

It was not a question he'd ever really asked himself

before. He'd always thought he knew the answer, but now he wasn't sure.

Did he really only want revenge . . . ?

The cavern echoed with the previously unacceptable half of the question and, to his surprise, he found it much easier to face than he'd expected.

Did he really only want revenge on Brax for having chosen another seer to protect?

The muting effect kept his mind unusually calm and focused as he examined the question from all sides.

Was he really that pathetic? And that . . . petty? What would he do if he actually achieved that revenge on Brax? What would he be; anything at all? Would he really die? And would any of it matter once he left this strange muting cavern where he could think like other people did for the first time in his life? Would he even remember it this clearly when his mind took wing on its familiar, chaotic flight again or would it just be another image in the storm of confusing images that swirled around him without pause? What, if anything, could he use to focus his thoughts and remember something as insubstantial as this? There was no stag beetle or turtle shell here, he'd long ago forced his fingers to stop their focusing tapping against his thigh, and no Anavatanon, Yuruk, Amatus, or Volinski form of prophecy could help him find one. Even the Godling had faded from his senses.

What did he want?

When the answer came, he wasn't sure he wanted to accept it, but it remained, stubbornly unwilling to be banished, as familiar as the image of the dark-haired boy who'd graced his dreams since he'd been three years old.

He wanted Brax. Then and now. Boy and man. But whether he wanted him alive or dead was still uncertain.

Opening his eyes, he turned a belligerent glare on Dar-Sayer, who merely nodded.

"Now that you've faced what you truly want," the oracle said calmly, "the knowledge can never make you vulnerable to the spirits." Holding out his hand, he allowed Nir to help him from the pool.

"And here is something else to consider," he continued. "If he has haunted your dreams all these years, perhaps you've haunted his. And, if so, perhaps this bond you share will bring him to the same understanding."

"What understanding?"

"Whether he wants you."

He smiled at the expression on Graize's face. "I'm ready to teach you now."

As Graize accepted Nir's aid in turn, he felt the familiar prescient chill work its way across his shoulder blades, and frowned, unsure if Dar-Sayer's words were true or not. This knowledge, this understanding, might not make him vulnerable to the spirits, but it could certainly make him vulnerable to others. To one other. His experience in the pool forced the recognition of the name, and with a resigned sigh, he allowed it to break across his conscious mind like a cold wave. To Spar. But . . . his thoughts continued, if he and Brax really shared a bond, then that bond could make Brax vulnerable as well, and if Brax were vulnerable, then so was Spar.

Because revenge was still a driving force in his life, not just revenge against Brax, but revenge against Spar. As Nir wrapped him in woolen blankets once again, he sank onto the sheepskin and, with great effort, forced his mind into a tighter focus than he'd ever achieved before. Calling up the image of the dark-haired man, he spoke to him directly for the first time in years, willing his thoughts out past the muting effect and across the miles.

"We have a bond," he mouthed. *"A future just as I told you we did long ago. But bond to this: you betray, you abandon, it's what you do, come to that understanding if*

you can. You'll betray and abandon Spar just like you did me."

Accepting a cup of hot tea, he hunkered down, his plans for the future unchanged. He would have Brax or kill him. Either way, Spar was not going to win this time.

11

Alev-Hisar

AT ALEV-HISAR, BRAX stood the dawn watch, looking down on the two villages that enjoyed Alev-Hisar's protection. Kinor-Koy, the smaller of the two, was surrounded by walled orchards and garden plots. With most of its inhabitants sworn to Havo, it tended toward solitary gardeners and market farmers. In contrast, Ekmir-Koy was the largest village on Gol-Beyaz. It had a reputation for the best horses and cattle on the western shore, and its sheep, with their distinctive tawny-colored wool and flavorful meat, were in high demand. The shepherds of Ekmir-Koy had made use of the easternmost foothills to pasture their flocks for centuries and, in the past, had done a brisk trade with the Petchans of the Gurney-Dag Mountains. Many of the villagers shared their blond-haired, blue-eyed features and their love of brightly embroidered felt clothing.

But that had been in the past. Now the flocks of Ekmir-Koy were guarded by armed militia and the lake people did not mingle with the mountain people, not even for trade.

Turning, Brax stared at the darkened hills once again, wondering if Graize really was hidden in some mountain village stirring up trouble among the Petchans as he had among the Yuruk.

As he leaned forward, eyes narrowed, a sudden fluttering of ethereal wings past his face made him scowl.

Ever since Spar had squeezed his unwilling promise of help from him, Hisar had been buzzing around his head like an overlarge wasp every time he'd left the confines of the temple buildings. But It had disappeared again once he'd taken ship for Alev-Hisar. Brax had assumed that was because It had gone back to hovering around Spar, but now he wondered if it was because of Gol-Beyaz. Hisar hadn't come off very well the last time It had faced a God—his God—above the silver lake. Maybe it was skittish.

"Maybe It was scared."

The unwanted thought passed across his mind, and he scowled resentfully. It wasn't his business if Hisar was scared. It was Spar's. And probably Graize's. They'd built It, or raised It, or done whatever they'd done to forge some unbreakable bond with It. Let them sort out how to take care of It.

"Hisar's young and doesn't understand how easy it is to get taken in by lifters and tricksters."

"Then it's high time It learned."

"Especially God-lifters and tricksters."

"Not my problem."

"You promised."

Stepping out of the sentry box, he raised his face to the sprinkling of rain, feeling the now-familiar flutter of wings across his cheek. "All right, enough," he snapped. "You want something; spit it out."

"As long as It doesn't get too close. Or actually talk to me."

"Shut up."

The flutter of wings paused. Turning slightly, he glared at the shimmering figure hovering in midair like a ghostly dragonfly just out of reach beyond the tower wall. His chest aching with the remembered chill of Its touch, he crossed his arms and waited, an unimpressed expression on his face.

After a moment, Hisar dropped until It paused a few

inches from the battlements, taking on a misty seeming of Spar's pale-haired features.

Brax narrowed his eyes in warning and It quickly took a different form, but when Its Graize-seeming drew an even deeper frown, It chose and abandoned several more before It finally settled on a ghostly seeming of Jaq standing on his hind legs. Since Brax's wide-eyed response seemed neither hostile nor suspicious, only surprised, It grew more confident, becoming slightly more solid in the moonlight.

Brax raised an inquiring eyebrow. "Well?" he demanded. "What do you want?"

The Jaq-seeming attempted an innocent shrug and Brax shook his head with a snap. "You got a voice, use it, otherwise, piss off. I'm on duty, and I don't have time for stupid games." Then his expression suddenly changed as a thought occurred to him. "Is Spar all right?"

Hisar blinked in surprise. It spent a moment working out the dynamics of the Jaq-seeming's muzzle, then just gave up. "Spar's fine," It answered, Its voice, a tinny soprano, echoing from the dog's closed mouth. "Why wouldn't he be?"

Brax frowned at It. "Why else would you show up here without him and looking like that?" He stabbed a suspicious finger at the Jaq-seeming's chest.

Clearly unsure of the significance, Hisar turned the seeming in and around on Itself causing Brax to have a moment of uncomfortable vertigo. "Spar's fine," It repeated finally, turning to face him once again, most of the seeming's limbs back in their proper positions.

"So what do you want, then?"

"Nothing. Really. Much." The Jaq-seeming's features were not up to the variety of expressions that Hisar put it through and finally It shifted to a seeming of a young, Yuruk girl of about fourteen, long black hair falling over an olive-skinned oval face with almond-shaped brown eyes. "I just . . . had questions."

"About what?"

It jerked Its head toward Alev-Hisar's First Day torches, gutted now that the celebrations were over.

"And?"

"And . . . I watched. It was . . ." Hisar paused, obviously searching for the right word. "Big."

"Big?"

"Um . . . momentous?"

"Could be." Brax narrowed his eyes, curious despite himself. "Did it *feel* momentous to you?" he asked with deliberate emphasis.

Hisar chose and discarded several responses, then gave Brax an uncertain look. "It was momentous for you," It answered hesitantly. "I . . . felt that."

"Because of before?"

Hisar blinked again. "Before when?"

"Before on the battlements." Brax waved his hand in front of his chest. "A year ago," he finished between gritted teeth.

"Oh. Yes, because of that."

"Do you feel everything I feel?"

Brax's voice was flat and emotionless, but Hisar paused nevertheless, sensing a potential trap. "No," It said slowly. "Not everything, just the really strong feelings, and only when we're close. Like when you have sex," It continued, encouraged by Brax's lack of an angry response. "You know, yesterday when the twins and that . . ."

"Yes, I remember," Brax interrupted. "So you feel it every time I have sex?"

"No." Hisar's own voice was petulant with impatience now. "I told you, only when we're close. I don't always come around you when you're having sex, you know, I have other things to do, too."

"Like what?"

"Like talking to people, *other* people, people who want to talk to *me*."

"People like Spar?"

"Yes."

"And Graize?"

Hisar opened and closed Its mouth a few times. "No," It said finally, Its voice subdued again.

"But you do ... hover around him, right?" Brax pressed.

"Yes."

"But you don't talk to him?"

"No." Hisar frowned at him. "I told Spar I didn't talk to Graize. Didn't he tell you?"

"Spar doesn't tell me what you two talk about."

"Oh."

"Why don't you talk to Graize?"

Hisar made the girl-seeming's right shoulder shrug in a passable imitation of Spar. "Just because. *You* don't talk to everyone either," It added in an accusatory tone.

"I talk to everyone I'm close to."

"About everything?"

"No," Brax allowed. "Not everything."

Hisar's girl-seeming wavered and then grew steady once again. "Did you talk to Spar?" It asked. "About me?"

"You mean, did he ask me to help you?"

"Yes."

Brax nodded.

"And?"

"And I said I would, for whatever good it will do. I still don't have any idea what you could need help with."

"Spar said you would help turn me gold."

Brax gave It a puzzled look. "What does that even mean?" he asked.

Hisar shrugged again. "I don't know, but Spar does. Spar's wise, he *knows* things."

"He does at that."

Hisar hesitated a moment, then gave Brax a suspicious look much like his own. "So if you don't know how to help me," It demanded, "why would you say you would?"

"Because Spar asked me to."

"That's all?"

"That's enough." Turning toward the north, Brax saw the quiet darkness of Estavia-Sarayi in his mind's eye, wondering if Spar were asleep in the small delin-alcove they used to share, or whether he was sitting on some temple rooftop staring south, imagining Brax in turn; maybe even seeing this conversation in his own mind.

"Like you said," he continued. "Spar knows things. So when it's time for us to know things too, he'll tell us."

Hisar chewed this over for a few moments, then nodded. Spar had said that very thing.

The two of them stood in silence for a while, each staring out at the moonlit fields, before It returned Its attention to Brax once again. "Are you going to try and kill Graize?" It asked abruptly.

Taken aback, Brax paused a moment to collect himself. Choosing and discarding as many answers as Hisar had earlier, he finally settled on a similar, one-shouldered shrug. "Yes," he said just as bluntly.

"Why?"

"Because he's our enemy."

"Our?"

"Mine and Spar's."

"What if he kills you first?"

"Then Spar will kill him afterward."

"It's that easy?"

"What is?"

"To decide to kill someone?"

Brax rubbed at his elbow. "No," he said, his voice more careful now. "It's not that easy. It takes years to come to that kind of a decision." His eyes narrowed. "Why," he demanded, "is Graize planning to kill me?"

Hisar frowned. "I don't know. He thinks about you all the time, but his mind is . . ."

"Twisted?"

"Conflicted." It fell silent. "You know, *Spar* wouldn't care if I talk to Graize," It said after a moment.

"Has Graize ever asked if you talk to Spar?"

Hisar shook Its head.

"So you haven't told him?"

Hisar shook Its head again.

"Why?"

"I dunno."

The studied carelessness of the response was so similar to Spar's that Brax found himself giving a snort of disbelief. "Bollocks," he stated.

Hisar reared back, an affronted expression on the girl-seeming's face. "Why is it bollocks?" It demanded.

"Because you do know."

The girl-seeming cast him an injured look before dissolving into the shimmering dragonfly form once more, and Hisar took flight off the battlements with a snap of ethereal wings.

As It disappeared into the darkness, Brax was left wondering why he suddenly felt as if he'd just been mean to a child.

✦

Two days later, Kaptin Majin of the Alev-Hisar garrison called a general council.

Brax met up with Brin and Bazmin as they came off duty, handing them each a piece of tripe stuffed in a pita for their noon meal. Both twins gave him an identical questioning look, but he simply shrugged.

"You're the ones who hear things. If you don't know, how'm I s'posed to?"

"There was a messenger from Estavia-Sarayi who disembarked just after the Morning Invocation," Brin pointed out between bites. "We saw her head into Kaptin Majin's office. She was dressed in Sable Company black."

"Moments later, messengers rode north and south to fetch Militia-Kaptins Carz of Kinor-Koy and Esin of Ekmir-Koy," Bazmin added.

"They've been closeted ever since."

Brax shook his head. "You two should never be allowed to stand sentry anywhere with a view," he noted.

"So we were wondering what you'd heard down here on the ground," Bazmin continued, ignoring Brax's comment.

"You figured I was listening at the keyhole?"

Brin snickered. "You? No, but someone had to have been."

"Someone always does," Bazmin added.

"Yes, they do," Brax agreed, "but those someones were leaning over the watchtower battlements risking their necks. I hope one of you at least was facing the mountains like you were supposed to."

Both twins waved dismissive hands at him as the rest of their troop fell into step beside them, and moments later they joined the stream of warriors and militia passing under Alev-Hisar's vaulted entranceway. As they crammed into the main hall, Brax glanced around, allowing his eyes to adjust to the low light levels.

Taking up the watchtower's entire ground floor, Alev-Hisar's council chamber was similar to the one at Estavia-Sarayi; built for function and defense rather than for light or comfort. Three of the four walls were unadorned gray stone blocks reinforced with thick wooden beams, but at some point in its history some priest or artisan of Ystazia had attempted to brighten up the gloom with a huge mosaic of Gol-Beyaz on the fourth wall.

Craning his neck to see past Brin's shoulder, Brax allowed that it certainly was bright. The silver lake had been depicted in the traditional style with hundreds of tiny blue, green, and white marble chips drawn from the lake bed. The surrounding villages and watchtowers had been painted on plaster, and Anavatan, with its three great watchtowers of Gerek-, Dovek-, and Lazim-Hisar, had been overlaid in gold and silver leaf.

Idly wondering how much the whole thing had cost to install, Brax turned his attention to the people already in place at the front of the room as Brin threw one arm over his shoulder, effectively blocking his view of anything else.

The handful of Sable Company seers attached to Alev-Hisar were sitting with the twin's mysterious messenger, a sixteen-year-old seer-delinkos new to Estavia-Sarayi that Brax remembered Spar telling him was named Gul. They were deep in conversation, the messenger doing her best to appear calm and mature, but, from the stiff set of her shoulders and the way she clasped her hands together in her lap, Brax assumed that this was her first assignment. As the watchtower doors boomed shut, she gave a startled jump, then pulled herself together as Alev-Hisar's kaptin entered the hall.

As one, the gathered warriors and militia came to attention and even Kaptins Carz and Esin stood when she strode past.

Kaptin Majin of Sandiz-Koy had served at Estavia-Sarayi as Sapphire Company's Birin-Kaptin until she'd lost an arm protecting her home village in a Yuruk attack twelve years ago. She'd run Alev-Hisar for a decade since with a blunt, uncompromising efficiency that was legendary among the watchtower garrisons. And, it was rumored, she was equally blunt and uncompromising in her criticism of Estavia-Sarayi's policies regarding the Petchans.

Now she stood, sweeping her cold gaze across the gathered who instantly silenced. "It's no secret that there's been increased raiding from the Gurney-Dag Mountains this season," she began without preamble. "And no secret that we've been completely useless in putting a stop to it. Now the activity's stepped up, and so our defense is going to step up as well, finally to the point of offense."

Brin elbowed Brax in the ribs as the gathered soldiers began to murmur their agreement, but Kaptin Majin's eyes flashed dangerously, and silence instantly reigned once more.

"To that end we've received a timely message from Estavia-Sarayi," she said, gesturing at Gul. "A second contingent of Sable Company seers, under Estavia-Sarayi's Birin-Kaptin Nicurz, will be arriving within the week as well as reinforcements from Indigo Company and a contingent of mounted Warriors from Bronze Company to bring the fight to the Petchan villages for a change. Until they arrive, Alev-Hisar is to coordinate increased militia patrols from both villages with those of the watchtower garrison. These patrols will go out on four-day rotations in order to expand their circuit to include the lower foothills. Any Petchans, no matter how ingenuous they may appear, are to be taken prisoner and brought back to Alev-Hisar, no exceptions. In the meantime, our own Sable Company seers will be increasing their prophetic vigilance. Birin-Kaptin Corzin will explain further."

She gestured at Alev-Hisar's ranking battle-seer who stood.

Birin-Kaptin Corzin was a lean, gaunt man in his mid-forties, his dark brown hair already streaked with gray and his eyes half-clouded with the white mist of prophecy. A shiver went through the assembly as he swept the room with the inward yet intense gaze of a seer, but when he spoke, his surprisingly rich voice filled the room with warmth.

"As the kaptin's already told you, we'll be increasing our forays into prophecy," he said. "Most of what we discover, however, will remain undisclosed until Birin-Kaptin Nicurz's had a chance to review our findings." When an involuntary murmur of disappointment rippled across the room, he held up one hand.

"Be patient," he advised. "The Petchan seers are extremely sensitive. We don't want to tip our hands by solidifying the streams with too many minds working in tandem. Even if they are untrained infantry minds," he added with a smile. "Now, I understand that a few of the temple's ghazi-priests have been briefed on how to increase their own sensitivity," he continued, nodding toward Brax's company. "And we'll be working with them at a later date. In the meantime—and I cannot stress this enough—everyone must behave in as routine a manner as possible. When not on patrol, stand your duties and keep any speculation or expectations to yourselves. Better yet, put them out of your minds completely. They'll only solidify the streams as I said before, making it easier for the Petchan seers to gain an understanding of our intentions.

"As soon as you need to know the plans of your superiors, you'll know them.

"Now, are there any questions?"

A tall, thin, militia-delinkos wearing the insignia of Kinor-Koy raised a hesitant hand. When the kaptin acknowledged him with a sharp nod of her head, he coughed nervously.

"Um, will we be asking the village priests of Incasa for their help in prophecy, Kaptin?" he inquired.

A new, cold silence descended on the room, and he glanced around, his face going red with embarrassment. "I only wondered," he continued, his voice cracking with uncertainty, "because my oldest kardos is a seer-delinkos at Incasa-Cami. And if we need to know what the Petchans are doing, shouldn't we use every . . . resource available?" He glanced about as nobody spoke, then raised his chin defensively. "Well, shouldn't we?" he demanded in the direction of his own abayos who was glaring at him from the other side of the room.

The kaptin gestured at Corzin who turned his misted gaze on the hapless young man.

"It's Quarzi, isn't it?" he asked. When the delinkos nodded stiffly, he smiled at him. "This is only the first step, Quarzi," he answered, his voice carrying only the slightest hint of a remonstrative tone. "Once we've determined what level of threat the Petchans represent, we'll know whether the situation requires resources beyond those available to the traditional protectors of

Gol-Beyaz—that being the Warriors and Battle-Seers of Estavia and the village militias."

He raised a hand to forestall any muttering that might break out. "That being said," he continued in a louder tone, "should any of Incasa's people wish to share their prophecy with us, we'd be more than willing to take it under advisement, but I think we have everything under control for the time being."

He caught Quarzi's eye once more. "However, I would ask that you keep this suggestion to yourself, Delinkos, and not discuss it with your kardos until your abayos gives you leave."

Quarzi shuffled his feet resentfully. "Of course I won't discuss it, Birin-Kaptin," he said stiffly. "I was only asking for clarification."

"Well, now you have it."

"And that's everything, people," Kaptin Majin added, sweeping her cold gaze across the room again. "The updated patrol schedules will be posted presently. In the meantime, you have your orders. Carry out your duties and remain vigilant. That's all."

As Quarzi's abayos moved purposefully through the crowd toward him, the gathering broke up, heading with obvious relief for the cool air outside the watchtower.

✦

The messenger caught up with Brax just as he and the rest of his troop emerged into the outer courtyard, pushing through the press of people to catch him by the arm.

"Ghazi, a word?"

She drew him away to a quiet corner, much to the annoyance of the twins, but when she held out a small vellum missive, Brax nodded.

"I'll meet you all later," he told them, then turned his back on them firmly as she passed him the missive.

"It's from Seer-Delinkos Spar, Ghazi," she said unnecessarily. Her brows drew down over brown eyes already flecked with white as she glanced back at the twins, standing with arms crossed and pointedly not withdrawing. "I'm sorry, but he said I was to give this to you in private. He was very insistent about that."

"I'll bet he was." Brax jerked his head at the twins who reluctantly moved out of earshot.

"He, um, gave me further instructions," the messenger continued, "but . . ." She paused, obviously discomfited, and the corners of Brax's mouth quirked upward.

"Did he say something rude?" he hazarded.

She frowned. "No, not exactly rude, Ghazi," she explained. "But possibly inappropriate."

"Better just spit it out then."

"His exact instructions were that I was to stand over you while you read it."

"Ah. Sounds remarkably polite for Spar actually."

"I imagine he might have been more . . . direct with you in person."

"I imagine you're right." Brax chuckled, but he obediently cracked the plain wax seal and opened the folded message. It contained two simple sentences.

There's a runaway cart coming. Don't do anything stupid until I see you.

Brax glanced over. "Do you know what this says?" he asked.

She shook her head. "Does he say to tell me, Ghazi?"

"No."

"Then his message is for you alone." She waited a moment, then sighed. "Am I to take a message back, Ghazi?" she asked patiently.

"What? Oh, no."

"Then I'll leave you to your duties." Gul turned to go, then turned back, an uncertain expression on her face.

"Um, might I ask you something private, Ghazi?" she began.

Brax nodded.

"It's about Spar."

"What about him?"

"You and he are kardon, yes?"

"Yes."

She nodded more to herself than to him. "Does he ... I mean, is he ..." She glanced at Brin and Bazmin who were now flirting with the watchtower's gooseherd amidst a flurry of white wings. "Is he interested in women ... do you think?"

Brax grinned despite himself. "He might be," he said noncommittally. "Why? Are you interested in him?"

She smiled shyly back at him. "I might be," she replied in turn. "In a few months or so. He's still a little young."

"How old are you?"

"Sixteen and a half."

"He's just turned fifteen."

"I know."

"But you do want him?"

She shrugged. "It's more that I'm thinking about being interested in wanting him ... at some point," she allowed. "If he's interested in women."

"Well, at some point, you should think about asking him yourself."

She gave him a scandalized look. "It's not that simple," she pointed out tersely.

"Why not?"

"Well, for one thing, because he might say no."

"But he might say yes."

She shook her head in exasperation. "No offense, Ghazi, but it's easy for you. You've probably never had to risk asking for it in your entire life."

"What?" Brax drew back, a little amused and insulted at the same time. "Of course I have."

"When?"

"Well ..."

"Aha!" She jabbed a finger at him, then remembering herself, pulled it back with an abashed look.

"I had to ask for it the first time," Brax continued, ignoring her expression. "But, regardless, this isn't about me, is it? It's about you and Spar. If you want something, you should reach for it, and if you want Spar, you should reach for him. Besides . . ." He grinned at her. "I thought you were a seer. Can't you just prophesize what he'll say?"

She squirmed uncomfortably. "It doesn't work that way, Ghazi, and besides . . ." She trailed off.

"Besides?"

"Besides I already tried," she muttered, going red.

"And?"

Her mist-flecked eyes flashed. "And nothing. Like I said, it doesn't work that way. I wish it did," she added in a dark mutter.

Brax snickered. "Well, why don't you ask the priests of Incasa for help?"

She sniffed dismissively at him.

Leaning against the trunk of a nearby plane tree, he cocked his head to one side.

"So tell me," he asked, "at the risk of asking the same stupid question twice, why don't we ever go to the Incasa-seers for help?"

Her brows drew down again. "Because we don't," she said, her expression betraying her obvious discomfort with the question. "We don't have to, do we?" she added when he raised a quizzical eyebrow at her. "Traditionally, the priests of Incasa come to us when they have a prophecy they wish to share; we don't go to them."

"So we never work together?" he pressed. "Not ever?"

"Well, of course we do. I mean, I'm sure we have in the past, when the threat's been great enough. But we don't ask, they offer."

"Why?"

She frowned at him. "Well, because, just . . . because that's how it's done," she said, impatience adding the beginnings of a sharp tone to her voice. When he continued to look mystified, she shook her head. "All right," she began very slowly as if she were speaking to a child. "Traditionally, the priests of Incasa are ..." she paused, obviously loath to say the words, "*perceived* to be the most powerful and the most talented seers in the land. Oh, don't be so dense," she snapped, forgetting herself once again as he opened his mouth to protest. "It's easy enough to understand why. A person wishing to serve Estavia serves as a soldier first and a seer second. Without that initial desire to live a martial life, a person with prophetic ability swears to Incasa because Incasa's people are seers first and foremost. Look at me." She gestured at herself. "I've been at Estavia-Sarayi for two months and I've had twice as much martial training as I've had prophetic training. A seer-delinkos of Incasa would have had two months of intense prophetic training and nothing else. They're not even allowed to leave the temple grounds in their first year, never mind being sent all over the lake with messages for one tower or another."

"So you're saying that if the Petchans are dangerous enough to threaten our security, the priests of Incasa will see it first because they're more highly trained?" Brax asked.

She sighed. "No, Ghazi, I'm saying that, if they have a part to play in meeting the Petchan threat, they'll come to that understanding first. And if they do, their leaders will contact our leaders with a very carefully worded suggestion of a joint venture that won't infer that either temple is subordinate or beholden to the other. It's political. It's always political."

Brax shook his head. "In other words, it's all about power. If we ask, we look weak and they look strong."

"Essentially."

"Why didn't you say that in the first place."

"No offense, Ghazi, but why didn't you figure it out for yourself in the first place?"

"Point," Brax acknowledged. "But, on the other hand if, while we're being political, the Petchans are working together and not wasting time on how things look, who's really weak and who's really strong?"

"I don't know, Ghazi," Gul sighed. "Maybe they have their own political problems. All I do know is that if the Gods' people are truly in danger, then the Gods will bring Their temples together as one in whatever manner, political or otherwise, They see fit. The protection of Their worshipers is paramount to the Gods."

Brax straightened. "Yes, and on that note, one last piece of advice, Seer-Delinkos?"

"Yes?"

"Don't talk about this sort of thing with Spar."

She grinned at him. "Actually, Ghazi, I wasn't planning on talking with Spar about anything beyond the question of your bed or mine sometime this winter."

"A good plan." He glanced over as Kaptin Majin's own delinkos emerged from the watchtower, blinking painfully in the bright sunlight as she looked about with an impatient expression. "I believe you're wanted," he observed.

She straightened as well. "Yes, I'd better go. The kaptin will have a pouchful of missives for me to take back to Anavatan. Thank you for your advice, Ghazi." Laying a hand against her chest, she bowed.

Brax echoed the motion with as serious an expression as he could manage. "And thank you for your explanation, Seer," he replied with a smile.

They made to go their separate ways, but a flash of iridescent light caught Brax's eye as the plane tree branches above their heads shimmered in the afternoon sun. He frowned up at them for a moment, then continued on his way as Brin and Bazmin fell into step beside him in their usual half-protective, half-intimidating manner. There would be time enough to deal with eavesdropping God-creatures, he decided, after he dealt with the twins and their insatiable gossip mongering.

✦

Hidden in the tree's highest branches, Hisar remained absolutely still until Brax had rejoined the twins—both of them obviously bursting to know what had been contained in Spar's letter—then turned Its attention to the seer as she disappeared inside the watchtower.

It had watched her arrive from the same vantage point as the twins themselves; hovering so close to them at one point that It had ruffled Brin's thick black hair just to see if It could get a reaction, but both ghazon had been riveted on the seer below, so It had eventually given up and peered down at her as well, wondering why they found her so interesting. She'd not been anything like Elif. Elif had been all mist and secrets and metaphysical potency hidden behind physical fragility; like an ancient cinar tree with the sap running deep inside a great, gnarled trunk. This seer was young and strong, but her power was green and unseasoned, more like a sapling's than a grown tree's.

The metaphor pleased It, and It puffed up Its iridescent chest in pride. Panos wasn't the only one free to draw new meaning from dissimilar sensations; Hisar had tasted the wind and the rain and knew what kinds of songs they sang just as she did.

The memory of the southern oracle, her arms entwined about Illan Volinsk's body, suddenly made the twin's behavior more understandable. They probably just wanted to have sex with the seer, like she wanted to have sex with Spar, everyone wanted to have sex with Brax, and he was happy to oblige anyone who asked.

Having sorted that out to Its satisfaction, Hisar now took to the air, soaring high above the watchtower battlements to watch the clumps of warriors and militia fighters scurrying this way and that. The air of excitement on the wind was almost palpable. Something was happening that everyone was happy about.

Alighting on the very top of Alev-Hisar's flagpole, It watched as a number of black-clad seers—looking for all the world like a flock of ravens—gathered together on the shore. It shivered.

Ever since Spar's warning at Elif's deathbed, Hisar had been very wary of seers. When Spar looked into prophecy, his eyes went wide and black, showing him a world that no one else could see: the dark place. Spar was cold and dangerous in the dark place, and Hisar had learned to be very careful around him whenever he went there. In contrast, the eyes of the God-sworn seers were white in the physical realm and a nearly transparent silver, like a mirror's, in the prophetic realm. Hisar had originally thought that this blinded them to more than just the physical world, but Spar had told him differently. Their silver God-gifted vision gave them the power of the Gods, and that meant that, like the Gods, they could hurt Hisar.

It shuddered. For all his advice, Spar had not helped It against Incasa or when Estavia had turned on It. For all his silences, Graize had. Graize had held It and soothed It, running hands half in and half out of the world along Its length and sending rivulets of unfamiliar physical sensations through Its body that It didn't fully understand until It had calmed. He had stayed, holding It like that, all night long while the storm raged above them, soaking into his hair and clothes and puddling all around him.

But that had been before Dar-Sayer and the muting cavern that kept them apart.

Hisar had spent the last few days flying back and forth between Alev-Hisar and the Gurney-Dag Mountains, waiting for Graize to come out and feeling lonely and unhappy. Its conversation with Brax hadn't helped, and It had flown north to question Spar only to find him inexplicably closeted with Kaptin Liel and a new and scary seer with a shining, silver mind that burned like fire.

Knocking a few of the watchtower's slate tiles loose

with a petulant swing of Its tail, Hisar frowned. Nobody seemed to want to talk to It. And even when they did, they were all wearing those stupid little beads that tasted of barriers and control like they didn't trust It. It wasn't fair.

Looking out past the battlements, It saw Brax take leave of the twins at Kinor-Koy and took flight into the air at once, reaching the village paddocks in a few seconds. It waited until the twins had entered a low, timber-and-wattle building, then swooped down, buzzing around Brax's head in much the same way as It would have done to Graize if It were annoyed with him.

Brax swatted irritably at It and It solidified into the Yuruk girl-seeming again, hovering a few inches in front of his face.

"Did you just have sex with them to distract them from Spar's message?" It demanded, the last two days of solitude making It sharp.

Brax pressed his fingertips to the bridge of his nose, clearly counting to ten.

"Yes," he answered just as sharply.

Hisar moved back a step, surprised by the honesty of his answer.

"And what are you all doing now?" It asked.

Brax gave It a flat look in return. "What does it look like we're doing?" he shot back.

"Running around like ants that have just had their anthill kicked over."

Brax snorted. "That sounds like one of Spar's observations," he noted.

Hisar sniffed. "He might have said that to me once," It allowed. "About something or other." It glanced back toward the watchtower looming over the paddock fence. "That seer you were talking to," It said. "Graize would have called her a baby-seer."

"Graize is a rude little shite," Brax retorted.

"Was she a temple-seer?" Hisar continued, refusing to be distracted.

"You mean a Sable Company seer? Yes."

"There are a lot of them here. And more are coming on barges. Why are they coming?"

Brax narrowed his eyes. "Why do you want to know?"

Hisar paused, Its initial pique evaporating before a wave of unfamiliar feelings. "I dunno," It said after a moment, falling into Brax's own Dockside accent. "Seers are . . . seers," It finished weakly. "They . . ." It frowned, unsure why It didn't want to tell Brax how the seers made It feel. It flickered from one seeming to another until it settled on Its usual Caleb-seeming. "Sometimes they make me feel . . . scared," It admitted.

"Why?"

Brax's tone was no longer belligerent, only curious, and Hisar made Its version of Spar's one-shouldered shrug. "I dunno," It said again. "They can see inside things. I don't like being seen inside."

Brax snorted. "Who does?"

"I don't know. Who?"

"What?"

Hisar blinked Caleb's almond-shaped eyes in confusion. "You asked me who does? I don't know, do you know?"

"No. I was just being . . ." Brax frowned at It. "I was just being sympathetic," he said through gritted teeth. "I don't like being seen inside either."

"Oh." Hisar blinked again, this time in surprise. "Um, thank you?"

Brax shook his head. "Look, Hisar," he said as gently as he could, "I don't think it's a very good idea to talk to me right now." He started walking again.

Hisar followed him, floating a few inches off the ground. "Why?" It demanded.

"Why?" Brax stopped to glare at It. "Because you're in contact with the enemy, that's why."

Hisar drew Itself up. "I told you, Graize and I don't talk," It said huffily.

"Maybe not now, but what happens when you do, when Graize does ask you what we're doing here? Asks about our battle plans and our troop movements? What will you tell him?"

Hisar paused. "I don't know," It said truthfully. "He's never asked me that sort of thing before."

Brax crossed his arms over his chest. "How long do you think it'll be before he does—before he decides to use you to spy on us and on Spar? He's crazy, but he's not stupid."

Hisar gave him a resentful look. "He doesn't even know I come here," It sniffed. "And besides, he's all busy right now *learning to be a better seer*," It added with a snarl, "He hasn't got the time to talk to me even if he wanted to. Which he obviously doesn't. And neither does Spar," It added. "He's too busy too, talking to all those blackbird seers he's never wanted to talk to before. Probably learning to be a better seer, too."

Brax paused, several conflicting desires warring inside his head. But finally, remembering his conversation with Spar and his promise, he sighed again. "Come over here," he growled, indicating a small meditation garden built in the corner between the God-Wall and the paddocks. Hisar eyed the wall with some trepidation but finally hovered to one side of it while Brax seated himself on the wrought-iron bench beneath the branches of a young lime tree.

"Look, you shouldn't say things like that," Brax said once they were settled.

"Like what?"

"Like what Spar's doing and especially what Graize is doing. If you're Spar's friend, you won't tell people what he's doing, not even me. And as for Graize . . ." He took a deep breath. "I'm his enemy, I told you that before, and we're about to go to war. If you tell me things that Graize is doing, that will give me an advantage over him.

"Now I want an advantage over him," he admitted

bluntly. "I want to ask you what he's doing, what the Petchans are doing, where they are, what kind of weapons they have, how many, and what *their* troop movements are. And if you keep hanging around me, I'm going to ask you; it's my duty. And you're going to have to decide how to answer me."

He shook his head as Hisar continued to look mystified. "Look, Spar asked me to help you, and I promised him I would, so I'm giving you this warning: Go away. If you come back, I'm going to ask you, point-blank, what Graize is up to."

"And if I don't tell you?" Hisar asked, Its voice both challenging and fearful.

Brax met Its gaze with a firm stare of his own. "I don't know," he said honestly. "But I do know that you can't be on both sides in a war. You have to choose one side or the other, and if you choose Graize and the Petchans, you can't choose me and Spar. You'll be our enemy, just like him, and the only one I know who can defeat you is Estavia. And, Hisar, I *will* call Her if I have to."

As agitated by his threat as by the sudden use of Its name, the Godling lost control of Its seeming. It flickered from one form to another, then finally disappeared altogether.

As a snap of wings knocked his hair into his eyes, Brax was left feeling, once again, as if he'd been deliberately cruel to a child. With a sigh, he stood and headed back for the watchtower where his troop was waiting. Things were getting far too complicated. He needed to be somewhere where he could think clearly, but there was no time. He'd have to face them as he always had, on the fly.

✦

High above the clouds, Hisar streaked northward, both hurt and confused by Brax's words. But as the cold upper wind poured across Its wings, It decided that It didn't care. It didn't care if Brax wouldn't talk to It, and

It didn't care if Spar or Graize or even Estavia wouldn't talk to It either. It would go to Cvet Tower and watch Panos and Illan having sex. That, at least, was a sensation It was starting to understand.

A single thread of potential tickled against Its belly as it sped past Estavia-Sarayi, and It almost checked Its flight, but at the last moment It shot back up into the clouds. It didn't care what Spar was up to. If he didn't want to talk to It, It didn't want to talk to him. Shifting forms to that of a simple, wild lands spirit, It put on a burst of speed and soon left both the mountains and the silver lake behind.

12

Sable Company

IN THE HUSHED, central atrium of Estavia-Sarayi's armory tower, First Oracle Bessic stood, politely inspecting a long, jewel-encrusted sword that had reputedly belonged to Kaptin Haldin, while inwardly studying the youth who stood a few feet away from him, clearly sizing him up in return.

Neither spoke.

Last night, Bessic had dreamed of the Battle God's temple. Incasa Himself had walked his First Oracle to the gates where they'd been met by the armored child and shimmering tower of Battle-Seer Elif's vision. When the messenger had arrived this morning with Marshal Brayazi's invitation to meet with Battle-Seer-Delinkos Spar, Bessic had merely inclined his head in gracious acceptance.

They'd walked over together, the older man taking some perverse pleasure in the young messenger's obvious discomfort. Now, standing amid a millennium's worth of battle trophies, Anavatan's premier seer turned the power of his prophetic sight on Anavatan's most enigmatic and intractable delinkos.

At first glance, the youth seemed somewhat of a disappointment. Smaller than average, with slender arms and legs sticking out of a blue tunic that, although well made, still managed to hang on him like a sack. Blond hair and blue eyes betrayed his possible Ekmir-Koy or even Petchan bloodline, and the slightly hollowed cheeks betrayed his earlier life on the streets, competing with the guarded expression that betrayed nothing of his inner thoughts or abilities whatsoever.

To Bessic's prophetic sight, however, Spar blazed with latent possibility. His body merged and shifted from the boy he'd been in the past to the man he'd be in the future, the blue tunic nothing more than a wisp of smoke swirling about the present. His blond hair spoke of centuries of trade and conflict, and his blue eyes were shrouded in a darkness so complete that it was as if he were a delos peering out from within his aba's cloak. His prophetic abilities shone with such intensity that Bessic almost had to squint to look at him, but wrapped about that intensity was a street-born, cynical wisdom steeped in self-interest and subtle manipulation that belied his age.

Here was no ordinary seer-delinkos and Bessic would have to use all his own considerable talents if he was to bring him into Incasa's fold. Tucking his hands behind him in a fair imitation of parade rest, the First Oracle waited for the youth to make the opening move.

"Elif and Freyiz talked about me," Spar said almost at once, his voice echoing in the lofty room.

Bessic nodded. "And Freyiz spoke to me of their conversation," he offered.

The youth turned away for half a moment, clearly uncertain of how much information to impart this early in the proceedings, and Bessic smiled to himself. Spar was subtle and cautious, but he was still very, very young.

"I was learning under Elif," the youth said finally. "But now she's gone."

Bessic nodded.

"I don't need a new teacher," Spar continued, betraying some vehemence in the tone of his voice. "But . . ." He paused; then, with a short one-shouldered shrug, he held out his hand to reveal a pair of small stained wooden dice nestled in his palm. "I threw them into the silver lake. Incasa threw them back."

The First Oracle smiled. "He gifted them to you?" he asked.

The youth frowned. "He put them where I would find them," he allowed.

"And you want to know why?"

Spar shook his head. "I can figure that out for myself. What I want is to tell you that I know something's coming, something big. Incasa's involved; so am I, and so's my kardos."

"Temple Ghazi-Priest Brax of Cyan Company."

The tiniest blink was Spar's only reaction. "We made a deal about Brax four years ago, Incasa and me. Now we have to make another one."

"And you want me to be your broker?" Bessic asked, allowing his humor at this request to color his voice.

Spar gave him a serious look in return. "Yes." Glancing about the armory, his eyes lit upon a heavy, bejeweled book sitting on a silver stand. For a heartbeat his expression grew hungry, but when he turned back, his expression was as guarded as ever.

"I have a year before I have to make any real decision about my life," he stated firmly. "And I want every one of those days. But I have to make some decisions now. The future won't wait.

"I won't come to Incasa-Sarayi," he continued in a dark tone, "but if Incasa helps, I won't stop Hisar from going to Gol-Beyaz either."

Bessic raised an eyebrow. "Could you stop the Godchild from coming?" he asked more as a reproach than a question.

Spar just shrugged. "I can get in the way. I have. Hisar asks questions, I give answers."

"And those answers are?"

"That It doesn't have to do anything It doesn't want to or follow anyone else's orders."

"Hm." The words babies raising babies came to Bessic's mind, but he carefully kept it from his features. It was well known that Spar of Estavia-Sarayi exerted some influence over the young God of Creation and Destruction. What wasn't so well known was just how much influence that was.

"So you would stop saying that?" he hazarded.

Spar frowned. "No. But I would try and be . . . more . . . neutral about it."

Bessic could see how hard the words had been and disciplined himself against the urge to smile. "And what do you want from Incasa in exchange?" he asked.

"If the future holds danger for Brax, I want Incasa to tell me," Spar replied at once.

Bessic's eyes widened. "You want to receive visions from the God without giving oaths to the God?"

"I want a heads up, yeah." When Bessic's eyes widened further, Spar scowled at him. "He started it," he said flatly. "He sent the dice back. If I use the dice, I'm doing what He wants, so He can do what I want; he can tell me what it means when I use them; plain and simple without any cryptic crap, I mean cryptic . . . imagery," he amended looking slightly embarrassed for the first time.

"And where do I and Incasa's temple fit in?"

The youth cocked his head to one side, his eyes narrowed. "There were birds," he said. "Gulls and ravens and pigeons. I didn't see the rest, but I'll bet they were there."

Bessic nodded at once, and Spar's eyes showed a brief flash of pleasure at not having to explain himself.

"We will work together, Spar-Delinkos," the First Oracle said formally. "With no bonds of obligation expected and no pressure exerted. If you need my help, you have only to ask for it."

Spar nodded.

"For one year," Bessic continued. "After which time I will be formally offering you a place as temple seer-delinkos at Incasa-Sarayi. The God has already gifted you with both favors and indulgences." He paused, then gave a passing imitation of Spar's own shrug. "You'd be wasted here," he said bluntly.

He turned to go, then turned back, his white-shrouded expression serious. "As you've said, you don't need a new teacher, but if I may offer you a piece of advice?"

Spar nodded cautiously.

"Prophecy is the art of reading the odds. If the odds are unpredictable, so is the outcome. And even the Gods can be unpredictable."

✦

The next day, three seer-delinkon clambered up to Spar's place on the battlements to tell him that Sable Company was gathering in their shrine for a mass seeking in preparation for the mobilization of troops to Alev-Hisar. Every temple-seer was required, including himself.

Despite his better judgment, Spar fell in beside them, casting a withering glare at the oldest who'd tried to discourage Jaq from following them.

✦

After Bessic had withdrawn, Spar had gone to see Kaptin Liel and Marshal Brayazi, sketching out their conversation in as few words as possible, and leaving both with the impression that he was considering accepting the First Oracle's offer.

As expected, the temple-seers had reacted by drawing their ranks in around him, bringing him into as many of their seekings and trainings as possible and making it clear that they considered him to be a valuable member of Sable Company.

Now, however, when the three seer-delinkon took their places with the rest of their year at the back of the shrine, Spar purposely tucked himself and Jaq to one side of the door where they could make a quick getaway if necessary and tried to ignore the sudden sense of foreboding that traveled up his spine. A deal with a God was dangerous enough, a deal with a God of Prophecy was worse, and Incasa had yet to exploit the opening Spar had given Him.

The door closed with a muffled thud, and he felt the gathered seers' disquiet slowly ease in the face of familiar ritual. He himself felt anything but eased. The shrine was crowded with people and, as the scent of incense attacked his nostrils, he fought down a sudden, panicked constriction in his chest, forcing himself to breathe deeply and evenly. After a while his heart rate calmed enough to take stock of his surroundings.

The seer's shrine was deep in shadow, the sunlight filtering in through the three, narrow windows unable to compete with the mass of light-absorbing black-clad bodies.

On the field, the battle-seers of Estavia formed themselves into a number of tightly controlled circles to better focus the power of their God; during Invocation, they stood in ranks with the rest of the temple-warriors; but in the privacy of their shrine, they came together in three loose and informal groupings: commanders, battle-seers, and delinkon.

Today, the commanders stood before the altar in full ceremonial garb: an embossed black leather cuirass worn under a heavy black tabard with Estavia's crimson eyes embroidered on the front above Sable Company's raven symbols of rank outlined in silver: four for Kaptin Liel, three for Birin-Kaptin Nicurz, and two for the four ikin-kaptins. The battle-seers, making up the bulk of the gathered, stood in the center of the shrine, dressed in training leathers, while the delinkon milling at the back, wore simple black tunics and sandals.

In contrast, Spar stood out like a songbird in a flock of crows, but until he was sixteen, he had the right to wear the bright blue tunic of Kemal and Yashar's infantry company, and he had no intention of being pressured out of it. He was not a Sable Company seer. Not yet.

Standing in Its shadowy alcove at the far end of the shrine, the eight-foot-tall statue of Estavia seemed to stare knowingly down at him, the hanging lamps to either side making Her ruby eyes glisten with a strangely cold light. The statue's twin swords, one pointing down toward the altar and the other pointing up toward the domed ceiling, gleamed with a sharp-edged menace and he stilled a new shiver of foreboding. Estavia might not be the God of Prophecy, but She had prophets of Her own and She was just as greedy for more as Incasa was. He would have to move very carefully now if he was to keep himself independent of either of Them.

A signal from the birin-kaptin drew him back to the present as the gathered straightened in anticipation. The seniormost delinkos grasped a rope leading to the shrine's bronze bell and pulled just as Kaptin Liel's tenor voice sounded the first note of the seeking, a command to attention meant to bring them all together to a single purpose. A tremor ran through the room, reflected unwillingly in Spar's own body, as the combined tone of bell and voice compelled his breathing to the same rhythm as the others.

The bell sounded again, Kaptin Liel sang the second note: a recognition of obligation to Estavia, and the hairs on the back of Spar's neck rose as he felt the assembled seers offer up their individual power to Her service. Suddenly afraid, he opened his mouth to spit out a denial, but the force of their combined will held him silent.

The third note sounded; as each of the battle-seers joined their voices to that of their kaptin, the entire room vibrated with the power of their abilities.

In battle, the fourth note would be a call to arms taken up by every warrior on the field, a preparation for the final note of summoning that would call Estavia to the fray. Today, the end was much more subtle: to touch the dreaming mind of the God without drawing Her from the waters of Gol-Beyaz. Spar felt his own abilities swept along with the rest as the fourth note, deep and soft, lifted their minds and bore them, very quietly and very carefully, to the silver lake. As one, they sank beneath the waves, then as one, they reached out for the slumbering presence of their God.

For a single heartbeat, Spar found himself within their midst. He touched the vast and untamed mind of a being so alien that it made his stomach flip with vertigo, and then he was slapped back into his own body as Estavia's battle-seers were pulled into Her embrace by the power of their oaths.

Without him.

The separation was like a blow to the chest and the bout of longing it invoked enough to make him snap his teeth together in rage. Fighting a wave of dizziness that threatened to drop him to his knees, he struggled to bring his own considerable abilities back on track, then, as the fifth and final note sounded, his mind rose up again, to hover just above the others like a footpad waiting for a gathering of marks to reveal their shine.

Below, the fog that had mystified and angered the temple-seers all season undulated back and forth, obscuring their vision, but events were now in motion and, empowered by their God, they forced their way through it just long enough to see the future it concealed: the Gurney-Dag Mountains and a wave of Petchan raiders sweeping down from the foothills toward the villages of Ekmir-Koy and Kinor-Koy. Numbers, tactics, and objectives streaked past them like a rain of fire and Spar could feel Sable Company's commanders study each one before it was quenched in Gol-Beyaz with a hiss. As the vision came to an end and the fog closed in again, the gathered seers drew back, their satisfaction apparent in the smoothness of their ascent.

Spar remained where he was, his naturally suspicious nature sniffing the breeze in disbelief. It all seemed too easy somehow and no more than they'd already figured out through other means. His own vision had a more specific target in mind and so, resisting the urge to slip into the dark place—he was far too close to both

Sable Company and the Gods to risk its discovery—he reached out toward the streams as a simple street seer might do and spoke one word.

"GRAIZE."

It had been years since he'd sought prophecy this way. The streams which appeared before his eyes writhed like snakes, refusing to be compliant to his will, and with a grimace of impatience, he plunged his hand into their midst, jerking up an entire handful from the depths of Gol-Beyaz. At his command, they froze, then laid their individual potential open for his inspection, but as he bent to study them, the smell of burning swept over him, and he dropped the fistful of streams with a shout.

Years ago, Illan Volinsk had used a vision of burning fields and tumbling stones and dust to terrify a young and untrained seer into submission. Spar had fought him with every ounce of strength he possessed, but it had taken both Elif and Chian to finally drive the northern sorcerer away. But Spar's two protectors were both gone to the dark place now.

A cloud of smoke billowed up around him, stinging his eyes and filling his lungs with a searing heat that made him choke. He couldn't see, couldn't breathe. Far away, he felt Jaq scratching at him desperately, trying to pull him back to the seer's shrine, but the smoke was all around him and he was lost within it. The smell of blood and death filled his nostrils and the sounds of screaming warriors and horses filled his ears. He saw Brax rise up out of the smoke, sword raised, and threw a hand out to him, but then he saw him fall back again, a spray of crimson flying from his mouth transformed to droplets of silver rain. He saw Graize and Hisar appear, saw them leap on the droplets like sharks. He saw Brax die, and then the smoke broiled up again, obscuring everything in his sight.

Falling to his knees, Spar fought to bring the vision back under his own control and then, suddenly, an icy cold wind slapped the smoke away in a whoosh of frigid air. Looking up, he saw the God-Wall looming high above his head as it had done five years before, and with a shout, he leaped, hands and feet scrabbling for purchase against its smooth surface, the clear, open sky beckoning far above him. For one brief moment he broke free, and then the smoke rushed in again and he was falling.

He hit the waves of Gol-Beyaz with a smack that drove the breath from his lungs. The streams became a mass of entangling water reeds, closing over his head, and icy cold water poured into his throat, freezing his mind and body. Darkness rushed over him, but the memory of Brax's impeding death compelled him upward. He shot to the surface, mouth agape, eyes gone as white as any seer's twice his age, and reaching out, he caught up a second fistful of potential streams-cum-water reeds and squeezed.

The reeds writhed and snapped, cracking against his face in their struggle to pull free and then, one by one, they wilted under the pressure of his fist, giving up their tiny allotment of prophecy. A dozen futures laid out like strands of gold-and-silver thread as yet unwoven into the fabric of the world.

In one strand he did nothing and Brax died, in another he was too late and Brax died again. In the third, he called—as Brax had called—to Estavia for salvation, and Brax lived, but behind this future lay years of martial and prophetic training under the command of Sable Company and in the service of the God of War. He saw himself a man, cold and harsh, dressed all in black; embossed leather cuirass beneath a black tabard embroidered with four silver ravens, hurling his abilities against the enemies of Gol-Beyaz. But on the inside, he saw a man he knew, closed off and angry, a jug of raki in one hand. He almost balked, then forced himself to watch as this future unfolded until a battle where, for all his strength, he dropped his guard; where he turned aside for just one moment.

And Brax died. Again.

In the fourth strand, he turned to Incasa and Brax lived, but entangled in that temple's political agenda, Spar saw himself move farther and farther away from his original purpose, and in the end he wasn't there and Brax died again, driven by his oaths to defend their city, alone.

Almost screaming in frustration, Spar hurled these strands aside and bore down upon the rest, demanding a better choice, any choice. He raised and rejected strand after strand, always with the same result: the Gods came to his aid unasked, Illan Volinsk took his service, the Petchans took his life, a golden-haired woman took his hand, but every time his payment was not enough, and in the end Brax still died.

And finally, as he jerked a new handful of reeds from the depths, he saw Graize. Baring his teeth, he shook them until they rattled, knowing that he'd found his answer.

Graize. It always came back to Graize.

Again, the water reeds gave up their prophecies at his command. In the first, he saw Graize leading an army drawn from every people who'd ever called themselves the enemies of Anavatan. He saw Hisar mature in Graize's care to become the first and only undisputed God of the western wild lands and the southern mountains. He saw It reach the God-Wall and, with one blow, smash it to pieces. He saw a flood of spirits sweep across the city and saw Hisar rising over dark and bloody streets as a fleet of ships closed in from north and south. He saw Brax stand alone as the champion of the Gods. And he saw Brax die.

In the second, he saw himself wrest control of Hisar away from Graize, leaving his old enemy dead on the battlefield. He saw Hisar rise up to become the new Deity of Expansion and Conquest, independent of the Gods of Gol-Beyaz. He saw It reach out greedily for followers and he, Its senior-priest, burning with the power of his worship, swept all Its enemies into the sea. This time Brax stood beside him, strong and blazing, but in the end, he fell again, only this time he fell conquering others instead of defending them.

The wind began to howl all around him, tearing at his face and hands. A single reed, caught in the maelstrom, spun in front of his eyes, but bent double above the blood-soaked waves, he couldn't bring himself to reach for it. Beating his fists against his temples, he tried to drive it all away. There were too many futures, too many possibilities. Gasping for breath, he raised his head, eyes gone as black as pitch, and reached out finally for the dark place, too desperate to care who might be watching. There were too many possibilities but there had to be a place, a time, an event where they all came from, something he could focus on to make it all stop. The dark place loomed up before him, promising quiet, peace, and stillness, and he almost fell forward in his relief, but just on the edge, he paused as another chill wind cleared his mind.

A place, a time, an event, or a person; one person. Cursing himself for a panicking idiot, he stood shakily as the wind withdrew and the streams grew still. He'd reached into prophecy as a seer would reach but, knowing all along what he was really looking for, he'd spoken a single word. He'd said Graize and his vision had shown him Graize, but Graize in the distant future.

No, he corrected sternly, pulling himself together; Graize in a distant future of his own design. In the present, Graize was still in the Petchan mountains striving to bring that future into being. He had no great army, not yet. The one place or time or event that each and every stream depended on had not happened yet. Pulling back from the edge of the dark place, he let the color of his eyes return to a seer's white, then stepped forward.

Into the warmth and haze of a High Summer's day. The sky was a pale blue, the clouds a fine, thin line, and the lush grasslands stretching unbroken from the multihued God-Wall in the east to the gray-cast Gurney-Dag Mountains in the west undulated in the breeze. There was no sound of birds or insects, no scent of flowers or grains or animals grazing on the wind, only the vaguest sense of an approaching storm, a charge in the air that made his stomach tighten. In the distance, a small group of figures made their way toward the foothills; figures armed and armored and dressed in tabards of blue and black; a patrol of temple ghazi.

Unnoticed a mile away, the shimmering heat gave the illusion of movement, but as Spar bent his focus toward it, it became a series of mounted figures. For a moment he thought his vision had steered him wrong, that he was reliving the Yuruk attack on Serin-Koy four years ago, but then he realized that, instead of the tall, black-haired nomads of the Berbat-Dunya, these riders were shorter, stockier, with blond hair, pale features, and brightly colored clothing worn under padded jerkins. Petchans. But the weapons they carried were frighteningly similar and so was the danger.

And then he saw Brax in the midst of the patrol. Like a bad dream, Spar saw him moving toward the raiders, but Brax couldn't see them. Clouds covered the sky, casting long shadows across the ground, obscuring the riders still further. It grew dark and cold. Night fell. A three-quarter moon broke from the clouds to illuminate the leader of the Petchans as he stood in the saddle, one hand raised in a gesture so familiar that it made Spar's blood grow cold. He tried to shout a warning, but it was already too late. As the Petchan riders engulfed the much smaller patrol in a cloud of obscuring dust, he thought he saw Hisar soaring high overhead, and then both the riders and the Godling suddenly winked completely out of sight.

"I don't get blocked."

His own words shouted in his mind, repeated over and over, and growing louder and louder until he had to press his hands over his ears again. The wind rose up again, shrieking and howling as the waters of Gol-Beyaz churned and boiled beneath his feet, slapping against his mind with all the power of a typhoon. He screamed out his denial until his voice cracked from the strain.

✦

And then he was back in the seer's shrine, gasping and choking, with Jaq frantically scraping the blood from his mouth where his teeth had gashed his lip, and Kaptin Liel holding him tightly, one hand pressed against his forehead, the other wrapped about his chest.

"I've got you, Delin, I've got you. It's all right now, you're safe now."

Slowly, his breathing calmed. When he slumped, Kaptin Liel turned him and raised his chin with two fingers to meet his white, unfocused gaze.

"Come back, Delin. Spar, come back."

As Spar's eyes slowly cleared, the kaptin gave him a faint, reassuring smile.

"What did you see?"

Spar shook his head, unable to speak, but the kaptin bore down.

"You need to speak of it quickly, or it will haunt you and paralyze you when the time comes to act against it. Now tell me, Delin, what did you see?"

Spar ran one shaking hand across his mouth, smearing blood across his bare forearm. "I saw death," he whispered, his voice a ragged rasp of pain.

"Whose death?"

"Brax's. It's always Brax's." He shuddered. "He was out on patrol and they were ambushed."

"When?"

Spar blinked. "What?"

"When, Delin?" the kaptin repeated firmly. "In the present or in the future?"

Spar forced his mind to relive a small portion of his vision." "In the future," he answered, the relief almost making his knees weak. "In the near future, but in the future."

"And the cause?"

He shuddered. "Our enemy," he whispered.

"What enemy? Give me a name, Delin."

The name was almost impossible to speak out loud, but finally he gasped it out. "Graize."

Once spoken, the fear of it swept away in a rush that made him dizzy. He looked around in confusion, noticing the crowd of seers that crouched around him with a scowl, then pulled away from Kaptin Liel's arms. "It's always Graize," he finished in a stronger voice, pressing his other hand against his throat which throbbed every time he spoke.

"And in how many futures did you see that it was always Graize?" the kaptin asked gently.

Spar blinked again. "What?"

"Futures, how many future did you see, Delin?"

"I don't know." Grimacing, Spar pushed Jaq's head away from his face. "Stop it, Jaq; I'm fine; lay down." Once the dog had dropped reluctantly to the floor, Spar glared at the kaptin resentfully. "Does it matter?" he demanded.

"Yes."

"A dozen, then, I guess. Maybe more."

"And did any of them offer up an alternative? Think, Delin, concentrate. Did any of these futures offer up an alternative to Brax's death even in the short term?"

When Spar nodded slowly, the kaptin straightened. "Good, then the future isn't set, is it?"

"But the alternatives . . ." Spar swallowed unable to face the flood of images again.

"Are ripples in the waters of undesirability," the kaptin finished in a firm voice.

"What?"

"Remember your lessons with Elif, Delin. An alternative stream is shallower, less navigable than a wider, more established stream, but its presence means that the actual future has no set course laid out for it just yet. Its current is still navigable. If that current is undesirable, you can still create a ripple that might change its course and change the future." The kaptin sat back. "Now, reach inside to the place where Brax resides inside your abilities and ask yourself if he is still safe. Come on, Delin, you have a great talent. I know you can do this."

Feeling incredibly exposed in the face of so many watchful eyes, Spar did as he was told, then sagged in relief. "He's safe," he answered. "The ... established stream is there. He hasn't moved out into it yet, but he will soon."

"Good, then we have time."

Spar scowled. "To do what?" he demanded.

"To create the ripple that changes the future. Again, remember your training, Delin, the future is always malleable; our actions make it so. Tomorrow will be different than it might have been because of actions and decisions based on discoveries we make today. That's why we have to keep seeking.

"So we will act on this new discovery to change the future to one we desire," the kaptin continued. "That's what seers do."

Spar's scowl grew deeper. "We cheat?" he asked belligerently.

Kaptin Liel gave him a wide grin, clearly pleased with the word we. "Of course we cheat. We cheat and we spy. The alternative is to allow the future to run about unsupervised like an undisciplined delos, free to do as it pleases to whomever it pleases. Would you rather have it that way?"

"Of course not."

"Then come." Taking his elbow, the kaptin drew him to his feet. "The marshal's sending a contingent of Sable and Bronze Company reinforcements to Alev-Hisar at dawn tomorrow. You'll go with them. In the meantime, I'll send a courier at once with a message for Kaptin

Majin to keep Brax there until we can navigate Estavia's Champion and, by so doing, his entire patrol into an alternative stream that will widen into a safer and more established current. One with no surprise Petchan ambush to be found, yes?" The kaptin gave him a brief grin. "Of course, how you handle his anger at being singled out in such a manner is your own affair."

Spar shrugged dismissively, recognizing the kaptin's attempt at levity while around him, the gathered seers chuckled. Fighting the sudden panicked realization that he was still the center of so much attention, he glanced about at the company he'd spent the last five years avoiding, taking note of the various stages of outer blindness in their eyes with a new understanding.

"I don't get blocked."

No, he allowed, but he could get distracted and so could they. And just as he'd been certain that he'd find Graize at the center of his vision, so they'd been certain that they'd find an organized threat in the Gurney-Dag Mountains poised to strike in the center of theirs, and even now with this new revelation, they weren't looking any further beyond a raid against two villages or a single ambush because they didn't believe—they couldn't believe—that the Petchans, no matter how organized they might be, could be any real threat to the Warriors of Estavia.

A chill wind whispered through his thoughts and he shuddered.

"Seers hate secrets."

Because seers act to change the future to one they desire, and they can't do that if they don't have all the information.

"Their shielding's not strong. If we all work together, it can be easily overcome."

But again, only if they have all the information.

"Obscurity's not found in prophecy, but in the prophets who seed their own desires into their reading of it."

"Yeah, I get it, shut up."

Feeling like he was standing on the edge of a precipice, he pushed the sudden vision of himself wearing the four silver ravens of Sable Company's kaptincy away, and did something he'd never done in his entire life before.

He told them everything he'd seen.

✦

The next evening, standing by the barge rudder, Spar stared at the western shoreline as if he could push the barge faster by will alone. The wind that had sped Brax south had vanished, leaving the surface of Gol-Beyaz glittering with a mirrorlike finish. In the distance, Orzin-Hisar rose above the village of Serin-Koy, the sunlight warming its stone walls in bands of reflected fire. Spar peered out at it, his eyes squinting against the glare and his thoughts in turmoil.

"Don't do anything stupid until I see you."

Shaking his head, he wondered what on earth had prompted him to write Brax such a self-fulfilling prophecy. He might as well have told him to go out and do something reckless on purpose.

But had he?

Closing his eyes, Spar sank into himself, feeling for the present and the future the way he'd done as a child, his abilities spread wide like the whiskers on a catfish, sensitive to any ripple of disquiet that might alert him to approaching danger. Nothing stirred and, pressing his fist against his chest as a focus, he sank farther down, reaching for the place where his sense of Brax resided; a place built of shared memories and experiences; a small delin-alcove off their abayon's room, both warm and safe.

The vision steadied, reflecting Spar's sense of his elder kardos: solid, strong, protective, and confident. There was no accompanying sense of danger or loss, and he breathed a sigh of relief. Although the potential for both still glittered in an unformed future, Brax hadn't done anything yet to bring them into being, either by chance or by design. He was still safe—poised to act—but safe. Spar still had time to deflect this future if he could reach Alev-Hisar before Brax moved. But time was running out; he could feel it.

A breath of hot air flowing across his ankles interrupted his thoughts and he glanced down just as Jaq—ever sensitive to his moods—dropped his muzzle onto his foot.

Spar smiled. "Yes, Delin," he said fondly. "I know, you'll keep me safe from too much melancholy, won't you?"

As Jaq grunted his agreement, Spar glanced past the animal's great square head to Kemal and Yashar talking to the barge-kaptin and Birin-Kaptin Nicurz by the larboard railing. Feet planted on the deck, Yashar's arms were crossed in obvious belligerence and Kemal's right hand rested on the pommel of his sword while the left punctuated his words with short, choppy gestures. They stood side by side, shoulders touching, taking strength in each other's presence, arguing, demanding, that the barge continue on its journey throughout the night. Brax was in danger, Spar had seen it, and their abayon were tired of waiting for Sable Company to decide when to ride to the rescue.

Spar frowned, reluctant to bring the temple-seers to mind but unable to keep himself from watching Birin-Kaptin Nicurz shake her head. She wanted to put in at Serin-Koy for the night, no doubt to convene a seeking at the chapel in Orzin-Hisar. Seers did not like to go anywhere blind.

Around her, the contingent of battle-seers bound for Alev-Hisar crowded the railings, their eyes ranging from clear to opaque as their age and abilities dictated. Seers did not take the world as it came; they knew more than anyone that, even with the aid of the Gods, the world could not be trusted. It was a dangerous place and any heads up, no matter how small, was important.

It was one of the few thing that Spar had admitted to having in common with them because, like it or not, he was one of them; he was a seer. But also, like Kemal and Yashar, he was tired of waiting.

Pressing his back against the railing, he sank down until he sat on the deck beside Jaq. The dog immediately dropped his head into his lap, and stroking the dog's long, soft ears, he lifted his face to the faint breeze coming off the lake. But the warm summer air did little to cool the heat that suddenly rushed into his cheeks. He had taken a single reluctant but significant step toward Sable Company by allying his vision to theirs, regardless of any obligation he may have forged with Incasa and First Oracle Bessic, and there would be no more holding his cards close to his chest now. They knew what he could do, they wouldn't underestimate him again, and it had left him feeling sick to his stomach.

Opening his eyes, he stared deliberately out at the sparkling waters of Gol-Beyaz until he was half-blinded by the glare. *"What's done is done,"* he told himself sternly, shaking off the fear that threatened to constrict his breathing again. *"And this isn't why you're sitting here fretting yourself into a frenzy. Think, stupid; you're missing something, something important, something about Brax."*

He frowned. The only thing he hadn't shared with Sable Company was the one thing he'd missed before, the one thing he'd wanted to miss: the single reed, caught up in the maelstrom, spinning before his face, the alternative that was not his future, but was Brax's, the one alternative that Graize had seen and told Brax about so many years before. The one alternative that Spar had never seen until now. It hung by a single thread of potential so fine that it could still be severed by a breath of air and drowned in the sea of bloodshed that churned all around it, but it was still there.

A brown-haired man, Graize, but older and clear-eyed, armed with steel and stone, standing by Brax's side on a snow-capped mountain ridge.

In this reed's allotment of prophecy, Brax lived.

Knowing what was going to come of it, Spar was barely able to even look at it but it unfolded nonetheless, pressing itself into his vision like a seal in wax. Brax lived and Graize won. Everything. At least everything important. Graize won Brax.

"Don't do anything stupid until I see you."

Rubbing his temples with the tips of his fingers, Spar shook his head. Would Brax even recognize what was stupid and what wasn't in the middle of all this?

"He said he saw us together, him and me."

"He told me that, too. He was always pulling that game, trying to split us up."

"It wasn't a prediction."

Laying the back of his head against the railing, Spar shook his head. "Yes, it was, Brax," he whispered. "And it doesn't matter if we like it or not, because you live, so it has to come true."

The only problem was that he had no idea how to make it come true.

As he closed his eyes, he felt the barge turn in the slow upper current. Birin-Kaptin Nicurz and the barge-kaptin had made their decision. They would put in to Serin-Koy for the night. Sable Company would get its seeking.

Suddenly afraid of what they would find, Spar wrapped his arms about Jaq's neck, and tried to ignore the lump of fear growing in his belly.

13

The Godling

ACROSS THE NORTHERN sea, Hisar reached Cvet Tower as the afternoon sun cast a net of fire across the waves. A solitary figure stood on the rocky shore below. Keeping as quiet and as insubstantial as possible, the Godling held back as the strength of Panos' visioning rippled through the physical world like a stone thrown into a river.

Panos closed her eyes, watching with her inward sight as the ship that was to carry her away to the warm sand and clear turquoise waters of her own lands docked easily, a dozen brightly colored ribbons streaming from its main mast in a rainbow of musical notes.

It wasn't there. Not yet. But it was coming.

Standing on tiptoe, Panos watched the ship waver in and out of sight and then disappear, leaving only the musical ribbons behind. They played a melancholy song of parting before vanishing as well and, as the empty green sea lapped against her mind, she blew it a kiss and turned away, made sad and wistful by the imagery.

King Pyrros of Skiros hovered beneath the surface of her augury like a shark. He would want her by his side when he snatched up his latest prey, the island of Ithos, so dangerously close to Gol-Beyaz. He would want her prophecy and her advice, so she would sail south, away from Volinsk and the man who made her body sing like a nightingale, past her mother's land of cool white pavilions and peaceful daydreams to stand by a royal father made of sun and ice. A father who demanded much and gave very little in return. But that was going to change. She was not a child anymore to be satisfied with a smile and a nod. She had tasted too much of life's bounty. She would not go hungry again.

Reaching down, she ran her fingers along the spiraling outline of an ancient snail shell pressed into the rocks so tightly that it was now nothing more than the shadow of itself. As she spiraled south, so Illan would spiral north, caught up in the twists and bends he himself had set into motion years before. They would meet in the middle, but by then, much of their outline would be lost and their ribbons would be playing two different songs.

Still, she noted, they could be made to play in harmony again. The rocks could press all they liked, but two determined snails might still find their way to the sea. North or south, it hardly mattered if they were together.

Straightening, she plucked two golden hairs from her head and, plaiting them as one, blew them from her fingertips. The breeze spun them toward the water, and she watched until they disappeared. Then, humming contentedly, she made her way back up the path to Cvet Tower as the shadows caressed her ankles. It could be done, and it would be done, prophecy was often as much about action as it was about reaction.

✦

She found Illan in his study, standing before his beautifully drawn map of the southern Deniz-Hadi Sea. The creamy-smooth vellum had been finely detailed by her friend and protector, Hares of Amatus, showing the coastal holdings of the Skirosian dominion at the time. Hares had since added the island of Thasos off the western coast and the seven-island chain of Katus off the east. Only Ithos remained before King Pyrros would become the dominant power in the south. And only Anavatan remained before Prince Illan Dmitriviz Volinsk would become the dominant power in the north. As Panos skipped lightly over the tower's uneven nineteenth step to stand, framed in the doorway, her lover turned to smile at her, his gray eyes warm.

Illan had changed little in the four years since he'd welcomed the seventeen-year-old Oracle of King Pyrros to his solitary home. At twenty-five, his lean face showed no more signs of aging than it had at twenty-one, although his chest and shoulders had filled out and he'd grown his hair, wearing it long and loose in the southern style as she'd asked him to.

"There's a change on the wind," he noted, his well-modulated voice tinged with controlled excitement.

She smiled back at him, coming forward to flow into his arms. "The wind's always changing," she answered, laying her head on his chest and breathing the aromas of wool and leather and the bright scent of pears in brandy that was uniquely his. "It cannot stay still or it dies," she added.

"But when it changes, it grows and sweeps up everything in its path," he replied. "And sometimes they die instead." Stroking her golden hair, he laid his cheek against her forehead. "Vyns tells me your ship has been sighted off the northern coast of Barachois," he said.

"Yes. I dreamed of it last night." She looked up at him, her black, fathomless eyes sparkling with unshed tears. "And of this, our last night together."

He met the prophetic intensity of her gaze with a steady expression of his own. In the last four years, he'd grown accustomed to the sense of light-headed dissociation that came whenever he looked into her eyes; confident that, for him, they held none of the perilous secrets that other people feared.

"You're all packed?" he asked unnecessarily.

She nodded. "Hares had all my things squared away in a musty old sea trunk by yesterday noontime. He's eager to return home."

"But you're not."

"I might be if you were coming with me."

"You know I can't, not yet. I have a journey of my own to make."

"Yes." She pressed her ear against his chest, listening to the strength of the earth pulsing in time with his heartbeat. "To the capital to be presented to your brother's new co-ruler, Tonja of Rostov."

"Halv's death left a convenient political void," he allowed. "I was encouraged to learn that Bryv's advisers had managed to fill it with a marriage rather than a traditional and utterly untenable invasion attempt. Now, for the first time in a century, Volinsk and Rostov are at peace, and we can finally turn our attention to Anavatan."

"As you've planned for so long," she observed, turning to gaze at the atlas table, the carved figurines on its surface already displaying the new political situation: armies drawn back from the borders and a fleet of ships poised to move south. "All the little pieces trotting obediently forward at your command."

"And their first few steps are crucial. I need to be at Bryv's side before Tonja's advisers turn his attention elsewhere. As we've envisioned, there'll be a child within the year, further solidifying their alliance. Before that happens, I need him committed to the invasion of Anavatan. Dagn will help me there, but it will take both of us. We need to be ready to move by the time the spring thaws unlock the sea."

His lip curled in distaste. "The palace will be crowded with people of every description this winter, cluttering up the halls and trampling the gardens, expecting to be feasted and entertained and straining coffers that might be better spent elsewhere."

Reaching up, Panos caught a lock of his hair, curling

it about her fingers until he smiled. "You have no love for people," she noted.

"Not in large groups, no," he allowed. "They muddy the possibilities with their chatter, creating waves of intrigue and chaos in their wake."

"Like a great flock of seagulls, flapping and squawking over a catch of fish," she noted.

"A good image."

Panos smiled dreamily. "And like seagulls," she continued, "they no more influence the possibilities in any lasting way than their feathered counterparts influence the catch."

"They can gobble it all up if there's enough of them," Illan replied dryly. "That would influence the catch."

"Hm, perhaps you need to set a dog on them then to make them mind."

"Perhaps I do," he agreed, "but my very best dog is currently herding Petchan shepherds toward Gol-Beyaz and cannot be spared." He glanced at the atlas table. "The Anavatanon Gods are unsettled with the latest of their number still unbound. The Petchans of the southwest are a visible threat, and the Yuruk of the Berbat-Dunya can be reawakened at a moment's notice. With their enemies closing in from all sides and the center collapsing, the Anavatanon will have no choice but to surrender control of the silver lake to Volinsk when our fleet sails down the Bogazi-Isik Strait."

Reaching up, Panos drew his face to hers until their lips touched.

"How you sparkle with ambition," she murmured. "Like the very stars themselves."

"When I've taken the power of Gol-Beyaz for my own," he agreed, his voice grown thick with the nearness of her, "the strength of my prophecy will shine just as brightly."

Her eyes sleepy with anticipation, Panos flicked the tip of her tongue out to trace the line of his upper lip. "Make love to me," she demanded. "Here by the fire so that the memory of your touch will be as warm as the memory of your ambition when we're parted."

They sank to the floor, their bodies cushioned by the soft, fur rug before the hearth. As they came together, Panos caught sight of a flickering shadow hovering at the window and smiled, her eyes gleaming with a predatory light. Graize's little eavesdropper always added a touch of aggression to Illan's lovemaking almost as if her northern sorcerer could sense Its presence.

It tiptoed across her consciousness, leaving tiny footprints of peppermint and jasmine behind, and she smiled again.

The creature had spent much of Its time with Graize in the last four years, draped about his neck, or flitting about his head as he walked and rode and climbed the rough hillsides around Cvet Tower, seeking the solitary places as many prophets did, where he could read the future unimpeded. Panos had watched Its form grow ever stronger and more corporeal as the months had passed.

She shivered with pleasure. It was so close to discovering the gratifications of the physical for Itself. So very close. If It was lucky It would avoid the nasty, silver mortar the Gods of Gol-Beyaz were mixing up to turn It into a good little tower because that mortar would kill any potential It might have for the physical. It would fix It firmly in the silver lake, leaving no more footprints to mark Its passage, and that would be such a shame. Perhaps she should help It. She liked peppermint and jasmine.

One hand kneading the nape of Illan's neck, she turned and beckoned at the window with the other, inviting and daring the half-grown creature to join them.

With a startled flutter, the shadow disappeared and Panos began to laugh.

✦

Rattled, Hisar sped back across the northern sea. It had watched the two foreign oracles having sex many times, sometimes alone and sometimes in the early days in concert with Spar, holding a tendril of the boy's mind up to the window so he could see. This was the first time It had ever been discovered.

It froze, a new thought sending a shiver of anxiety down Its ethereal spine.

Or so It had thought.

Buzzing the western coast of Barachois Island, It circled uncertainly above the ruins of an old stone fishing village. Panos had stared right at It with her deep, black eyes, so like Spar's when he visited the dark place. Stared at It like she knew It, like she'd seen It before, like she'd seen *inside* It before. And maybe she had. Maybe she'd seen It every time. Maybe this was just the first time she'd let It know she'd seen It.

Beating Its wings against the air current to stay in place, It struggled against a rising tide of panic. If that were true, why would she reach out to It now?

It paused, allowing the wind to push It backward toward the open sea.

Because It was alone.

The panic receded as a frown darkened the iridescence of Its dragonfly form. Did that mean that she wanted to talk to It or, like Incasa, she wanted to harm It?

And could she really harm It? Was she as powerful as a God?

And why was It afraid that she could? Couldn't It hurt her back, or even first?

It beat the air with Its wings once more, anger darkening Its form still further Why, It demanded of Itself, was Its first reaction always fear?

In a shower of iridescent feathers, It spun about and shot south again. It needed to talk to someone, to ask someone. Spar was sailing down Gol-Beyaz; It could feel the pressure of the Gods' domain pressing against Its breast. Brax didn't want to talk to It at all. That left Graize hiding out in his mountain cavern like some kind of great gray bat. Graize would answer Its questions whether he wanted to or not, even if It had to smash through the muting effect on that cavern like It had smashed through the wards on the Hukumet's vision-house. Graize had told It that nothing could keep them separated if either of them desired to come together. And It desired to come together. Now. It was tired of waiting.

Catching the wind, Hisar made for the northern coast of the Berbat-Dunya and from there, to the Petchan Mountains, feeling both anger and apprehension in equal measure.

✦

In the darkened waters of Gol-Beyaz, Oristo stirred, made uneasy by the strength of Hisar's loneliness and confusion. Rising to the surface, the God of Children stared out at the distant mountains with a frown then, drinking in the strength of the people settling before their fires and into their beds for another night, lifted one ruddy-brown hand in readiness. The delos had called and Graize, Its abayos, would answer. Whether he wanted to or not.

✦

Miles away, seated on Dar-Sayer's rug, Graize let out his breath in a fine, controlled stream. He had no idea how many days or nights he'd been here. He slept and dreamed, awoke and dreamed. Nir brought him food and drink and helped him in and out of Dar-Sayer's steaming pool while the oracle spoke to him in a low voice filled with secrets and the past crashed over him with the force of a hailstorm. But afterward, wrapped in woolen blankets before the fire, he floated in a silence so complete that he sometimes wondered if he'd actually died in this place.

Slowly, so very slowly that he could not have said when it happened, he began to perceive the tiniest bits of prophecy that had somehow managed to worm their way through the muting effect. They flickered in the silence all around him like delicate, silver fireflies and, as he breathed them in, they flowed down his throat like ice, blossoming in his mind with a familiarity that made him bare his teeth in pleasure. They were not spirits, not yet, and their tiny allotment of power did little more than reawaken his hunger, but they would do for now.

Carefully and very, very slowly, he began to weave them together in much the same fashion as he'd woven Hisar all those years ago, but this time, instead of merging them together, he held them separate but connected so that their combined power would not trigger the muting effect. And bit by bit, he came to understand their essence.

The water spirits of the mountains streams ran in silver torrents down the crevasses and gullies during the spring thaws and autumn rains. They filled the rivers and tributaries that eventually found their way to Gol-Beyaz, bringing the seeds of the mountain's muting effect in the bits of rock and sand that tumbled in around them. But unlike the spirits of the mountains who feared this muting effect, the Gods had found a way to fashion it to Their own design. They had used it to build a great wall of power and protection which held the weaker members of Their kind at bay.

Clever Gods.

But over time, the smallest of the wild lands spirits, born of storm and sky rather than earth and ice, had wormed their way through the Gods' wall and had come together to become one vast, swarm of destructive instinct. His tiny fireflies could be made to do the same.

For him.

Time passed. Graize ate and slept and worked and slept again. Using the combined power of his fireflies as a shield against the muting effect, he sent his mind out to flit around the cavern, keeping it well away from Nir and Dar-Sayer sleeping to either side of him. The tunnel mouth beckoned, and slowly he drew closer, testing the strength of his woven shield with every inch. It held, and he made his way down its length with greater and greater confidence. The nearer he got to the outside world, the stronger the shield grew and the weaker the muting effect became until, finally, he hovered at the very edge of the cavern, the two held in perfect balance within his mind. Then, reaching out, he began to weave them together in a more intricate pattern of symmetry and strength. When the pattern solidified, he slid back down the tunnel and into the cavern once again, drawing it behind him.

As he rejoined his body, the pattern remained, the two conflicting elements fused into a single, workable whole containing both protection and power. Almost like a wall, he noted, only better, lighter, more flexible, and more portable; like a cloak providing both clarity and deflection.

The secret of the Petchans?

He nodded to himself. He could leave now, he thought. If he wanted to. Dar-Sayer had nothing more to teach him. He could take this new power and use it to defeat his enemies and silence the memories that echoed through the chambers of his mind; silence the memories of the dark-haired boy and remake him in the image of the man he should have been, or silence him altogether. Once and for all.

If he wanted to.

A single thread of prophecy feathered through his mind, whispering of many paths not just the one he'd set his feet upon, but he ignored it. To win the game, he needed a single path that was clear and simple, a single path to win the shine he desired: possession and revenge.

Reaching out, he drew that path from their midst: a waning moon still bright and clear that shone down on his present and his future. With that decided, he had all he needed to win the game and that was all that mattered. Satisfied, he drew the cloak tightly about his mind until its essence merged with his, then gave himself over to the deep, dreamless sleep it provided.

✦

What seemed like hours but might have been no more than a few moments later, a silvery presence he'd not felt since he was a child—not icy cold, but warm like the banked coals of a cami's fire—brushed against the edge of his perception.

Graize opened his eyes, taking a moment to orient himself to the unfamiliar clarity of the cloak's perceptions, all his senses suddenly, painfully alert. The orange glow from the coals warmed the hanging rock pillars above his head in layers of shimmering fire that burned his eyes, while the damp scents of rock and water mingled with the pungent aromas of goats hides and sweat, so strong it made his head ache. To either side of him, Dar-Sayer's breathing—deep and calm—and Nir's—higher and more shallow—sounded like thunder in his ears. He tasted the hint of copper on his lips and felt the rough fibers of his shirt catch against the hairs along his arms, and deep within his mind, he felt a heavy, resonant pounding as if another's heartbeat competed with his own.

Raising himself on one elbow, he stared into the darkness. The silvery-warm presence, held in check by the cavern's muting effect, pressed against the opening in his mind, created by his memory. Unable to do more than amplify the pounding, it bent to that task until the sound reverberated through his body; urgent, demanding, and familiar. Eyes narrowed, he shook off the blanket, then stood and headed down the tunnel.

Even before he reached the opening, he knew what he would find.

✦

Taking the form of Maf's hunting eagle, claws out-stretched, beak open wide in a shriek of frustration and outrage, Hisar hurled Itself at the cavern mouth for the dozenth time, hitting the muting effect head-on. The impact sent It flying backward to slam against a jut of rock thirty feet away. Wobbling slightly, It rose into the air, turned, and hammered against the muting effect again. And was thrown back again, one limb twisted un-naturally behind It, onto the same jut of rock.

Reflex snapped It into Its most familiar Caleb-seeming, but older now and with a greater understanding of physical wounds, the boy's past bound and broken arm sent a shock of pain through the Godling's twisted limb and It gasped in surprise. It struggled a moment, Its misty chest rising and falling in the parody of panicked breathing; then it finally lay still, spent and weak.

Its various seemings flickered over Its body until It settled on Kursk, the strong and pragmatic Rus-Yuruk leader who had given his life to save Caleb's four years before. The new form brought a wave of calm to combat the pain, and eventually the latter faded to a resentful memory. Rising to Its knees, Hisar considered the cavern mouth with a dark but even expression. It was still resolved to force Its way to Graize, whatever it took, but if It couldn't batter Its way in, perhaps It could sneak in.

One by one, It considered each of the human-seemings in Its arsenal: Kursk, Ozan, Danjel, Rayne, Caleb, Brax, and even Spar and Graize, then rejected them. If Maf's eagle couldn't get through the muting effect, a person couldn't; clearly they were too big.

As for animal-seemings, Jaq wouldn't do either. Hisar hadn't managed to work out the dog's seeming to Its satisfaction yet; Its animal form coupled with its nearly human emotions and reactions were harder to hold to-gether than they appeared.

Hisar's dragonfly form was strong and resilient, but It had tried to enter the cavern in that form at the beginning and been hit harder than It had in the eagle form. It needed something smaller, something tighter, something less obvious, simpler and more ... physical.

The memory of Graize and Danjel sitting on a similar rocky ledge made It pause. Graize had called Danjel swallow-kardos after the wyrdin's birth fetish creature. Swallows were small.

Hisar narrowed Its eyes. And Caleb's mouse fetish was smaller still.

Rising into the air, It flew to the mouth of the cavern in eagle form, landing just shy of the entrance. Then, taking the mouse-seeming, It crept forward more slowly this time, feeling the pressure of the muting effect press against Its chest like a great hand. The mouse-seeming wavered, but Hisar bore down, holding the form steady as It pushed on, one tiny footstep after another, as if It were fighting Its way through high winds.

Pressure became pain radiating down Its back and limbs in waves of disruption. The memory of Incasa's attack filled Its mind, trying to force a change to Its tower form, but with streaks of silver light sparking off Its body, Hisar ignored it. The tower form was strong and impervious, but it couldn't move forward, and Hisar was determined to move forward. Another step, another wave of pain. It stumbled, and another memory rose up, silver like Incasa, but warm instead of cold, one of Graize's memories from years ago. It beckoned to the Godling, offering strength and comfort, and Hisar paused, uncertainty causing Its seeming to waver once again, but eventually It ignored the silvery warmth as well. Hisar did not know this presence, but It knew enough to know that it was of the Gods and so could not be trusted; Graize and Spar had both taught It that.

Hisar pushed on, the pain radiating across Its tiny form in pulsing waves of fire and ice, growing with every step. Finally, it became too great, the mouse-seeming disintegrated, and the muting effect rushed in to slap It down like a great hand. For a split second, the Godling was outlined in a blazing conflagration of gold-and-silver agony, then It collapsed. As It opened Its mouth to scream, a sudden gout of power shot out from the tunnel entrance, and the pain snuffed out like a candle. A familiar presence snatched It up, wrapping the tattered remnants of Its essence in bands of strength and comfort. As Its form solidified once more into Its dragonfly-seeming, It looked up into Graize's wide gray eyes, clear and even for the first time in Its very short life. Under the pressure of his gaze, Hisar changed.

✦

Standing just out of sight, Graize had watched, fascinated, as the Godling had fought the muting effect, beating the mountain's natural defense against Its kind, slowly but surely, one inch at a time. The urge to go to It and to protect It as he had after the Hukumet had scrabbled against his conscience, abetted by the unwelcome silvery-warm presence of his childhood, but his curiosity to see what would happen next had held him immobile. Staring through the cloak's new perception, he'd watched as the Godling's form had wavered, melted, and solidified, over and over again.

The silvery-warm presence, unable to do more than buzz against his mind like an angry wasp, had grown more and more agitated as he'd remained unmoved, but he'd ignored it. Finally, however, as the very fabric of the Godling's being had begun to unravel, he'd thrust the presence aside impatiently and stepped forward. The mouse-seeming had disintegrated and the Godling had taken the full force of the muting effect's attack against Its immature body. It had opened Its mouth to scream, and then Graize had caught It up in his arms, his new protective cloak wrapped about them both like a balm. The Godling had opened Its glazed and pain-filled eyes to stare into his, and something deep in Graize's own eyes had caused a shudder to run through Its body.

It changed.

And Brax stared up at him, the ethereal red-lined scar across his cheek standing out in sharp relief through an unfamiliar growth of beard.

Graize drew in a hiss of breath. He stared down at It for what seemed like an eternity until he spat out a single word, "Why?"

The Godling flinched away from the harshness in his voice, but spent and exhausted, It continued to stare up at him in mute entreaty, the Brax-seeming's dark eyes dull with the memory of pain. Breathing deeply, Graize used his new clarity to smooth his own expression to one devoid of anger and suspicion.

After Its final birthing on the battlements of Estavia-Sarayi, the Godling had formed human-seemings to bond to a physical form, including Brax's. But Brax had been fifteen that night, as young and clean-shaven as Graize himself had been. This seeming was older, Graize's age as he was now.

An unfamiliar growth of beard.

Graize narrowed his eyes. Unfamiliar to him, but clearly not unfamiliar to the Godling. A more important question than why suddenly filled his mind.

"Have you seen the man who wears this form?" he asked, biting back a snarl as he heard the quaver in his voice.

The Godling nodded weakly.

"When?"

The creature stared searchingly up at him, a dozen conflicting emotions chasing themselves across Its face, the pain and weariness in Its eyes causing the Brax-seeming to age a dozen years at once. Above them, the silvery warmth moved closer, drawn by Its distress, to become the shadowy outline of a ruddy-hued figure cradling bread and fire in Its arms.

Graize bared his teeth at It. "Back off," he snarled, using the muting effect inherent in the cloak's protective focus as a weapon. "You're not wanted here—by either of us."

The Hearth God's image grew faint but, held by the Godling's distress, stared down at him coldly before turning to Hisar. The Godling blinked in surprise yet managed another weak nod, and slowly, the ruddy-brown face displaying little beyond suspicious disapproval, Oristo disappeared again.

Graize sat down with his back pressed against the outer wall of the cavern, the Godling still cradled in his arms, his own expression dark and thoughtful. "Interfering know-it-all Kitchen God," he muttered.

A shudder traveled the length of the Godling's body, and Graize found himself stroking Its tangled hair almost absently. "It's all right, little Spirit-Delin," he said. "I'm not mad. Well, not at you, anyway," he amended. "But this seeming is Brax, not Brax on the battlements, but Brax as he might be today. Have you seen him recently, Delin?"

After a moment, the Godling nodded once again and Graize frowned. Five years ago, when the creature had been little more than raw potential created by Graize's own manipulation of the wild lands spirits, It had formed words in his mind, eager and impatient to know his thoughts. But since that time It had kept predominantly to Its dragonfly form and Graize had all but forgotten that It could speak at all.

"When?" he pressed. "Tell me in words; I know you have words, you pooled enough of them into my head in the past. When did you see him last?"

The Brax-seeming's eyes showed surprise. Its throat worked silently, and then the Godling whispered one word. "Yesterday."

Yesterday. Graize stilled the urge to tighten his grip as a surge of shock and jealousy threatened to overwhelm his newly found clarity, but the protective cloak held, and he took a deep, quieting breath and forced his fingers to relax as a new thought fought through the jealousy. *The Godling had seen Brax yesterday, and nothing in his prophecy had given him warning. Clearly, the muting effect was a dangerous and double-edged sword.*

Not trusting himself to look down into Brax's face for fear the jealousy would cloud his thinking once again, Graize stared sightlessly at the dawn-streaked mountainsides all around him, feeling for the familiar sense of the Godling's essence, *his* Godling's essence—instead. "Where was he?" he asked as casually as he could manage.

"On a tower."

"In Anavatan? In the shining city?"

"No. Beside the shining lake."

A village tower, then.

"Did he see you?"

There was a long pause. When the Godling finally spoke, Graize could hardly hear It.

"Yes."

"Did he recognize you from the battlements?"

Again the quiet affirmative.

Graize frowned, his new clarity unable to compete with the multitude of questions and unwelcome emotions this revelation evoked. Finally, he brought up the old familiar image of his stag beetle to calm his thoughts and once the questions had receded, he took another, quieting breath.

"Why ... ?" He paused, uncertain of how to even phrase the question. He was not used to asking for knowledge. That wasn't how the game was played. In the game you studied the marks carefully, pretending that you already knew the answers, leading or tricking them into revealing what you needed to know. You found out what they wanted—by prophecy or any other means available—and you used it to get what you wanted. And you never, ever betrayed your own ignorance.

But the rules of the game didn't apply to the Godling, he suddenly realized, because he didn't actually know what the Godling wanted.

It had never occurred to him that It might want anything at all. And so the Godling had reached out to get what It wanted—*what It needed*—from ... Graize's lips peeled back from his teeth at the thought. *From Brax.* And he hadn't seen it.

Two serious mistakes he'd never made before. His expression hardened. And he would not make again.

Closing his eyes for a moment to recalibrate his position, Graize then deliberately stared down at the creature's Brax-seeming.

"What were you doing at a tower off the shining lake?" he asked, keeping his tone as even as possible.

The Godling squirmed in his arms. "You were gone from me," It said in a petulant tone. "You said we couldn't be kept apart, but we were. And I had questions. I couldn't go to Panos or Illan. I tried, but they were having sex, and besides, I've never talked to them before. I'm not used to talking." It trailed off, the unfamiliar flow of words too much for It in Its weakened state.

Graize gave It a firm look, refusing to be sidetracked with new questions about Panos or Illan. "You asked Brax questions?" he pressed.

The Godling looked away. "You were gone from me," It repeated quietly.

"What did you ask him?"

The same conflicting emotions chased themselves across the Godling's features, but eventually It gave a one-shouldered shrug that seemed strangely familiar. "Nothing. He started talking about other things and I got confused."

"He started talking? To you? What about?"

"Just things. I can't remember."

A sharp, spiking headache began to throb at Graize's right temple. He tried a different tack. "What did you want to ask him?"

This time the Godling closed Its own eyes briefly. "Why ... I can be hurt?"

Graize sighed. "Because you exist, Delin," he said simply.

"But I'm not physical."

"No, you're not, but you're not metaphysical either, not completely. Not anymore."

"Because I fed from Brax?"

Graize stilled a thrill of warning. "Maybe," he allowed cautiously.

"I never tasted anything like his essence before," the Godling admitted. "That's why I talked to him. It was strong. I wanted more."

"All the Gods want more."

"Is that why everyone's always thinking about him," It asked in a hesitant voice, "because they want more, too?"

Graize blinked rapidly. This was not the question he'd been expecting. "Who's always thinking him?"

"You; all the time."

"No, I'm not."

"Yes, you are."

"No . . ." Graize shook his head irritably to rid it of the sudden feeling that he was nine years old. "I think about Brax sometimes," he allowed.

"Why?"

"For different . . . complicated reasons. But not because I want more of his . . . essence."

The Brax-seeming gave him a disbelieving look. "Do you want to have sex with him?"

Unaccountably, Graize found himself growing red. "Why do you want to know that?" he demanded. "No, forget it, it's not important. Why do you want to know why I think about Brax?" He caught the Godling in a penetrating stare. "Does it bother you?"

The Godling squirmed uncomfortably in his arms. "No. Not . . . really."

"Not really but really."

"No, it's just . . ." The Godling gave Its one-shouldered shrug again. "It's physical, and the physical is . . . confusing."

Graize gave a bark of laughter. "No, it isn't." Resting
the back of his head against the cool rock of the cavern
entrance, he stared out at the rising sun, his expression
amused. "The physical is easy," he said. "It's obsessed
with its own needs and those are too simple for words:
food, drink, comfort, safety."

"And sex?"

"Most definitely sex."

"But not essence?"

"No, not really."

"Then why?"

"Because it feels good."

"That's all?"

"That's everything."

"Essence feels good."

Graize nodded. "Yes, but sex feels better."

"Oh." The Godling sounded unconvinced but did
not press the issue, and after a moment, Graize looked
down at It again.

"Back to the point on the table, little Spirit-Delin."
Catching the Godling's face between his palms, he
stared deliberately into Its dark eyes, willing the creature's essence to overshadow Brax's memory. "You said
you saw Brax yesterday and that the two of you talked.
So he knew what you were, but he didn't try to hurt you
or drive you away?"

"No." The Godling answered the question at once,
but Its voice was a little unsure and Graize cocked his
head to one side, schooling the predatory gleam in his
eyes to one of mere curiosity.

"No?"

"Not . . . at first."

"But later."

"Yes. The next time."

The next time. Graize pressed his fingertips to the
bridge of his nose as the throbbing in his right temple
moved across to his left. The surprises were coming
thick and fast today. It was clear that there were a dozen

different subjects to explore, the one leading to another and that one to yet another and another yet again, like picking up whelks in the sand, but each one leading you farther and farther away from the safety of the beach until the tide took you unawares. Graize narrowed his eyes. He was never taken unawares. He kept his focus on the game, whatever else might be happening all around him, and he always got away safely with his whelks intact.

"Place your shine, place your shine."

The memory of a thousand screaming spirits tearing at his mind and body whistled through his thoughts like the wind through an empty hall, and he shoved it aside with an impatient grimace. He'd won that fight, and the only reason to revisit the battlefield was to plan a new engagement against the opposing general.

Under the familiar pressure of his thinking a single prophetic image squeezed through the protective cloak: a moon, almost full in a cloudy sky. He nodded.

"Do you know where Brax is now?" he asked, catching the Godling in a firm stare.

The Godling shrugged uncomfortably. "No."

"But you *can* find him?"

"Yes."

"Without him seeing you?"

"Yes."

"And are you strong enough to make the journey now?"

"I think so."

"Good." Graize stood, the creature still cradled in his arms. "Why don't you go do that now, then come and find me?"

"Why?"

"Because I want to know where he is. For those complicated reasons I mentioned before," he added.

The Godling eyed the cavern with trepidation and resentment equally mixed. "Where will you be?" It asked, the petulant tone back in Its voice.

"I'll be following a moon back to Chalash to reconvene the Hukumet."

The Godling blinked but, used to Graize's multilayered comments, shook Its confusion off quickly in the light of a more important concern. "You won't be gone from me again?" It demanded.

"No." Graize caught the Godling in his new even stare again. "I'll never be gone from you again."

Its expression still uncertain, the Godling nodded, then, returning to Its dragonfly-seeming, rose slowly from Graize's arms, hovered a moment, and headed east.

Graize watched until It was out of sight, then began to make his own way down the cliff face, his expression dark. *"I won't be gone from you again,"* he thought, *"and you won't be gone from me either. Brax is not going to take you from me again."*

14

The Grasslands

HISAR FLEW SLOWLY over the mountaintops as the rising sun painted the sky with streaks of pink and yellow. Its sense of Brax told It that he was moving west and so, wheeling about in an awkward bank, It headed off on a course that would intercept his trail, Its form still trembling in the wake of Its earlier struggle.

It faltered for a moment as the memory took possession of Its limbs, causing It to lose altitude until It hovered no more than a few inches off the ground. The pain at the cavern's mouth had been even more frightening than Incasa's attack and had lasted far longer. Graize's interrogation had been just as distressing, coming as it had so soon after Brax's warning. The need to be comforted warring with a newly-forged instinct to be cautious, Hisar had fielded his questions as best It could. And in the end both the pain and the questions had been worth it. Graize had come back and had promised that he would never go away again. That was all that mattered.

Heartened by Its victory, the Godling rose into the air once more, snatching at a few stray spirits made sluggish by the dawn. Their power gave It new energy and with a burst of speed, It cleared the mountaintops, the rugged landscape below passing by in a blur of indistinct green-and-gray shadows. Within a few moments It had reached the foothills and, after taking the form of a wild lands hunting hawk, It made for the line of silver light on the eastern horizon that betrayed the presence of Gol-Beyaz to Its spirit-born eyes.

By the time the sun had reached its zenith, It had spotted the shape of a militia patrol in the distance. Wheeling about, It caught an updraft which carried It close enough to find Brax's distinctive gait among the other helmeted, armor-clad figures and, with a triumphant cry, It folded Its wings and dropped.

✦

On the grasslands, Brax watched a marsh hawk disappear into a thick patch of grass before returning his attention to the western sky. The midday sun was a brilliant disk of white-and-blue fire shimmering through a thin layer of cloud and he stared up at it until his eyes were dazzled by sunspots then looked away.

Beside him, the twins plucked strands of fine grass from the fields, plaiting them into rings before throwing them at each other while the five older members of the troop looked on, amused. Despite their status as full temple ghazi, Brin and Bazmin had always enjoyed the role of precocious delinkon.

A quarter mile ahead of them, Sarqi and Khair, the patrol's battle-seer and mounted militia scout, walked their horses together, scanning the skies and talking quietly. A bank of storm clouds was gathering to the far west above the distant mountaintops, flashes of lightning skipping back and forth with the barest hint of thunder to mark its passage, but here on the grasslands, everything slumbered in the summer haze; quiet, still, and peaceful.

Brax stifled a yawn.

They'd left Alev-Hisar immediately after the Morning Invocation, one of five units sent out on the first of the four-day patrols ordered by Kaptin Majin. Stirring up clouds of insects, they'd made their way through the cultivated fields and into the grasslands beyond just as the dawn sun had lit up the morning mist in a fine spray of golden dust.

Glancing back at the watchtower's tall black silhouette, Brax had wondered where Spar was at that moment.

"Don't do anything stupid until I see you."

Brax shrugged. If Spar were taking ship that morning, he would reach Alev-Hisar tomorrow noon at the very latest. He'd be upset to find Brax gone, but there was no helping that. Brax was a ghazi; he went where he was told to. Spar would spend his time fretting and rehearsing what he would snarl at him when Brax returned, but there was no helping that either. That was what Spar did. That was what all seers did. They fretted and they snarled.

Catching one of the twins' rings, Brax twirled it about his finger as the patrol began to ascend a small rise. The grasslands were not as flat as they appeared from a distance; the ground undulated up and down, sometimes quite steeply. Any number of these shifts in elevation could hide a Petchan patrol. Standing at the top, one fine hand shielding her mist-covered eyes from the sun, Sarqi scanned the surroundings carefully before pointing to the west.

"Do you see that collection of rocks in the distance?"

The rest of the patrol squinted in the direction she indicated, but only Khair nodded from his extra vantage point above his mount.

"The ground rises to that spot," she continued. "It would afford us a full view of the area all the way to the edge of the foothills were we to make it our sentry place."

"I mark it a day and a half's travel away," Khair agreed. "Barring any unforeseen delays due to weather, of course," he added with a dubious look to the west.

As the wind picked up, rustling the grasses around their feet, Sarqi frowned. "The haze does seem to be thickening rather than receding," she allowed. "And there's a growing sense of expectation in the air."

Scratching absently at the faint scar across his cheek, Brax squinted at the shimmering horizon. "A storm, Seer?" he asked.

She shrugged, "Most likely, Ghazi," she answered, but her expression remained unconvinced.

Behind them, the troop exchanged a knowing glance; seers hated committing themselves in case they were wrong, and seers hated being wrong.

"There's no cover, Seer," Brin now pointed out in a hopeful voice as if Sarqi were capable of redirecting the weather. "If a storm catches us here, we'll spend a wet time out in the open."

One of the older ghazi gave an unimpressed snort. "Do you melt, Ghazi-Delin?" he asked in a sour voice.

Unoffended, Brin just laughed. "Not at all, Feridun-Sayin, but I squelch and my leathers squeak. You would find it highly annoying after a mile or two, I think."

"Not I; I've been deaf to such noises for years."

"I envy you."

"Enough." Sarqi turned an impatient scowl on them both. "Come, we have a lot of ground to cover before nightfall unless you really do want to be caught out in the open."

Without waiting for an answer, she urged her mount down the other side of the rise and, after shooting a warning glare at both Feridun and Brin, Khair followed.

The two shared a philosophical shrug. "It's as I've often said," Feridun observed, his voice as sour as before, "seers have no appreciation for a good argument."

"And riders have no appreciation for those who move on foot," Brin agreed. "I'll bet those rocks are more like two days away than a day and a half and no real cover to speak of, anyway, once we do reach them."

Feridun snorted again. "I'd take your bet, Ghazi, if I could even see those rocks," he groused.

"But you've been blind to such sights for years as well, Sayin?"

"At the very least. Besides, it matters little to me. One day out or two days out; it's all the same. I'm no scout. My duty is to protect my home from the enemy, and I can hardly do that from so many miles away."

"I suppose," Brin replied carelessly, catching up another blade of grass. "My home is Adasi-Koy, and I haven't been back for two years."

"You're young. It's your duty to endure long absences without complaint until you're old enough to earn it."

"That's true, and it makes me a much more pleasant traveling companion in the meantime."

"Hmph." Turning his back on this last comment, Feridun fell into step behind the others who'd already started down the rise and, with a smug expression at having gained the last word, Brin went after him.

Brax gestured the rest of the troop to follow, then paused as a strange noise at his feet made him turn. He stared a moment at the undulating grasses around him, but when the noise was not repeated, he shook his head. The haze was changing and amplifying everything so that even the most ordinary sounds seemed alien. With an irritated sigh, he made his own way down the rise after the others, catching another of the twins' grass rings as it was tossed back to him.

✦

As the patrol headed across the grasslands again, Hisar rose from the grass beside the imprint of Brax's left sandal, hovered a moment, then sped off toward the distant mountains, the flickers of lightning in the distance reflecting off Its gossamer wings with a scattering of metallic brilliance.

✦

"He's on a rise in the middle of the grasslands with nine others."

"Warriors?"

"All but one."

"Are they mounted?"

"Only two of them."

"But not Brax?"

"No."

Graize smiled.

✦

The Godling had returned to him just after midday. Standing under a narrow outcropping of rock where he'd taken refuge after a heavy summer storm had swept across the mountains, he'd spotted the creature swooping in and out of a heavy cloud bank to the east. He'd given a piercing whistle. Dropping from the sky, It had accepted a small seed of power, then spun about his neck like a living scarf, Its earlier trauma forgotten in Its eagerness to give Its report.

"One of the riders is a seer," It added now, Its voice buzzing musically in his ear.

"A patrol," Graize noted with satisfaction, "and straying ever so far from home." Catching up a fallen tree branch, he stripped the leaves away, one by one, with a thoughtful expression. "How long do you suppose it might take to reach this patrol?" he asked after a moment.

The Godling considered the question. "Two days maybe, but they're coming even closer than that, to a pile of rocks at the edge of the foothills," It added. "They'll be no more than one day's ride away then. They think they'll reach it by dusk tomorrow. Then in the morning they're going back to their tower. I heard them talking about it while I was hiding at their feet as an insect." It added proudly. "They never saw me."

Graize gave It a lazy smile. "That's very good, Delin," he crooned, reaching up to stroke Its flank. "But can you do one better? Can you go back and keep an eye on them for me, secret, secret like a little mouse, then come and find me as soon as they reach that pile of rocks?"

"Yes."

"Good. Go do that."

The Godling lifted into the air with a snap of Its iridescent wings, disappearing into the bank of clouds a second later.

Graize watched It go, then continued on his way with a satisfied expression.

In the game you found out what the mark wanted, and you used it to get what you wanted.

He nodded to himself. He'd been momentarily nonplussed to think that the Godling might not be playing by the same rules as everyone else, but he should have known better. Everyone played by the same rules: people, Gods, spirits, and Godlings. Now that he knew what his Godling wanted—attention and approval like any other delos—the game could continue on as smoothly as before.

Pausing on the edge of a narrow crevasse, he gave in to the deep chuckle of greedy anticipation that was rumbling inside his chest. Brax was coming to within one day's ride away. *One* day.

Closing his eyes, he rolled the words silently around his tongue, savoring the sense of electric excitement they evoked. The timing was perfect. His Petchans were ready and eager to ride. A dozen raiding parties could be sent out by dawn tomorrow with a handpicked band of his own heading straight for the Godling's pile of rocks. Plenty of time to set up a proper greeting for his old acquaintance and no time at all for Brax's vigilant, little street-rat baby-seer to do anything about it even if he discovered it.

Opening his eyes, Graize reached up to caress the thick bank of clouds above his head with his fingertips. Especially if he discovered it, he added gleefully. And he would discover it; Graize would see to it that he did. It was too easy. All he had to do was lay his plan out as simply and directly as possible with none of the shrouding layers of subterfuge and deception that he usually employed to befuddle his enemies. The little rat-seer was always sweeping his beady little prophetic eyes back and forth, always on the lookout for the slightest sign of danger to himself and his beloved Brax. With the bait left lying so clearly in the road like this, he'd be hit with all the force of a runaway cheese wagon and before he knew it he would be a squashed and flattened little rat-seer because Brax was one day's ride away and Spar, wherever he might be, was not.

As his plan took shape in his mind, new elements appeared, scattering across the protective cloak like a handful of stars scattered across the night's sky. Under the cloak's focusing power, they came together with a speed he'd never experienced before. The moon he'd seen at the cavern mouth rose from the depths of his prophecy, blazing out through a break in the clouds with a near physical intensity to illuminate first an expanse of grasslands and a jumble of black rocks and then a small cave, which, like Dar-Sayer's cavern, winked in and out of sight like a lantern swaying in the wind.

Graize began to laugh, throwing his exultation at the surrounding mountainsides in near hysterical triumph. He'd waited so long and soon his revenge would be complete. The moon had shown him the way.

Leaping the crevasse, he continued on his way to Chalash at a run, eager to reach the Hukumet and set his plan into motion.

✦

Away to the east the sun made its slow journey across the sky, sending long fingers of shadow stretching over the grasslands whenever it managed to break through the gathering bank of storm clouds above.

Sarqi called a halt just after dusk. After setting the watch, Brax filled his waterskin at a nearby stream, watching the sun's pale light disappear behind the distant foothills with a frown of unease as behind him the patrol made a cold camp, sharing a meal of flatbread and salted pork rather than risk a fire that might reveal their position to an enemy patrol. Ever since their conversation on the rise, he'd kept an eye on the western sky, noting how the summer haze had risen to meet the gray clouds until it was hard to say where one ended and the other began.

Sarqi was right, he mused; there was something on the wind. Not so much a sense of expectation to his untrained mind as one of apprehension. It had grown throughout the day until they could all feel it. It was making everyone argumentative and edgy and not even the Evening Invocation had been enough to relieve the tension; the God had been restless and edgy as well, and that had only made matters worse.

Pressing his hand against his chest, Brax felt for the tingle of Estavia's lien against his fingertips. Her presence had felt sluggish all day as if She'd labored to reach him so far from Gol-Beyaz and that had made him even more uneasy. He'd never thought to ask Kemal or Yashar if distance might impede Her touch. He might as well have thought to ask if it would impede his own breathing.

His throat constricted at the thought, and he shook off the accompanying lump in the pit of his stomach with an angry jerk of his head.

"Stop acting like a seer," he snarled at himself, his voice falling strongly flat in the still, evening air. "You're Hers; you'll always be Hers, and She'll always be able to reach you, no matter what the distance is. She feels sluggish because you're tired. That's all." Purposely turning his back on the hovering storm clouds as well as his own sense of apprehension, he headed back to camp, his jaw set.

✦

"You'd better get some sleep while you can," Bazmin mentioned when Brax made his way through the gathering dusk to the shallow, sheltered place where the twins had already laid out their bedrolls. "As you wanted, Abbas and Zeineb are on first watch with Khair, then Feridun, Berar, and myself; Brin's with Jejun, and then you, our beloved ikin-kaptin, get to keep company with our humorless battle-seer until dawn."

Shedding his leathers, Brax laid his weapons carefully to hand before lying back, his hands tucked under his head with a carefully crafted air of disinterest. The twins were like dogs on a scent; if you piqued their interest, they never let up on you.

"It suits me," he answered around a yawn. "I'd rather have an unbroken night's sleep, however short, than have it hacked to pieces in the middle. I hate the midnight watches."

"The midnight watches are usually the quiet ones," Bazmin pointed out. "Most people don't attack in the pitch-dark. They wait until dawn."

"It won't be pitch-dark tonight; the moon may be waning but it's still nearly three quarters full."

"Three quarters full but shrouded in clouds."

"Point, I suppose."

Having won the argument, Bazmin fell silent and, for a moment, Brax thought that both twins had actually fallen asleep, but after working one toe free of its blankets, Brin nudged him in the leg.

"You spent an awfully long time staring at nothing today. Do you think something's up?"

Brax sighed. So much for maintaining disinterest. "A storm," he answered shortly. "Just like Sarqi said."

"Sarqi didn't seem any too convinced of her own words, whatever she might have said."

"Yeah, well, you know how seers are. They always see omens on the wind and dangers in the shadows."

"And what did you see on the wind and in the shadows?"

"Why should I have seen anything more than you did?" Brax demanded querulously. "I'm no seer."

"You're Estavia's favorite," Brin pointed out. "And

Kaptin Liel said you took to the stillness training better than any of us."

Brax snorted. "That's like saying I was the best at breathing underwater because I was the last to drown," he sneered.

"Regardless, you must have gleaned a bit of something," Bazmin added.

"Well, I didn't . . . Though . . . no, I'm not sure," Brax began, and the twins shared a triumphant expression. "It's more like a tickle at the back of my neck than anything else," he continued, ignoring them. "Like I have a louse in my hair that I can't reach, you know?"

"Now that's a lovely image," Brin replied in a disgusted voice.

"You did ask."

"I didn't ask for street poetry."

Brax raised himself up on one elbow. "Tell me you haven't felt the same all day," he demanded.

"I certainly will. There's no lice in my hair," Brin retorted indignantly. "All I felt today was bored and footsore. Hey, Baz." The toe now poked the other twin in the leg. "Maybe we'll meet a Petchan fighting party tomorrow. That's what this patrol needs, you know; in the absence of sex, a bit of bloodshed always puts things to rights."

"You shouldn't wish for such things, Delin." Feridun's sour, disapproving voice floated up from the darkness. "You might end up shedding more of your own blood than you'd anticipated."

"We fight in the name of the God of bloodshed, Sayin," Brin called back with a laugh. "To wish for mine or the enemy's is to do Her homage."

"To throw your own away on a whim is to diminish Her strength," the older man admonished angrily. "And that does Her no homage at all."

"Point," Brin acknowledged, although the laughter remained. "I apologize profoundly, Feridun-Sayin."

When an incoherent mutter was the only reply, Brin

leaned toward Brax, whispering so that only he and Bazmin could hear. "But my own point still stands. If the Petchans are such a great threat, then they should come out from behind their mountains and be a great threat so that we can defeat them, go home, and get laid by half a dozen grateful villagers each."

"Point," Bazmin agreed emphatically. "The Petchans are being very disobliging."

"That's all I'm saying."

Ignoring the ensuing conversation which swiftly degenerated into an explicit speculation about who the twins might have sex with on their return to Alev-Hisar and how quickly, Brax lifted his face to the night breeze. A cool hint of moisture feathered across his cheeks. It felt like rain, or at the very least a heavy dewfall by morning.

The faint scar on his cheek throbbed in the damp air and he scratched at it in absent irritation. Brin was right, he thought with a sigh, what he needed was bloodshed. He never felt more clarity than when he was in the middle of a battle, and clarity was what was wanting right now; he felt like his head was wrapped in gauze.

"The worst of it is that we have to wait three whole days," Brin now moaned beside him in response to a suggestive remark of Bazmin's, and an explosive snort sounded from the darkness.

"Tomorrow at least would come that much sooner for all of us if you would just shut your mouths," Feridun snapped. "Now go to sleep before I knock your heads together like two of my own delon."

Laughing, Brax pulled the blanket up over his ears, blocking out Bazmin's protesting response. Feridun was right, he thought, the morning would come that much sooner if he slept and perhaps, as Brin hoped, there would be a fight tomorrow that would put everything to rights.

Deep within him, the Battle God's lien buzzed Her eager agreement, and he smiled in relief. The sluggishness he'd sensed was nothing more than his own anxiety caused by Sarqi's approaching storm, just as he'd said. If there was any real danger, Estavia would tell him. She would tell them all. She always had.

As the last of the evening's light disappeared, he closed his eyes and willed himself to sleep.

✦

Crouched in the underbrush, as still as the mouse-seeming It wore, the faint glow of Its eyes masked by a thick tuft of grass, Hisar watched the rise and fall of Brax's chest growing slower and deeper.

It had followed the patrol all afternoon just as Graize had asked, keeping as close as possible without alerting Brax or the seer to Its presence. Although It had not understood much of what they'd talked about, It had eavesdropped on their conversations regardless, paying particular attention whenever Brax spoke, but learning little beyond what It already knew: they were making for the rocks at the edge of the foothills; they were nervous, although none of them could explain why, and most of them were itching for a fight to relieve the tension.

"You're Hers; you'll always be Hers, and She'll always be able to reach you, no matter what the distance is."

Hisar lifted Its tiny face to the darkening sky, wondering why that phrase kept echoing in Its mind. Something in Brax's voice had caused a thrill of excitement to chase down Its ethereal spine. What would it be like to have someone be yours so fully that they never doubted your presence, It wondered? And did that mean that you never had cause to doubt theirs?

"I'll never be gone from you again."

The Godling shook Its head, the fine whiskers of Its mouse-seeming trembling at the movement. That was different. Graize had never pressed his hand to his chest to feel Hisar's presence. He could promise to never to be gone again all he liked, but there was no lien made of blood and power and obligation to bind him to his word as there was to bind Brax to his. Their connection was more in the mind and less in the body. It was less ... physical.

A stray thought splashed across the surface of Its thoughts like an errant fish. Would that change if Graize ever swore to It the way Brax had sworn to Estavia? Would it make their connection more physical. Would it make Hisar Itself more physical?

And why did that cause the same thrill of excitement to run down Its ethereal spine?

Rubbing irritably at Its trembling whiskers with one slender paw, Hisar pushed the thought away before it could fully form. Graize would no more swear to It than Spar would. Expecting it, wanting it, maybe even needing it a little bit, wouldn't change that. It wasn't who they were.

But maybe, the thought persisted, It could ask him why now that they were talking.

Hisar's form grew indistinct as the mouse-seeming began to change to the dragonfly form. There would be little enough conversation and no movement by Brax's patrol until dawn. It would be safe to leave for just a few hours.

Hovering just above the tuft of grass, the Godling paused uncertainly. Graize had asked It to follow Brax's patrol and return when they reached the pile of rocks at the edge of the foothills. This was the first time Graize had ever asked It to do anything, the first time he'd ever treated It differently than the way Spar treated Jaq. Hisar had liked that. It had made It feel ... needed, powerful even, and just a little bit hungry for more. If It went to him before Its task was complete, he might not ask again. And It needed him to ask again although It couldn't have said why.

Sinking back into Its nest of grass, Its form returned to the mouse-seeming. There would be time enough to ask questions later. And time enough to experience the answers.

So why was It feeling so anxious, It thought, wondering at the sudden lump of fear that constricted the mouse-seeming's tiny throat, causing Its entirely illusionary heartbeat to hammer so painfully in Its chest. Anxiety was a physical response felt by ... people—not by spirits and not by Gods.

Gaining enough corporeal form to catch up a stalk of grass between Its teeth, the Godling bit down, severing the stalk from the ground. It would be the first to admit that Its experience with people and the emotions that drove them was limited. Although It had eavesdropped on any number of relationships: Kursk and Ayami's, Danjel and Yal's, Panos and Illan's, It had formed no more than three actual relationships of Its own in Its very short existence: with Graize, with Spar, and most recently, with Brax, but the rivalry between the three of them had colored every one of their actions and decisions with so much misunderstanding, jealousy, and lately, sexual tension, that even the most experienced observer would have become confused about how to act toward them.

Nibbling on the stalk of grass, Hisar admitted ruefully that It actually understood less about sex than It did about any other physical concern. Graize had said it was simple: a physical need that felt good, but if that was all there was to it, then why did he and Brax insist on making it so complicated? They mixed emotions and past experiences into what should have been a purely physical desire. Graize wanted Brax—that much was obvious—but he hated him. Likewise, Brax wanted Graize—that was just as clear—but he hated him right back. And to confuse matters even more, Spar loved Brax and hated Graize but didn't seem to want either one of them.

And none of them were doing anything about what they wanted or how they felt, Hisar added with a flash of irritation, except whine and complain, and then deny that they were doing either.

It bit the grass stalk in two with a disgusted snap of Its front teeth and spat it out onto the ground. The animals whose seemings It sometimes adopted never bothered with this kind of nonsense; if they wanted something, they went after it, be it food, shelter, or sex. For that matter, so did most of the people. Caleb, Rayne, and the rest of the Rus-Yuruk never allowed emotions to get in the way of what they wanted, and from what It had seen of the Petchans, neither did they, nor did Brin or Bazmin, Illan or Panos; especially Panos. So if this problem between Graize, Brax, and Spar wasn't about sex, then what was it about? Love, hate, want, and need, why did they have to throw everything into the mix all at once, anyway?

Hisar glanced around, noting the tiny sparks of silver light that betrayed the presence of the grassland spirits hovering all around It. Did the spirits feel such things, It thought; did the Gods? When Incasa had snatched It out of the air and slammed Its consciousness into that of His seer, Freyiz, It had felt a terrible kind of wild possessiveness coming off the Prophecy God like icy smoke, but was that the same thing as hate? And when Oristo had appeared before It at the cavern entrance, the look on the Hearth God's face had seemed to be one of concern, but was that the same as love?

Regardless, it didn't seem as if the Gods would let anything get in the way of what They wanted either.

Hisar paused in the act of catching up a second stalk of grass, wondering suddenly where It fit into all of this; not truly God, nor spirit, nor physical creature, did It love, hate, want, and need and if It did, did It allow emotions and misunderstandings to get in the way of what It wanted?

And for that matter, what did It want, anyway?

Releasing the stalk, It examined the questions carefully, running through Graize's earlier list, one at a time: food, drink, comfort, safety, and sex. The raw spirits from both the wild lands and the mountainsides provided It with as much food and drink as It needed; although food and drink weren't entirely the right words, especially when there was far stronger and more tempting fare just out of reach. As for comfort and safety, It hadn't needed either until recently and Graize had provided both. That left sex. Did It want to have sex? And who with? That evening Brin and Bazmin had mentioned almost every person they'd ever met and seemed willing to have sex with each and every one of them. Hisar thought It might be a bit more ... discriminating, but then It had only ever really met three people.

Hunkering down, It considered each one.

Of the three, It felt the closest to Graize, but he often treated It more like a half-tamed hunting hawk than anything else, tending to Its needs much as he might have tended to an infant's. Hisar struggled with the image of an adult bird feeding its young, then decided that this was the best way to describe how It felt about Graize. Graize fed It.

Spar talked to It like an equal but rarely showed It any real warmth or concern. Likewise, Hisar tended to treat Spar like he was a teacher, not a friend and certainly not a ... lover. Like Graize, Spar fed It, only Spar fed It knowledge and understanding while Graize fed It ... purpose.

As for Brax, he was the most mercurial of the three of them, by turns either hostile or polite, professing to dislike and distrust the Godling while at the same time offering It help and advice. He invited, even initiated conversation, then drove Hisar away just when that conversation was becoming interesting. He didn't feed It, not by a long shot. But he had once long ago, however unwillingly, and the memory of that feeding colored Hisar's dreams with longing. He was frustrating and confusing, but for all that, there was something physically compelling about him, more than just his dark, fathomless eyes, wide shoulders, and thick, tousled hair that drew so many people to him.

Hisar had watched Brax having sex any number of times, noting how often these encounters were initiated by others. They would draw close, their eyes lingering over his body almost hungrily, make some casual remark, and then, if he responded—or rather, when he responded—a not so casual suggestion, and the next thing Hisar knew they would be seeking some private corner or empty chamber, emerging a few moments later looking rumpled and sated.

Looking fed, It decided. Did Brax feed them with sex the way he'd fed Hisar with essence, only willingly?

Hisar wrinkled Its tiny muzzle. That was what It wanted, It decided. It wanted to be fed, by wild lands spirits and mountain spirits certainly, but also by Graize and Spar and especially by Brax. It wanted to be fed knowledge and purpose but mostly power by anything and everything that carried even the tiniest scrap of it. It was hungry and It wanted to be fed.

Changing to Its dragonfly-seeming, the Godling rose silently over the campsite, careful to avoid the sharp gaze of the three hidden sentries just in case they had enough prophetic sensitivity to spot Its shimmering form. The sky above was shrouded in darkness, both starlight and moonlight stifled equally by the gathering clouds. The only illumination came from the host of grassland spirits that sparkled like fireflies all around It, and taking wing, the Godling swooped down among them, snatching them up, one by one, much like a lake gull might snatch up a catch of fish on Gol-Beyaz. Then calmed and strengthened, It flitted across the sleeping figures of the patrol until It hovered just above Brax's head.

Graize had asked It to follow him, to spy on him just as Brax had said he would, and Hisar now understood the driving force behind the familiar, wild light glowing in Graize's eyes. Like Itself, Graize wanted to be fed; maybe not by the streams of golden-red fire that still pulsed beneath Brax's chest, hidden from the world by the heavy confines of Estavia's lien, but by something very much like it, and Hisar wasn't so naive as to believe he didn't mean Brax any harm by it. Graize had a plan, Graize always had a plan, and it always involved harming Brax, feeding on him, consuming him the way the spirits of the wild lands had tried to consume Graize himself. He had learned that from them.

Hisar frowned as a new, unfamiliar feeling trickled through Its ethereal body. It didn't think It liked the idea of Graize feeding on Brax. Brax was . . . Its to feed on.

The dragonfly's wings beat the grass around Brax's prone body with a gentle whoosh of air. Brax stirred with a frown but did not awaken, and Hisar backed away carefully. When It had fed on Brax four years ago, It had done him harm, It considered. The memory of it still echoed in his gaze whenever they locked eyes. By spying on Brax, Hisar was helping to do him harm again. Did that mean that Hisar felt the same way about him that Graize did, both wanting him and hating him at the same time?

It didn't think It did. When Brax had stood by the stream, staring into space, obviously concerned about something, Hisar had almost approached him to ask him what was wrong. It had almost wanted him to ask It to make it better.

Almost. Their last conversation where Brax had sent It away remained fresh in Its mind, so It had taken on the mouse-seeming instead and crept up so close to him that It could have run across his sandal.

Hisar snickered at the memory. It had almost given in to the temptation, feeling a thrill of pleasure at the thought of startling Brax that way, but at the last minute, It had changed Its mind. Graize wouldn't have liked it if It had been discovered, and Brax might have been able to recognize It through the seeming. He had before. So Hisar had just followed Brax back to camp, listening to him talk and wondering what it was that was making him feel like he had a louse in his hair.

And wondering absently what it might feel like to be that louse.

A scattering of stars appeared above Its head, shining weakly through the thick bank of clouds, and Hisar stared up at them, their faint light reflecting in Its shining eyes. It knew what It wanted now, but It didn't know how to get it. Ordinarily It would have asked Spar; Spar understood the multiple layering of the physical world and didn't mind being asked about sensitive subjects—and feeding off Brax the way It had fed four years ago was definitely a sensitive subject—but his presence on the silver lake had cut him off from the Godling more effectively then Dar-Sayer's cavern had cut off Graize. No need, no matter how great, could compel Hisar to make an attempt against Gol-Beyaz.

Not yet, anyway.

Still, It considered, Spar had to disembark eventually. In the meantime, Hisar would do as Graize had asked It to; It would follow Brax until he reached the pile of rocks. After that It would just have to see how events unfolded.

Taking the mouse-seeming once again, It hunkered down in a new patch of grass, watching the rise and fall of Brax's chest again and listening to him breathe.

✦

The night passed uneventfully. Each watch handed their duty over to the next until the faintest line of pale gray brushed the eastern sky. Standing above the camp, Brax rubbed his left elbow with a grimace. The old injury always stiffened painfully when he slept outdoors and the preceding hours spent standing still never helped.

"Well, that's what you get for being a guard," his mind supplied with an unsympathetic snort worthy of Spar. *"Porters, laborers, servants, even priests sleep the night away."*

Beside him, he could just make out Sarqi staring out

at the distant foothills, her opaque eyes gleaming softly in the darkness.

"Seers don't count," his mind argued. *"They've all gone a bit soft in the head from staring at things that don't exist yet. Besides, I think they can sleep standing up."*

He cast her a sideways glance. The seer had maintained her position, unmoved, for most of their watch as if the mountains could be made to give up their secrets by sheer willpower. And for all Brax knew, they could. In the past Spar had stood in much the same way for as many hours, staring at the obstacles between himself and the shine he wanted until he found a way to overcome them. And he always did. It would be the same with Sarqi. Only seers had the kind of patience that came with foreknowledge. Everyone else had to make do with what their eyes and ears gave them. Seers cultivated stillness.

Taking a deep breath, Brax closed his own eyes for a moment, concentrating on one thing like Spar had told him, allowing his ears to bring him the sounds of the grasslands. As he'd told Brin, he preferred the late night watches, and not just because it afforded him an unbroken night's sleep but because, in the peace of the predawn hours, he could think quietly and prepare for the coming day. In the past, he and Spar had stood like this every morning, unmoving and unspeaking, until the younger boy had been satisfied that the hours to come held no hidden danger.

Of course, in the past they'd stood above the streets of Anavatan, the silence broken only by the occasional whisper of a bat's flight above their heads, or the sharp scratch of a rat's passage in the walls. Here in the countryside, it was never completely silent. Even when the air was still, the constant hum of a thousand insects, rodents, and frogs going about their business through the underbrush seemed magnified and every cry of a predator or its prey echoed like an approaching army no matter how far away it might be.

Five years ago he'd lain awake, overwhelmed by all this noise, but he'd long ago learned to block the sounds out, concentrating instead on the steady thrum of Estavia's lien within him, but they still caught him unaware from time to time. He imagined they always would. He wasn't used to that much life rustling about in the darkness all around him. It didn't seem . . . natural.

Smiling at the thought, he cocked his head to one side, listening for the faint sounds of the other eight people sleeping either restlessly or deeply all around him. In a few moments the silence would be broken by the sounds of coughing, grumbling and urinating, but for now, the entire world seemed to be holding its breath as the sun crept slowly toward the horizon. It would be the same across the shores of Gol-Beyaz from Anavatan to Anahtar-Hisar, he considered. Only guards, seers, and thieves kept company with the night.

An owl hooting in the distance caused Sarqi to finally stir beside him.

"It will be a foggy morning," she noted, more to herself than to him, her voice sounding hollow in the translucent, predawn air.

Brax just nodded. Having grown up on Anavatan's western docks, he could sense the moisture in the air even without a seer's abilities.

"There shouldn't be fog on the grasslands," Sarqi continued peevishly, "Fog's a water sign. There should be mist on the grasslands, but not fog. It muddies the streams."

Brax shrugged. Mist and fog were much the same as far as he was concerned. "What does fog signify on the water, Seer?" he asked, more to keep her talking than from any real desire to know the answer, much as he might have done with Spar. Like Spar, Sarqi took a while to get to the point.

"Hidden agendas," she answered.

"And on land?"

"The same, only more convoluted. All mixed up together until it's hard to see one from the other."

"Well, that fits."

"Yes, it does. That's why I don't like it. You can't see outward or inward in a fog."

"But neither can the enemy."

"The enemy's sight doesn't concern me," she replied. "The enemy knows the terrain. The enemy doesn't need to see to be a danger to us."

"Are we in danger?" he asked bluntly, just as he might have asked Spar.

She frowned impatiently. "We're always in danger when we step outside the protection of the God-Wall, Ghazi."

"That's why we go armed, Seer," he replied with a grin.

She glared at him for a moment but, as his grin remained unchanged, she favored him with a sour smile in return.

"Yes, I suppose it is," she allowed.

"Do you sense that the enemy is near?"

She frowned. "I can sense that something is near," she answered after a long silence. "Beyond that, we'll have to ask the God." She jerked her head in the direction of the camp. "If you would be so kind as to awaken your patrol, Ikin-Kaptin; we've just enough time to eat and break camp before the Morning Invocation."

"I can do that."

As he moved off, a faint shimmering behind him caused her eyes to narrow suspiciously. She watched him go for a long moment and then, reluctantly, returned her gaze to the western foothills.

✦

The day passed in much the same way as the day before had done, with Khair and Sarqi brooding over the distant clouds, Feridun and the twins sniping at each other to the amusement of the others, and Brax wrapped in his own thoughts, feeling restless and worried. The Morning Invocation had offered up little in the way of comfort. The God was fractions, refusing to give Sarqi any answers to her questions, and that in turn had made the seer terse and uncommunicative herself. After a few sharp rebuffs even Khair had backed off.

Now they moved in silence, the sense of unease growing. Like the day before, the haze refused to burn off, making everything seem faint and unreal. There was no wind, and Brax began to feel like he was walking wrapped in blankets; his ears kept popping as if he were slowly going deaf, allowing a faint buzz to resound just beyond his hearing before it was blocked again

They paused briefly at noon, then carried on. The collection of rocks that Sarqi had noted the day before were now clearly visible to them all, standing out in the distance fog like tiny islands rising up from a mist-covered sea. But the closer they came, the more reluctant they seemed to reach their destination until, finally, Khair gave a snort of impatience and set off at a gallop, his horse's hooves sending up swirls of mist in his wake.

"Show-off," Brin muttered, but not even Feridun felt like taking up the complaint and they continued on in silence.

✦

The shrouded sun had not yet touched the horizon when the rest of the patrol finally reached the rocks. Sarqi dismounted, scrabbling up the largest until she stood at the very top. Khair paused below, hesitant to dismount.

"Do you see anything?" he called.

She narrowed her eyes. "A single hawk hunting in the sky and the heat shimmering in the distance. Nothing more."

"Should we make camp?"

She scowled at the setting sun. "Our orders were to travel two days out and two days back," she answered. "We have at least another hour before sunset. Another hour closer to the foothills and I might be able to glean a better knowledge of this sense of ..." She paused with a frown; expectation was no longer an appropriate description. "Apprehension," she finished, her tone still unsatisfied as if even that word was too mild.

"Told you it would take more than a day and a half," Brin muttered to no one in particular as the rest of the patrol began to glance about uneasily, clearly unhappy at the thought of passing from even the minimal safety of the rocks but unwilling to voice their concern in front of each other.

Finally Brax turned. "This is a better place to mount a defense should that sense of apprehension evolve into real danger, Seer," he offered.

Sarqi paused, her white-covered gaze tracking across the terrain, then nodded. "I suppose. Yes, we will make camp here tonight," she decided reluctantly. "I'll ask the God for clarification during Evening Invocation. Perhaps She'll be more obliging at that time." Leaping down, she lead her mount to a small stream on the eastern side of the rocks without another word.

Brax nodded at her back. "Abbas and Zeineb, you're on first watch."

As the others began to make camp, Brax took Sarqi's place, the sluggishness he'd experienced before even stronger now as he felt rather than saw the sun descend farther toward the horizon. Above him, the hunting hawk sent one long cry echoing across the sky, and he watched it bank and turn for a moment before returning his gaze to the hills, an involuntary shiver running down his spine.

✦

In the sky, Hisar wheeled back and forth, buzzing with pleasure at the near-physical sensation of the wind rippling through the hawk's flight feathers. It circled once around the camp, so high that It was little more than a speck in the clouds, sending a cry of jubilation into the air, then turned and made off toward the mountains. Brax and his patrol had reached the rocks at last. It could return to Graize without fear of reproof and then It would seek out Spar.

Turning, It shot through a bank of clouds, scattering a host of spirits in Its wake. A sense of unease whispered across Its mind, causing It to pause for a moment as an errant breeze from the east bought It the faintest taste of disquiet, then It shook the feeling off and carried on, eager to discharge Its duty.

15

Champions

MILES AWAY, STANDING on a rise in the middle of the grasslands, Spar squinted in the fading daylight, staring out at the gray-draped foothills in the distance and feeling the dread broil in the pit of his stomach. Beside him, Kemal and Yashar watered their mounts at a small stream, equally reluctant to pause, but knowing that they could go no farther tonight. The horses were done. Closing his eyes, Spar forced down the growing sense of panic that had been with him all day.

He was going to be too late.

It had been a frustrating two days for everyone. Once they'd docked at Orzin-Hisar, Birin-Kaptin Nicurz had rounded up every battle-seer available. Estavia's Evening Invocation became a seeking with the God towering a hundred feet in the air, the minds of Her seers flying around Her like a flock of agitated ravens. But the future to the west had been concealed by a dense mental fog of unusual strength, and they'd fallen back, thwarted and confused.

Spar had spent a restless night with Kemal's family at Serin-Koy, staring sightlessly up at Bayard's dark, beamed ceiling, his mind replaying his vision over and over again until he'd wanted to scream. The faintest hint of dawn had sent him back to haunt the wharf, pacing the wooden dock impatiently until the others had joined him.

They'd loaded quickly, and the barge had set out directly after the Morning Invocations but the upper current had been as sluggish as the day before. They put in to Alev-Hisar well past midday only to learn that Kaptin Liel's messenger had arrived too late. The first of Alev-Hisar's patrols, Brax in their midst, had gone out the morning before.

Reinforcements had been sent out at once, but the odds of finding a single patrol on the grasslands was slim. The battle-seers called yet another seeking, but when dawn brought no more clarity than before, Spar'd had enough. He went to his abayon and demanded that they head out to find Brax.

"I don't care how much fog they've wrapped him in. I can find him."

That had been good enough for Kemal and Yashar. Using their status as senior temple ghazi, his abayon had managed to commandeer a militia scout and seer and, with Spar mounted behind, had set out for the distant foothills, Jaq loping stubbornly along beside them.

But it had been slow going. Neither Kemal nor Yashar were used to riding and the obscuring fog was proving more difficult than Spar had believed possible. As the sunlight began to dim, the growing awareness that they'd fallen too far behind became more and more impossible to ignore. When Kemal'd finally called a halt at dusk, Spar had dismounted stiffly and walked a few hundred yards more, the long grass wiping at his bare calves before he'd come to a reluctant halt, Jaq pressed tightly against his side. Behind him, he'd heard Yashar begin a subdued Invocation to Estavia and for the first time in his life, he'd wished he could join in.

Because for all his powers, and for all of Kaptin Liel's assurances, he was going to be too late.

He closed his eyes with a grimace, fighting off a wave of useless regret that threatened to close his throat.

All his life he'd stood apart, if not physically, then at least emotionally, from the Gods and Their Invocations. He'd shielded his prophetic abilities from Their sight day after day, first on the streets of Anavatan to protect his small family of lifters from the garrison guards of Estavia and the abayos-priests of Oristo, then in the courtyards of Estavia-Sarayi and every watchtower from Gerek-Hisar to Anahtar-Hisar. But why, he demanded silently, to protect himself or simply to deny that the Gods had any right to a part of his life?

He didn't know. And until today he hadn't cared. He'd always believed he didn't need Them and didn't want Them, but now . . .

Grinding his teeth, he glared back in the direction of the silver lake. The seer-priests of both Incasa and Estavia believed that prophetic ability was a gift from the Gods. Spar had always sneered at the idea, but he hadn't been able to deny that, as his abilities had grown with each passing year, so had his sensitivity to Their touch.

When the gardeners and farmers along the shores of Gol-Beyaz joined Havo's priests each morning, his mind would fill with the relentless and methodical passage of time; birth and growth giving way to decline and death. The power of their song would demand a response each time, but before he could accept it or deny it, Havo's worshipers would finish and the voices of Oristo's abayos-priests would rise up, promising comfort and security and bringing a host of unwanted memories in their wake. He often felt as if he were drowning in them, but just as quickly, they would give way to the eerie, frightening control of life and death wielded by the physician-priests of Usara.

The subsequent martial shout that took the place of singing for the Warriors of Estavia was a familiar battering ram against his senses, but followed as it was by the soft, seductive call to craft and learning sent up by the artisans of Ystazia, it left him weak and reeling.

Ripe for a final attack by the Oracles of Incasa.

The hair on the back of his neck would stand on end as he'd feel rather than hear them begin their call: a low, deep-throated hum more than an actual song. His own abilities would struggle to join them, his throat working to voice the same invoking note, knowing that it would strengthen his prophetic powers to a degree that he could never hope to achieve alone, but every day and every night he managed to overcome his desire for it. He might be a seer, but he was not and never would be a seer of Incasa. But what did that leave?

"If it's not gonna be a Sable Company seer, what's it gonna be, then?"

Brax's voice echoed in his head so loudly he might have spoken the words directly beside Spar.

"I don't know," he snarled back, his own voice falling flat in the heavy air. "But there has to be another choice."

But his choices were running out because he was going to be too late.

✦

The sun slowly set behind a heavy bank of storm clouds. With the Evening Invocations over, Estavia hovered above the surface of Gol-Beyaz a frown marring the perfection of Her ebony visage. Far to the west, lightning danced across the clouds, reflecting in Her crimson gaze as dozens of tiny, silver specks—each one a temple warrior or village militia sworn to Her service—glittered across the grasslands. They were searching for the single speck that shone with the fiery light of Her regard.

It sparkled like a gem on the very edge of the foothills, and She'd turned the attention of Her people that way in every seeking and Invocation for the last two days. With no battle to be joined, however, Her understanding of their difficulty was limited. Brax was there; Brax was safe. What else could they want? Together, She and Incasa had pierced the fog that had so frustrated Her seers, revealing the Petchan threat grow-ing in the mountains. That was why Her warriors now prowled the grasslands. If they needed Her in battle, they would call. If Brax needed Her in battle, he would call. With one last irritated glance at the shrouding fog that had continued to hover above the distant foothills, Estavia returned to the depths of the silver lake.

✦

And in the center of the waves, Incasa caressed the mind of His First Oracle with a single thread of waking. The Champions were coming ever closer to each other. It would soon be time.

✦

Far to the west, shining above the muting fog, the moon of Graize's vision was bright and clear, showing its face in three-quarter profile as a sitter might for a portrait painter in Anavatan's artists' market. It was not yet fully realized, but it soon would be; Graize could feel it trembling on the very edge of being. He chuckled in gleeful anticipation.

Crouched beside him in the lea of a small hill, Danjel and Yal glanced over, but when he made no further sound, they returned their attention to the jumble of rocks in the distance. Around them, the rest of the Petchan raiding party—junior sayers all—lay, wrapped in hide blankets, waiting for the word to attack. As the sun touched the edge of the horizon, Graize contin-ued to gaze lovingly at the agent of his desire. So very soon.

The cry of a hunting hawk brought him back to the physical world; as he lifted his face to the evening breeze, he saw the Godling circling high above his head. He raised his hand and, streaking from the clouds, It lengthened Its form to wrap about his neck, whispering in his ear even before It grew still.

"They're there."

It repeated all that It had overheard on the grasslands, and Graize nodded silently. He could sense Brax and his patrol as keenly as if they were standing right beside him, and the power of his new protective cloak allowed him to feel the full force of his response: ancient, simmering resentment, possessive jealousy, and heated desire that made him want to bare his teeth.

Brax would be standing on the highest rock, staring into the evening mist, unaware that his oldest enemy was crouched nearby but still feeling the cold hint of foreboding raising the hair on the back of his neck.

Very soon he would know the reason, Graize promised silently; as soon as the moon broke from its concealing clouds; the moon that had followed him all the way from Dar-Sayer's cavern and finally revealed itself on the path to Chalash. It had been then that he'd known he could not fail. The moon was a constant. It would be there whatever other factors might introduce themselves later. Twisting his head, he stared back at the way they'd come, seeing the events of the last two days unfold in his mind's eye.

He'd reached Chalash just after dusk had finished filling the vale with shadow. Standing on the top of the log-step path, he'd watched the smoke rising from the double line of clay chimneys to either side of him, breathing in the scents of cooking meats, spices, juniper, and cedar with a thrill of purely physical pleasure before making his way down to the village square.

He'd found Las waiting for him by the central pool, a piece of flatbread in his hand.

"The elders saw your coming in vision, Graize-Sayer," the boy'd explained, handing him the bread. "The Hukumet is waiting for you."

Graize'd nodded. "Then let's not keep them waiting a moment longer," he'd answered, tucking the bread into a fold in his shirt for later. "Night is falling, and the omens are gathering like blackbirds in the trees."

Las laughed, and together they crossed the vale with as dignified a pace as the boy could muster.

The atmosphere inside the vision-house had been one of expectation; the elder sayers huddled in their low chairs by the fire, wrapped in shawls, their bows lying still and unstrung across their knees now that their visioning had been completed, the junior sayers hovering dutifully behind them, their eyes bright with anticipation. In the center, the fire-tending delinkon had raised such a cloud of aromatic smoke that Graize's eyes had begun to sting almost at once. As he'd entered the main room, Haz-Chief had gestured him over immediately.

✦

"Dar-Sayer has released you in good time," the older man noted, his sharp gaze tracking across Graize's face as if he could see right through to the changes within his mind. "Our scouts have returned with word of several enemy patrols scouring the grasslands to the east. All that's wanting now is the addition of your own vision to ours."

Graize inclined his head with a regal gesture. "My vision showed me a dozen Petchan raiding parties sweeping those enemy patrols away like so much chaff, Haz-Chief," he answered, dispensing with his usual cryptic response. "But most especially it showed me a patrol of particular importance no more than one day's ride from this very spot. Eight warriors, a militia scout, and a sayer of some small talent. I would, if you would have it so, grant them our most particular attention."

"And this sayer of some small talent will not discern our most particular attention?" Haz-Chief asked dryly.

Graize lifted his head, his eyes misting over until they were the opalescent white of a senior Anavatanon seer. "She's already discerned some of it," he said, his voice echoing in the wide empty space around them. "But she can't identify what it is. She feels it gnawing at her, tickling the back of her mind like a fine hair might tickle the back of your throat if you tried to swallow it, but the muting effect blankets her abilities like a fog. She won't truly know what she's discerning until it's too late.

"If the Hukumet sends out raiding parties to engage the other patrols scouring the grasslands at the same time," he added, "her prophecy will be even more muddied. And if those who ride against her patrol are sayers wielding the muting effect against her specifically—say a dozen besides myself and Danjel-Wyrdin, she'll never see us coming."

Haz-Chief glanced over to the old man seated closest to the fire. "And what say you, Fal-Sayer?" he asked respectfully.

The old man spat a gob of spittle into the flames in a gesture that said he'd already known what Graize would reveal. "We've seen this patrol in vision," he said in a dismissive tone, a peevish expression on his leathery face. "They're making for the Gathering Stones; and yes, they're but one day's ride away and both powerful and vulnerable in equal measure."

"How so?"

Fal-Sayer twitched his shawl more tightly about his shoulders with an impatient growl. "Powerful because its members carry oaths and obligations which bind them to the lake dwellers' God of Battles," he answered slowly and deliberately as if Haz-Chief were a child. "If they call, She'll answer. Vulnerable because . . ." He gave a thick, ropy cough, then gestured irritably at Graize as a junior sayer bent to wipe his lips with a scrap of cloth. "The boy here is better able to explain that to you," he rasped once he'd gotten his breath back.

"They're vulnerable because they rely on Her response to such a degree that should She not appear when they call Her, it would shake them to their very core and weaken them more surely then even the spilling of their blood." Graize answered easily. "Which would also weaken them quite nicely, come to think of it," he added with a pleased smile, more to himself than the older man.

"And why would She not appear?" Haz-Chief demanded. "I thought these oaths obliged Her to appear?"

Graize showed his teeth. "They oblige Her to respond," he said, "but She can't appear if She can't find them. The Gods don't venture far from the wellspring of Their power and so Their worshipers have no idea just how strong a barrier the muting effect really is; as strong as their own Wall of Power. Strong enough to deny the power of a God," he added, his eyes gleaming in anticipation.

Haz-Chief caught him in an even stare. "The muting effect is indeed strong," he allowed, "and has kept us safe from the Gods of Gol-Beyaz and Their worshipers for many centuries, because, as you say, they don't know how strong it actually is. If all goes as you would have it, they would soon discover it."

Graize returned the chief's expression with an open expression of his own. "Yes, they would," he said bluntly. "But that discovery would not galvanize them to action, it would shatter them." He waved a dismissive hand at the east. "Almost every one of the lake dwellers is among the sworn," he expanded. "It's more than just words. The Gods live inside them all the time; eating, sleeping, working, screwing. If that bond were suddenly severed . . ." He drove the edge of his hand down sharply. "They would be struck down, frozen in their tracks, unable to move, vulnerable and afraid. And it would shake the very Gods Themselves."

"You believe this, but you haven't actually seen it come to pass," Haz-Chief pressed.

Graize shrugged the detail off with casual disdain. "I was raised by priests; smug and arrogant in their belief that all it took to be strong and safe was a personal bond with a God—any God. They could never see the inherent weakness built into that belief. This patrol will be no different. It will fall as surely as a leaf falls when the tree beneath it is cut down."

"And pray tell us what makes this patrol of such particular importance to your vision, other than its proximity?" Fal-Sayer demanded.

Graize glanced down at him before answering, and the elder sayer graced him with a toothless smile of malevolent challenge in response.

"At its heart is one highly favored by the God of Battles," he replied. "A blow struck against him will have the greatest effect on them all."

"Highly favored by the God of Battles and highly disfavored by yourself. Is that not true, Graize-Sayer?" Fal-Sayer asked with an evil chuckle.

"I'm not saying that I wouldn't enjoy it, Sayin," Graize answered, falling unconsciously back into an earlier speech pattern. "Only that he represents the point of greatest weakness for the greatest reward."

"And does his patrol carry anything in the way of *physical* reward?" Haz-Chief interrupted in a dry tone, "to make it enjoyable for us?"

Graize inclined his head. "The warriors carry weapons and armor worthy of their status. The scout and sayer ride two fast and powerful horses bred for the battlefield. And since they're delivering them practically to your doorstep," he added, "how much more enjoyable could it be?"

Haz-Chief chuckled. "You make a convincing argument, Graize-Sayer," he allowed. "Very well. As we have come this far with an attack in mind, you shall have your dozen sayers. We strike as many Anavatanon patrols as we can find, especially your particular patrol by the Gathering Stones and we will see how enjoyable it is for both of us and how vulnerable and afraid it truly makes them. In the meantime, the Hukumet will remained convened to shield our purpose until your return."

"That would be of great assistance, Haz-Chief," Graize responded. He inclined his head once more, but as he turned to go, Fal-Sayer abruptly shoved his vision-bow into Graize's hands.

"You'll need this," the old man growled by way of explanation. "I've only one vision left, and I don't need prophecy to see it; it's staring me right in the face." He pointed a gnarled finger at the younger seer in warning. "Your path isn't as clear as you think it is, my arrogant little mountain goat. And all paths can change within the space of a single heartbeat. Even Gods can be unpredictable. Take care you don't fall into a sudden crevasse when you finally come face-to-face with your adversary."

Graize smiled down at him, matching the old man's earlier challenging expression, his eyes glittering in the firelight. "My thanks, Fal-Sayin," he answered with exaggerated formality. "I'll be sure to use your gift to shoot a bridging line across any suspiciously new path before tossing my adversary into that crevasse."

One hand on his chest, he made the old sayer a low bow before exiting the Hukumet without another word. Fal watched him go, rheumy eyes narrowed, then spat another gob of spittle into the fire.

"Mountain goats, eagles, turtles, wisps of smoke; all I need now are some vegetables to become a hearty stew," Graize murmured to himself. Heading back up the wooden steps, he wove the still unstrung bow back and forth in front of him, watching as it sent faint trails of disturbed prophecy spiraling through the air, and wondering if Fal-Sayer's death would thicken the broth or thin it. Reaching the top of the steps, he leaped sideways, scrambling up the steep, slippery mountainside until he found a shelf of rock from which he could watch the vale below.

The word went swiftly after the Hukumet's decision, spreading out from the vision-house like ripples of water. They would leave at dawn. Figures moved from house to house and stable to stable, making ready.

Fishing the flatbread from his shirt, Graize chewed at it reflectively, watching the activity below until he recognized the hint of a familiar pipe smoke on the breeze and saw Danjel and Yal leaving Maf's small dwelling on the far side of the village. He gave a piercing whistle, grinning as he saw Danjel's head snap up. The Yuruk wyrdin was not used to seeking people in mountainous shadows, but Graize saw Yal point toward him immediately. Resisting the urge to move to a more precarious location, he waited as the two of them began to climb the wooden steps, Yal in the lead.

They reached the shelf a few moments later, Yal leaping up as agilely as a goat, Danjel following more carefully a moment later. Once they'd settled themselves beside him, they sat in silence for a time, Danjel's smooth, beardless features lit by the occasional flare from her pipe.

Yal glanced at the bow in Graize's hand without comment, then tipped her head to one side. "Where's your tamed spirit?" she asked.

Graize waved a hand in the direction of the wind. "Doing my bidding elsewhere."

She considered his words with a pensive expression, then fixed him with a penetrating stare. "Is It really a God?" she demanded.

He finished the last of the flatbread before giving a careless shrug. "An immature God," he allowed.

"And It still does your bidding?"

Beside him, he saw Danjel watching him carefully. "Yes," he answered.

"Why?"

"Because It's mine."

"Like a hunting eagle?"

Remembering his conversation with the Godling at the mouth of Dar-Sayer's cave, Graize shrugged again. "More like a delos, a child," he replied.

Yal fingered the protective beads in her hair uncertainly. "But you're certain It won't turn on us?" she pressed.

Graize gave her a lazy smile. "Have you ever turned on Maf?"

"I've disobeyed her."

"It won't disobey me."

"Will It fight beside us against your Anavatanon patrol?"

"Us?"

Yal tossed her head at him impatiently. "Possibly," she said in an irritated tone. "I haven't decided yet. Will It fight beside the Petchan raiding party you and Danjel are leading against the Anavatanon?"

"Yes."

"Why?"

"Because it pleases us both for It to do so."

Yal glanced at Danjel who shrugged in turn. "Eventually you just have to trust in his prophecy and in your own," she replied. "Or stay at home."

"I'm not a sayer," Yal answered in a sour voice. "I have no prophecy to trust in."

"Then trust in mine."

The Petchan woman was quiet for a moment, then she nodded. "Yes, I can do that," she decided, catching up Danjel's hand in her own. "If your prophecy tells me that it's safe to trust this God-spirit, then I believe you."

Danjel's green eyes warmed as they met the bright blue of the other woman's gaze. "The spirits of the Berbat-Dunya are not so wild nor so strong as they are here," she admitted. "They can be bribed and tamed to some degree, but they're still creatures of power, driven by hunger. This God-spirit was born of a thousand such creatures and was fashioned by the blood and will and strength of Graize alone. Whatever It may become, for now, If anyone can control It, he can."

"Your prophecy tells you this?" Yal pressed.

"No, my experience. My prophecy tells me that the wind's at our back driving us forward. It may change in the future, but for now, the grass is bending in the same direction as our horses' hooves are pointing. And in the same direction that the God-spirit is flying," she added.

"And you'll tell me if the wind changes," Yal asked, "or if the God-spirit does?"

Glancing meaningfully at Graize, Danjel nodded. "Yes. I will."

Yal sat back. "Then I'll trust your prophecy," she decided, plucking Danjel's pipe from between her fingers and taking a long draw. "And come with you to fight against this Anavatanon patrol."

✦

Now, hidden beneath an undulating rise, their mounts tethered nearby, Yal gave Graize a narrow-eyed look and he smiled innocently back at her.

"Destiny begins today," he intoned.

Beside them, Danjel gave a cynical snort. "I thought you believed that destiny began the night you were attacked by the wild lands spirits?"

Graize shrugged. "Destiny has many beginnings. This is tonight's destiny." Swinging Fal-Sayer's bow back and forth in front of him, he closed his eyes, a sleepy expression on his face. "My moon will rise within the hour," he said, the singsong cadence back in his voice. "But it will be another two before it shows its face to the world. As soon as darkness falls, we can pad forward on silent feet, softly, softly like foxes on the hunt, to a hollow that will shield us from the sharp and fearful gaze of our prey until my moon shines down upon them, and then . . ." He mimed snatching something from the air and Yal's pale brows drew down in a doubtful expression.

"At night?" she asked.

He nodded. "Oh, yes. *The late night watches are usually the quiet ones. Most people don't attack in the pitch-dark. They wait until dawn,*" he explained, his voice taking on a new timber as he repeated the Godling's report. "Once we're in position, the clouds will part and my beautiful, prophetic moon will spill light upon their campsite, illuminating each and every one of our adversaries as if the dawn sun were shining in their faces.

"Then my spirit-delos will fly above them as silent as the wind. Won't you, Delin?" he crooned to the Godling still wrapped about his neck. He ran a hand along Its flank and It stretched in pleasure like a cat, turning Its metallic gaze on Yal with an alien expression. "And gift us with a single target for each of us for a swift and coordinated attack that will overcome anything their sayer tries to bring into the fray," Graize finished.

Yal frowned at him. "I thought you said the muting effect would be enough," she accused.

Graize shrugged. "One false die is good, two are better."

"What?"

"It pays to be cautious around sayers," Danjel explained. "And old habits die hard," she added, shooting a sour glance at Graize.

"Because people—Petchans included—die so very easily," Graize replied. "Don't forget, Kardos, the purpose of the game is not to play, it's to win. And the best way to win is to account for every possible move and hold the winning combination for each one.

"They tried to find us, you know," he added suddenly.

"Who did?"

"Our flock of blackbirds to the east. They flew in even greater agitation than when their eldest raven died."

"When?"

"Last night. Knowing that something was amiss and feeling it deep within their feathers, they even called upon their Carrion God and She bent all Her attention to the west, but the Hukumet was standing sentinel in the darkness and She passed them by."

Danjel's green eyes narrowed. "Why didn't you tell us this before?"

Graize shrugged. "It was like the butterflies, Kardos; not the least bit important. They couldn't find what they were seeking for, and so they're still seeking it, unable to move forward until they find it." He began to laugh.

"And their little baby rat-seer is going nearly mad from the strain of waiting." He cocked his head to one side as if listening for something in the distance. "He'll break soon, I should think," he mused. "I wonder what he'll do."

He stood abruptly, spilling the Godling into his arms in a heap of sinuous coils. "Come," he ordered. "Darkness has fallen; it's time to be foxes." Tucking the bow under one arm, he headed for his mount without another word.

After exchanging a glance, Danjel and Yal rose and followed him. One by one, the rest of the raiding party fell in behind, and soon they were making their way, single file, through the whispering grasses as the sun slowly set behind the horizon.

✦

Night closed about the grasslands like a cloak. A heavy, oppressive stillness filled the air, weighting everything down until even the insects ceased their singing. At either end of their makeshift camp, Abbas and Jejun stood staring into the distance while, at their feet, the rest of the patrol slept fitfully in the lee of the great rocks. The shrouded three-quarter moon rose, giving off a pale nimbus of light that slowly grew as it emerged, bit by bit, from its nest of concealing clouds. The cry of a hunting hawk sounded in the distance and then there was nothing but silence once again.

When the attack came, it took them completely by surprise.

A dozen Petchan raiders erupted from the grasslands all around them. Abbas went down with an arrow in the throat. Jejun managed a single cry before being cut down in turn. The patrol jerked to their feet, eyes clouded with sleep, hands scrambling for their weapons, but it was already too late. They were outnumbered.

Khair died before he even made it out of his blanket, killed by a blow to the head that nearly sliced his skull in half. Sarqi fell less than a heartbeat later as Yal and Danjel drove a pair of long, wicked knives into her chest. The seer collapsed against them, blood spraying from her mouth, unable to cry out the name that might have saved her, and Danjel laid her body on the ground, almost gently.

On the other side of the camp, Berar grappled with her own attacker, then fell to another who came at her from behind, while Zeineb knocked his first attacker to one side. Before he could bring his blade up, another took her place, slashing at his exposed abdomen. He stumbled back screaming and clutching at the terrible wound that spewed blood and organs between his fingers. He was dead before he hit the ground.

Beside them, Feridun managed to throw his shield up, deflecting a blow that streaked toward his head. He kicked out blindly, connecting with his enemy with a grunt, then surged up to drive the point of his sword into the Petchan's chest. Overbalanced, they fell together as a blow from another whistled over his head. The second blow hit its mark.

Brin and Bazmin were not where they should have been, and this saved their lives. Two raiders fell upon their empty blankets only to be attacked in turn by the twins who rushed in on them, swinging wildly. They cut both raiders down, then turned on the two bending over Feridun's prone body, killing them as well. As Brin held off another, Bazmin dragged Feridun to the dubious safety of the rocks, then fell into a defensive position beside Brin.

Tangled in his own blanket, Brax slashed at the legs of a raider rushing past him, catching him across the calf. The man went down with a scream. Brax was on his feet a second later, whirling to meet another attacker.

And came face-to-face with Graize.

He had an instant to react before his oldest enemy swung at him. Knife blade hit sword blade, Brax twisted his wrist reflexively, knocking Graize's weapon aside, then slashed at him in a tight arc. Graize leaped back, allowing the blow to fly harmlessly past him. He lunged forward, feinted to one side, then drove his right elbow into Brax's left with a sudden snap of his arm. The old injury gave way, and Brax jerked back with an involuntary cry. Graize's downward stroke caught him in the thigh, the leg twisted out from under him, and he fell.

Graize loomed above him, knife in hand, face twisted in a terrible grimace of rage and hate. He raised his arm, then drove it down with all his strength but, at the last moment, Brax jerked away and the knife point slammed into the ground an inch from his cheek just as shaft of moonlight lit up his face.

Graize froze. Staring down at Brax, his own face shifted from one emotion to another with lightning speed, then Hisar was suddenly between them, screaming in rage.

"Mine! Mine, Mine, MINE, MINE, *MINE!"*

Graize staggered back in shock, then thrust the half-ethereal, half-physical creature away from him, his knife jerking up in instinctive defense.

Brax used the distraction to kick out with his good leg, knocking the other man off-balance. The knife went flying into the grass and, for a moment, Brax was clear. He tried to rise, but his injured leg refused to move. He made to call out to Estavia then, but suddenly Graize was surging upward, shouting out a single word. A great, suffocating fog rushed over him, followed almost at once by an empty, enshrouding darkness so complete it was as if he'd fallen off the very edge of the world. He never saw the next blow coming.

And then he felt nothing at all.

On Gol-Beyaz, Estavia shot from the waves, screaming in outrage as a great hole was torn open in the very center of Her power, while on the grasslands, Spar jerked awake with an echoing cry. But there was nothing either one of them could do. Brax had disappeared. As the enraged scream of a hunting hawk tore through the air, Jaq began to howl.

16

The Tower

IN ORISTO-SARAYI'S SUMMONING Chamber, Tanay winced as Oristo's lien cracked against the back of her mind with the acrid odor of burned toast. Taking a deep breath, she sent a thread of calming power out toward the Hearth God as she waited for First-Abayos-Priest Neclan to begin the song that would link Anavatan's chamberlains to their God.

She'd been driven from her bed in the middle of the night by the pressure of her half-latent prophetic abilities. A tight lump of fear growing in the pit of her stomach, she'd thrown an old tunic on and headed for the central courtyard, joining a number of Sable Company seers already outside.

✦

The reason for their disquiet became obvious seconds later when Estavia exploded above the eastern battlements, dwarfing walls, turrets, and even Lazim-Hisar to the north. The God let out a deafening scream, throwing the more powerful seers to the ground in pain, and destroying a dozen windows before vanishing again only to reappear to the west, ripping up shrubs and trees in Her wake. Seconds later, driven to the same rage by Estavia's destruction, Havo flew at Her, hands outstretched like claws, calling up a great wind of rain and hail which tore across the city, smashing chimney pots and wresting tiles from the rooftops. This brought Ystazia and Usara into the fray, and as the four Gods came together in a cacophony of shrieking, Anavatan erupted in chaos.

Tanay turned and ran for the kitchens as she felt Oristo and Incasa rise behind Them.

She met Monee, bleary-eyed and frightened at the door to the spice room.

"What's happening," the older woman wailed.

"I don't know. Something's angered the Gods. I'm going to Oristo-Sarayi. I need you to keep order here until I get back. Can you do that?"

Monee's eyes were wild, the whites showing clearly around her brown irises, and Tanay resisted the urge to shake her.

"You're senior cook," she pressed. "The others will obey you. I need you to keep them calm." She glanced around quickly. "Get the bake ovens fired up. That mess will have awakened everyone by now, so the bakers should be here at any moment to check on their ovens. Then start breakfast. The appearance of normalcy will calm everyone down, and they'll respond to being fed. Monee . . ." She took the woman by the shoulders and stared firmly into her eyes. "They're all used to being told what to do by the Servers of Oristo. This will be no different. Feed them. By the time that's done, their own leaders will have restored order."

"But what's wrong?' Monee insisted.

"With the Gods? I have no idea. But it better be good," she added with a growl, drawing a reluctant half smile from Monee. "Now, I'll either be back or send word as soon as I know what's going on," she continued. "In the meantime, the Servers of Oristo will do what we do best, we will serve food. Yes?"

Monee straightened her shoulders. "Yes."

"Good." Tanay turned on her heel. Behind her, she heard Monee begin to give orders to the dozen cooks, bakers, and delinkon who had stumbled into the kitchens, her voice growing stronger as the commands calmed both her and them. A sense of busy industry descended almost at once, and Tanay smiled as she slipped through the receiving door, gesturing at a delinkos to follow her. Together, they ran down the long tunnel to the kitchen wharf, their bare feet slapping against the cold stone.

The moon was hidden behind the city wall, and it was very dark when she stepped outside. After ensuring that the delinkos closed and barred the door behind her, she made her way down the wharf by memory. Then, dropping down onto the cool wooden planks, she pushed off.

The stones shifted under her feet as she landed, but years of going barefoot in the shoals of Ekmir-Koy found her footing for her and she hurried south along the narrow strip of beach. The waterside was the fastest and most private way of reaching Oristo-Sarayi from Estavia-Sarayi and this hadn't been the first time she'd taken this path.

The noise from the city was dampened behind the high temple walls, but that she could hear it at all was worrisome.

Her feeling was echoed by Oristo. Everyone should be asleep in their beds at this time of night, and she could feel the Hearth God turn in growing agitation from the other Gods to the people of Anavatan, like a frantic chicken scrambling about an overturned nest. Tanay quickened her pace. She needed to get to Oristo-Sarayi before the chicken caused even more damage.

A few moments later, she ducked under the first of Usara's wharfs, half expecting Rakeed to join her. But the sound of shouting from behind the Healer God's walls made it clear that he had not been able to restore order quite as quickly as she had—physicians being harder to distract with food and drink than soldiers. She hurried on, careful not to walk headfirst into the other two wharfs that served Usara's temple and brain herself.

The strip of pebbled beach narrowed as it began to angle southwest, and she felt a deep muted sensibility settled over her prophetic abilities as she stepped into Incasa-Sarayi's domain. Those seers not sworn to the God of Prophecy tended to keep well away from His territory, and Tanay stilled a sudden chill of disquiet as she passed the huge, ornate main temple wharf, striding under it without the need to duck her head in the slightest. Tanay was tall, but Incasa's main wharf was another foot above her head. His great marble statue loomed so high above her that it could have blotted out the moon had it been behind Him and His wide, white gaze made her shiver.

The sense of foreboding only passed when she crossed into Oristo's dominion. Usually this invoked a sense of peace and well-being, but tonight all she felt was the Hearth God's own anxiety increase.

As she'd expected, a pair of junior guards of Estavia were waiting with a server-delinkos when she vaulted onto the temple's plain and serviceable main wharf. They gave a crisp salute that belied the time of night as the delinkos came forward.

"You're expected, Sayin," she said formally. "I'm to take you to the Summoning Chamber at once."

"Have any of the others arrived yet?"

"Not from this gate, Sayin. You're the first."

"Very well. Lead on."

✦

Unlike Estavia's temple, the mood inside Oristo-Sarayi was one of tightly reined composure. Although many more people were up and about than was normal, everyone carried themselves with an air of—albeit strained—dignity and purpose as they dealt with the crowd of people spilling in through the main doors.

Chamberlain Kadar met her at the entrance to the Summoning Chamber, dismissing the delinkos back to her duty by the lake wharf.

"We're to wait within until the others arrive."

Together they slipped inside.

Oristo-Sarayi's Summoning Chamber had been fashioned to resemble a private sitting room, with an eye for comfort and serenity that echoed the Hearth God's passion for order and security through familial surroundings. The room was paneled in warm, somber woods and the carpet which ran the entire length of the room was woven in deep jewel tones. The cushions were firm, fashioned to support the spine and buttocks and, after bowing to Senior-Abayos Priest Neclan, Tanay took her usual place, trying to bring her thoughts to some order. A carafe of light wine and a plate of cucumber slices and yogurt sat in the center of the low, mahogany table in the center, but no one touched them. Together, Tanay, Kadar, and Neclan waited silently for the other chamberlains to join them with word from Anavatan's temples.

They weren't long in arriving, but their news was far from reassuring. Driven to distraction by Estavia's destructive path, Havo had sent a storm of seasonal proportions slashing across the city; hail as large as pigeon eggs had been seen smashing through the marketplaces and injuring dozens of people. As a consequence, Ystazia and Usara's temples were in an uproar with their Gods' followers crowding their main courtyards in panic.

But the most disturbing news had come from Incasa-Sarayi.

There was no news. After last night's Evening Invocation, the Prophecy God's temple had closed its doors, its senior priests had gathered in its central arzhane chamber and there they'd stayed. When Estavia had exploded from Gol-Beyaz, dragging the other Gods with Her, not a single seer-priest or seer-delinkos had reacted. The servers, artisans, gardeners, physicians, and sentinels who tended Incasa-Sarayi were told to return to their beds. Everything was under control.

To illustrate the point, Incasa was the first of the Gods to return under the waves, compelling Havo, Usara, and Ystazia to follow. This left only Estavia raging across the grasslands and Oristo, ruddy-brown feet planted firmly on the God-Wall, refusing to be moved.

As Neclan and her abayos-priests began the Invocation that would bring them into concert with the Hearth God, a shriek of possessive fury reverberated from the west.

✦

"Mine! Mine, Mine, MINE, MINE, *MINE!"*

The dawn sun lit up the grasslands in a wild pattern of sunlight and shadow as the Godling screamed the words at Graize, battering at his senses, both physical and mental, until the seer spun about in the saddle, lips pulled back from his teeth in a rabid snarl, and shot a bolt of pure power directly into Its face.

Hisar went flying backward, then collected Itself in midair and sprang forward once again, still screaming.

Behind them, Danjel held Brax's unconscious body in the saddle before him, one arm wrapped about his chest while Yal and the rest of the Petchan sayers maintained a protective, muting circle around their captive.

They'd been riding throughout the night, making for the protection of the mountains. Early on it had become clear that their combined power over the muting effect and Danjel's wild lands blood had kept the Godling as well as Estavia at bay. Enraged, It had renewed Its attacks against Graize, but so far It had been unable to win out against the man who'd fashioned It. Now, as they reached the edge of the foothills, Graize raised himself up and caught the Godling in a blazing stare.

"Stop, or I'll kill him."

Hisar froze in mid-strike.

"He's not yours," Graize continued in a snakelike hiss. *"He's mine."*

"I FED FROM HIM. You GAVE him to ME."

Graize's eyes narrowed. *"I did not* give *him to you; I* allowed *you to feed off him. And when I'm finished with him,"* he added as Hisar made to protest, *"I may allow you to feed off him again, but not before. Now, go and find Spar and return to me with his whereabouts."*

"WHY SHOULD I?"

"Because I asked you to."

Seer and Godling stared at each other until, with a snap of Its ethereal wings that knocked Graize's hair into his eyes, Hisar shot into the clouds. Graize watched It go with a baleful expression, then gestured sharply at the others.

Sharing an apprehensive glance, they followed as he urged his mount forward.

✦

Movement brought pain and pain brought a soupy semi-consciousness that forced its way through the darkness. Brax reached out, but there was nothing in the darkness except pain and a deep, hollow, echoing emptiness as if he were nothing more than a shell, lying shattered on the ground. He wasn't dead; there'd be no pain in death, only the all-embracing power of Estavia's final embrace. But he couldn't be alive because Estavia was gone and Spar was gone. The place where their presence should be felt scoured and raw as if all his organs had been torn from his body. Unable to face the pain alone, Brax fell back into unconsciousness.

✦

Below on the grasslands, Estavia screamed in impotent rage, the signs of Her anger spread out in a dozen-mile radius with great channels gouged in the earth and the sky filled with flying debris. Towering a hundred feet high, the Battle God spun Her swords until the air grew hot, sparking a dozen grass fires with every pass and churning up a vortex of wind and rain that rivaled even Havo's Dance. One by one, Her patrols were plunged

into the depths of Her anger and, as their search for
Her missing Champion continued to turn up nothing,
Her fury increased.

◆

An hour's ride from the rocks, Kemal reined up, feeling scorched and exhausted by the Battle God's anger.
His face was caked with dried blood from where an
eight-foot strip of brush, rent from the ground directly
beneath his horse's hooves, had thrown him from the
saddle, and his mind throbbed as Estavia's screaming
reverberated through Her lien.

FIND HIM!

Holding his hands cupped around his mouth, he
shouted so that the others could hear, then pointed to
a low rise a few hundred yards to the west. They turned
their mounts that way and pushed on, eyes narrowed
to slits against the storm, Estavia's rage driving them
forward.

FIND HIM, FIND HIM!

They'd been riding all night ever since Spar had
awakened crying out for Brax. He hadn't spoken a
word since and now sat numbly in front of Yashar in
the saddle, cradled in the older man's arms as he'd been
as a child with Jaq padding along beside them, whining
loudly. Every now and then Yashar would glance down
at him with a questioning murmur, but when Spar remained unresponsive, his abayos would return his own,
distraught gaze to the empty landscape while Spar continued to stare sightlessly at nothing, his eyes wide and
blank and as black as pitch.

◆

*The dark place stretched out before him, the echoing,
empty silence thundering in his ears. One by one, the
ghosts of his past were dragged up from the black
waters, only to stare mutely back at him and be flung
back in disgust, his rage as violent as the God's. They*

could not help him; no one could help him, but he still reached for them, unable to believe that Brax was really gone.

✦

They made the rise just as the dawn sun broke the horizon. Pausing in the lee of its minimal protection, Yashar turned to Kemal.

"Do we stop for Invocation?" he shouted over the wind.

His arkados shook his head. "No," he shouted back. "We sing in the saddle!"

"And the wards?"

"We couldn't manage it in this weather, Yash! They'll have to wait! She'll understand!"

Throwing his arm up to deflect a piece of flying wood, Yashar winced. "How long can she keep this up?" he shouted.

"As long as we can!" Kemal called back. "She must be tapping into every one of Her sworn to maintain a physical presence this long. Start the song, Yash; it should lend us all some extra strength!"

The older man nodded. Gesturing at the others, he took a deep breath, then began to sing Estavia's Morning Invocation, struggling to be heard over the screaming in his own senses.

"FIND HIM!"

✦

A voice cut through the dark place, Yashar's, deep and compelling, almost desperate. Kemal joined in a heartbeat later. Spar stood staring at the horizon, certain that Brax would join in. But when the dark waters revealed only his own, shrouded reflection, he sank to his knees on the cold, black sand, fists pressed against his eyes to block out the sight of . . . nothing.

✦

The rocks came into view an hour later. The Invocation seemed to have calmed Estavia somewhat. She still raged across the grasslands, but at least She'd stopped screaming and the angry shriek of Her swords had eased, bringing the wind down to a manageable level. With a fresh burst of speed, they reached the rocks, then froze as the signs of battle came into view.

Blood covered the ground with streaks of dried gore ending at a line of bodies covered in blue cloaks.

The two militia threw themselves from their saddles at once. Kemal followed more slowly, accepting Spar's limp weight from Yashar before the older man joined him on the ground. As he tucked the youth into a protective hollow between two hillocks, he whistled for Jaq, who immediately placed himself between Spar and the rocks with a warning growl, all the fur along his neck and spine bristling angrily. Leaving him in the dog's protective care, Kemal then followed Yashar around the main bulk of the rock pile.

They found Brin and Bazmin huddled to either side of Feridun. The man was unconscious, his face bleached of color and Bazmin's eyes were tightly closed in pain, but Brin had managed a defensive position against the rocks, sword pointed outward, although the blood-spattered hilt was propped against the ground to keep it from falling.

At the sound of their names, both twins stirred weakly.

✦

Slowly Brin fought upward from a hazy world of fatigue and pain.

It had taken some time before the twins had realized that their attackers had withdrawn. Brin had managed to climb the rocks just high enough to keep watch for a fresh assault while Bazmin had stumbled from one fallen comrade to another, using the moonlight as a guide. But they were all dead except for Feridun.

After binding his wounds as best they could, they'd dragged the others to a shallow depression on the other side of the rocks, laying Khair, Sarqi, Abbas, Jejun, Berar, and Zeineb together, weapons at their sides, and covering them with their own cloaks before slumping down beside Feridun, too exhausted to even whisper the Morning Invocation.

At first, Yashar's appearance registered as nothing more than a dream, but when the dawn sun shining off the two silver swords worked into the front of his leather cuirass proved that he was really there, Brin began to cry.

✦

The militia made Feridun as comfortable as possible while Yashar forced a mouthful of raki down first Brin's throat and then Bazmin's, gently cleaning the blood from Bazmin's face where a nasty head wound had caked over the twin's eyes and mouth. Kemal had glanced wordlessly at the line of bodies, then crouched down beside them, taking note of the familiar sword and shield laying beside Brin.

"Brax?"

Brin pointed weakly in the direction of the foothills. "Gone. Taken."

"But alive?"

"Alive."

"How many?"

"A dozen Petchans. Maybe more. I'm not sure. It was dark. But, Sayin." Brin struggled to rise, clutching at Kemal's sleeve in agitation. "It was Graize; Brax's enemy, Graize. He took him."

Kemal glanced over his shoulder at Spar. "We know, Ghazi." Straightening, he gestured the two militia over. "Menaz, send your bird with our position. Cenk, can you reach another seer's mind from here?"

"Now that the muting fog has lifted, I can, Ghazi."

"Then do it. Tell them to send word to Estavia-Sarayi

that we're heading into the western foothills to find Brax. Anything that Sable Company can do to aid in our search should be done at once. After that, do what you can for Feridun and keep watch. When reinforcements arrive, return to Alev-Hisar with the bodies."

"Yes, Ghazi."

Bazmin rose blearily on one elbow. "Should we come with you, Sayin?"

Kemal shook his head. "No. Rest if you can, follow with reinforcements."

"Yes, Sayin."

Both twins sank down again, reluctant relief showing clearly in their dark eyes.

Catching up Brax's sword and shield, Kemal returned to Spar.

"Delin, can you hear me?" he asked gently, laying one hand on the youth's arm and the other on Jaq's head to still his growling. "Brax is alive. Taken prisoner, but alive."

Slowly, Spar focused on his abayos' face, the blue of his eyes rimmed with a frightening darkness that made Kemal shiver.

"I can't feel him," he whispered hoarsely. "I can always feel him. Why can't I feel him, Aba?"

Kemal glanced to the east where Estavia still raged across the grasslands. "I don't know, Delin," he said gently. "But we're going to find him. You rest now for just a few moments, all right? And then you eat something for your abayon, yes? After that, we'll push on and we'll find him, I promise you."

Spar nodded wearily. Closing his eyes, he leaned against Jaq's flank and, whining quietly, the dog turned to nuzzle the side of his face, his nose knocking against the blue-and-green beads wound into a lock of his hair. Spar made no response, and Kemal shared a worried glance with Yashar before rising to unpack a flask of water and a piece of bread from his saddlebags.

Deep within him, Estavia's lien continued to force its demands into words.

"*FIND HIM.*"

Pressing his hand against his chest, Kemal nodded. "I will," he promised.

✦

In the dark place, the faintest of green lights suddenly sparkled at the very edge of the horizon, casting a pale sheen across the water for the space of a single heartbeat. A hunting hawk's dark silhouette hovered high above it, but wrapped in his own despair, Spar did not see either of them.

✦

Something stirred in the darkness; the faintest sense of something, of someone Brax had sworn to protect, no matter what the cost, so many years ago. He reached for it, desperate to catch hold of anything that would fill the empty, bleeding place in his body, but just as quickly, it was gone. With his mind twisting in despair, Brax fell back into the darkness again.

✦

High above the grasslands, in the guise of a hunting hawk, Hisar watched Spar's people move about the rocks, Its expression twisted in uncertainty.

The last few hours had confused It terribly, and It had no one to turn to for answers. It had never felt so alone, and the pain of it threatened to knock It from Its seeming every time the winds of Estavia's wrath slammed against Its focus. Snapping Its wings closed, It dropped a few hundred feet, trying to find a calm air stream where It could think clearly.

The battle had gone exactly as had Graize had said it would. Hisar had given over the position of each and every one of Brax's patrol and then withdrawn to the air to watch, Its duty done.

But then everything had gone horribly wrong.

Hisar had seen violence before. It had been born in the rage and fury of a wild lands storm, and been fashioned by the power and madness of Graize's glittering, unpredictable ambition. It had fought at the battle of Serin-Koy before It had even known what battle was and had stood Its ground on Estavia's own temple battlements for the right to feed from Her Champion and grow strong. And last night, as the moon had risen over the grasslands, and each of Graize's enemies had fallen, giving their spirits over to the Battle God far away, Hisar had felt nothing more than a vague excitement and a curiosity at their fragility.

But then Graize had risen over Brax like a leviathan, his face contorted in hatred, his mind screaming promises of bloodshed and death, and Hisar had suddenly known a fear so overwhelming that it had knocked It from the sky. On the heels of that fear had come a possessive rage, white-hot in its intensity, and after that had come the hunger; the desperate, mythic, starving hunger of the wild lands spirits denied the essence they craved century after century; the hunger that had created the Godling five years before; the hunger that had driven It against Graize in the very beginning of Its consciousness. Terrified and furious that Graize might actually kill Brax and deny Hisar that essence once again, the Godling had thrown Itself at him screaming out Its fury, half-in and half-out of the physical world.

"Mine! Mine, Mine, MINE, MINE, *MINE!"*

Because no matter how powerful the Battle God's lien might be, and no matter how strong Graize's hate might be, Hisar had tasted Brax's essence on the battlements of Estavia-Sarayi, and that very act had bound them together forever. Brax belonged to Hisar, and Hisar could not leave him to face his enemies alone. The muting effect had deflected the Battle God's lien, but it would not deflect Hisar's. Hisar had fought it before and won through it, and so the Godling had faced Graize down and saved Brax's life. For now.

But Graize was a powerful seer, capable of throwing an entire pantheon of Gods into confusion and capable of blocking his own ties to the Godling by wielding the muting effect like a sword thrown up between them, and so Hisar had obeyed his last order out of fear, flying back across the grasslands to find another of his enemies.

To find Spar.

It shuddered, dropping a hundred feet in Its distress.

Spar; as powerful in his love and desperation as Graize was in his hate and need. Spar; who wielded an even more terrible weapon in the dark place than Graize had in Dar-Sayer's cavern: his sticky black net of prophecy. Spar was coming closer. His mind was filled with a paralyzing fear for Brax's safety that rivaled Hisar's own, but as soon as he overcame that fear, he would reach out for Graize's death. Hisar could see that as clearly as if It were a seer as well. And It couldn't allow that because Graize was also Hisar's.

But Spar was not.

Gaining altitude, the Godling soared high above the rocks as It mulled over this new revelation. It could feel no ties of power and obligation to Spar deep within the center of Its being. It could, if It wanted to, fly back to Graize and tell him where the rival seer was and how distraught and vulnerable Brax's capture had made him. It could, if It wanted to, lead Graize to Spar's position and help him kill Spar. It could.

If It wanted to.

But Spar had talked to It, had explained things to It, and had convinced Brax to help It.

It didn't want to help Graize kill him.

It wanted Spar to belong to It, too; Spar and Graize and Brax, Its three Champions just as Incasa had shown It.

Hovering miserably in midair, Hisar wished It knew how to sort out all these frightening new feelings and make them stop hurting.

But It had no one to ask. Wheeling about, It made for the clouds above, trailing distress like a tail of a fiery comet.

✦

Far to the east, pacing the shores of Gol-Beyaz like an angry guard dog, Oristo, God of Emotional Succor, heard the crying of one of Its children and turned only to see Incasa rising from the waves, His own icy gaze riveted on the western grasslands. The Hearth God leaped instinctively between the God of Prophecy and the half-made Godling of Creation and Destruction at once, lips drawn back in a defensive snarl.

Incasa glared back at the younger God, His stance demanding acquiescence, but Oristo was the God of Children and so the two stood facing each other like a pair of angry cats until, very slowly, each one reached out for Their chosen avatars.

At Incasa-Sarayi, First Oracle Bessic and his senior seer-priests channeled more power to their God, waiting for His signal to act, while at Oristo-Sarayi the Hearth God's chamberlains prepared to answer their God's most recent demand: to help the God-child, Hisar.

✦

Hisar was flitting unhappily through the clouds east of Spar's position when the hazy outline of the figure It had seen before Dar-Sayer's cavern suddenly material- ized in front of It. The Godling snapped backward in alarm, but when the figure remained still, It paused.

Everything both Graize and Spar had ever told It had made It mistrustful of the Gods, but Brax trusted at least one of Them completely, so when Oristo made no hostile move toward It, Hisar drew closer, drawn by the Hearth God's air of unwavering composure. When

It was no more than a few hundred yards away, Oristo turned and began to slowly move west. The Hearth God did not turn to see if the Godling was following, but little by little, the two of Them returned to the sky high above the rocks where Spar's patrol was making ready to move out.

Hisar looked down at the young seer, then turned to Oristo with a questioning air.

The Hearth God gestured.

"ALL YOUR QUESTIONS MAY BE ANSWERED THERE, DELIN."

The words echoed in both the God and Godling's minds, sending ripples of near-physical response ebbing back and forth between Them that neither one accepted nor resisted until they stilled.

Hisar was the first to recover, shaking Its head as Jaq might shake off a swarm of meadow bees.

"I can't go to Spar," It complained, speaking out loud, even though It knew instinctively that the Hearth God could have heard Its thoughts.

"YES, YOU CAN."

"He'll be mad at me."

"WHY?"

"Because I betrayed Brax."

Oristo paused a moment, considering without question or judgment, then shrugged. *"ASK FORGIVENESS."*

"How?"

"WITH WORDS, THEN WITH DEEDS."

"But why would he forgive me?"

Hisar's voice was so plaintive that Oristo smiled down at It with an expression of indulgent exasperation. *"BECAUSE HE IS YOUR ABAYOS, DELIN."*

"But his mind is too far away in the dark place."

"HIS MIND WILL RETURN. I WILL SEE TO IT."

"But . . ."

"NO. DO AS I SAY."

Anxiety spat out the same words Hisar had thrown at Graize moments before.

"WHY SHOULD I?"

"BECAUSE YOU WANT TO."

The Hearth God gave Hisar a shove in the direction of the young seer, then disappeared.

✦

At Oristo-Sarayi, Tanay stiffened as Oristo's intent filled her thoughts, then, using the God's lien as a springboard, flung her mental abilities out toward Spar.

✦

A hooded figure suddenly appeared before him, the waters of the dark place lapping against the hem of her brown robe. Caught up in his own misery, Spar ignored the figure at first, but when Tanay dropped her hood with a meaningful cough, he glanced up.

"A fortune for fifteen gift from the Hearth God," she said firmly.

Spar blinked, his hand reaching instinctively for the beads tied into his hair.

"You have the other one I gave you?"

Spar's own voice echoed in his memory, causing the still waters before him to ripple as if he'd thrown a pebble into their midst and, far off on the horizon, a pale green light glowed in response.

He frowned as Brax's voice now sounded overloud in his ears.

"On a cord around my neck, one green bead to go with the brown one you gave me before."

As Spar's expression signaled his understanding, Tanay nodded. "Good," she said. "Then use it as a bridge between you and go find him."

✦

On the grasslands, Spar opened his eyes to see Yashar, his bearded face lined with worry and fatigue, bending over him.

His abayos made a strained attempt at a smile. "You cried out," he said.

Spar nodded. "Brax is alive."

A wolfish gleam suddenly shone in the older man's eyes. "Where is he?"

"I don't know, not yet, but I will."

"Good enough." Yashar turned. "Kem!"

His arkados came running at the urgency in the older man's voice.

"What is it?"

"We ride. Now."

✦

The sun was near its zenith when Kemal called a halt on the edge of the ragged foothills. Accepting his abayon's help, Spar dismounted stiffly, crossing to a fast-running stream, Jaq tight on his heels. He crouched down, lifting a handful of water to his mouth and winced as the near-freezing liquid burned his throat. The old injury to his calf throbbed from so much unaccustomed time in the saddle, and he kicked off his sandal, thrusting his foot into the stream up to his knee. The frigid water cleared his mind with a snap as quickly as it numbed the pain in his leg. When he couldn't stand it any longer, he pulled his foot out, staring down into the water thoughtfully.

He could feel the power within the stream, so similar to that in Gol-Beyaz, shimmering just below the surface; the power of the spirits and of the Gods. Using the slap of it against his mind to fuel his own abilities, he closed his fist around the beads in his hair and reached out for the two tied about Brax's neck.

The reassuring sense of the other man that had lived within him ever since he'd been four years old stirred weakly in response and he swallowed hard against the lump in his throat, feeling the rush of relief that made his head spin.

Brax was alive, barely, but alive. That was all that

mattered. That was all that could matter. Until he found him. His sense of him was so faint that anyone else might have missed it; anyone but Spar. It was still too weak to lead Spar to him, but it would be enough to fuel his search. Whatever power was blocking him would be smashed to pieces. He would save Brax, and he would kill Graize. Opening his eyes in the darkness, Spar sent a thread of strength and comfort toward his only kardos, then, standing, he returned to his abayon, accepting a handful of dried dates with a savage expression.

The other sense, as familiar as his own, reached out, and this time Brax managed just enough strength to snatch it up, holding it to him as tightly as possible. When the darkness closed over him again, he took Spar with him. He felt the youth open his eyes, felt him size up the darkness in a single heartbeat, then heard him speak.

"Don't be afraid. I'm coming."

✦

High above, Hisar felt a shiver of fear as Spar's renewed sense of purpose reached out to It on a ribbon of power. Oristo had told It to go to him, but It was still afraid. What if he wouldn't forgive It? What if he turned It away? What if he demanded that It help him kill Graize? Or worse, what if It hesitated too long and Graize hurt Brax or even killed him because Hisar hadn't returned to him with word about Spar.

Dropping lower with each unanswered question, Hisar began to tack back and forth in growing agitation.

✦

Kemal was the first to spot the strange shimmering in the air above them. Crouched by the stream filling a waterskin, he raised his head slightly.

"Spar?"

Alerted by the warning in his abayos' voice, the youth

spun about, his eyes black with the power of the dark place.

Spar had told his abayon about his relationship with Hisar on the voyage south down Gol-Beyaz, holding nothing back for the first time. Now, as they moved to stand behind him, forming a solid presence at his back like a pair of marble pillars, he locked his emotions behind an impenetrable barrier of icy control, calling on his years of fleecing Dockside marks to convey the proper stance and attitude to get what he wanted. Hisar was not naive, nor was It stupid; It might not have been involved in the attack on Brax, but It would know what had happened and that would make It wary of his reaction. It must be made to tell him what he needed to know as quickly as possible.

Crossing his arms over his chest, he watched with narrowed eyes as the Godling's dragonfly-seeming wavered in and out of focus a few yards away. Under the pressure of his regard, It hovered for several moments more, flipping back and forth from one seeming to another, until It finally settled on the form of a fierce-looking Yuruk girl.

The two youths stared at each other silently, until Spar raised one lip in a calculated snarl.

"Brax," he demanded.

A flash of hesitation came and went across Its face. "Alive," It answered.

"I know he's alive. Where is he?"

"Heading into the mountains."

"Is he injured?"

The Godling chewed at Its lip in a purely human gesture of uncertainty. "Yes," It said finally.

"Is he dying?"

Spar's voice was flat, his expression carefully neutral, but the underlying threat of violence was so obvious that the Godling moved back a step as if propelled by the wind.

"No," It said a little too quickly, then straightened Its own shoulders. "No, I would feel it if he was."

Spar considered his next question carefully, then caught the Godling in a baleful stare. "My sense of him is weak," he admitted deliberately. "Why is that?"

"The muting effect." Hisar's voice was strained, but It met Spar's gaze with an even expression of Its own. "The mountains block a seer's abilities, even a God's sometimes if the Petchan sayers are controlling it."

"Are the Petchan sayers controlling it?"

"Yes."

"They're that strong that they can cut off the Sworn from their Gods?"

"This close to the mountains, yes, they can."

Spar shook his head. "And all this time the Anavatanon seers had no idea. They just thought the Petchans could block the prophetic visions of enemy seers."

"They can do that, too."

Spar's eyes narrowed dangerously. "Well, they won't block mine," he snarled. "You'll take me through their muting effect to find Brax."

Hisar's form flickered in uncertainty. "Graize is with him," It said finally.

"Good." Spar's eyes darkened still further and the Godling shivered as a ripple of power passed between them.

It rose a few inches above the ground, Its Rayneseeming overlaid with Jaq's as It struggled to contain Its response. "I can't let you kill him," It said finally.

Kemal and Yashar glanced down at Spar as the youth leaned casually back on his good leg. "Really?" he asked in a deceptively conversational tone. "How did you plan to stop me?"

"I won't take you to Brax unless you promise not to kill Graize."

"I see." Spar's head turned very slightly. "Aba-Kemal, can you bring me my bow and quiver, please?"

Hisar watched, Its metallic gaze flickering with suspicion, as the man complied.

Once Spar had the bow in his hands, he strung it, then

turned back to Hisar. "Do you know how accurate I am with this weapon?" he asked.

Hisar's own eyes narrowed. "I've seen you practice," It said defensively.

"Do you know why I'm so accurate?" Accepting an arrow, Spar notched it, holding it to the string between finger and thumb. "When I take aim," he said, "I speak the name of my target in the dark place, binding it to the arrow in my hand. The two become one."

"You can't shoot me," the Godling said hotly.

"Maybe not. But if I bind this arrow, neither you, nor Graize, nor a host of spirits, Petchans, or Gods will stop it from reaching its target, even if it takes a hundred years." He stared long and hard at the Godling as if measuring the distance between them. "And the longer I wait, the longer Brax is in danger, the more likely I am to do just that."

"You helped Graize take him," he said, his voice echoing from the dark place to buffet against the Godling's mind like a typhoon. *"I can see it in your eyes."*

"I kept Graize from killing him," Hisar spat back at him, rearing up take the form of a tall black tower, strong and unassailable.

"Then help me free him."

The tower disintegrated in the wake of Hisar's obvious agitation. It chose and rejected a dozen forms until It finally took the seeming of a young Yuruk boy with a broken arm.

"Promise not to kill Graize, and I'll take you to Brax," It said quietly. *"Please, Spar. I don't want any of you to die."*

Spar considered his answer for a long moment, then gave a sharp nod, his eyes returning to their usual color as he withdrew from the dark place.

"If Brax is alive, I won't kill Graize," he promised. "But only if Brax is alive."

Reluctantly, Hisar nodded as together they headed for the horses.

✦

In the dark place, a child armed and armored and a shimmering tower, strong and defensible, turned toward a snow-clad mountain covered in a crimson mist of danger and of death. And in Gol-Beyaz, the God of Prophecy rolled His dice, watching as they came up six and one just as expected. It was time for the Gods to take the field. Reaching out, He touched the mind of His First Oracle with a single tendril of prophecy.

17

Hisar

MOVEMENT CEASED AND HE felt himself lifted, then laid upon the ground. Something was pressed against his lips, and a warm liquid forced its way down his throat, making him choke. A pressure on his leg caused the pain to ease off temporarily and then he was being lifted once again and carried into a new darkness. A muting oblivion even more powerful than the first closed over him, threatening the tiny spark of Spar that he'd held onto so desperately, and for the space of a heartbeat, panic was the equal of pain. But then the sense of Spar steadied and, using the strength of Spar's promise, Brax began to fight his way back to consciousness.

"Don't be afraid. I'm coming."

◆

Crouched in a tiny, hidden cave, Yal forced another infusion between Brax's teeth, rubbing his throat like a baby bird's until he swallowed, then made her way outside. Much smaller than Dar-Sayer's home, the cave barely fit two people, so Yal and Danjel had taken it in turns to see to it that Brax didn't die of his injuries before Graize decided what to do with him.

As she emerged into the bright, afternoon sun, she met Danjel's eyes and the Yuruk wyrdin shrugged philosophically. Graize would make up his mind as soon as his mind explained what his choices were. Danjel had long ago stopped wondering at the process.

Pulling out her pipe, the Yuruk made herself comfortable with her back against a tree while the rest of the patrol made camp, sending the youngest back to Chalash with word of the attack, and setting up sentry positions against the rescue attempt Graize had assured them was coming.

Meanwhile, Graize sat just inside the cave entrance, watching Brax's inner struggle with a frown and wondering at his own motives. The protective cloak was torn from his conflict on the grasslands; madness bubbled up through it like water in a leaking boat, and he watched it as dispassionately as he watched Brax.

Beside him, Brax moaned, and with a snap, Graize's mind came back to itself.

He had intended to kill the other man right there at the rocks. He'd seen it, planned it, and all the pieces had fallen into place with prescient perfection. He'd found his enemy, fought him, and felled him just as he'd envisioned. Rising above him, he'd delivered the killing blow, but at the last moment, Brax had jerked aside and the traitorous moon had shone full upon his face and Graize had found himself ricocheted into the past. The cold rain of Havo's Dance had swept over him and, once again, he was a frightened little boy, crouched in a doorway, abandoned and alone. The familiar sense of powerless vulnerability had enraged him, but before he could strike again, another traitor, this time the Godling, had flung Itself between him and the object of his wrath.

But nothing, not Brax, the past, the Godling, nor his own twisted emotions could distract him for long. He'd recovered, and shouting out the single word of command necessary to separate Brax from Estavia, he'd thrown the muting effect at the other man with all his strength. It had all but severed Brax's connection to the Battle God, and the other man had gone down like a felled ox. Far to the east, Graize had heard an unearthly scream of loss that had echoed through his mind like a storm of cinders. It had thrown up his vision from the road to Chalash: a tiny cave that winked in and out of his vision like a lantern. And then he'd understood.

In his eagerness to destroy Brax, he'd forgotten about Spar. The other seer was still in the game; injured, maybe even crippled by this latest move against Brax, but a dangerous enemy notwithstanding. There were still important moves to be made if he were to finally overcome them both. Giving the order to withdraw, he'd caught Brax up and all but thrown him at Danjel, then remounted. The game begun on the grasslands with Brax's defeat would end in the mountains with Spar's.

✦

Kemal called a halt at the edge of the foothills. Dismounting, he and Yashar watered the horses while Spar stood, staring up a winding path, his expression grim. Hisar hovered in dragonfly form to one side, agitation causing Its wings to buzz intermittently. Finally, Spar spoke without turning.

"He's there?" He indicated the path with a flick of his head.

Hisar nodded. "In a cave. It's strong with the muting effect. I can't go in."

"But you can lead me to it?"

"Yes." The Godling hesitated for a moment, clearly torn. "You know they'll be waiting for you," It warned. "Graize and the Petchans. They know you're coming."

Spar gave his familiar one-shouldered shrug. "It doesn't matter."

"How will you get past them?"

"You're going to tell me where they are."

"So you can ... kill them?"

The anxiety in the Godling's voice finally made Spar turn his head. "No. So I can elude them."

"What if they see you?"

"They won't."

"What if they do?"

"Kemal and Yashar will kill them."

"There's a dozen of them. And they're seers, every one. They control the muting effect."

"And I control the dark place. If I have to, I'll fight them from there."

"But . . ."

Spar raised a hand, and Hisar subsided. As the wind caught Spar's hair, knocking the beads together with a soft, clacking sound, the Godling shifted to Its Rayne-seeming.

"Why do you wear those?" It asked plaintively.

"They were a gift."

"They taste like weapons."

"Weapons?"

Hisar nodded, Its features clouded, but encouraged that Spar had not rebuffed It, It drew closer. "When you wear them, it feels like there's a big hand trying to grab me."

Intrigued despite himself, Spar cocked his head to one side. "Why?"

"The Petchans make them to use against the spirits."

"But you're not a spirit."

Hisar gave an impatient snort. "I'm more than a spirit," It said haughtily, "but I'm made of spirit. Everything is: the Gods, the land, the people. And everything feeds on it. Everything *needs* to feed on it," It added, baring Its teeth like a cat drawing in a disconcerting scent. "The unformed spirits most of all. That's why they attack anything unprotected. They have to have it, and if they can't get it, the nearness of it drives them mad. If it's really strong or close to the surface in a person, they can use it, like the way your seers and priests use it to control the Gods."

"Control?"

Hisar echoed Spar's own one-shouldered shrug. "They

let the Gods come inside them and feed on them, so the Gods protect them from anything else that might want to feed on them, but the people feed the Gods so they have the power; they have the control. It's no different than with Jaq," It added, waving a hand in the dog's direction. "You feed him and he guards you. And," It added pointedly, "he guards his food supply."

"Point," Spar acknowledged with a cynical sneer.

"The Yuruk wyrdin make power on the outside to feed the spirits and the spirits answer questions for them," Hisar continued, pleased to be the one passing on knowledge for a change. "The spirits don't protect them, but they do leave them alone."

"And the Petchans?"

"The Petchans make the beads to help them control the spirits without feeding them. They use the brown ones for protection." It tipped Its head to one side in a thoughtful gesture. "It feels like the hand's trying to push me away. Brax wears one of those," It added with a scowl.

"I notice that it didn't push you away very effectively on the battlements four years ago," Spar observed in a dry tone.

"It tried," Hisar sniffed. "But I pushed back. I'm stronger than some stupid little bead, and far stronger than any mountain spirit, no matter how wild it might be."

"So the brown ones feel like they're pushing you away, and the others feel like they're trying to grab you?" Spar asked.

"The blue beads do. The Petchan sayers use them to focus their own spirit to control the mountain ones, and the green beads help them capture dreams; dreams are made of spirit, too. And prophecy," It added, a faraway look in Its eyes. "I guess prophecy is like the dreams of the earth and sky."

"Poetic."

Hisar glanced up quickly to see if Spar was being

sarcastic, but the youth's face held the same faraway expression and the Godling smiled shyly.

"I guess."

"I wonder if that's why I can see a green light when I think of Brax," Spar wondered aloud. "Because we're both wearing green beads."

"Maybe. Maybe he's dreaming of you. Graize wears a green bead, too. Maybe he's thinking about you both and the beads are linking up."

"Maybe. Where did Graize get his green bead?"

"The Petchan chief gave it to him. He has green and brown and blue," Hisar replied, oblivious to the sudden gleam of interest in Spar's eyes. "Every color but red; red's just for chiefs and senior sayers. But the other colors poke at me just the same," It complained. "He shouldn't wear them. None of you should."

"What do the red ones do?"

"They have bits of raw spirit trapped inside them. The Chalash's chief called it spirit-blood."

Spar's eyes widened. "Spirits have blood?"

"No, they don't," Hisar snapped impatiently. "They probably just say that because it's red. All I know is that it's supposed to be the strongest."

"So how do the red ones make you feel?"

Hisar frowned. "They . . . don't. That's . . . odd."

"Yes, it is." Pulling the cloth bag from his belt pouch, Spar drew out a small red bead flecked with silver, and the Godling took an involuntary step backward.

"Tanay gave me four," Spar told It. "Gifts from Oristo for my fortune for fifteen. She said I would know what to do with them. I gave a green one to Brax, I put a green and a blue one on, and this one . . ." He jiggled it in his hand. "I don't know, it felt like I should wait."

"I thought you hated Oristo," Hisar accused, Its voice thick with suspicion.

"I don't *trust* Oristo," Spar corrected. "I don't trust any God. But I trust Tanay. She wouldn't have given them to me if they weren't important. Like the brown ones four years ago; they helped link Brax and me together. So will these."

Hisar nodded. "I can feel them," It said. "The green one itches, like how you might feel if there was a louse in your hair."

Spar raised an eyebrow and Hisar shrugged. "It was something Brax said last night. He said he felt a tickle in the back of his mind, like how a louse feels in your hair. A tickle of danger. He knew something was wrong." It frowned. "But he's not a seer, is he?"

"No, but he's had a little training. *Cultivating stillness.*"

"Maybe that's why you can reach him."

"Maybe. But I'm no Petchan sayer. I'm . . ."

He suddenly went very still.

"What?" The Godling drew closer. "Spar?"

"Wait." Closing his eyes, Spar stepped into the dark place. The waters stretched out before him, his past hovering just below the surface and, with a simple gesture, he reached out. The warmth and safety of Tanay's kitchen enveloped him, smelling of bread and spices and woodsmoke. He felt the sting of the injuries he had taken five years ago in the spirit attack on Liman-Caddesi, and then he heard Brax's voice.

"Cindar thought Spar might have mountain blood."

He nodded. Neither one of them knew who their first abayon had been, but they'd always assumed that Spar's blond hair and pale eyes had come from either Ekmir-Koy or Gurney-Dag mountain people. They'd talked about going to Tanay to find out, but what Spar hadn't told Brax was that he could have found out any time without her help if he'd wanted to.

But he'd never wanted to until now.

He stared into the depths for a long moment. Then, as the sense of Tanay's kitchen faded with his answer, he cleared his mind the way a diner might clear his palate for another course. Then he reached out, this time for the green bead around Brax's neck instead of for Brax himself.

It flickered in the darkness like a distant beacon.

"The Petchans make the beads to help them control the spirits without feeding them."

"And the Anavatanon let the spirits come inside them," Spar whispered. "And I am also Anavatanon."

Drawing his sense of Brax's bead into his mind, he cupped his mental powers about it like hands around a flame until it glowed with a strong, green light. Then, drawing up a vision of strength, he sent it toward the light on a trail of shared experience.

And opened his eyes.

Hisar had withdrawn back into the sky. Instead, Yashar stood before him holding a piece of bread.

"Eat," his older abayos said gently. "Then we'll carry on."

Spar nodded.

✦

A bright green light burned in front of Brax's eyes, hot and insistent. He tried to turn away, but everywhere he looked, the light followed, and so finally he gave up and stared belligerently into its depths.

"What?"

Spar's voice crackled through his mind.

"You cultivate a single thought about one thing, anything: a . . . sword or a word or . . ."

A memory.

With the bond between them revitalized, Brax opened his eyes as Spar had. And saw Graize crouched beside him in the darkness, his pale eyes glowing eerily in the faint light. Their eyes locked, and Graize tilted his head to one side like a bird.

"How does it feel?" he asked almost conversationally.

Brax stared up at him unblinkingly, refusing to follow the question down to any form of pain, physical or otherwise.

"To be alone," Graize expanded. "To feel nothing, not your precious God of Battles or even your more precious little street seer? How does it feel to have lost them all?"

The darkness threatened to swallow him up again, and Brax fought his way back, using the green light and the memory of his conversation with Spar to hold himself steady. Spar was not gone, and so Estavia couldn't be gone either. When the panic and despair receded once again, he stared back at Graize.

"What did you do?" he croaked.

The other man showed his teeth at him. "I took them away from you," he answered. "I took them all away." He leaned forward. "I guess the Gods aren't as powerful as you thought they were, huh? You should have remembered what Cindar taught you. Besides how to fall down drunk in the street, that is," he added, his eyes gleaming maliciously.

Brax shook his head wearily. "That was a long time ago, Graize," he said, unable to speak above a whisper. "What does Cindar's weakness matter now?"

Graize reared back as if stung. "Weakness breeds weakness," he retorted.

Brax smiled faintly. "So what does my weakness matter now?"

Graize made to speak, then just shook his head, his right pupil narrowing to a pinprick. "It matters," he said quietly.

Leaning his back against the cavern wall, he regarded Brax again as his right pupil snapped back into line with the other. "It matters to Spar," he said, the conversational tone back in his voice. "He'll be going out of his mind looking for you, as impotently as your Carrion God," he noted. "But they won't find you, not here. Here they're as weak as you are."

"They'll keep looking."

"Of course they will. That's why I haven't killed you yet. You see, if I kill you, it will be over; your spirit will flutter off like a little butterfly to Gol-Beyaz, and Estavia and Spar will mourn you and that'll be that." Graize leaned forward. "But I don't want that to be that. Not by a long shot of thats."

"Why?"

Graize blinked at him. "Why what?"

"Why can't it be over?" Shifting a little, Brax gave an involuntary hiss as the movement grated on his injured elbow. For a moment, the pain swept across his mind like a wave of fire, then ebbed. When he could focus again, he saw that Graize had returned to his position against the wall.

"It can't be over because my vision says it isn't over," Graize answered. "We're being swept along by the tide and we sweep the tide along with us as we go. Three ragged little street lifters, but the Gods fight over us like fishmongers fighting over fish in a net. Isn't that strange? But while They keep Their eyes on the three little fish, the enemy sends in reserves to flank them from all sides. Weakness, Brax, breeds weakness—and the fish, the fishmongers, even the net, will be lost."

Brax gave his head a weary shake. "So stop being a fish and start being a man," he rasped, the words grating in his throat like dust but too annoyed by the other man's tone of distant self-pity to care.

Graize gave a sigh of real regret in reply. "I think it's probably too late for that now. We might have managed it, you and I, if we'd stood together a long time ago. I told you before; I saw it and Spar saw it."

"Spar didn't see it," Brax countered. "He told me he didn't."

"Ah, you did get up the courage to ask him, did you?" Graize shrugged. "If he didn't see it before, he's seen it by now. It's the only way you'll get out of here alive."

"Spar and Estavia will find me," Brax repeated, and Graize gave a bark of derisive laughter.

"Really? How?" he demanded. " This cave's so full of the muting effect that I can barely even see you and I'm sitting right beside you. Your God will rant, and scream, and rip up trees, and then She'll forget all about you. The Gods are like cats, Brax. They'll slap you about until you stop moving, and then they'll wander off in search of more lively prey."

He showed his teeth at the other man. "And as for Spar," he continued. "He could fall into this cave and he still wouldn't see it or you.

"Besides, I have the edge. I have a spy. That's right," he sneered as Brax's dark eyes narrowed. "My Godling—I'm told you've met It. Well, It is, at this very moment, searching out Spar's position. That's how I defeated you and your precious little patrol, by the way.

"Never trust a God, Brax, not even a Baby-God."

"So why do you trust It?" Brax countered.

Graize snorted. "I don't trust It; I control It."

He laced his fingers behind his head. "So there you have it," he said. "I win. Now, I imagine you'll need more water and someone to check that nasty wound on your leg for you. I would hate for my little bait fish to bleed to death before Spar gets here with his fishing line."

He giggled, and the pupil of his right eye narrowed once again. "Now, don't be stubborn," he chided as Brax's jaw tightened. "You can't be rescued if you die. Never give up hope, Warrior of Estavia, that's probably the worst kind of treason. Well, that and out and out changing sides," he amended. "Which you just might do before this is over."

He stood before Brax could answer. "I told you: I saw it and Spar saw it. When you finally see it, let me know." He stared down at the other man for a long moment as if about to say something else, then turned abruptly and ducked out of the cave.

Brax lay, breathing carefully so as not to reawaken the pain in his arm, then closed his eyes. Reaching out, he drew the green light toward him, using it like a candle flame to chase away the darkness. Then pulling the last of his strength around him like a cloak, he waited.

✦

Beyond the cave, the sun began its descent as Brax's small family made their way through the foothills and into the mountains. They rode the narrow, winding goat path silently, led by Spar's renewed sense of Brax and aided by the Godling who flew above them so high they could barely see the shimmer of Its wings in the cloudy sky.

As the path steepened, Spar rubbed his eyes in frustration. The higher they climbed, the greater the mountain's natural muting effect became. Already it pressed against his abilities, causing the distant peaks to wink in and out of his physical sight as well as his prophetic vision, and it took all his concentration to keep them in view.

Finally, when the Godling swooped down to stand before them in Its Rayne-seeming, he dismounted, throwing himself down on the path beside Jaq and pressing his fists to his temples to fight off the pain that was beginning to radiate across his forehead.

Hisar gave him a curious look, then turned to Kemal and Yashar.

"Another three hundred yards and they'll see you," It said bluntly.

The older man nodded. "Then this is a good time to pause and discuss our strategy."

The two men dismounted. As they saw to the horses, Hisar returned Its attention to Spar.

"You promised you wouldn't kill anyone," It reminded him.

Panting slightly, Spar raised himself up. "If everything goes smoothly, I won't have to," he agreed, but the tinge of uncertainty in his tone caused Hisar to widen the Rayne-seeming's eyes in alarm.

"Why wouldn't everything go smoothly?" It demanded. "You said that if I told you where they were, you could elude them."

Spar winced as Its shrill voice added a new layer of pain to his headache. "I can."

"But?"

"But they can't."

Youth and Godling turned as one to regard the two men with them.

"I thought they were your backup against the Petchan seers."

"They were, but you told me yourself that the Petchans control the muting effect. If they control it in battle, then it won't matter if we know where they are. There are a dozen of them. Are they entrenched?"

"Yes."

"Expecting a rescue attempt?"

"Yes."

"Then Kemal and Yashar will be overwhelmed."

He glanced back at his abayon. "So they can't come."

Hisar wrinkled Its brow in a deep frown. "How are you going to stop them? You can't just sneak off; they'll follow you, and sooner or later they'll walk right into a Petchan ambush."

"I know." Spar scrubbed irritably at his eyes. "The natural muting effect's only going to increase, and the Petchans' control makes it even more dangerous for them and for Brax. They have to be made to see that." He raised his head. "Aban?"

Yashar looked over immediately. "What is it, Delin? Do you see something?"

"No, but I need to talk to you about something very important. Will you hear it?"

"An interesting way of putting it," Kemal observed. Seating himself on the ground beside the youth, he gave Jaq a scratch beneath the collar before indicating that Spar should proceed.

"A dozen Petchan seers guard the cave where Graize is holding Brax. The only way to get him out is to sneak in and steal him out because if they throw the muting effect against you, they could block your bond with Estavia just like they did with Brax. And if Estavia reacts the way She did on the grasslands, She'll give our rescue attempt away and Brax could get killed."

Kemal and Yashar exchanged a glance. "Then we'd better make sure they don't throw it," the older man replied with a dark expression.

"You can't kill a dozen seers undetected, Aba," Spar said gently. "Not in their own territory. They'll sense the first attacks even before you make them. And besides, you can't sneak, neither one of you, you're too big, you wear too much armor, and you carry Estavia's lien within you like a beacon. You're warriors; warriors march into battle carrying flags and waving swords."

"So, what do you suggest?"

✦

"No."

"But, Aba . . ."

"No. We will not allow you to go into the mountains alone, and that's final, Delin."

The three of them had been arguing for nearly an hour while the shadows lengthened around them. Spar had been adamant that they could not risk Estavia giving their position away and his abayon just as adamant that they would not send him into danger alone.

Finally, Spar threw his hands into the air in frustration. "Aban, I know what I'm doing, I'm a thief!" he all but shouted.

"You're not a thief," Yashar snapped back. "You're a warrior-delinkos."

"Not yet I'm not, and that's our edge, can't you see that? I know you want to save Brax and keep me safe, but this is the best way, the only way, to do it!"

"And you think Graize doesn't know that?" Kemal

countered. "If he's as powerful a seer as you say he is, won't he be expecting this kind of an attempt?"

"Yes."

Both men drew back, surprised by the admission.

"He'll know I'm coming," Spar agreed. "He'll know I have to come," he added quietly. "And he'll be waiting for me with this muting effect all ready to throw at me like a giant net. But what he doesn't know is that I can block him as easily as he can block me. And he doesn't know how I can do it."

"How can you do it?"

"With the dark place."

✦

The explanation took longer than Spar would have liked, with both men interrupting more often than they listened. Finally Kemal stood, rubbing at the small of his back with a grimace.

"I still don't like it," he said.

Spar opened his mouth to argue, and his abayos raised a hand to forestall it. "I'm not saying that your argument doesn't hold merit," he said. "Just that it hinges on too many variables."

"Variables are good, Aba; they confuse the streams of prophecy."

"I know. But you're forgetting the most important variable of all: Hisar."

"Me?"

The Godling had returned to Its dragonfly-seeming during most of the argument, weaving back and forth as the breeze took it. Now, wearing Its Caleb seeming, It turned an indignant look on the three of them.

"What do I have to do with this?" It demanded.

"What don't you have to do with it?" Kemal countered. "You move back and forth between Spar and Graize at will; we know that. We also know that Graize fashioned you, and that on the temple battlements four years ago, he set you against Brax and that Brax nearly drowned as a result. We also know that you know more about this recent attack than either you or Spar have admitted to us. But what we don't know is whose side you're on. So tell us, Hisar, whose side are you on?"

The Godling reared back, clearly agitated by the question. "I'm not on anyone's side," It protested.

"No? If you lead Spar to Brax's position and help him rescue him, you betray Graize. If you lead Spar into a trap and help Graize kill him, then you betray Spar. Now you've brought us this far without having to do either, but the time is fast approaching when events will force you to show your hand. What will it be?"

"Spar promised that he wouldn't kill Graize. If Graize doesn't catch Spar, then he won't kill him either."

"That's a pretty big if, considering that Graize knows he's coming."

"He doesn't know when. He sent me to find out, but I haven't told him."

"Why not?"

"Because I don't want either of them to die."

"Again, why not?"

"Because! Just . . . because," Hisar muttered sullenly, hunkering Its shoulders.

"Do you see what I mean about being an important variable?" Kemal told It gently. "How can we send our delos into danger without knowing whether you'll betray him or not?"

"I could say I won't betray Spar, but why would you believe me after I said it if you don't believe me now?" Hisar countered.

"We need to hear you say it to gauge the honesty of your reply," Yashar answered.

The Godling narrowed Caleb's almond-shaped eyes. "I don't think I've been in the world of people long enough to lie all that well," It said stiffly. "I think it takes a few more years of experience to learn how to do it as convincingly as most people do it."

Kemal chuckled. "Point," he acknowledged. "So," he

crossed his feet at the ankles, reaching down to scratch Jaq under the collar again. "It comes down to whether we trust you or not. Spar does, but he may be trusting you out of desperation."

The Godling whirled on Spar. "Are you?" It demanded.

The youth had been listening to the debate with an impatient expression on his face. Now he met Hisar's angry gaze with an even one of his own.

"No," he answered.

"And are you lying to me?"

"No. I've never lied to you, and I know you haven't lied to me. My abayon don't know you. They're afraid for my safety. That's all."

Hisar shook Its head. "People are too complicated," It accused. "They say one thing and mean another. Act one way when they ought to act another. They talk until their mouths grow tired and never say anything useful. They hide what they feel and pretend it doesn't bother them.

"And you and Graize and Brax are the worst," It added, stabbing one finger at him. "You love each other and hate each other and drag everyone else into danger."

"I didn't drag anyone anywhere," Spar retorted, growing angry in his turn. "I'm the one who got dragged."

"Then it's all Graize and Brax's fault," the Godling snapped. "That suits me just fine. They should have sorted out all this jealousy and sexual . . ." It flung Its arms wide as It lost the words in Its frustration, flickering from one seeming to another until It became Rayne again, ". . . whatever a long time ago," It finished with a dark and angry grimace.

Spar blinked at It. "What sexual whatever?" he demanded.

"She wanted Graize," Hisar spat, jabbing the finger at Its own chest now. "She would have chosen him to birth a delos with. He could have made a life in the Rus-Yuruk with her or with Danjel. He could have been an important wyrdin, but no, he's too consumed with Brax to see anything else because Brax led some priest to him and saved his life when he was little, and so Graize thinks that means they should be together forever. But he won't go to him and tell him that, will he? Of course not! That would be the *sensible* thing to do!"

"Graize is mad," Spar answered, taken aback by the vehemence of Hisar's outburst.

"Only sometimes," Hisar snarled. "And he can control it if he wants to. He just doesn't want to because he knows his movements can't be tracked by seers if his movements are always chaotic. He stays a variable *like me*."

"Point," Kemal observed mildly and Spar stilled a growl in response.

"And Brax," Hisar continued, refusing to be distracted, "will have sex with anybody, and I mean *anybody,* who even hints at an offer. I've seen him bed three different people in one day . . . before dark! Anybody except Graize, because Brax always has to protect you from him! I'm getting fed up with both of them! I kept Graize from killing Brax! I should have just flown away!"

Hisar threw Itself down on a nearby rock, seemingly exhausted, while the three people stared at each other, unsure of how to react. Finally, Kemal looked over.

"Brax and Graize have a conflicted relationship," he allowed. "It's very difficult for people to overcome such things, even if they recognize that they should. Especially when they're very young."

Hisar gave him an unimpressed snort.

"So, if you should have just flown away," Kemal continued, "why did you stop Graize from killing Brax?"

Hisar shrugged, Its features flickering uncertainly. "I told you, I don't want anyone to die."

"Why?"

"Why, why, why!" Hisar threw Its hands into the air angrily. "Why do you keep asking me that?"

"Because I want to know the answer. Don't you know why?"

"Of course I do!"

"Then ... why?"

"Because! Because Brax is *mine!*" Hisar glared at him. "I tasted him. He's mine, all right?"

"Tasted him? On the battlements, you mean?"

"Yes. Graize took me to Gol-Beyaz to drink from the silver lake of power and grow strong enough to come fully into the world."

"But you didn't drink from Gol-Beyaz."

"No."

"Why not?"

Hisar glared at him. "The Gods were in the way. And besides, it didn't feel right, not then. I drank from Brax instead. That felt right."

"And now you feel an obligation to protect him?"

Spar glanced over at Kemal wondering where he was going with this line of questioning, but Kemal was staring intently at the Godling.

"Sort of," It acknowledged cautiously. "Maybe."

"Sort of ... maybe you feel an obligation to the man who fashioned you and the man who gave you strength. You feel their needs, yet you can't answer those needs because you don't understand them, and so you get angry and wish you could just fly away, but you can't."

"Yes." Hisar continued to glare at him. "How do you know these things?" It demanded.

"I'm a priest, a ghazi-priest, but still a priest. You're a God, a young God but still a God. The Gods answer the needs of their people. It's what They were fashioned to do."

"But Brax is not one of Hisar's people," Spar pointed out, his expression alarmed.

"No," Kemal agreed. "He's one of Estavia's people."

Hisar glared at the ground. "I don't care," It muttered. "He's still mine, too. She should share."

Kemal disciplined a smile. "She does share sometimes,"

he allowed. "Brax is one of Her favorites, but She might be convinced to share a little of him if Brax himself were willing."

Spar opened his mouth to say something, but subsided when Yashar put a hand on his arm.

"Wait," he said quietly.

"We're only the God's if we choose to be, no matter how much of us the Gods might taste," Kemal continued. "Brax is only yours if he agrees to be yours. Has he?"

Hisar made to answer, clearly planning a reply full of bravado, but something in Kemal's expression cause It to slump back down again. "No," It said grudgingly.

"Have you asked him?" Kemal pressed, ignoring the self-pitying tone.

"No."

"Why not?"

Hisar gave one of Spar's patented one-shoulder shrugs again, and now it was Yashar's turn to discipline a smile.

"It costs little to ask," he prompted and Hisar turned Its frustrated look on the older man.

"It costs *everything* to ask," It retorted, Its voice clearly showing Its opinion of Yashar's intelligence right then. "He might say no. And besides, why would he ever say yes," It added in a more subdued tone. "He has everything he needs already: a family, a God, lots of sex. Why would he need me?"

"He needs you to rescue him," Yashar answered quietly. "If you don't, Graize will kill him, or he'll die of his injuries."

Hisar shot him a resentful look. "I already told Spar that I would help rescue him," It replied. "He asked me to. I don't need Brax to ask."

"Why? Because Spar is yours, too?"

"No." Hisar glanced sideways at the youth, trying to gauge his emotion. "Because he's . . . my friend, I guess."

"Good enough." Yashar stood, stretching his back and neck out carefully and Hisar looked from him to Kemal and back again.

"That's it?" the Godling asked with a frown.

Yashar cocked his head to one side. "That's what?"

"You trust me after one conversation?"

The older man chuckled. "Like you said, it takes years of experience to learn how to lie well, and I've had years of experience learning how to judge someone's honesty. I trust that you don't want to see any of the three people you care about get hurt.

"That being said," he continued, "we need a proper plan of action and not just one that involves Spar sneaking through an entrenched line to take on an enemy who knows he's coming, no matter how much help you might be able to provide."

"So what do we do?" Hisar demanded.

Kemal pressed his hand against his chest, feeling Estavia's lien warm his palm. "We ask for help," he said simply.

"What about the muting effect?"

"We get past it."

"How?"

"We ask for help," Kemal repeated.

✦

In the arzhane at Incasa-Sarayi, First Oracle Bessic took a deep breath as he felt the streams finally begin to merge.

He'd been leading the High Seeking for nearly twenty-four hours, his mind deep in concert with the God of Prophecy while an army of seer-delinkon had seen to his physical needs. As a new delinkos slid in behind him, pressing his back against her chest so that some of the burden might be relieved, he felt Incasa stir.

"It's time."

Bessic's inner voice alerted his senior seer-priests so

that when the God of Prophecy finally spoke, they were ready to receive Him.

When they came, Incasa's words sent a shock of surprise through their ranks, but Bessic dutifully turned to the delinkos standing by the arzhane's door.

"Send messengers out to all the city's temples at once," he croaked, his outer voice little more than an exhausted whisper. Tell them, they must make ready to send their strength to the Gods at a moment's notice. The God of Creation and Destruction is at a crossroads, and we must all work in concert if we're to keep It from straying in the wrong direction."

"Yes, Sayin."

As the youth disappeared through the door, Bessic resisted the urge to stretch his muscles. They weren't finished by a long shot, and the renewed blood flow would only bring a new wave of pain to distract him. Laying his head against his delinkos' shoulder, he allowed himself a moment's break in concentration to find the tiny speck of potential shining on the grasslands: Spar, still seeking, still fighting, still standing stubbornly alone. But the time was coming when he would have no choice. He might not ask for help, but he'd have to accept it whether he liked it or not because the God of Prophecy had entered the field.

Closing his eyes, First Oracle Bessic returned his full attention to his God as Incasa pulled strength from His High Seeking to manifest before the God of Battles.

✦

On the grasslands, Estavia paused as Incasa rose up before Her, His intent flowing from His mind on a breath of ice-cold prophecy. Where it touched Her crimson gaze, it took fire, merging and changing until it became first response and then action more in line with Her own domain. Her eyes narrowed as She considered the repercussions, then with a violent motion, changed the intent still further until it coalesced into a simple directive then, as Incasa returned to Gol-Beyaz, She flung it toward the most receptive of Her favorites.

✦

Standing on the path, Kemal's head suddenly jerked back as Estavia's intent smacked into his mind like a blow.

"I have an idea," he said, blood welling up from where his teeth had snapped against his lip. "But we have to get closer and we have to wait until dusk."

Yashar met his eyes with a dark frown. "I hope Brax has until dusk," he grated.

"So do I, but it can't be helped. We have to wait."

Kemal headed for their mounts without further explanation; after giving a small growl, Yashar did the same.

Hisar glanced over at Spar for some explanation, but the youth just shrugged. "They trust each other," he said simply.

"And you trust them."

It wasn't a question, but Spar nodded anyway. "They're my abayon." Standing, he whistled for Jaq before following the two older men, leaving the Godling to shake Its head in confusion before It followed them as well.

18

Seer-Priest

IN THE CAVE, A THIN shaft of sunlight crept across the floor, marking the passage of time. Brax tried to ignore it, concentrating instead on the memory's instruction; cultivating stillness and focusing on a single thought, that Spar and Estavia were coming.

But the pain was getting worse. His elbow throbbed from wrist to shoulder, and his leg felt like it was on fire. It was making it harder to think about anything else.

A shadow fell across his face. A pair of hands lifted his head, then pressed a waterskin to his mouth. He drank, and the hands and the shadow withdrew.

The sunlight began to creep along the far wall, and he squinted up at it. His vision seemed blurrier than before. The cave lurched sideways, so he closed his eyes against the motion; it was making him feel sick to his stomach. His face felt hot, but his body felt cold. He began to shiver, and the shadow returned to drape some kind of a cloak or blanket over him. The fabric fell across his wounded arm and the darkness rushed in again on a tide of agony.

✦

Danjel emerged from the cave, a frown marring the smooth contours of his face.

"He's feverish," he observed.

Seated cross-legged on the ground, Graize laid his

three turtle shells in a line before him, then began to weave Fal-Sayer's bow back and forth above them.

"How long are we going to wait here, Kardos?" Danjel prodded.

"Until we leave."

"Which will be when?"

"When Spar reveals which shell he's under."

"And Spar is coming?"

"He's coming. He's creeping under a shell at this very moment."

"And you've seen this?"

Graize smiled sleepily. "I don't have to see it, Kardos. I know it." He tipped his head up to regard the other seer with a challenging smile. "And what have you seen, Wyrdin-Kazak of the Rus-Yuruk?" he asked in mock formality.

Taking the question seriously, Danjel glanced over at the western sky, streaked red by the setting sun. "I've seen a flock of silver birds flying above the foothills," he answered. "They've been coming together and breaking apart for the better part of the afternoon."

"They can't settle," Graize agreed.

"Ordinarily, such a flock might signify that a storm was coming."

Graize gave a snort. "The Yuruk think every movement in the sky means that a storm is coming."

"That's because there are many storms, and their coming always causes movement." Walking forward a few paces, Danjel frowned again. "Something's happening," he said in a quiet voice.

"You've said that before. Does it feel like the same something?"

"It does." He turned. "Where's your Godling?" he asked suddenly.

"Where indeed."

"Shouldn't It be back by now?"

"Yes."

"And Its absence doesn't worry you?"

"No. Its absence tells me more than anything Its presence might impart."

"Meaning?"

"Meaning . . ." Graize began to weave the three shells back and forth. "Place your shine, place your shine," he sang. "Meaning," he repeated, "that It's with Spar."

"And this doesn't worry you either?" Danjel pressed.

"No." Graize held up the cracked shell. "I broke this, remember?"

"I remember."

Graize nodded. "I broke it, and only I know how to fix it." Tucking all three shells back into his belt pouch, he unstrung the bow carefully, then stood. "But you're right," he allowed over his shoulder as he headed back into the cavern. "Something is happening. The sun's going down. You'd better have the others make a fire and prepare for the attack."

✦

One hundred yards away, Yashar glanced up at the sky with a worried expression.

"It's almost time for Evening Invocation, Kem," he whispered.

"I know."

They'd left the horses and most of their gear in Jaq's reluctant care and crept cautiously forward until Hisar had warned them that any further movement would be discovered. Now they hunkered down in a narrow gully beside a fast-moving stream, sharing a meal of flatbread and water and waiting for nightfall. Above them, the setting sun lit up the mountain peaks in streaks of fire. Spar kept his eyes glued to the path, Yashar watched the sky, and Kemal watched Hisar.

The Godling had become increasingly agitated as they'd drawn nearer to Graize's position. Now It flitted back and forth, unable to keep to a single seeming.

Within him, Kemal felt Estavia's lien begin to stir and nodded more to himself than to Yashar.

"The priests of Havo will be climbing the steps of the city's minarets now," he said, just loud enough for Hisar to hear him without the sound of his voice carrying past the gully. "Feeling the mood of their God on the evening breeze and preparing themselves to receive word of the night's weather. Will it be fair, will it storm, can the ships and market stalls be left as they are, or should they be battened down?

"On a night like this," he continued, "with all the Gods in an uproar, the song will be strained with worry, but centuries of practice will fill it with images of fruit trees and vegetable gardens and that will strengthen the God of Seasonal Bounty.

Yashar glanced at Hisar, who was staring intently at Kemal, then nodded.

"The priests of Oristo will be standing by their hearths," he replied. "The afternoon's tasks fulfilled, the evening's tasks yet to be done. The bustle in kitchens and larders will pause, though there'll always be someone to make sure the pot doesn't spill over or the kettle boil dry. Oristo's a practical God and so are the abayos-priests. When they sing their Invocation, they summon a practical response: to keep the people warm and fed, their delon safe from harm, their pantries full, and their livestock strong and healthy.

"But tonight Oristo will be fretful, and so the abayos-priests will croon a lullaby of peace and comfort that will strengthen the God of Hearth and Home."

Hisar now turned Its wide-eyed attention to Yashar, Its form holding steady in Its Caleb-seeming.

"The physician-priests of Usara will be just finishing their rounds," the older man continued. "They'll have a few moments before their Invocation begins, and their infirmaries need constant care. Usara watches with them always, and they know that He's given them everything they need to ease the suffering of the sick and wounded and to comfort the dying.

"Tonight their song will be particularly important because when Usara is agitated the sick do not sleep easily, but the physician-priests will sing for patience and compassion and time and that will strengthen the God of Healing.

"For time?" Hisar asked quietly.

"For time to reach those who need them before it's too late and sickness and injury lead to death," Yashar answered pointedly.

"Oh."

"And after Usara comes Estavia," Kemal now said. "Her Warriors will be standing in battle formation in Her temple, on Her ships, in the village squares, or on Her tower ramparts; wherever their duty finds them. They'll be tired, *we'll* be tired," he amended, "from fueling Her manifestation all day, but we'll never waver." He placed a hand on his chest and Yashar did the same, causing Hisar to swallow hard.

"And when we sing to Her," Kemal continued, "we'll offer up our lives, and She'll take every ounce of strength and power we can send to Her and gift it back to us tenfold; enough to stand as steadfast as the God-Wall itself against our enemies.

"Tonight She's almost mad with worry, but we'll sing of action and rescue and that will strengthen the God of Battles.

"Then the artisans of Ystazia will raise up a song filled with poetry," Yashar said before Hisar could react too strongly to the mention of rescue. "Standing by their tables and their tools, ensuring that each brush is dry, each knife is sharp, and each book has been returned to its shelf, ready for tomorrow's task. They'll sing along with their priests so that Her gifts will flow smoothly through their hands and out to their work.

"Tonight they'll distract Ystazia with all the color and

texture of the world and that will strengthen the God of the Arts."

Yashar's voice had become a low, singsong tone and, under the spell of his imagery, Hisar began to weave slowly back and forth, Its eyes closed and Its expression peaceful.

"And finally, Incasa," Kemal said, and the Godling's eyes snapped open at once. But it was Spar who spoke instead of his abayos.

"The seer-priests have listened to all the others," he said solemnly, "hearing their prayers and weighing the answers. They're standing on the very edge of prophecy beside their God, and when He throws his dice into the future, they'll follow.

"Tonight they've focused all their formidable abilities to a single purpose," he said, feeling the truth of it whisper through the tentative bond he'd forged with their First Oracle, "and this will strengthen the God of Prophecy and Probability."

He shook himself as a shiver went up his spine, and Hisar echoed the motion. "A single purpose," Spar continued. "To fulfill a vision of importance to the Gods and to Their followers."

"A child of great potential still unformed standing on the streets of Anavatan," Kemal said.

The wind picked up, spinning his hair into his face, temporarily obscuring it from sight. "The twin dogs of creation and destruction crouch at its feet," he continued. "The child is ringed by silver swords and golden knives and its eyes are filled with fire."

A fine shaft of sunlight lit up the gully, causing a red mist to dance over the stream at their feet and he stared down at it intently. "It drew strength from Anavatan's unsworn and was born under the cover of Havo's Dance."

He looked up, meeting Hisar's eyes. "You came into the world just as Freyiz-Sayin predicted. Now you're here, but that isn't the end of it. A child armed and armored and a shimmering tower, strong and defensible, standing before a snow-clad mountain covered in a crimson mist; a mist of danger and of death. A child and a tower raised to defend the City of the Gods."

"Elif's prediction," Spar allowed. "She believed that I was the child and Hisar was the tower." He smiled faintly. "But seers often seed their own desires into their interpretations. Hisar could easily be both child and tower."

"The Gods take our form because the pressure of our needs is what fashions Them," Kemal agreed.

"Hisar's not a God, not yet."

"No, Delin, Hisar *is* a God, a young God, a *child*-God, but still a God. It can already feel Its abayon pushing It toward a true form, and It can't help but try and respond."

"No." Hisar backed up a step, shaking Its head, Its expression close to panic. "The Gods are scary," It hissed. "They want to hurt me, take me over, make me do things. I don't want to be one of Them."

"All delon feel that way about their abayon sometimes. And sometimes it's true, but abayon also want to protect their delon, raise them, teach them, and make them strong enough to walk their own paths in the world."

"No."

"We're close to Invocation, Hisar-Delin," Kemal said gently. "What do you feel?"

Hisar shuddered. "Like I can't breathe," It whispered. "Like my chest is being pressed down by a huge hand."

"What will it take to breathe, to push that hand away?"

Hisar tipped Its head back, eyes closed, teeth bared in a grimace of pain. "Power," It whispered.

"Whose power?"

"Everyone's, anyone's." Its eyes began to glitter with a bright, metallic light. "I'm so hungry," It whispered.

✦

Across the shores of Gol-Beyaz, the priests of Havo reached the tops of their towers and minarets while on the silver lake, Incasa rose silently from the waves, dice held high in the final act before casting. As the first note sounded across the waters, Havo rose beside Him. Under the pressure of their song, green-tinged eyes turned to the west, and the God of the Seasons looked upon Hisar.

✦

The Godling began to shudder as It felt Havo's regard rumbling like a thunderstorm in the distance. "It won't be enough," It gasped. "The Gods are formed. I'm not formed." It gave a faint whimper. "It hurts."

✦

Under Incasa's direction, Havo sent a cold wind sweeping across the mountain path, thrumming through the cave. Graize stood with a frown, his abilities quivering like whiskers on a cat.

✦

"What do you need to be formed, Delin?" Kemal pressed.

"Power," Hisar repeated. "Unformed power."

"The power of Gol-Beyaz?" Yashar asked.

Hisar gave a jerky nod. "But I can't go there," It whimpered. "They won't let me."

"Who?"

"The Gods. Estavia smacked me last time I went near Her temple and Incasa'll only let me drink if I do what He wants."

"Would that be so bad?"

Hisar bared Its teeth and, for a second, Spar's own image overlaid the Caleb-seeming. "Yes," It grated. Then Its form solidified for just a moment as a memory trickled past Its eyes. "Graize says . . . the spirits flow through the mountain streams down to Gol-Beyaz . . . and the Gods feed on them there."

Yashar glanced at the stream flowing behind them. "Can't you feed on them here?" he asked.

"I can. I have. It wasn't enough."

"Did you feed during Invocation?"

"No."

"Try it now."

✦

The priests of Havo finished their song, but remained in place as the Gods of Prophecy and Harvest continued to stand motionless above the waves. When the abayos-priests of Oristo began their own Invocation, led by the combined power of Anavatan's Temple chamberlains, Oristo rose to join Them. Expression a mix of anxious determination, the Hearth God stepped up onto the God-Wall to stare out to the west, directly at Hisar.

✦

The faintest odor of baking bread brought Graize from the cave, his face clouded.

Danjel glanced over at him.

"What is it, Kardos?"

"Something." Graize walked a few paces, stopped, turned in a slow circle, stopped again. The western sky glowered with a sullen, uncommunicative glow that made him clench his teeth. "Something," he repeated.

✦

The Godling made to enter the stream, but as It touched the water, the natural muting effect caused the Caleb-seeming to disintegrate and It gave a faint moan as It fell back.

Spar jerked forward, hands outstretched as if to catch It up in his arms, his face twisting in frustration as his fingers passed right through It.

"Why can't I touch It?" he demanded.

"Because the Gods aren't physical beings, Delin," Kemal answered gently.

"But They can affect the physical world and it affects Them."

"Only when They have access to the vast stores of power granted to Them by Their worshipers."

Spar's eyes narrowed. "I have access to vast stores of power," he grated.

✦

On Gol-Beyaz, Usara rose to stand above His temple as the physician-priests' quiet song echoed from every hospice and infirmary along the lakeshore. Glancing at Incasa, the God of Solace raised His staff toward the distant gully, sending out a single impulse on the wind: to heal.

✦

Standing by the fire, Graize tasted a strange sensation on the breeze, and taking a deep breath to focus his mind on the protective cloak, he reached out for his connection to Hisar.

✦

In the gully, Yashar's eyes widened as he realized what Spar was suggesting. "You're only fifteen, Delin," he protested.

Spar's head snapped up. "So? Brax was only fourteen when he swore to Estavia."

"It's not that simple."

"Yes, it is. Hisar's made of spirit, but isn't spirit; It's a God, remember? Everyone and anyone's power won't do. It needs power freely given, power that's pure and unbound. Power that's unsworn. It needs mine."

As Hisar stared up at him in surprise, Kemal caught him by the arm. "Swearing to a God can't be taken for anything else, Delin," he said urgently. "And if you're only doing this to save Brax, you'll fail."

With an angry jerk, Spar shook him off. "I won't fail," he snarled. "Hisar'll take my oath, and I'll keep it, for Brax."

Dropping to his knees, he pulled the red bead from his bag, slipping it onto a piece of cord before draping it over Hisar's neck.

"What are you doing?" It whispered.

"Spending my fortune for fifteen present."

The red-and-silver bead came to rest against the Godling's chest as if Hisar were a physical being, and Spar laid a hand on Its shoulder feeling it as a tingle of warmth through his palm. "If the red ones have bits of raw spirit trapped inside them," he reminded It, "they're trapped in physical form. This will help keep you in physical form. Now get up."

✦

At Estavia-Sarayi, Marshal Brayazi sang the first note of the Battle God's Invocation. As each and every one of Her Warriors added their voice to their marshal's, Estavia swept Her crimson-eyed gaze across the grasslands until it lit upon Hisar and, with Incasa's intent swirling around Them both like a forewarning of Winter, She raised one sword above Her head. Hisar tried not to flinch as it streaked down to hit the red bead with an explosion of fire.

"FEED!"

✦

Graize leaped forward, his eyes wild, but he was too late. Hisar rose up, Its form outlined in God-wrought fire, turned, and dove headfirst into the mountain stream, taking Spar with It. With a scream of rage, Graize hurled all His formidable powers out to stop them.

✦

Spar half fell into the stream, fighting to keep his own head above water as Hisar struggled in his arms, keening and shrieking in desperate hunger, Its need to suck up the few mountain spirits It could reach in the icy stream driving It almost mad once It had begun.

A furious, hateful presence swept over them, and Spar knew Graize had discovered them. The muting effect rose up like a vast gray fog.

Then froze as a rainbow of incomparable brilliance suddenly arched out from the east. As Ystazia held the muting effect at bay, Spar jerked Hisar into the dark place.

"I GIVE YOU MY WORSHIP!" he shouted over the Godling's frantic screaming. *"I GIVE YOU MY POWER! COME FULLY INTO THE WORLD! DO IT NOW!"*

A huge tower exploded from the waters at once, changing from black to red to black again in the space of a heartbeat, its immature lien tearing through Spar's body like a hurricane. The tower rose a thousand feet in the air, its sheer sides crackling in a conflagration of gold-and-silver fire. The barrier between the dark place and the physical world began to bow under the pressure, and then the tower slammed against the muting effect's impenetrable wall.

With a shriek of pain, the Godling vanished only to reappear immediately in the physical world, when, glutted with the power of His seer-priests, Incasa hurled His dice directly into Its face. As they hit, Hisar catapulted across the grasslands into Graize with a force that threw them both to the ground.

"HELP ME!" It shouted, still writhing in pain.

Graize fought to regain his balance throwing all his power against Hisar as Its panic smashed through the protective cloak, shredding it to pieces.

"IT HURTS! HELP ME! *MAKE IT STOP!*"

The turtle shells clattered to the ground, the broken one on top of the pile.

"YOU PROMISED YOU'D NEVER BE GONE FROM ME AGAIN!"

"I won't," Graize gasped.

"MAKE IT STOP!"

"How!?"

"BE MINE!"

The image of Spar's oaths swept over them, and Graize screamed in rage. "No! He can't have you!" he shrieked. "He won't have you! You're mine, only mine! *My God!"*

The power of his oath destroyed his hold on the muting effect, carving Hisar's lien through his body and shredding the icy pathway formed by Incasa five years before. Every injury he'd taken in the spirit attack on Liman-Caddesi outlined in lines of golden fire, Graize's head hit the ground, his back arched and, as he began to seizure, Hisar tore Itself away from him, ricocheting off the mountainsides like a comet hitting the earth.

✦

In the gully, Yashar pulled Spar from the stream. "Go!" he shouted at Kemal, "Go for Brax! Graize will be distracted, go! We'll follow!"

Kemal hurled himself up and over the embankment at once. Yashar followed, Spar weaving groggily in his arms as above them Hisar continued to shriek, snapping from one seeming to another too fast to make them out.

Struggling out of Yashar's grip, Spar fell to the ground, then threw his arms wide. With a cry, Hisar slammed into him. Together, they tumbled into the dark place.

Splayed out on the black sands, under the pressure of Spar's abilities, Hisar changed forms again.

✦

At the cave, the clouds above parted and wind and rain hammered down on the clearing as Danjel shouted at the others to withdraw.

"Get out, all of you! Get back to Chalash!" Lifting

Graize's unconscious body as if it were no lighter than a child's, he ran for their mounts, his green eyes wide with prophecy. As he all but hurled Graize over his pony's back, Yal caught him by the arm.

"What's happening!" she demanded.

"An Anavatan God has just come into Its own! We don't want to be anywhere near this place!"

"What about him!" She jerking her head at the cave.

"Leave him to his people! They're coming for him!"

The Petchan sayers melted away at once, the Yuruk wyrdin following behind with the body of his kardos just as Kemal stumbled into the clearing, his sword drawn.

He let them go. As the rain gutted out the fire in the center of the clearing, he threw himself into the cave just as Estavia appeared before it. She reached in, catching up Her favorite in an all-encompassing embrace that nearly shattered his tenuous grip on the world. But Kemal's arms were equally strong, and after a brief struggle, the God gave way, and it was his abayos that drew Brax from the cave.

Kemal fell to the ground, his delin cradled in his arms, just as Hisar reappeared, Its body that of a tall, golden youth with eyes as gray as the ocean waves. It reached for Brax, and suddenly Estavia rose between them, Her eyes flashing fire. With great reluctance, the newly formed God of Creation and Destruction withdrew back to the arms of Its first Anavatanon priest.

✦

Night fell across the grasslands. With Estavia's powerful lien throbbing through his body once again, Brax drifted in a feverish dream, unwilling to come up back up to consciousness despite Kemal and Yashar's ministrations. But finally, when Spar reached for him through the dark place, he opened his eyes to stare up at his only kardos. Spar placed an old, worn sword in his arms, wrapped Brax's fingers around it when it was clear he didn't have the strength to hold it, then wrapped his own arms around him in turn.

Held safe, Brax slept.

✦

Much later as the stars shone down from a cold, clear sky, Spar and Jaq joined Hisar on a narrow outcropping overlooking the grasslands. Casting a perfect shadow in the moonlight, the young God twisted around, trying to see all Its new form at once: Caleb's body clothed in Brax's olive skin tinged with gold, Spar's blond hair streaked with silver, and Graize's pale gray eyes. The form flowed from male to female, from Caleb's features to Rayne's, until It finally settled on Caleb's.

"Am I a golden tower now like we wanted?" He asked, one hand clasped about the red-and-silver bead to help focus His voice in the physical world.

"Not big enough to be an actual tower," Spar answered in a dry tone, glancing down with a pointed expression. "But close enough, I suppose."

Hisar looked down as well, then gave Spar an unimpressed snort.

"That's not what I meant."

She cocked Her head to one side as Her features flowed into Rayne's once again. "The world seems different," She said after a moment.

"Different how?"

"More clear and less . . ." Hisar struggled to put how She felt into words. "Real. I can see things as they are and as they were all mixed up together."

Spar's eyes narrowed. "What about things as they will be?" he asked.

Hisar frowned, returning to the Caleb form. "Sort of. Everything's hazy."

"Like it hadn't come to pass yet?"

"I guess. Is that how seers view the world?"

"No."

"What about the Gods?"

Spar shrugged. "I don't know." He turned, his eyes white. "Cultivate stillness," he said, purposely sending a stream of power out from the newly-formed lien. "And try it now."

Staring out at the silent grasslands, Hisar's eyes widened with an inward gaze that Spar recognized at once.

"What do you see?" he demanded.

"A storm coming in from all sides, driving a fleet of white ships and a fleet of brown ships before it and a wall that's too cracked and leaking to stand against them. It won't hold if we don't do something to repair it. Things could go either way."

"Creation or destruction?" Spar asked.

"Maybe. How will we know?"

"We won't. Not without help."

"Whose help?"

Spar made a sour expression. "Bessic's. We can't afford to stand alone, not anymore. We need Incasa's help."

Hisar nodded, back in Her Rayne form again. "And Graize's," She said, glancing back at the dark, impenetrable mountains. "He's good at this sort of thing. We need him."

A brown-haired man, Graize, but older and clear-eyed, armed with steel and stone, standing by Brax's side on a snow-capped mountain ridge.

Spar scowled at the memory, but simply nodded.

"I need him," Hisar added quietly. "He's mine now. Really mine. Though I'm not sure that's what he meant," She added.

"The oath wouldn't have taken if he hadn't meant it," Spar pointed out.

Hisar gave him a cynical glance that rivaled one of Spar's own. "He meant it deep down," She answered, "I just don't think he meant it higher up."

"Well, wherever he meant it, he won't come over to us easily," Spar replied. "Not now."

"Then we'll have to convince him."

"How?"

Hisar gave one of Spar's one-shouldered shrugs. "Incasa still wants me in Gol-Beyaz. That might give me enough power to convince him."

Spar frowned. "Do you want to go to Gol-Beyaz?"

Hisar shrugged again. "Maybe, I don't know. They're like me and not like me. It makes me feel safe and restricted at the same time."

Spar snorted. "Welcome to fifteen."

"What?"

"Fifteen, almost an adult but not completely; not yet. And that reminds me ... Traditionally it's silver, but in this case I think this might be a better symbol." Fishing into his belt pouch, he pulled out the pair of old, wooden dice. "Here," he said placing them in Hisar's palm, "fortune for fifteen."

"Fortune?"

"We make our own."

Hisar jiggled them in his palm, watching the numbers change back and forth with the movement and changing form with them. "Dice are Incasa's domain," He pointed out, back in his Caleb form.

Spar shrugged. "Dice can be a lot of things,' he replied. "Give them your own meaning and they'll become your domain, too. At any rate, you've got a year to decide."

Hisar tipped His head to one side. "Does that mean I don't have to make any decisions now?" He asked hopefully.

"Yes, but it also means that those decisions are coming, whether you like it or not, so you have to be ready for them."

"Just make a strong choice, that's all I ask."

Elif's image wavered in the dark place, and Spar nodded. "We're trying, Sayin," he whispered. "But at least we're trying together now.

"Come on." He jerked his head toward camp. "I don't

want to be away from Brax for too long." He headed back to camp, Jaq at his heels.

Hisar followed, but at the edge of the firelight, He paused. "What is it about Brax," He demanded suddenly. "Why does everyone want him so badly?"

Spar shook his head. "You asked me that before," he pointed out.

"Yes, but you didn't answer me."

Spar shrugged. "Because he gives himself so completely. That's rare. Anything rare is valuable."

"Did he give himself to Graize all those years ago when he saved him?"

"I don't know. Did he save him?"

"Graize thinks he did. He thinks he led a priest of Oristo to him in a doorway during Havo's Dance when they were children."

"So you said. He was probably just running from the priest himself and stumbled across him," Spar snorted. "But he would have saved him," he allowed quietly. "Brax is like that."

"Things would have been different if he had."

"Maybe."

"Do you think he might give himself to *me*?"

Spar snorted. "Well, you can take physical form now," he noted in a cynical voice. "And you yourself said Brax would have sex with anyone who even hints at an offer. Make an offer."

Hisar took an involuntary step backward. "That's not what I meant," She protested again, Her annoyance snapping Her into the Rayne form.

"No?"

"No, not . . . exactly."

"Well, you have a year to figure that out, too, then go ask him."

Spar glanced toward the east, his blue eyes dark with prophecy. "If your vision-storm gives us that much time," he added. "But I don't think it will."

His eyes narrowed. "Seers seeding their own desires into their interpretation of prophecy," he whispered. "Or refusing to seed them. I saw it, the reed that held the answer, but I didn't believe it. The Gods helping, unrequested. If the odds are unpredictable, so is the outcome, and even the Gods are unpredictable." He shook his head. "Brax is alive for now, but the danger's still out there."

A brown-haired man, Graize, but older and clear-eyed, armed with steel and stone, standing by Brax's side on a snow-capped mountain ridge.

"*I know,*" he told it peevishly. "*Shut up.*"

He turned. "Come on, we need to get back." He and Jaq crossed into the firelight and, after a moment, Hisar followed.

✦

Far to the east, Incasa stood above Gol-Beyaz, staring past the shimmering God-Wall, to the west, a satisfied smile on His icy features. Champions were moving ever closer. The Petchan threat had been nullified. He turned to the south. The Skirosian threat was still in its infancy. He turned to the north. The Volinski threat was close to entering the streams of possibility. It would be next.

Drawing on the strength of His senior seer-priests, the God of Chance rose up until His icy form blotted out the moon, then sent one single bolt of pure prophecy hurtling across the sea.

✦

At Cvet Tower, Illan Volinsk's atlas table suddenly shattered, sending pieces flying across the room. Three hit the map above the hearth and hit the floor together: the silver, gray, and black champions.

✦

Incasa threw back His head, laughing at the foreign seer's consternation. The odds always favored the House and the God of Prophecy always controlled the House. With one last glance north, He descended into the silver lake without a ripple to mark his passage.

Fiona Patton

The Warriors of Estavia

"In this bold first of a new fantasy series... Court intrigues enrich the story, as do many made-up words that lend color. The smashing climax neatly sets up events for volume two." —*Publishers Weekly*

"The best aspect of this explosive series opener is Patton's take on relations between gods and men."
—*Booklist*

"Fresh and interesting...I look forward to the next."
—*Science Fiction Chronicle*

THE SILVER LAKE

978-0-7564-0366-9 $7.99

THE GOLDEN TOWER

978-0-7564-0577-9 $7.99

To Order Call: 1-800-788-6262

www.dawbooks.com

Fiona Patton

"Rousing adventure, full of color and
spectacular magic" —*Locus*

*The Novels of
the Branion Realm*

THE STONE PRINCE
0-88677-735-6 $6.99

THE PAINTER KNIGHT
0-88677-780-1 $6.99

THE GRANITE SHIELD
0-88677-842-5 $6.99

THE GOLDEN SWORD
0-88677-921-9 $6.99